ACROBAT

GONZALO LIRA

St. Martin's Paperbacks

Library of Congress Catalog Card Number: 2001058862

ISBN: 0-312-98971-7

Printed in the United States of America

St. Martin's Press hardcover edition / May 2002
St. Martin's Paperbacks edition / May 2003

St. Martin's Paperbacks are published by St. Martin's Press, 175 Fifth Avenue, New York, NY 10010.

10 9 8 7 6 5 4 3 2 1

FOR ANA ANDRADE

Everybody's got a plan until they get hit.

—MIKE TYSON

PART I

Ideas of Order

We don't have enemies anymore, said Tom Carr. The whole world's on the same page—even the Commies in China are coming our way: Democracy, capitalism, human rights, all that other good shit. That can be bad for Central Intelligence.

You figure? asked Duncan Idaho.

Tom Carr nodded. It robs us of a reason for being. When people don't have a purpose, they get ideas.

CHAPTER 1

Tuesday Morning at Times Square

Tom Carr was the first to arrive at the rendezvous point: The Red Line platform at the Times Square subway station in New York City. It was not quite ten in the morning, a Tuesday, the platform lightly populated with the after-rush-hour crowd— messengers on their way to deliver packages, random tourists getting a leg up on their Manhattan excursions, retirees waiting to do whatever lonely tasks they'd set for themselves this sunny spring morning. In the dark recesses of the subway platform, trains were coming down the tracks a little less often than just a few minutes ago. And as the subway doors opened and closed, people flowed to and fro in a soothing, uncluttered rhythm, unconscious of Tom Carr.

He wasn't one to stand out. At fifty-three, Tom Carr had a comfortable potbelly that oddly suited his five-foot seven-inch frame—a fighter's frame: Bantamweight. He had sandy brown hair touched with gray at the temples, parted to the left and thinning on top; thick fingers and stubby feet; and, by the way he carried himself, you could tell he ordinarily wore conservative suits and ties. As it was, this morning he was wearing a sports jacket and khaki slacks, looking a bit like what he was—an out-of-towner, dressed down.

He discreetly looked around the platform, looking for the members of his work-group: The CIA work-group known as Acrobat.

Deep in huddle-cuddle mode, standing about twenty feet

away, Duncan Idaho and Monika Summers stood waiting in the middle of the platform for Tom's signal to get going.

"I missed you," Monika was saying quietly, squeezing Duncan's waist.

Duncan Idaho looked down at his girlfriend. "Yeah?" he asked, amazed.

"Yeah," she said. "Did you miss me?"

"No, not really," he teased.

Monika gave him bright and shining eyes before hiding against his chest, murmuring and squeezing his body until she got him to squeeze and hold her in return.

Monika Summers was American sunshine—blonde and happy, athletic and uncomplicated. A scholar-athlete, a sorority sister on a corporate detour before suburban bliss, she didn't put much stock in things abstract or intangible, Monika being one of those very practical people who looks at the world directly, and without undue complications.

That straightforwardness was probably why she and Duncan Idaho were together.

"We made it," she was saying quietly, looking up at her boyfriend as he scanned the platform, Monika resisting an urge to brush his tousled blond hair out of his eyes.

Duncan Idaho looked down at her and then sighed before looking around the platform some more. "Almost, but not yet," he said, making Monika tense in his arms. So he turned back to her and soothed her with a smile. "But it won't be long now."

"Mmm," said Monika, taking a deep breath of his leather jacket as she tried to relax, leaning into him, loving the solidity of him.

Duncan Idaho looked like he was used to the rough and tumble, willing to get banged up by the ways of the game. A little over six feet tall, he was good-looking without being perfect, a decent, playful guy: A guy's guy, with deep-set eyes that squinted in the sun and a wide-open smile that could drive any woman to distraction.

Of the six members of the Acrobat work-group, Duncan Idaho was the only one who hadn't gone to college. Instead, he'd spent seven years with the Army, six of them with Special Forces, before moving on to the CIA. In fact, Tom Carr had been his CIA recruiter.

"Do you think he'll find us?" Monika asked him quietly, her voice muffled against Duncan's old leather jacket.

"Who, Denton?"

Monika nodded against his chest.

Duncan exhaled. "He'll find us only if we let him. So we can't let him. We *won't* let him. Not if we stay sharp anyways."

"Duncan, I'm so tired," she said. "I was so *scared*."

"I know," he said, rubbing her back and breathing in the smell of her maple blonde hair, hair that was such a warm color it gave the impression that it must be dyed; it wasn't. "I know I know I know—but it won't be long now, okay?"

"Okay."

Beyond them, about twenty feet farther down the platform, the other Acrobat couple, Russell Orr and Ljubica Greene, stood together, looking bored, like a couple who've been together for a while now, now used to each other's company, now not quite so lovey-dovey this early in the morning.

"Tom's here, but I don't see Tobey anywhere," said Russell, a big, hulking man of thirty-two, with a completely shaved skull and perfectly round, gold-rimmed glasses.

Ljubica didn't say a thing, standing there and staring at Monika Summers and Duncan Idaho through the thin crowd of people waiting for the subway train. Monika and Duncan were in the middle of a kiss. Blinking, Ljubica turned away, her eyes flickering on Russell as she scanned the subway station platform.

Ljubica. Though she was an American girl, through-and-through, her name was Croatian, and it was pronounced "you-*vit*-za," a name that sounds as absurd in its way as cartoon characters running fast enough to cross an invisible bridge spanning a yawning canyon. But that was her name, a name that required a kind of faith in the manipulations of the tongue. You-*vit*-za: Ljubica.

And then there was Russell, Russell Orr. He stood about

six feet five, his body as massive as a linebacker's, easily tipping close to three hundred pounds, none of it flab. He wore round John Lennon glasses not because he needed them—he had better than perfect vision, tested in flight school at 20/5. But glasses eroded his height and his size in the minds of the people who encountered him. There was so much of him too— he was so big, he needed something to bring him back down to a manageable size. Hence the glasses with clear lenses. His father had been black, his mother white, so his own skin had turned out a creamy café au lait color, perfectly splitting the difference, his features narrow and sharp, his body bulky and athletic.

Ljubica ("You*vitza*"), on the other hand, was so white that her skin could have been mistaken for flexible porcelain. And like a porcelain figurine, she seemed perfect, possessing a poise, a coolness, an aloofness that was a little eerie, as if she'd been carved from stone a little more precious than most mortals. She had lazy eyes shaped like upturned almonds, and her hands, her limbs, her entire body seemed stretched some-how: Somehow too impossibly long and tall and thin to be real, her arms and legs looking as if they were too fragile to stand any but the gentlest weight.

But she wasn't fragile—she was a woman: She only seemed so. Though her body might look like a faggot of twigs, snap-breakable at the hint of pressure, there was an impossible distance in her eyes that turned her very being into an optical illusion: The closer you were to her, the farther away she ap-peared, like a hard and chiseled statue that is so perfect it seems animate from afar.

That hardness, that distance was what had attracted Russell to her. There used to be a soft center there. But now, for Russell, she was all hard as stone.

"Transportation's all set," he said with the self-conscious eagerness of a teenager. "What about gear?" he asked a little too quickly, wincing at his words.

"God you're annoying," said Ljubica a little more sharply than she'd meant to, her deep, smoky voice lashing out like a lazy whip through the air between them. "You saw me get the gear. You saw me stow it. We were there together."

"I didn't mean it that way," said Russell. "I meant—Let's just drop it," he said.

Ljubica said nothing as she stared down the tunnel of the platform, her straight blackish brown hair coming over her face like a curtain.

Russell looked at her, feeling as if a spot on his brain had been scraped raw. Like the other members of the work-group Acrobat, they had been on the run for the last four days, ever since Nicholas Denton, their boss at CIA, had blown them out of the water.

But unlike the others, Russell and Ljubica had been together during that whole time. And it had taken a toll.

Russell took a breath, as if about to say something more, then thought better of it, the right side of his face flinching as he turned away and stayed silent.

Ljubica turned to Russell. For a fraction of a second, her face seemed to collapse in upon itself. She looked as if she was going to cry. Then she looked away.

Monika, hiding in Duncan's arms, saw the whole thing with one eye. Still staring at them, she said, "Russ and Yuvi are at it again."

"Mmm," said Duncan, without looking at them, kissing Monika's hair as he looked around, as if to tell her that that would never happen to them.

Monika continued to stare. God help her, a flash of satisfied *glee* zipped through her body: Glee that it was *them*—and not her and Duncan—who were busily chopping and hacking away at the love between them.

With a guilty wince, Monika looked away from her best friends, spotting their work-group boss, Tom Carr, who was looking around the platform.

Where's Tobey? Tom Carr was wondering, slowly turning around to scan the platform, hitching up his khaki trousers beneath his little pot-belly as he looked for the last member of his Acrobat work-group.

Speak of the Devil, just then, Tobey Jansen came down onto the subway platform, looking tall and geeky and ridiculously high-strung, twenty-five years old and clueless, rubber-necking around the platform and unable even for a second to hide the relief he felt when he caught sight of all the other members of the Acrobat work-group.

He might have gone right up to his friends and yelled, "Hiya guys!" if Tom Carr himself hadn't shot him a look and given him a short, furious little wave.

Tobey stopped and stared, his face wide open and as easily read as a billboard: "Oh, okay, yeah, sure, I'll stay put, you betcha—I can pretend we're not all together, sure, I'm a CIA employee, a *field agent,* I can fake stuff, *sure* I can!—absolutely!—no sweat!"

Tom Carr frowned, then sighed and shook his head: *Fucking moron.*

"God what a geek," said Duncan Idaho.

Monika Summers smiled and squeezed her boyfriend's waist.

Duncan—surprised at how relieved he was that Tobey was okay—gave a shaky sigh and murmured, "A *total* super-geek."

And indeed he was. Tobey Jansen had started life at CIA as an analyst, which was why he wasn't too bright. In fact, he was an accountant, though he didn't look like one, what with his shaved head and his six-inch-long goatee that stuck out straight from his chin like a spike, the gelled goatee dyed platinum blond. He looked like the love child of Sid Vicious and Martha Stewart.

In a gesture that was sort of like the reset protocol on some temperamental machine, Tobey Jansen pulled back his maroon red baseball cap over his shaved skull before pulling it back down again. Then he shoved his glasses up the ridge of his nose with the tip of his middle finger, looking as if he were flipping the world the bird as he looked around the platform.

I'm here, guys, his posture seemed to be saying. *Now what?*

To Tobey's left, Tom Carr stood alone. To his right, Duncan and Monika were gently swaying in each other's arms, slow-dancing to a tune only they could hear. Russell and Ljubica stood together, though without touching or looking at each other, about twenty feet farther on down the platform.

Tobey, Duncan and Monika, Ljubica and Russell—everyone was there. So Tom Carr hitched up his pants one last time and looked up and down the platform, confidently slapping his potbelly.

Okay, he thought. *Time to go.*

None of them saw Amalia. She was standing in the shadows behind one of the platform stairs, watching Tom Carr and his work-group, as unnoticed and lethal as an incubating disease.

Even if she had been spotlit, it would've been hard to notice her. Small, mousy-looking, Amalia had straight, shoulder-length, field-mouse brown hair; and with her wide-eyed face and her flat breasts and narrow hips, she looked younger than she was. She looked almost like a girl pretending to be an adult in her severe, unadorned gray flannel suit.

If you'd happened to run into her on the street, you would have paid her no mind; and if you'd managed to corral her at some party she never would have gone to in the first place, all her answers to your prodding or flirtatious questions would have been monosyllables. She would never have asked you a single question in return, just as she never would have allowed herself to spend any time with you. Which might have been just as well—for you.

Casually, as if she were covering a discreet cough, Amalia said into the transmitter tucked away in her sleeve, "I'm in position. What's going on."

A voice, out of breath and running, said into her ear, "We're up top at Forty-fourth and Broadway—give us ninety seconds."

"I don't have ninety seconds," she answered right back. "They're all here, and they're about to move."

On a different frequency, a different voice, a voice full of a weird, funky humor, said into her ear, "If they move, function. Priority list."

"Yes sir," said Amalia as she stood there, waiting for either her back-up to arrive or her targets to move.

Just then, the rattle of a downtown Number Two train

started to fill the platform of the station, deciding things for everyone.

"Okay," said Monika Summers with a smile, looking at the others on the platform. "Fuck you, Nicholas Denton," she said to Duncan.

"Absolutely goddamned right," said Duncan Idaho.

"A train is arriving, sir," said Amalia into her transmitter, waiting for the man with the funky voice to give her her orders.

"Go to it," was all Nicholas Denton said.

"Yes sir," she said as she began to walk toward the work-group Acrobat through the scattered civilians standing around on the platform.

Everyone seemed to converge. As the express train rattled closer, the people standing on the platform gently surged forward, getting ready to board it.

Without a break in her stride, with only a quick glance down the platform at the other targets, Amalia walked straight toward Tom Carr, her primary target.

Foolishly, in Amalia's eyes, Tom Carr and the members of his work-group were all looking at the approaching train, not at the platform around them. As she walked toward Tom Carr, she changed direction slightly as she aimed for Tom Carr's blind side—just behind him and to his left.

Duncan Idaho was the only one who saw Amalia. Glancing to his left, over Monika's head, he saw a small woman he had seen somewhere before but could not place, a woman in a conservative suit walking quickly toward Tom Carr, accelerating as she drew closer. Duncan only had time to frown as suddenly this small, mousy woman raised her hands and gave Tom Carr a terrific shove.

"*Tommy!*" he screamed.

Tom Carr never knew what hit him. All he heard was the clicking, the clicking of a woman's heels on the concrete of the platform. And then suddenly the surprise of falling into the path of the oncoming train.

He fell on his side, his head bouncing on the farther rail, inches from the electrified third rail, his knee slamming hard against the nearer track rail. He could feel that the rail ties underneath his belly were wet, the combination of water and oil soaking his shirt. As he put his hands on the ties to get up, he felt the terrible rattle of the approaching subway train. Looking down the length of his body, behind him, he saw a subway rat huddled under the platform. The rat was watching Tom Carr get to his feet.

His left knee was killing him, and it nearly buckled under him as he stood up and turned around. On the platform, people were staring down at him, their eyes and mouths in *O*s of surprise. He looked to his left. The train was screaming toward him, not thirty feet away. Though it was hard to see him through the glare of the oncoming headlights, the subway engineer was staring at Tom Carr. The engineer was screaming.

Tom Carr bobbed on the tracks, the blow to his head and the surge of adrenaline making him dizzy as he took a quick but unsteady step forward and put his palms flat on the platform. The platform's edge had yellow concrete bubbles to prevent people from slipping when they stood on it. They dug into the heels of his palms as Tom Carr jumped up with all his strength and speed, trying to get back up onto the platform. The edge of the platform scraped into the bottom curve of his potbelly; his hips and his legs were still in the well of the subway tracks.

Then the train hit him.

It collided against his hip, spinning him around as the subway car ground his body against the side of the platform. Tom Carr's arms thrashed the side of the car and the edge of the platform as his body was spun around and around, the subway car twisting him like a child's top. His legs, completely shattered and turned to mush by the force of impact, twisted themselves into each other as he was spun down the length of the platform, braiding into each other like strands of a young girl's ponytail.

There wasn't any sound, or at least none that Tom Carr could hear. He felt as if he were in a washing machine, twisting around with only the hum of his heart to keep him company. Though there was no time to make even a single logical thought, time seemed to have turned malleable and plastic, almost jelly-jam-like in its crazy rhythms as Tom Carr continued to spin against the subway car and the station platform. It all seemed to go on forever, and with no hurry, yet quickly too, and impatiently.

When the subway train finally came to a stop, it was leaning slightly away from the platform. And when the automatic doors opened, the surprised passengers, about to step off, looked down to see a middle-aged man seeming to come out of the gap between the platform and the subway car.

The man—Tom Carr—looked up at the passengers disembarking. He blinked, then frowned, not quite clear as to what had just happened.

"Hello," he said automatically at all the surprised eyes that were staring down at him.

Then everyone screamed.

The screaming was not high pitched and abrupt, but rather, it began like a low moan that quickly rose into a terrified peal, like the sound a man makes when he has been set on fire. The passengers of the car screamed this way, as did the people on the platform. Monika Summers screamed, and so did Russell, and Ljubica, and Tobey Jansen, too. Everyone was screaming uncontrollably, staring at Tom Carr, who looked like a jack-in-the-box come out of the subway to play, a child's toy designed by some supremely malevolent demon, looking for a laugh in a world underground.

The screaming didn't sound like it was going to end anytime soon.

And in the middle of all of this, there were only two people who were watchful and sensate—Amalia and Duncan Idaho.

This is what happened.

"Get down get down get down!" Duncan screamed at Monika, pushing her out of his line of sight as a GLOCK 9 mm appeared in his hand as if by magic, Duncan quickly squaring up in a policeman's stance as across the platform Amalia was ready for him, Amalia with a gun in her hand, firing before Duncan had the chance—*PLACKPLACKPLACKPLACK*—going right for Duncan's head and missing, one of her bullets

neatly nipping off his earlobe, taking his earring and a pinkie-nail piece of flesh with it, her bullets shattering the tile wall-covering behind him as Duncan goes for Amalia—

—*WEET*—he fired back, a single shot, missing Amalia altogether and Duncan now not daring to fire again, too many real people in the way and in the background as the entire platform became a mess of panicked mushrooms.

Russell Orr too squared up, moving extraordinarily quickly for such a big man, a gun in his hand, pointing down the platform and trying to get a line of sight on Amalia—but he was farther away, with even more civilians blocking his firing line.

"Getouttatheway! - Getouttatheway! - Getouttatheway!" Russell screamed at the civilians.

"Go!-Go!-Go!" Duncan shouted at Russell, dealing with Amalia.

"What?" shouted Russell.

"GO!" yelled Duncan.

Russell turned and grabbed his girlfriend, Ljubica Greene, pulling her behind him as he led the way away.

Tom Carr—pinned between the subway car and the platform—turned to see geeky little Tobey Jansen running toward him—Tobey squatting in front of him—Tobey trying to pull him out—Duncan behind him and trying to get a line of sight at Amalia through all the screaming, stampeding civilians running in a panic on the subway platform.

Tobey was grabbing Tom's arms, and he was pulling.

"C'mon," Tobey grunted, yanking at Tom Carr.

"Go, I'm dead already," Tom said calmly into Tobey's frightened eyes.

"Huh?" was all the boy managed to say, still yanking at his boss and friend.

Tom Carr twisted his arms around Tobey's, grabbing his biceps and pulling him to his face.

"Tell the others," he said, suddenly fierce, "27-13."

Tobey's face crinkled into a frown. "What?"

"Listen!" Tom Carr hissed. "It's at box 27-13. Tell the others; they'll know what to do. Remember: 27-13. Repeat it."

"27-13."

"Good. Now go," he said, knowing full well what he was saying, understanding it all very, very clearly now. "*Go*, Tobey—you can still get away."

Tobey frowned down at Tom, his eyes blinking behind his glasses, his gelled goatee vibrating like a tuning fork.

Looking over Tobey's shoulder, Tom Carr saw blonde Monika Summers running up to Tobey and grabbing his shoulder as she looked right at Tom Carr.

"*Come on!*" she shouted at Tobey as her eyes continued to stare at Tom's shattered body, her eyes wanting to linger as the rest of her wanted to get away.

Tom released Tobey, who fell on his backside before he turned and got back up, running down the platform and away from the firefight between Amalia and Duncan, never once looking back at the dying Tom Carr.

Duncan couldn't get a shot as he kept screaming at the mushrooms, "*Get-down-get-down-get-down!*" to no avail, the civilians on the platform and the train too terrified to listen, as frightened as stampeding bison, running without sense, making it impossible to shoot and kill the calm, well-dressed woman-child assassin.

Amalia had no such qualms—*PLACKPLACKPLACK-PLACK*—she fired again, again missing Duncan even as she clipped the elbow of an older lady in an avocado-green cardigan, the old bird caroming and falling and—

—Amalia fell to the ground, tackled from behind by a civilian, a big burly construction-type workman, his panting breath in her ear as he tried getting the gun away from her—

—Amalia screamed, enraged and panicked, slithering in the construction worker's arms 'til she had turned around, solidly connecting her knee to his groin, getting up, losing a shoe, picking up her weapon, firing into the construction worker's head—*PL-PLACK*—killing him on the spot, whirling around—

—Duncan gone, the rest of Acrobat gone, lost in the panic on the platform—

—Amalia—*PLACKPLACKPLACKPLACKPLACKPLACK*—

into the corpse of the construction worker, she starts running up the plat——

—*"Drop your weapon—DROP IT!"*

—NYPD SWAT surrounding her, black helmets and bullet-proof vests, frightened eyes behind clear visors, and automatic barrels aimed right for her heart—

—*"Not ME!"* the diseased Amalia screams in frustration, pointing up the platform with her gun arm. "THEM!"

—but they are gone.

Through the Red Line platform, up the concrete stairs, through the lower level of the station, across the wide expanse of columns and people and flower vendors and street musicians, they are running, running, running to get away from Amalia and whoever else will be joining her, running and running away in a long thread of souls that Russell leads fifteen yards ahead, Ljubica behind him, Monika pulling at the terrified Tobey Jansen, Duncan tail-gunning as SWAT give chase, Duncan yanking and tripping passersby to the ground and into the path of the rushing SWAT while Russell runs far ahead, Russell looking for the exit, looking for the getaway, looking for a way out, looking and looking and finding the staircase that will lead up and away, up and away, and Russell follows it, rushing up the electric escalator into the sunlight, the shiny steel turnstiles there, up and over them in a single leap, bursting out of the glass doors and into the sunny spring morning outside—

—Times Square's full of people and cars and tourists and hot dog vendors as Russell, the first outside, is looking for transportation, people *everywhere,* the light and sun flooding his eyes this bright and dazzling morning as he looks up and down Forty-second Street, the colorful street-signs and advertisements as psychedelic as a trip, his gun at the ready, inconspicuously at his side as he steps off the curb and looks for a way—

BLAAAAAAAAHHH!!!—screams a yellow taxicab—horn—screeching to a halt—behind him—whirls around—gun in hand.

"Out of the car—NOW!" shouts Russell Orr—a gigantic

café au lait man aiming a firearm at the taxicab that has nearly
run him over—the cab's front bumper just two feet from his
knee as he goes 'round to the driver's side and opens the door,
using his enormous bulk and his ugly gun to bully the terrified
Russian cabby out the passenger-side door—*"Out out
OUT!"*—and out of the cab the driver goes, falling to the
ground and slithering backward on all fours, like a man pretending to be a spider.

Ljubica, Monika, and Tobey rush out of the station, and
when they see Russell in the taxicab, they stop, waiting for
Duncan, who's been covering their flank but is now nowhere
to be seen, Russell roaring, *"What are you waiting for—get
in get in get in!"*

The three of them jump into the back of the cab just as
Duncan reappears, Duncan getting to the top of the electric
escalator and running to the turnstiles, getting to the turnstile
and leaping over it, getting to the doors of the station and—

—Duncan stops suddenly and deliberately turns around just
as two SWAT officers come rushing toward him just beyond
the turnstile, their automatic weapons rising to aim at him,
ready to shoot him, Duncan's own weapon ready to kill—

(—*I won't kill them, I won't kill them, I'll lie down before
I kill them*—)

Duncan Idaho tosses his hair out of his eyes and pops both
SWAT twice on their bullet-proofed chests—*WEE-WEET!–
WEE-WEET!*—both of them going down in two untidy heaps,
their weapons flying out of their hands, the two of them yelling—

—*"Aw—SHIT!"*

—*"God that HURTS!"*

Right as rain.

—"Duncan, *come on!"*—

Duncan Idaho nods and runs out of the station and into the
shotgun seat of the cab—

—Russell floors it, the taxicab screaming like an agonized
refugee.

The oblivious civilians out and about this sunny May morning haven't yet realized what is happening, many of them stop-

ping and looking and staring at the taxicab, its sound ricocheting against the placarded canyons of Times Square, the cab tearing away from the grip of all those eyes that have latched onto it as it races down Forty-second Street, newly regentrified and Disneyfied, the cab on its way crosstown to Grand Central Station.

"Tom's dead," Duncan Idaho says out of breath, still not having realized that he is bleeding from his nicked earlobe as he checks his weapon and begins to reload.

"Yeah, I know," says Russell, concentrating on the road and casually noticing that his door is still wide open even as the cab starts passing the sixty mile an hour mark.

So he closes it, the five inside.

"We got company," says Ljubica in the back, her low, smoky voice even and relaxed as she looks out the rear window. The rushing wind makes her hair billow thin black-brown serpent strands across her face as she loads a round into her firearm and checks the safety with quick, practiced motions that are all arms and legs and elbows, impossibly long and thin.

Behind them, two cop-cars rush at them like hulking metal monsters, their sirens blazing red eyes that clear out the traffic in either direction.

Inside the cab, everyone's attention turns behind them, just as Russell casually says, "Up ahead."

Up ahead, at Forty-second and Sixth Avenue, two more cop-cars slam to a halt just at the intersection, thinking they'll block the cab—they think wrong.

"Hold on," says Russell as he pumps the gas and accelerates into a ramrod, smashing both cop-cars ahead of them—front end—rear end—both cop-cars spinning around in the middle of the intersection—out of their way, sweat-droplets of glass showering off of them from the collision.

"They're still behind us," says Ljubica as the cab screams through the city.

"Well then do something about it," says Russell to his girlfriend as Duncan beside him pounds his knee in frustrated agony, agonized because the dividing wall in the cab keeps him from getting into the backseat and dealing with the two chasing cop-cars—

But Ljubica and Monika can deal.

"Get down," says Monika Summers to Tobey Jansen, who is between both women, totally useless and in the way since he doesn't have a gun; Tobey crouching as Monika and Ljubica begin firing out the rear window, their first bullet shattering the glass, their subsequent bullets aimed at the two cop-cars that are chasing them, now joined by two more—

—*FLAK-FLAK-FLAK-FLAK-FLAK-FLAK-FLAK-FLAK!*— go their weapons as they fire on the four cop-cars, aiming for the tires and the engines, and something must have exploded on one of the cop-cars because its hood bursts open amid sparks and a smoke cloud, the cop-car drifting away with losing interest. Another one of the cars, one of the recent additions, takes a bullet in the wheel and falls askew like a drunken sailor as it too starts to fade as surely as a man who's had all the whores he can handle for the night—but that leaves two more cop-cars, and they are relentless.

Down on the floor in the rear seat, Tobey is looking up, covering his ears to the drum-splitting sound of the weapons being fired, his gelled spike of a goatee completely mushed, his maroon red baseball cap askew, Tobey happening to look up to see through the rear door window a helicopter—a helicopter?—pass by—a police helicopter?

"There's a helicopter up there!" he shouts, no one but the idle Duncan in the shotgun seat hearing what he has to say.

"What?" shouts Duncan.

"I said there's a helicopter chasing us!" Tobey shouts calmly above the roar of the firefight, making his soft and excitable geeky-kid's voice go hoarse.

Up in front, Duncan leans forward and looks out the window and indeed there is a cop-chopper buzzing around, joined by another chopper with white markings—

"We got a fucking, a fucking *news*-chopper, too," says Duncan, amazed.

"Pictures at eleven, great," mutters Russell, who is concentrating on the traffic on the road—

—*traffic,* traffic like a river chockful of logs, jammed up in both directions, Forty-second Street a vehicular nightmare of frozen patience as way down on the other end of the block, Fifth Avenue, more traffic, more cars, more nightmares—

"Watch out!" yells Duncan, Russell Orr turning this way and that, trying and failing to find a way to bypass all these stuck cars, the sidewalks brimming with pedestrians, the static traffic zooming at them at seventy miles an hour.

"Hold on," Russell shouts as he hits the brakes and twirls the steering wheel with all his strength, the cab sliding hard, slip-sliding across the pavement, smoke rising from the tires as the right side of the taxicab goes right to the rear ends of the stuck traffic—

Crau-HIH!!! goes the taxicab, the whole right side smashed, everyone inside getting tossed around—

—but they're already moving on, dealing with it, Duncan in the front seat slithering out the open window of the cab and onto the trunk of the car they smashed—*"I'll cover!"*—his gun in hand, he stands on the trunk's hood and aims his gun at the approaching cop-cars, Duncan not firing—not daring to—real people *everywhere*—but the cops in the cop-cars don't know about his self-control—the cop-cars swerve out of the way, their tires almost on fire as they brake to avoid Duncan and now Russell, who, too, has burst out of the cab with his gun in hand, both men in policemen's firing stance, using their guns and their stance to intimidate the cops, giving cover to the others—Ljubica, Monika, Tobey—so they can get out of the busted-up taxicab and run down Forty-second Street.

The pedestrians out and about: The drivers of the stuck cars: They've seen the crash, but now they see the men with guns, and they know enough to get out of the way, ducking and running, ducking and running and shouting and afraid.

"Go!" yells Duncan to Russell, Duncan knowing the pedestrian panic is the only thing that will save them.

Big Russell Orr turns and runs around the cab, following the others down Forty-second Street, the screaming, running, freaking civilians distracting the cops, who only have eyes for Duncan Idaho.

The two chasing cop-cars have stopped a good distance away—ten, fifteen yards—they're both regular NYPD, sirens blaring—Duncan hears more sirens on the way, the two cop-cars in front of him with two cops each, all of them hiding behind their open doors, Duncan, the last one there, with that perfect aim he learned when he was getting his master rifle-man's badge at Fort Benning, gets a bead on the closest cop-car, aims, fires once at the engine radiator—*WEET!*—all the cops flinch and duck some more as the radiator explodes white steam, the hood buckling, Duncan Idaho takes the opportunity to look over his shoulder at the members of his work-group, making sure they're getting lost amid the panicking pedestrians down Forty-second Street—

—a crazy-brave rookie punk, one of the cop-car drivers, makes a break for it when he sees Duncan look away and over his shoulder. This idiot of a rookie runs a zig-zag pattern (as if that would help!), running out from behind the open cop-car door as he rushes at Duncan, the moron-fool thinking that his Kevlar vest will save him, his speed will save him, his will and bravery will save him, this fool-rookie thinking he can tackle Duncan Idaho—

(—*tackle ME? That surely is some funky dung, look here*—)

—*WEET* goes a single, perfectly aimed bullet, right to the cop's sternum, breaking *all* his ribs with a single shot—the rookie'll be on the disability list for three weeks, desk duty for six more, but during the rest of his long, long life, he'll grow to love that perfectly round, half-inch-deep hole in his chest, the little hole he'll think of as his second belly-button.

Now, though, it hurts. *"MotherFUCKER!"* screams the downed rookie, his entire chest feeling like it got squeezed by an angry giant—

—but Duncan Idaho's already away, arms flapping like condor wings, running after the others down Forty-second Street.

The whole scene is taking place about a third of the way from Sixth Avenue to Fifth, one of the long blocks of Manhattan. So a funny thing happens: Though the mushrooms at *this* stretch of Forty-second Street know that a shoot-out is going on, the ones down the street have no idea. Not yet, at any rate. They'll get an education presently.

Acrobat's running. The stuck traffic's so thick, the sidewalk's so congested, it's easier to just run across the hoods and roofs of cars, leaping from car to car, hood to trunk, their feet never touching the ground—Ljubica, Tobey, Monika, Russell, Duncan: Acrobat.

The rookie-punk cop is down, rolling in non-fatal agony, but his three buddies are all chasing Acrobat, running like rats through a maze as they go between bumpers and then between columns of cars, neither side daring to let loose a single shot, the bright sunny sky big and wide, the canyon of the street filled—ant-like—with innocent pedestrians who have no idea what the commotion is all about, tourists automatically filming the action with their camcorders, ordinary New Yorkers averting their eyes and speeding along to their next appointments as the cops give chase, Acrobat running and jumping and leaping from hood to trunk to roof, suddenly all of it boiling down to who's in better shape and who is more desperate—

—Fifth Avenue and Forty-second Street, the lions of the Library just down the block, and up ahead, traffic semi-stopped—slowing—stopped—red light, the intersection empty as Acrobat run through the empty intersection—

—a high-pitched scream—*"AghYEEah—I'm hit!"*—Ljubica, her elegant face turned into crags of pain—her thigh gushes blood in rhythmical spasms—a sharp shard of glass-sensation zipping through her leg like an electric current that throbs before turning it numb. *Unbelievably* an idiot-idiot-*idiot* cop let go a shot as they were crossing the empty intersection, right in the middle of all those goddamned fucking civilians (someone ought to outlaw them altogether), a crazy, lucky shot, the slug is buried deep in Ljubica's thigh—she's lying on the ground, bleeding out at the intersection of Fifth and Forty-second—

—Monika Summers's there, holding her gun with both hands, firing—*plü-plück!*—right at the three chasing NYPD, who dive for cover, her bullets blowing out a couple of windshields, sending out the message—

"*Stop it!*" snaps Russell Orr, yanking Monika's arms down, keeping her from shooting again, the sweat droplets on his shaved café au lait dome shining individually as if they were each a tiny little light.

Geeky Tobey Jansen is already kneeling beside Ljubica, tearing off his own T-shirt, his maroon red baseball cap the exact same color of the blood coming out of Ljubica's thigh, Monika and Russell standing over them, covering them as the NYPD yell at each other, "*Don't shoot! Watch your civilians, don't shoot!*"

The civilians are wigging. *Now* they know what's going on.

All over the intersection of Forty-second and Fifth, people are running to get away, people ditching their cars, the whole intersection turning into a total mess—it looks like one of those pictures of the Russian Revolution, people running to and fro for no apparent reason other than mere survival.

Up above the impassive gray buildings that see it all with the indifference of elephants, news-choppers are alighting like flies, buzzing around with tethered cameramen standing on the running rails, catching all the late-breaking action.

Tobey has ripped his shirt into one long strip and tied it round Ljubica's wounded thigh right there in the middle of the street.

"*Tighter, tie it TIGHTER!*" shouts Ljubica, as Tobey tightens the knot of his shirt as hard as he can, his T-shirt now drenched in Ljubica's blood.

"You good to go?" Tobey asks her.

"I don't think it's broken," says Ljubica, meaning "Yes," as she struggles to stand up.

Russell Orr doesn't say a word as he bends down and scoops Ljubica into his arms, picking her up like a bridegroom carries his bride, a bloody wedding night as her thigh continues to bleed.

He doesn't notice the bleeding—he just runs with her, running just as fast as if he were carrying nothing, running as if he knows exactly where he's going: Running down Fifth Avenue.

"Where are you going?" Duncan Idaho yells at Russell.

Russell Orr stops, unsure. "This way—"

"Come on!" Duncan yells, waving his hand at Russell and Ljubica in his arms, forgetting that he's got a gun at the end of that hand. *"This way!"*

Russell, confused, turns away from Fifth Avenue and runs after Duncan, who is running down the north sidewalk of Forty-second Street, running through the pedestrians, running toward Madison Avenue, crossing the street at a dead run—

—running toward Grand Central Station.

Just before Forty-second hits Park, on the northeast side of the street, tucked away, hard to see, there is an entrance to Grand Central Station: A half-dozen double doors made of thick oak, the top third of each door having a pane of clear glass.

Duncan Idaho, the first to the doors, yanks one open, getting immediately swallowed up by all the pedestrians, who have no idea who he is. As soon as he's inside, he knows they'll be safe here.

One of the other doors has one of those handicapped signs, a big blue flat button beside the door. As Russell Orr with Ljubica in his arms gets to the entrance, he kicks the button, making the mechanical doors instantly swing open like the cave doors to a magi's fortune, Russell rushing in with Ljubica as behind them, Monika and Tobey cover their rear.

Tobey's ahead of Monika, and he gets to the handicapped door just as it begins to close. Once inside Grand Central, he slows down and stops.

The station is all champagne marble. Where Tobey is, oblivious pedestrians are swiftly walking along, paying shirtless Tobey no mind. The ceiling is high and distant, the hallway he is in about forty feet wide, lined by a couple of thick columns a good five feet in diameter.

Down the hallway, Tobey watches as Russell and Ljubica go to the very end, some three hundred feet away, to the top of some electric escalators that take them down. Tobey is about to follow when he thinks about Monika, wondering if she's okay, Tobey about to open one of the doors and see if maybe a cop tagged her, when she suddenly bursts through the oak doors, pedestrians flowing swiftly between them.

"Hey," says Tobey.

"Go, go, go," says Monika, waving Tobey forward to the electric escalators down the hallway as she looks around.

Perfect, Monika Summers thinks as she looks around, noticing the columns that can give her cover, looking at the volume of mushrooms passing her by, looking at the thick oak doors, thinking of the three cops still chasing them.

Perfecto-mundo.

Monika's tough. To look at her, she's a KKΓ sorority girl, but to know her, she's a CIA utility player. She has no one particular duty, no particular task, but all the tasks she does, she does exceptionally well.

Leaning against one of the champagne marble columns, Monika slips her firearm between her knees and reties her maple-blonde ponytail with an elastic scrunchie, keeping her eyes nailed to the half-dozen oak double-doors.

"What are you doing?" asks geeky Tobey Jansen, Monika not having realized that he's stayed behind with her, Tobey looking gawky as a teenager.

"What are *you* doing here, *go,*" she says, taking her firearm and waving it at Tobey—too late.

"Okay, stay, but watch out."

Manhattan: Not a single pedestrian even notices she's waving a gun.

The fleetest NYPD cop gets to the closed doors of the station and *not waiting!*—stupidly not waiting, Monika dashing to hide behind the marble column, her eyes on the door, the lone cop yanking open the wooden door, no hesitation, huffing and puffing and dumb as a post as he runs in pursuit—

Plück-plück-plück-plück!—Monika nails him right on the chest as she comes out from behind the column, her bullets not piercing the Kevlar vests, but so what? Know what a mule kick feels like? Know what four kicks in a row feel like? This NYPD cop knows: He's shouting pain, all the pedestrians suddenly *very* aware that Monika has a gun, everyone rushing to be gone—it's like a hundred particles suddenly deciding that *here* is not a place they want to be.

The cop flies right off his feet, the shotgun he was carrying flying out of his hands and clattering to the ground fifteen feet away, too far for Monika to reach for—

—Tobey Jansen's there, the super-geek with the zero cool. Using his toe, he flicks the sliding shotgun up off the floor and right into his expectant hands, the Gods of Grace smiling as they give him perfection this one time on spec, his goatee humming while his hands check the action of the rifle, Tobey walking right to the double-doors of the station, walking right outside—

"Stay away!" he yells to no one in particular, the civilians freaking out at the sight of this punk-rocking anarchist with the scrawny milk-white chest and the black shotgun, the cops in the distance running directly at him, diving for cover as they see him with a weapon, Tobey casually firing into the soft asphalt of Forty-second Street—*PAHM!*

Loud as he can (though not quite as loud as the shotgun), Tobey yells to the world, *"STAY AWAY!"*

No one contradicts him.

He lets the door close as he comes back inside Grand Central Station, he and Monika running down the hallway after the others, Monika's ponytail flopping like it would after a big win—she's looking like she's forgetting her pompoms.

"Smooth!" she tells Tobey, who pumps all the shells out of the shotgun as he jogs along, then takes the empty shotgun and slides it far across the brilliant champagne marble of the station, out of casual sight.

They get to the top of the escalator—just three hundred feet away from the action, and no one here has a *clue* what's happened: The beauty of a crowd in a fluid environment.

Monika and Tobey make their way through the civilians on the escalator, people shooting them angry eyes but not much else as they elbow their way down to the station proper.

"Pull up," says Monika, stopping on the escalator.

Tobey stops and looks at her, confused. "What?"

"Take a breather," she says, taking a deep breath herself.

"But what about the others—?"

"Be cool; they'll wait," she says calmly. "Take a breath. Relax."

Tobey considers this. "Okay," he says. He takes a breath and wipes his face. He realizes he has no shirt on, though he isn't cold.

Monika takes another deep breath, and then a last one, until her heart has stilled. By this time, the electric escalator is almost at the bottom, on the south side of the main area of the station.

Across it, the others are waiting for them: The work-group Acrobat.

They're right there at Grand Central where the brass clock shines the time at the round information desk. Up above, the ceiling is painted like the night sky, all the stars in place, the constellations ordered, while on either side of this pretty mural, towering windows glow with the morning light. The place is chockful of people, so no one's noticing a tousled blond man wearing a biker's jacket or his buddy, a big, bald, cocoa-colored man with a shaved head and gold-rimmed glasses. They certainly aren't noticing a thin, pale woman with stringy, black-brown hair who is standing between both men, carefully not putting any weight on her left leg. They're not noticing the blonde sorority sister who walks up to silently join this trio, nor the shirtless punk rocker who's walking with her, a rocker with a maroon red baseball cap, a spiked goatee, and a tattoo of a tumbling acrobat on his left shoulder blade.

Why would anybody notice them? Everyone is minding their own business, doing their own thing. No one sees which way they go. No one cares. They're there, yes, but then they're not there. The blindness of the crowd. The invisibility of being anonymous.

By the time the NYPD shows up in force, combing Grand Central Station like they really mean it, Acrobat is gone.

Down deep in the tunnels of the Times Square subway station, Nicholas Denton was a happy man.

He arrived alone, walking through the empty tunnels of the station with a big-fat-happy smile on his face, almost *skipping* on his way to see the dying Tom Carr. Not even the odd spookiness of the empty subway station could distract Denton from the sheer glee that he was feeling.

Boy-o-boy-o-boy, he kept thinking to himself.

Nicholas Denton was the Deputy Director for Counter Intelligence of CIA. He stood about six feet even, and he was rather slim, his blond hair slicked back, and a natural smile always on the verge of breaking out. It was his job to uncover, monitor, and if possible control foreign intelligence assets, and of course to police the Central Intelligence Agency itself. And though he himself was always the first to point out that he was just another Federal bureaucrat, underpaid and under-appreciated, there was a look of money to Denton; of money and casual, effortless ease. The best schools, the best breeding, all the accouterments that money and class could buy—that was Denton all the way: Choate, Yale, Oxford on a Rhodes, of the Social Registry Dentons of New York and Maine. Nicholas Andrew Denton III—the pleasure was all his.

He was that rarity, a naturally content man. He always looked as if he had just heard the funniest damn story, and there was an aura to him that made you want to be around him, maybe go up to him and ask him, "What was that story you heard again?" He looked happy, but he also looked like a man who knew his way around the world, like someone who could eat an artichoke or make a death happen without getting his hands dirty.

Like today.

"Oh *boy!*" he said to himself.

A nasty kind of morbid curiosity was making him go see Tom Carr; he couldn't believe the man wasn't dead already. And though he knew he shouldn't be here, he couldn't help himself. Because as surely as he knew his name, he knew he had to go see Tom Carr and gloat while he still had the chance.

The hard tattoo of Denton's leather heels clicked and clattered and bounced around the tiled subway station tunnels like a squash ball. As he got to the top of the stairs leading to the platform proper, hearing the firefighters talking and moving equipment around, Denton stopped and collected himself. He wiped the smile off his face, flicked his cigarette away, then slicked his hair back and adjusted his Paul Stewart suit. A tiny smile kept trying to break out, a smile at the thought of watching Tom Carr die. He wiped it off his face for the sake of propriety, then walked down the stairs to the subway platform.

The corpse of the construction worker Amalia had killed was gone, as was Amalia herself. The elderly woman who had been caught in the middle of the firefight was also gone, shot in the arm, the arm treated on the spot, hordes of newspeople waited to interview her.

But down on the platform, there were no news crews. The entire station had been evacuated and sealed off by the NYPD—an amazing feat, considering how crucial the Times Square station was to the whole New York City public transportation system. With no one around, the place was downright spooky, the ghosts of countless passengers hovering silently around, while Tom Carr waited to join them.

Tom Carr lay where he had stopped, the doors of the subway train left open so as not to crowd him, his right elbow on the subway platform, his left on the formica flooring of the subway train. A uniformed policeman in his mid-thirties was squatting next to him, talking soothing nonsense as Tom Carr lay there without much to do.

"You want me to go get somebody?" the cop was saying. "If you want I can go get somebody."

The cop squatting beside him was some beady-eyed little freak, one of those icky, ferrety little sons-of-bitches you just hate on sight. Joey Goldman was the name he'd given, and from the fatness of his face and his short, fat, grotesque little body, you just knew instinctively that this was one evil little demon. Now, though, the little fucker looked green and speechless, except for that one line he kept repeating: "You want me to go find someone? Go find your wife or kid or girlfriend or something? I'm serious, you tell me—you want me to go find someone for you?"

Find someone, thought Tom Carr. *That's a hoot.* There was no one left to go find.

Wife? Gone, both of them. Kids? Grown-up strangers he didn't have much to say to or much use for. Hometown friends and family? Left 'em going on near forty years ago, back when he had gone off to Vietnam and then to college. In fact, Tom Carr's only close relationships were with his Acrobat kids—Ljubica and Russell, Tobey and Monika. And of course, Duncan Idaho. Especially Duncan, his boy in all but name. The Acrobat kids were his kids . . . and from the way the New York City cops around the subway platform were acting, Tom Carr could tell that his kids had gotten away.

Just a few feet away from him, firemen were placing a hydraulic press in the seven-inch-wide gap between the train and the subway platform. None of the firefighters looked at Tom Carr if they could help it. They just concentrated on the machinery, all of them intensely, uncomfortably aware that Tom Carr was staring right at them.

"You sure you don't want me to get in touch with anyone?" the ferrety-looking cop kept asking Tom Carr.

"I'm sure," said Tom Carr, feeling no pain.

He heard someone behind him come onto the platform, and with difficulty, Tom Carr craned his neck around—

—and what he saw literally took his breath away—he simply could not believe what his eyes were registering.

About ten yards away, Nicholas Denton had come down the platform stairs and was now talking to a couple of firefighters and a policeman. The little group kept glancing at Tom Carr as they talked, but Denton stood with his back to him, his head bent, one hand covering his mouth.

He's laughing, thought Tom Carr. *The fucker's* laughing.

"You know he's laughing, don't you?" he managed to croak to the cop squatting beside him.

"Save your strength," the policeman said inanely.

Tom Carr sighed and let his chin slump onto his chest.

Presently, the ferrety little cop squatting beside Tom Carr was called away by the policeman speaking to Denton. And then Denton himself turned from the huddle and approached Tom Carr.

Only Carr could see his face. It was sharp and narrow, with clear blue eyes and an invisible nose. *He changed his hairstyle,* Tom Carr thought absently, as he noticed Denton's hair was slicked back over a head that was narrow at the jaw and wide at the brow. His lips were pale, and as he approached Tom Carr, those lips began to stretch into a smile.

Don't let me go like this, Tom Carr thought crazily, steeling himself for Denton. *Don't let me wimp out.*

"Well well well," he said, mustering all his courage to deal with his boss and enemy. "If it isn't Nicholas Denton, CIA's resident bogeyman."

"Hello Tom," said Denton, squatting to be at eye level with the dying Tom Carr. "You're looking good," he said, his evil smile growing all the wider.

"Amalia's getting sloppy," said Carr. "I should be dead already."

"You will be, soon enough," said Denton, smiling as he said it. "This way is almost better. A last chance for me to give you a merry sendoff before you go on your way."

The two men stared at each other without a word as, around them, the firefighters heaved and grunted and positioned the hydraulic press.

Finally, Denton broke the spell. "You know what's going to happen, don't you," he said casually, a leer on his face. "That hydraulic press is going to push the subway car away from the platform. And when that happens—*tock!*" said Denton, making a clicking sound with his tongue and the roof of his mouth. "Your insides will fall right out of your body. Fairly disgusting, and unbelievably painful, or so those fine gentlemen back there have told me," he said as he motioned vaguely to the firefighters behind him.

"You're sick," said Tom Carr disgustedly.

"Yes, I know," said Denton pleasantly. "But I can't help it. You had it coming, Tommy," he said, wagging his finger good-naturedly at Tom Carr. "You had it coming."

Denton. Nicholas Denton. He was smiling. He was *laughing*. It was all a big joke to him. He shook his head as he took out a silver cigarette case and offered it to Tom Carr, in a motion as casual as if they'd been down at the park, having a chuckle over some office adventure. Carr didn't even see the case as he stared at Denton, wanting above all else to kill him but knowing he would never get the chance.

"I can't feel anything below my chest," he said.

Denton hunched his shoulders in a wordless "Too bad" gesture as he took a cigarette out of his silver case and lit it with a white-gold DuPont lighter.

"Not a goddamned thing," Tom Carr repeated.

Snap! went the DuPont lighter as Denton replaced it in his jacket pocket and took a drag on his cigarette, staring all the while at Tom Carr. Denton's gold wedding band was half as thin as a key ring; his wristwatch—subdued and elegant, Swiss and expensive—had a black leather strap.

"How?" Tom asked finally, looking at Denton, afraid of the answer just as he suspected its shape already.

"How what?" asked Denton. "How did I know you'd be here?"

Tom only nodded with a grimace, as if the answer was going to hurt.

"Why, because one of your Acrobat kids belongs to me," said Denton.

Tom squeezed his eyes shut, blindsided even though he'd suspected as much.

"Mine from the start," said Denton easily. "I mean, really, you didn't think I'd let you go running around without knowing exactly what you were up to, hmm?"

Suddenly, it was too much for Tom Carr. Though he felt no pain, it was just too much. He started to cry as he lay there, his broken body twisted beneath him.

"It's not fair," he said softly.

" 'Not *fair*'?" said Denton, genuinely surprised by what he heard. " 'Not *fair*'? Oh-ho, that's a good one, Tommy. 'Not fair.' I'll be remembering that when I'm pissing on your grave."

"Mr. Denton?" one of the firefighters called out.

Denton stood up and turned around. The firefighter spoke to him briefly, his eyes constantly going to Tom Carr. Denton nodded solemnly, then he turned back to Tom Carr and squatted to whisper to him.

"It'll be soon now," he said to him. "Any final words? Last requests?"

Tom Carr looked up at the evil blond man staring down at him with a smile.

"My kids got away," he said.

Denton casually nodded as he took a drag on his smoke. "We have people looking for them," he said.

Tom Carr kept on staring at Denton as the smoke from the man's cigarette stung his eyes.

"Someday," said Tom Carr, unable to stop himself from crying, "someone will come looking for you."

Calm, relaxed, completely detached, Nicholas Denton said, "I'm sure you're right, Tommy. And when that day comes, I'll be sure to give them your regards. But right now, no one's here for me. Right now, I'm here for you."

"We're ready," said the firefighter as the hydraulic press was turned on, the sound a high-pitched whine that made the platform vibrate.

The two men stared at each other, the one crying, the one smiling.

"Good-bye, Tommy."

"Fuck you."

Denton's smile turned into a happy grin as he stared at Tom Carr. The hydraulic press must have changed a gear or something, because suddenly it whined powerful loud. With that, it began pushing the subway car away from the platform. And as it did, Tom Carr's entrails fell out of his body, and he died.

CHAPTER 2

Getting a Bead on Things

"... *The search for the suspects soon turned deadly, as law-enforcement officials were involved in a high-speed car chase through the streets of New York City* ..."

"A fucking miracle, that's all I can say," said Duncan Idaho. "Wipe my brow."

Tobey Jansen took a hand towel folded into a square and wiped Duncan's brow as the television droned on and on.

"Wipe my eyes too," he said, as he turned his face toward Tobey.

Tobey wiped Duncan's eyes. Then he hesitated, looking at Duncan's earlobe.

"Your ear's ... lemme get it," he said, wiping the earlobe Amalia had shot off, which was beginning to bleed again.

"... *Police have yet to identify the alleged bank robbers, who are believed to have participated in last November's failed assault on the Chase Manhattan branch on Water Street. In that incident, four well-dressed assailants carrying automatic weapons staged an early morning raid on the bank.* ..."

When Tobey was done, Duncan turned to Ljubica. "Hey, Yuvi, how you doing hanging in there?"

"Quit it with the chit-chat and get it over with," said Ljubica Greene.

She was stretched out on the bed, lying on her back and naked from the waist down, holding onto the headboard above her head, squeezing the pain away. Though the motel room they were in was cool, Ljubica was sweating, her stomach turning slow, nauseous somersaults.

"... *tonight there are unconfirmed reports that one of the suspects was in fact killed today by members of the police department SWAT team...*"

Kneeling on the floor beside her, Duncan held the clamp steady as he began digging through Ljubica's thigh, looking for a piece of metal that was stuck inside her leg.

"Wait, I'm gonna puke," she said.

"Don't move, this is delicate," said Duncan, as he continued trying to get the fragment out. Then he added, "If you're gonna puke, tell Tobey to hold you down."

"Hold me down," said Ljubica.

Without hesitation, Tobey grabbed her tight by the hips and held her down, putting the full weight of his body into it to keep her from moving.

"I got her," he said.

"Go," said Duncan.

With no fanfare, Ljubica vomited over the side of the bed, into a plastic garbage can that was a quarter full already with vomitus.

"Uhn," she said, spitting and swallowing and then spitting again. "Better," she said, Tobey releasing her and smoothing her wet hair, which was black and stringy with sweat.

"Thanks," she said to Tobey, looking into his eyes, trying to think of something else besides the pain. She noticed that sweat—cold sweat—was running down Tobey's brow and onto his glasses, a single droplet having made its way to the very tip of his goatee.

"Mmm," said Duncan, digging through the meat of her thigh, the clamp finally catching hold of the slippery little piece of metal. "Hold on," he warned, then yanked hard before she had had a chance to prepare.

Ljubica yelped once, then held it in, sweating even more but feeling relieved.

Like when you're constipated and it finally comes out, she thought, finding no humor in the analogy.

Duncan stared at the jagged hunk of metal at the end of the clamp, turning it this way and that, trying to figure out what it was.

"Well?" asked Ljubica, leaning her head up to see.

"I have no idea what it is," said Duncan.

Tobey, peering at it, said, "It looks like a piece of a car."

Yuvi plopped her head back down. "I don't care that much to figure it out. Just sew me up already."

Duncan tossed the clamp away and turned to a small tray lying on the bed next to Ljubica's feet, a tray woefully lacking in instruments.

"Try passing out," Duncan told her as he took up a spool of fishing line and a sewing needle. He began threading the needle. "It'll be easier if you're out cold."

"I-I-I'm not good at passing out," said Ljubica. "Just get it over with."

"Gimme some more wet towels," said Duncan. "And get rid of the puke while you're at it."

Tobey took the half-full garbage can and went into the bathroom. But there weren't any towels, at least none that weren't drenched in blood. So he went through the connecting doors to the other motel room, the room where Duncan and Monika would be sleeping, and found a stack of fresh towels. He threw them all in the bathtub and turned on the hot water, then threw Ljubica's vomit into the toilet.

Before he could help himself, Tobey himself leaned over the toilet seat and vomited in sympathy. He had never been shot at before. He had never seen anyone shot at either. *A lot of firsts,* he thought, retching again.

When he was through, he felt better—clear-headed and more alert.

"Where are those towels," Duncan called out from the other room.

"In a sec," said Tobey, spitting out the vomit from his mouth and washing his face in the sink. He grabbed the mass of soaking wet towels from the bathtub, squeezed the excess water out of them, then went back into the room.

Ljubica still lay there, staring at the ceiling. Duncan took one of Tobey's wet towels and started cleaning up the blood around her wound. Then he began sewing Ljubica up with the sewing needle and the fishing line.

". . . Cathy, authorities here are mum about this morning's deadly shoot-out. FBI agents have taken over the investigation, already gathering forensic evidence that might provide a clue as to who it was that turned a pleasant spring morning into a deadly shoot-out. . . ."

Duncan sewed in silence for about five minutes. He hadn't done any medical work in maybe ten years, back when he'd been a fresh-faced teenager humping the Special Forces course at Fort Benning. But Duncan was surprised by how much he remembered, his sutures remarkably even for someone who hadn't had any practice. He sewed in silence, but carefully leaning back so that Tobey could see exactly what he was doing. Duncan concentrated on Tobey, trying to ignore Ljubica's breathing—she kept yanking in a sharp shaft of air every time he pierced the skin around her wound, unnerving him.

"What do you do about a final knot?" Tobey asked quietly, gently combing Ljubica's hair as he watched Duncan.

"You tie it like this," he said, automatically tying up the fishing line after he'd done the last suture, not allowing his brain to get in the way of his fingers' memory.

"Cool," said Tobey.

"Don't call it cool," said Ljubica. "Call it anything but cool."

Duncan and Tobey smiled at her.

When he was done with the entry wound, Duncan gently slapped Ljubica's knee. "Roll over," he said.

With Tobey's help, she rolled onto her stomach, the bullet's exit wound on her left thigh farther from Duncan. So he scooted up, leaning on Ljubica's behind.

"Man, you've got a great ass," he said to Ljubica as he began on the exit wound.

"Shut up and get it over with," she said, her smoky voice serious and tired, her white-porcelain skin having turned ever so slightly yellowish.

"Monika's ass isn't as nice as yours, I'll tell you right now," said Duncan, as he continued his sutures. "But yours— whew! Nice and tight, and just round enough."

"Shut up, cowboy," Ljubica said into the pillow, laughing a little.

"With an ass like that, man . . . uh, look, Tobey, uh, mind giving us a minute?" Duncan asked without looking away or stopping what he was doing, only the tone of his voice betraying any humor. "I think, uh, Yuvi and me, uh—you know what I'm saying? So why don't you go get lost for a little while, huh? Say an hour?"

Tobey smiled. "An hour? Fifteen seconds is more like it," he said, taking off his glasses and wiping his face. "Monika tells me you're getting therapy for your problem. How's that going?"

"Goddamit, that's a vicious lie Monika's been spreading," said Duncan without taking his eyes off the suturing. "The truth is she's frigid, and that's a fact."

"Frigid?" said Tobey, mock-surprised, then mumbling, "You could have fooled me."

"Fooled—? So *that's* where those dinosaur undies came from."

"Shut up, both of you." Ljubica laughed, her words muffled by the pillow.

By the time Duncan finished suturing the exit wound, Ljubica was snoring into the pillow. With a pocket knife, Duncan trimmed the fishing line. Then he washed the wounds with one of the wet towels, before taking a bottle of peroxide and dousing the two wounds.

"AH—!" Ljubica yelped, waking to the pain.

"All done," said Duncan. From the tray, he took two big bandages and peeled the paper off them. They were just big enough for each of the wounds, which Duncan covered, pressing firmly on them to make sure they stuck. Then he took an Ace bandage and wrapped Ljubica's thigh.

"All done," he repeated.

Ljubica lay back and listened to the television blare on.

". . . Though the New York City Police Department has yet

*to release any official statement, unconfirmed reports indicate
that the bank robbery suspects are believed to have fled the
state and might be currently in New Jersey, or even in Pennsylvania. . . ."*

"Bank robbers," she said aimlessly.

"Denton's a clever guy," said Duncan, turning to look at
the television set and slumping to the ground, leaning his back
flat against the side of the bed.

"What," said Ljubica, surprised by Duncan's equanimity.

"You think Nicholas Denton is gonna tell the whole world
he's got a CIA operations-group running around, screwing
with his shit?" said Duncan. "No. Denton's smart. He tells the
world that we're bank robbers. That way the FBI, Secret Service, state and local police—they're all on board. They're all
out gunning for us, no questions asked."

Tobey nodded as Duncan shook his head in admiration.

"That fucker," said Duncan. "He's like an evil genius sometimes."

Tobey meanwhile stood and picked up the tray with the
fishing line and sewing needle and bandages. He set it on the
table and motioned to Duncan.

"Your turn, cowboy," he said, motioning to Duncan.

Duncan sighed and got up, walking over to Tobey and sitting facing him as Tobey proceeded to sew up his ear.

*"Once again, the failed arrest in Manhattan of five bank
robbery suspects has left two civilians dead and one wounded.
Frank, back to you."*

*"Thank you, Marcy—In other news tonight, a young man
with Down's syndrome has fulfilled a lifelong dream: Build
the world's largest ant colony . . ."*

Yuvi, Tobey, and Duncan turned and stared at the television
set.

Though it was well lit, the dark walls of the White House
briefing room seemed to vanish away from the oval conference
table at its center. The ceiling was low, the lights hidden and
shining down on the deep brown walnut burl table as about a

dozen people sat around it, waiting for the President to arrive. He was forty-five minutes late.

Par, thought Nicholas Denton, relaxed as he shot the breeze with the White House people.

On one side of the table sat a dragoon of White House political operatives who were nominally in charge of the Intelligence community. They were feeling very clever this afternoon, thinking they were riding the Intelligence pony, naively, charmingly unaware as to who was riding whom.

The four men sitting across from them made no effort to change their minds. These four men ran CIA and the FBI.

Christopher Farnham, the Director of CIA, was an extremely tall, pathetic old stuffed shirt, all-Ivy, alcohol besotted, in an Hermes suit and a Cardin tie. He was a huffy man, with wavy gray hair and without a sense of humor. His bright red face made you think he was well on his way to a high-blood-pressure nightmare of stroke and paralysis. Farnham didn't look like a particularly happy man.

To Farnham's right sat the Director of the FBI, Roy Livre, a lifelong Bureau man who'd risen through the ranks and was as straight as they come, the prototypical G-man, and sometimes waggishly dubbed as the long-lost love-child of Melvin Purvis and J. Edgar Hoover. He was crew-cut, and young, too, with the sharp eyes and aggressive movements of a man who has always been ahead of the curve and at the top of his class.

Beside him sat his deputy, Mario Rivera, the Deputy FBI Director, a heavy-set man with arms as thick as tree trunks and a sad face that was too used to too many barbecues; a very able man who, in a just universe, would have been born Sicilian and therefore eligible to become a mob *capo regime.*

And then there was, of course, Nicholas Denton, his slicked blond hair neatly in place, the only one of the four who looked smiling and relaxed. He hadn't changed since this morning's little get-together with Tom Carr. He was patiently waiting, toying with his white-gold DuPont lighter as they all waited for the President.

Though the two Directors and Mario Rivera were practically squirming in their seats, hardly saying a word, Denton had charmed the half-dozen White House staff people until they were all but rolling over and waiting for him to scratch their upturned bellies. He knew most of them already, and as always, the White House people were impressed with Denton's charm and looks and background and connections.

"We met at Kate Graham's," Denton was saying to one of the political operatives, one of the junior members of the group that Denton hadn't gotten around to cultivating.

"Yes we did," said the President's junior political operative, nodding as she recalled, discreetly but intensely attracted to the reptilian charm coming off of Denton like wisps of smoke coming off a block of dry ice.

"But you, Craig," said Denton, motioning to the senior man of the bunch. "You owe me a rematch—a one-putt win is no win at all."

"I beat you fair and square, Nicky," said the man, liking Denton very much.

"I'm a generous guy—I let you win," said Denton, everyone laughing at what they thought was a joke.

It was no joke. Denton *had* let the man win. Denton was perfectly content to let the little ones slide if it meant he'd win The Big Ones.

Finally, the President of the United States of America, God help us all, came into the room. Everyone rose as he walked in, and everyone nodded at his winning, plaintive smile so desperately looking for love in all the wrong places.

"Please be seated," said the President.

Farnham, the Director of CIA, was the first to speak up.

"Mr. President," Farnham began, "we at CIA called this meeting," he said, then he looked around the room at all the political people sitting in on the debriefing. "This is a national security meeting," he added, to get them all to leave.

"I trust everyone in this room," said the President. "Everyone here has Eyes Only clearance."

Farnham said, "Mr. President, if I may—there are four tiers of clearance above Eyes Only. The highest clearance level has a designated name that I cannot even mention in the presence of most of the people in this room. With all due respect, I would ask the people who do not have clearance to please leave. If they don't, my deputy cannot give this briefing, and we will all be wasting valuable time."

The President tightened his lips, already a little irritated, waving everyone away except for the four FBI and CIA men.

"This had better be good," said the President peevishly once they were alone, "not some national security bullshit."

"Uh, no, Mr. President," said Farnham. "We have a serious security problem, and we need your authorization to call in every single law-enforcement agency in the country. Nicholas?"

On top of the conference table, there was a television remote control. Denton scooped it up and pointed it at the television monitor on the far side of the room, the TV blinking on. Personnel file pictures of the Acrobat work-group came on one at a time as Denton began his briefing.

"This is Tom Carr, Duncan Idaho, Monika Summers, Russell Orr, Ljubica Greene, and Tobey Jansen," he said, clicking the remote between each picture. "These six individuals form Acrobat, a unique work-group at CIA. They did both Counter Intelligence work and operational tasks. They worked for Bart Michaelus, the head of the Operations Directorate at CIA. The job of this work-group was to find foreign agents, monitor them, and if possible either turn them over to our side or shut them down altogether."

"What do you mean by 'shutting them down'?" asked the President.

"They alerted Federal law-enforcement officials, who would arrest these foreign agents," said Denton. "These people are tough and they are resourceful, and they are traitors. And we have to find them. Now."

The President didn't even bat an eyelash. "So what'd they do?" he asked.

Only Denton was unsurprised, studying his very nominal boss.

Farnham spoke up. "They were supposed to investigate possible Chinese infiltration of the Skunk Works laboratories. According to information we have been able to gather, instead of investigating Skunk Works, these people took approximately sixty million dollars from the Chinese government. And in return, they broke into Skunk Works and stole some of the biggest secrets we've got."

"Chinese money . . ." said the President vaguely, vaguely worried as he started making out the outline of the wave that was about to crash on top of his head. "What's this 'Skunk Works' you're talking about?"

Deftly maintaining control over the meeting, Denton motioned to his FBI counterpart. "I think the FBI Deputy Director can answer that question. Mario?"

Mario Rivera shrugged and spoke. "Sure thing. Skunk Works: It's a laboratory out in California. Their emphasis: New technologies—the stealth planes, the U2 spy plane, the SR-71; all sorts of stuff, all designed at Skunk Works. Skunk Works also deals in avionics, satellite systems: Radar, PCB boards, electronic countermeasures—highly sensitive, very advanced technologies. Acrobat's involvement: We think they stole a whole laundry list of materials."

"From Skunk Works?" said the President.

"Yes," said Mario Rivera.

"Fuck," said the President, his bushy gray hair glowing in the relative contrast of light and shadow in the room. "*Fuck*—these people sold military secrets to the Chinese?"

"Yes they did," said Mario Rivera.

"How'd you let that happen?"

Rivera was unprepared for that question. "Acrobat's a CIA prob——"

"Huh?!?" the President grunted like a boar, a completely different man, his puffy face going nuclear-red as his own Chinese money problems and this Skunk Works mess threatened to snowball right before his eyes. "Answer me that, goddammit, how'd you let this happen? Any one of you, *how'd you let this happen to me!*"

No one said a word, everyone but Denton stunned by the change in the man. But Denton had anticipated the reaction, so he sat there quiet as a wolf, waiting for the President to ride it out.

"I just can't catch a break, can I," said the President, as petulant as a teenager. "I've got less than a year left in my presidency and this shit had to go happen to me? Is this the worst case of spying in American history or what?"

CIA Director Farnham—foolishly—answered the question. "Potentially, yes," he said.

"And it's all your fucking fault, you fucking asshole!" the President screamed. "This dickhead who works for you—the boss of these fucking Acrobat people—what's his fucking name again?"

"Michaelus," said Nicholas Denton softly, oh so softly. "Bart Michaelus."

"This Michaelus *fuck* works for you, doesn't he?" the President screamed at CIA Director Farnham.

Farnham cringed. "Yes he does, but—"

The President didn't even hear him. "Everyone's gonna say that it was on my watch that this happened, aren't they? *Aren't they?* And they're all gonna say it was my fault when it was *your fucking fault!*"

Everyone sat there, shell-shock quiet.

"I cannot catch a motherfucking *break!*" the President screamed.

Denton mentally counted to ten; then he shrugged with a perfect balance of detachment and rueful knowledge as he said, "We still have options."

The President looked at him, ready to pounce. "What did you say?"

Denton didn't meet his eye, looking down at the table with pained subservience. "We could, possibly, still manage to salvage the situation," he said, acting at once as docile as a dog and as wise as a genie. "We can still turn things to our advantage."

"What do you mean?" asked the President, unsure as yet whether to hug him or eat him.

Denton said, "The Acrobat work-group is on the loose—that's bad. The good news is they weren't able to pass along their information to the Chinese."

"How do you know that?" asked the President.

"Because I acquired the information before they could pass it along," said Denton, turning his head to CIA Director Farnham. "Isn't that right, Chris?"

Christopher Farnham took his cue like a good little boy. "Once we discovered the Acrobat problem, uh, our priority was to get our hands on the Skunk Works material. In trying to get at the material they had stolen, Acrobat got away. You may have heard of the, uh—the situation—in New York City this morning?"

"The gang of bank robbers?" said the President, confused. "That's them? They're robbing banks now?"

FBI Director Livre—a good man but a little punctilious—said, "They didn't rob any bank, Mr. President. That was a story the CIA concocted—over our objections, I might add. The FBI does not condone lying to the public, even in matters as sensitive as this one."

Denton said, "But because of our cover story, the press doesn't know about the security problem. With no security problem, there's no political problem."

The President was a bundle of ego-nerves—but he was no dummy. Far from it, he was as cunning as a troll. As Denton spoke, he suddenly realized who was really running this meeting.

He turned to Denton and said, "If you catch them . . . then there wouldn't be any political problem . . . would there?"

FBI Director Livre cut in. "No, there wouldn't, not for the time being," he said. "But once we capture the Acrobat group and put them on trial, that might be something else."

When FBI Director Livre spoke, Nicholas Denton clasped his hands on the surface of the conference table, staring at them, the tips of his thumbs gently bumping against each other. When the FBI Director finished speaking, Denton looked up and stared straight at the President.

The President stared straight back at Denton.

Denton's eyes were as clear as teletype. They told the President, "There will be no trial. There will be no trial because there will be no Acrobat. Not if we handle this thing just . . . *right*."

"Do it," said the President out loud. "Do whatever it takes to get these people—FBI, Secret Service—everything, everything. I want these people by the end of the weekend, you hear me?"

Everyone at the table murmured ascent, all but Denton surprised that the President hadn't wanted any more details. Denton had told Farnham not ten minutes before they arrived at the White House, "He won't ask for details—if he knows details, he won't be able to deny." And here he was, the President of the U.S. of A, doing exactly what he had predicted, trying to remain as uninformed as possible for the sake of deniability. If the Acrobat situation had happened under Bush, James Baker would have grilled them for hours, then gobbled them down when they were all nice and crisp. Not so now!

"I want progress reports every morning and every evening, is that clear?" said the current President, rising to go.

But the FBI Director would not give up the ghost on the cover story Denton had put out. "Mr. President, I have to insist: I really object to this cover story the CIA has concocted."

"Keep the cover story—I want this . . . investigation to be top priority, understand?"

"Mr. President, I have to insist, we cannot keep the cover story," said FBI Director Livre, shooting a glance at Denton and acting like the teacher's pet who was getting tarred with the bad-boy's misdeeds. "We are lying to the American public."

"No, we're not lying," said Denton.

"Oh, so then what are we doing?" asked FBI Director Livre. Everyone stopped and turned to Denton.

"We are simply . . . managing the truth for the time being," he said to the President.

" 'Managing the truth,' that's a good one," said the President as he led them out of the room, laughing at what Denton had said.

Not once had any of them called the President "sir."

The four Intelligence men stood in the hallway of the White House as they watched the President walk away, each of them thinking their own thoughts about the man.

Then Roy Livre, the FBI Director, turned to Denton and Farnham.

"Denton," he said.

"Yes?" said Denton, biting his inner lip to keep from smiling. From his look alone, Denton could tell Livre was about to bust a gut.

But Livre took a breath. "When I get hold of these Acrobat people of yours, I'm going to wring them dry. I'm going to get to the bottom of this thing even if it kills me. I want you to know that."

"Okay," said Denton simply.

Director Livre stood there and blinked. "I mean it," he added inanely.

"I believe you," said Denton, looking at him as innocent as a snowflake, Farnham and Mario Rivera wisely fading into the scenery.

The FBI Director suddenly leaned forward and spoke very softly, so as not to be overheard. "You're crayoning way outside the lines. This cock-and-bull story about how Tom Carr and his kids took sixty million—give me a break!"

Denton frowned good-naturedly. "You think I'm making this stuff up?" he asked.

Roy Livre crossed his arms and stared up at Denton. "You know something else? Yeah, I think you are making up these allegations. I think you're mixed up in something, and I don't know what it is, but I think it's dirty. I also think this Acrobat group is innocent, but I think you're using them to get away with murder. Or worse."

"I see," said Denton, nodding his head thoughtfully, looking at Livre with a little smile and flat eyes. "So let's just say, for the sake of argument, that they *are* innocent . . . then why would they be on the run?" he asked, with the reasoning of a sophist.

The FBI Director said nothing, staring at Denton. If it were physically possible, steam would be coming out of his ears. But since it wasn't, Roy Livre stomped away before he could say anything he might regret, walking over to his deputy,

Mario Rivera. The two FBI men huddled, their backs to the watchful CIA men.

"He's like a little baby, always throwing tantrums," said Farnham, standing a respectful step behind Denton.

"Mmm . . . ," said Denton, staring at FBI Director Livre with a thoughtful look.

"So is POTUS," said Farnham, referring to the President Of The US.

Denton turned and looked at Farnham, owning him. "Really," he said to Farnham.

"Yes," said Farnham, trying to curry favor with his own deputy. "He once slapped the NSA man in front of the entire National Security Council, for no reason whatsoever."

"Mmm . . . ," said Denton, turning to look after FBI Director Livre again.

"So, er, what did you think of the meeting?" asked Farnham.

Denton smiled and turned to his boss. "You did fine, Chris."

"I must say, Nicky, you must be psychic: Exactly like you said, he didn't even ask about details and proof and such."

"Chris, you know I don't like being called 'Nicky'," said Denton.

"Yes, of course, I'm sorry, Nicholas," said Director Farnham.

"Mmm . . . ," said Denton, mildly disgusted by Farnham's toadying.

Denton's method of controlling people was two-fold: Charm, and information. In other words, if he didn't seduce you into doing what he wanted you to do, he'd happily blackmail you instead.

Two years ago, Denton had come across some interesting bits of poop that he used to control Director Farnham. The poop hadn't been that awful to begin with, just enough to cause extreme though survivable embarrassment. But then Denton subtly deployed that embarrassing bit of information, maneuvering Farnham into outright law-breaking. That, of course, is how blackmail works, and that was how Denton had gained control over the Director of the Central Intelligence Agency.

He'd also broken him. From a straightforward, relatively upright man, Farnham had become a broken-down cart-horse. His drinking was getting out of hand; he was engaged in a shockingly sadistic sexual liaison with his own secretary (Denton had still pictures and videotape); his weekends in Atlantic City were becoming as long as they were expensive; and he had just discovered cocaine—in short, Farnham was turning into a mess. Lately, it was getting so bad it was downright embarrassing.

Farnham had been easy.

Not so the other Deputy Director at CIA, Bart Michaelus.

Michaelus, whom Denton had so neatly tarred-and-feathered with the mess of Acrobat, ran the Operations Directorate, the operational arm at CIA. And though he was high-strung and a lot crazy, Michaelus was a smart man: For close to three years, he'd managed to stay clear of Denton, sometimes through some pretty shrewd maneuverings, sometimes through sheer luck. But free he'd remained—

—And that freedom ensured his fate. Because the longer he stayed out of Denton's control, the more Denton had to destroy him. He just had to. It was his nature.

Denton smiled to himself, relishing how neatly he'd set Michaelus on the slide out, absently staring at CIA Director Farnham as he thought about Bart Michaelus.

You're going to have to grow a bigger brain than you've got room for if you want to get out of this one, Bart, thought Denton as he stared at Christopher Farnham, his putative boss.

"So what do you think our approach should be?" Farnham asked, clearly nervous about the stare Denton was giving him, mentally screaming at himself for having called Nicholas "Nicky."

"I think," said Denton, "that we should let the FBI deal with this problem, just as Director Livre said. We should just sit back, see how it unfolds."

"What about using our people?" asked Director Farnham.

"Mmm, we don't want to get splattered with shit, now do we?"

"No, I suppose not. Do you think I should talk to the FBI Director?"

"No no no, I'll handle it, Chris," said Denton. "I have a back channel I can tune in to."

Just then, FBI Director Livre shot a look at Denton and Farnham and walked away. His deputy, Mario Rivera, sighed before he walked up to the CIA men with a pained look on his face.

"And here comes my back channel now," said Denton, smiling at Rivera, liking him very much. "Hello, Mario, how are you?"

Mario Rivera stopped and nodded at Farnham and Denton, knowing full well how dangerous Denton was. They'd worked together before. "The word from Director Livre: I'm gonna be handling this on the Bureau's end. I wanted to talk to you about this Acrobat group."

"No problem. Would you excuse us, Chris?" said Denton, dismissing Farnham. "I'll see you back at the ranch."

"Yes of course," said Farnham nervously, wondering what Denton's stare had meant. That stare and the Nicky/Nicholas slip up would keep him awake tonight.

Farnham wandered off, leaving Rivera alone with Denton. "So, Mr. Denton—"

" 'Nicholas' is fine. How have you been?"

"Uh, okay," said Rivera.

"And how is Margaret Chisholm?" asked Denton.

Rivera looked at Denton, his gears spinning, warily wondering what Denton had in mind. "She's hanging in there," he said noncommittally.

"Good, good—she's still with your office?"

Rivera looked at Denton. "You know she is, Mr. Denton."

"That's good to know," said Denton, thinking through exactly how he was going to handle this thing.

Just as Tobey was done bandaging Duncan Idaho's ear, they heard two cars pull up outside their motel room.

They picked up their guns. Ljubica Greene kept on snoring lightly as Duncan and Tobey stood on either side of the window of the motel room and peeked out through the curtains.

Outside, Russell Orr and Monika Summers had just pulled into their room's parking slots, Russell at the wheel of a red-and-white pick-up truck, Monika driving a brand-new Toyota Camry sedan.

Tobey sighed, relaxing, carelessly dropping his right hand holding his firearm to his side as he touched and teased his spiked goatee with his left hand.

"Yo pardner, why don't you go put that weapon on safety before you shoot your toes off," said Duncan as he opened the motel room door.

"Right, right," said Tobey, putting the safety back on his firearm as Russell and Monika walked in, each carrying a pair of grocery bags.

"We're cool," said Russell as he walked in. He dropped his bags of groceries and walked over to Ljubica, kneeling beside her and combing her hair.

"Hey there, stranger," said Monika, walking in behind Russell and standing up on tippy-toes to peck Duncan on the lips.

"Hey there, cowgirl," said Duncan, kissing her back. "Whatcha got?"

They'd got plenty. Russell and Monika had gone to town and bought a carton of cigarettes; a carton of orange juice; a box of cereal ("Why'd you get the kind with raisins; I hate raisins," Duncan mumbled); a gallon jug of skim milk; a new orange T-shirt for Tobey with the famous Superman logo on the chest; a new pair of jeans for Ljubica; a whole bunch of gauze, tape, and disinfectant to change her field dressing; a bunch of bananas; a few apples; a loaf of stone-wheat bread; a jar of fat-free mayonnaise; a package of sliced, processed cheese; an assortment of lunch meats, all in their hermetically sealed packages; and a head of lettuce ("For the sandwiches," said Monika as she tied her hair with a purple scrunchie). And of course they'd also stolen a brand-new Camry sedan ("We even managed to switch the plates with another Camry just like it," said Russell, as he yawned and stretched, his body seeming to fill the whole room).

After Monika and Russell had oohed and aahed over Ljubica and Duncan's wounds, they broke out the cigarettes and sat around the room trying to figure out what had happened.

"We got set up," Duncan flatly stated.

Russell Orr just shook his head, raising his hands in a catching gesture, receiving Duncan's cigarettes and lighter in return.

Monika, sitting on the bed besides Ljubica, blew out cigarette smoke and said, "Duncan, honey, you're talking paranoid."

"That little woman knew *exactly* what she was about," Duncan insisted. "No hesitation—she *knew* we'd be there. How'd she know that? Someone told her so, that's how. We got set up."

"We heard you once, Duncan," said Russell dismissively, Ljubica Greene wincing and looking away.

Duncan looked at his friend. "Fuck you," he said.

Russell sighed. "Okay fine: So who set us up?"

Duncan fell silent, looking at Russell almost as if *he* had set them up.

But Russell went on. "Come on: You think one of us tipped them off? Was it you, me, Monika? Tobey or Yuvi? *Tom?* Who?"

"They weren't waiting for us," said Tobey Jansen, no one paying him any mind.

"I don't know," Duncan went on. "All I know is that they were just *there,* a'right? They were there like they were waiting for us."

"They weren't waiting for us," Tobey repeated, loud enough that they all turned to him.

Tobey sat there on the floor, his knees up, his arms around his legs, smoking a cigarette, his spiked goatee making him look like a wise young Mandarin. "They found us," he said, "but they weren't *waiting* for us."

Duncan sniffed and brushed his nose with his cigarette hand. "Tobey, you know I respect you, a'right? But this isn't your bag."

"If they'd been waiting for us," Tobey insisted patiently, "wouldn't they have had, like, twenty guys? And if there'd been like twenty guys, wouldn't we be dead already?"

Everyone blinked, checking the logic of this.

Ljubica nodded agreement as she sat up on her bed, her wounded leg propped up with a pillow under the knee. "Tobey's right."

Russell nodded. "From the mouth of babes . . ."

"Yeah," agreed Monika, crossing her legs Indian-style, her hands lightly resting on her knees. "There would have been a whole squad of people to wash us out."

Duncan thought a bit and smiled at Tobey, proud in an older-brother kind of way.

And relieved, too. It meant that they hadn't been betrayed.

"Yeah, I'm sorry, you're right—they must've tailed one of us. We must've gotten sloppy and they tailed us. Yeah," said Duncan, nodding almost as if he were convincing himself against his better judgment. "Everyone watched their rear, right?"

Everyone nodded casually as they all smoked, from their body language clear that they weren't followed.

Tobey suddenly frowned. "What about Tommy?"

"Tommy was a pro," said Duncan instantly, the one who had been closest to Tom Carr. "A real roadrunner."

"Well, maybe," said Tobey. "But when was the last time he did any field work?"

Duncan glanced at Monika, Russell, and Yuvi, a thought none of them had anticipated.

"The seventies?" said Monika reflexively. "Maybe the early eighties? I hate to say it, but Tommy probably gave us away."

Ljubica nodded grimly.

Duncan sighed. "Tommy . . . shit—Anybody ever seen that little woman before?"

"That's *your* bag, pal," said Russell.

"I've seen her before, I'm sure of it, around Langley or someplace; and when I see her again, I'm gonna shoot her in the cunt, just to watch her bleed to death."

"Don't say that word," said Monika. "I hate that word."

"I'm sorry, babe." Duncan walked over and hugged Monika, reassuring her.

Russell looked at the two of them, staring at them vacantly before snapping out of it and looking away as he spoke up: "We've got to get going, tomorrow morning at the latest."

Tobey blew a perfect smoke ring and fiddled with his gelled goatee, splitting it into three rigid strands. "Why?" he asked in his high, reedy voice, sounding more like a junior-high geek than an amazingly talented number cruncher. "We're lost in the boonies of Pennsylvania. You think they're gonna somehow find us here?"

"Yes, absolutely," said Duncan, for some reason unhappy that he was agreeing with Russell. "Tonight, they figure out we're in PA, if they haven't already. By tomorrow they'll figure we've stolen that Camry and the pick-up truck, and by Thursday, they've got the plate numbers. By Friday, they're rounding us up."

"Are you sure?"

Duncan winced and nodded. "We remain stationary, sooner or later, they're gonna scoop us up. With the TV coverage, we'll be all over if we don't shake a leg."

" 'Shake a leg'—is that the official CIA term?" said Russell, making Duncan, Tobey, and Monika look at him with a "What the hell?" look to their eyes. For a while now, Russell had been slipping with his friends. Once they'd turned to him as the Learnèd Voice of Reason. But lately, they'd been turning away.

Like now.

Dismissing Russell, Monika asked Duncan, "What TV coverage are you talking about?"

Russell too looked up and tried to pretend he hadn't said a thing.

"We were all over the evening news," said Duncan.

"They're saying we're bank robbers," added Tobey.

"Bank robbers, huh?" said Monika. "That's smart."

"They got pics of us?" Russell asked cautious-thoughtful.

"No," said Duncan, quick and dismissive.

"No?" said Monika, surprised.

"No," said Duncan, slowing down to think about that. "No pictures of any of us. Not yet anyway. And no names either."

"No names, no pictures . . . ," said Monika, suddenly lighting up. "They're trying to bring us back into the fold!"

Duncan tsked. "They are not."

"They are *too*," said Monika excitedly. "They would have plastered our faces and names all over if they didn't want us back!"

Behind her, Russell looked at Duncan and dimissively motioned to Monika, as if to say, "Why don't you put some reins on that crazy puppy of a girlfriend you got there."

Duncan Idaho ignored Russell as he spoke to Monika with a gentle voice. "Monika, babe, that's nuts. No one at Langley wants us back. Nicholas Denton's running things now, and he wants us six underground."

"It's Bart Michaelus; I'll bet you anything," Monika insisted. "Michaelus hates Denton's guts—he'd help us get back in and stick it to Denton—"

"Oh we're gonna stick it to Denton alright," said Duncan Idaho. "With or without Michaelus."

"What do you mean?"

Duncan Idaho said nothing, standing there looking at the ground and smoking his cigarette, avoiding Monika's look.

Ljubica and Russell were falling apart, but they could still read each other's minds. They glanced at one another, and then Russell Orr pointed to Duncan Idaho. "You're gonna tag Denton, aren't you," he said.

Duncan snorted. "I'm not gonna lie down for that fucker, if that's what you mean," he said.

Tobey Jansen was the most surprised. "Have you lost your mind?"

"I couldn't live with myself, lying down because I was too chickenshit to do something about it," said Duncan Idaho.

Tobey said, "It's one thing to be a chickenshit? It's another to be a fucking idiot."

Duncan said, "The fucker washed out Tommy, for crying out loud!"

Monika said, "Honey, tagging Denton is big-time crazy."

Even Ljubica looked nonplussed. "That's fairly radical," she said, studying Duncan.

"It's payback," said Duncan. "Payback for Tommy."

"It's stupid," said Monika Summers, clearly trying to control her temper as she sat in the middle of the bed. "It's stupid and dangerous and needless."

"But it'll make me feel real good," said Duncan, looking his girlfriend in the eye.

Calmly, Ljubica said, "I don't think tagging Denton should be our priority."

"Fuck priority," said Duncan Idaho, allowing his temper to bloom. "Don't *any* of you feel like we owe it to Tommy to put Denton in a box? I mean, it's like you're all chickening out or something."

No one said anything, but suddenly Russell, Tobey, Ljubica, and Monika gave Duncan a very serious Look.

"Sorry," he said with a sigh. "I didn't mean it that way. You know I didn't."

Seeing her opening, Monika Summers grabbed it. "Of course I want to stick it to Denton; that's not the point," she said, getting up off the bed and walking toward Duncan. "We might be able to tag Denton, but that would still leave us on the outside—more so than before, because everyone would know we'd done it," she said, wrapping her arms around Duncan's waist and pulling him close. "But if we blow him up from the inside, we make it all better for ourselves and still put some hurt on the guy," she said quietly, her face barely inches from Duncan's own.

Duncan stood there, Monika using all her willpower to get him to do what she wanted.

"Russ?" he finally asked, without looking away from Monika, "what do you think?"

Russell Orr, surprised at being pulled into this conversation, shifted where he stood, looking at the others rather sheepishly. Then he said, "Russell is undecided."

Duncan smirked. "Shit, 'Russell is undecided.' "

Ljubica winced at her boyfriend's answer. She looked down on her bandaged leg and took a drag on her cigarette.

"Guys?" said Tobey Jansen, sitting there on the floor. "There's something else?"

The Acrobat work-group looked over at him.

Tobey gulped. "Back at the subway station? After that whole thing? Tom told me to go to box 27-13. What does that mean?

The others looked around at each other, the pressure in the tidy little motel room going up like on a submarine going down.

"What did you say?" Russell asked quietly.

Ljubica snapped, "You heard him: Box 27-13." Then she blinked and looked away.

Monika sat there on the bed, looking stunned as she turned to look at Duncan. *Shit,* she silently mouthed.

Duncan nodded as he whispered, "Son of a bitch: He did it."

"What?" Tobey asked. "What did he do?"

Duncan Idaho was the first to recover. "Tommy promised us that if something bad ever happened—like a meltdown— like what's going on now—he'd arrange some gear for us, and he'd leave it in a safety deposit box in a bank off DuPont Circle?"

"What kind of gear?" asked Tobey.

Ljubica said, "Passports, plastic, walking around money, enough to keep us viable for a good long while." She looked over at Monika and Duncan, then over at Russell.

"A good long while," Duncan repeated, looking at Monika. "We could get it," said Duncan thoughtfully. "We could get it, and then go underground."

Monika looked doubtfully at Duncan, not saying a word.

Tobey looked at Monika and then at Duncan. "Get what?" he asked. "Get this gear? Will it be enough?"

Duncan looked over at Tobey and nodded as Ljubica again spoke up: "More than enough," she said, speaking to Tobey but looking at Monika.

Monika stared back at her friend. "What."

"Let's use it," said Ljubica, combing her sweaty, lank black hair behind her ear. "Grab our gear and then just go. Screw Denton, Michaelus, the whole Langley scene. Save ourselves while we still can."

Duncan, also looking straight at Monika, nodded at what Ljubica was saying.

"Just run for the hills, huh Yuvi?" said Monika, looking almost disgusted with the idea even as she looked a little rattled, getting squeezed between her lover and her best friend. "Who's chickening out now?"

The men in the room collectively winced, but Ljubica only sighed. "Monika, this country is so big," she said. "It's so . . . roomy. You can walk away from practically anything—even your own self. If my vote counts, I vote we get the gear at DuPont Circle and then walk away."

"I agree," said Duncan Idaho. "Just so long as we tag Denton before we go."

Monika turned on her boyfriend. "Duncan, don't you listen? I am not walking away—period. I am going to get back into the fold, alright? Maybe you guys don't want to, but I do."

Duncan said, "Baby, with the gear at DuPont Circle, we could head off into the sunset—maybe to Europe—together— we could go there—"

"Back at the ranch—"

"We could just *go*—"

"Back at the ranch," Monika insisted, interrupting, "there're all sorts of people who could help us—there's Dexter, Annie Roth, Joe McMillan, Joey Alvarez, Hillary Klein, Nancy LeBay—"

"But—"

"—all these people who could help us."

"Monika—"

"I am not leaving!" Monika Summers shouted out loud. "I'm not! This is where I belong—back at the ranch," she said, pausing to take a breather. "If we walk away from Langley, we walk away from everything else in our lives—our friends,

our families, everything. Now, I've always supported this
work-group—*always,* all the way, a hundred percent. But not
this time. I'm not walking away. I'm not going underground.
I'm not going to abandon my entire life just because it's convenient."

Duncan and the wounded Ljubica Greene looked at Monika; and all of a sudden, Monika felt very alone, sitting there
in the middle of the bed in a Lotus position, feeling the others
subtly pull away.

But she wasn't going to budge, and the others knew her
well enough to know that.

"What about you, Tobey?" said Duncan, surprising everyone by this change in tack.

Tobey Jansen sat there, his arms around his knees, looking
up at the others and not saying much—squirming, in fact. But
decided. "I'm with Monika," he said finally. "I want to get
back inside."

Duncan nodded at Tobey. "And why would you want that?"

Monika said, "Stop it—"

But Duncan Idaho cut her off as he spoke to Tobey. "I
mean pretty soon—maybe today, maybe tomorrow—Denton's
gonna put our pictures on TV. Once that happens, *no way* we
can get back inside the ranch, not in a million years—anyone
sees us after that, we're six underground. And even if we get
back inside, what are we going back for?"

Tobey looked up at him as if the answer were so simple.
"Duncan, I don't want to be on the outside. I just don't. I want
to be back on the inside where I belong—where we all belong.
I don't want to be a fugitive for the rest of my life."

"Tobey, think," said Duncan reasonably. "With the gear we
got at DuPont Circle, we won't be fugitives: We'll be brand-
new people. Yuvi—tell me if I'm wrong—the passports and
plastic are solid, right?"

"Completely solid," said Ljubica Greene, smoking her cigarette and studying Tobey. "And I know where we can get
some more papers, if need be."

"Right," said Duncan. "We're good to go, Tobey. And we
can go *now.*"

"I don't care," said Tobey, looking almost on the verge of crying. "I want to get back inside."

All of a sudden, Duncan Idaho took a couple of steps forward and squatted in front of Tobey. "Tobey look at me—look at me."

Tobey looked up at Duncan, wincing as Duncan pushed his best friend harder than he ever had before.

"You think it's even possible for us to get back inside?" he said quietly, talking to Tobey as Monika looked on.

"I don't know—"

"Even if it is," said Duncan, with professional reasonableness, "what are you gonna do? Tell me: You think it's gonna be like it was before? 'Cause I can tell you now, it won't."

Tobey looked at the ground uneasily.

Quietly, but firmly, Monika repeated, "Duncan, stop it."

"I'm just talking here," said Duncan, still squatting in front of Tobey.

Tobey squirmed, yanking nervously on his gelled goatee. Then he looked Duncan in the eye. "When you talk about walking away from everything? That's easy for you to say," he said, his voice going tight and reedy and softly supersonic. "You guys are together—you and Monika, Ljubica and Russell. You're not gonna be alone. But I will, Duncan. And I'll be looking over my shoulder every second of the day waiting for Nicholas Denton to catch up with me—"

"Well if we tag Denton then you won't have to worry about that—"

"I'm not afraid," said Tobey quietly, almost crying. "I just don't want to be alone. That's why I want to be back in the fold. I wanna be in a place where I . . . where I belong. So if there's a chance that we can get back inside? Then it's a chance I'll take. Because I don't want to be on the outside. I don't want to be—"

"You don't want to be a Drifter," said Duncan quietly, quietly capitulating, everyone else frowning at the term, having no idea what he was talking about.

Tobey bit his lip, staring right at Duncan.

"You want to be a Soldier," said Duncan. "Not a Drifter."

"That's right," said Tobey, barely one good shove away from crying.

Duncan Idaho looked at the ground, feeling his face go flush at bullying Tobey. *Like beating up on a little kid,* he thought, a little disgusted with himself. Duncan had no doubt that if he really wanted to, he could push Tobey into going along with him. Because Duncan knew that Tobey was weak . . .

. . . and therein lay all of Tobey's power over Duncan Idaho, ex–Special Forces, now ex–CIA: Tobey was the weakling little brother Duncan had never had, but could never refuse.

"Okay," said Duncan finally, nodding.

Tobey nodded at Duncan, thanking him.

"Okay what?" said Monika, surprised at how hurt she suddenly felt—hurt at this silent understanding between Tobey and Duncan that she wasn't a part of. Hurt that it was Tobey—and not her—who had changed Duncan's mind.

"We'll do what Tobey wants," said Duncan, standing up. "We'll go back to D.C., and then use Michaelus to try to get back inside."

Everyone just looked at Duncan, surprised into silence.

"What about you two?" he asked Russell and Ljubica.

Ljubica looked straight at Duncan. "What about the gear at DuPont Circle?"

"We'll get it, that's a given," said Duncan. "But we'll try to get back in anyway."

Russell almost said something, but then stopped, afraid. He looked instead at Ljubica, who spoke up for them both: "We'll go with you to D.C. When we get there, we'll decide what we'll do."

"Fair enough," said Duncan.

With that, he went to the groceries and began to make some cold-cut sandwiches, the others eventually following behind.

That night, Duncan and Monika made love a little sloppily, a little desperately, trying hard to forget about the horrifying day just past.

When they were done, Monika lay on top of Duncan, her ear against his chest, listening to his heart to make sure it was real.

She knew he was thinking about Tom Carr: She could feel it. So instead of that, she decided to bring up something else.

"What was that stuff about Soldiers and Drifters?" she asked softly, surprised it was the first thing that came to mind; surprised at the unexpected surge of jealousy.

"Nothing," Duncan murmured. "Just something Tobey and I talked about one time."

Monika nearly said something she might have regretted. But then Duncan sighed and spoke up. "Tobey thinks that in this world, you're either a Soldier or a Drifter. You're either part of an army, fed and clothed, marching in stride, doing what you're told, protected, but without any freedom. Or you're drifting along with no allegiances, no commitments, nothing to hold you back; free to do whatever you want, but without anyone who can watch your back; with no security and no guarantees."

Monika thought about what Duncan said; in her mind's eye, she saw a lone and eccentric hippy sauntering past a battalion of robotic soldiers marching in a perfect ten-by-ten formation; a surprisingly clear vision. "That sounds . . . kinda juvenile," she said.

"Tobey ain't a hundred percent grown up yet," Duncan agreed. "But I think maybe he's got a point. Anyway, get some sleep."

"Okay," said Monika.

They lay there quietly for a while, Monika looking at the hairs on Duncan's chest, oddly slanting moonlight threading through them. In her mind's eye, the hippy had become Duncan. And the soldiers at attention had just now noticed him.

"Promise me something," Monika said suddenly.

"Hmm?"

"Promise me you won't do anything foolish," she quietly demanded. "Promise me you won't make a move on Denton."

"I promise I won't do anything foolish," he said.

"Promise it like you mean it," Monika insisted, getting up

on her elbow and looking down on Duncan's face.

Duncan smiled at her, his thumb rubbing her nipple. "I promise," he said. "Okay?"

"Okay," she said, unhappy with his answer but knowing it was the best she would get from him. She plopped back onto her pillow, staring at the ceiling as she felt him holding her body. "You're all I've got, Duncan Idaho."

But that wasn't quite true. As she drifted off to sleep, Monika Summers thought of all her friends, all the people she knew at Langley and in Washington—all these sets and circles and cliques where she belonged. Girlfriends she shopped with; men she flirted with in friendly irony. All these people she knew. All these people she wanted to get back to.

"Baby, I'm so scared," said Monika sleepily, fighting to stay awake, knowing she ought to sleep.

Duncan didn't answer, lying there on the edge of sleep, too.

"Duncan?"

"Mmm?"

"Say something . . . say something comforting."

Duncan didn't seem to have heard, but then he spoke up. "I'm scared, too."

In the other room, Ljubica Greene lay curled up and sleeping, her back to Russell Orr.

The seconds ticked away in the total darkness. Russell was lying on his back on top of the sheets and blankets, his enormous body taking up more than half of the bed. He was thinking.

He did a lot of that. But more and more it didn't seem to help him much. Russell, like Monika Summers, didn't have any specific duties in Acrobat, but he had a very specific place within the work-group: He was the Voice of Reason, "with a capital 'V' and a capital 'R,' " as Tom Carr had told him more than once, slapping his massive biceps for emphasis. Duncan Idaho was clearly Tommy's favorite, but Tommy was wise enough to know that there isn't much of a line between what's brilliantly daring and what's downright stupid.

That's where Russell came in. Russell wasn't stupid. Far from it, Russell was as smart as they come, and cautious, too: The caution of a career Air Force flier.

Movies and TV might show crazy fighter-jocks doing crazy fighter-jock stuff. But real fliers are methodically cautious bores when it comes down to the job. The blue sky above is pretty darn big, but not so big as to allow any room for the sloppy.

That was Russell's bag: The cautious, methodical grind. If things had gone his way, he would have driven fighter jets for a decade or so, then gone on to the friendly and lucrative skies of commercial aviation, the embarrassing but very real reason he'd gone into the Air Force in the first place: He didn't want to be any kind of fighter-jock hero; he just wanted to fly from city to city, with the perfect excuse to avoid a kind but crazy drunk mother, the only person in his life.

But that didn't happen. Instead, his career was ruined by his own body: In his time at Colorado Springs, for no good reason, he gained four inches and over a hundred pounds. His shoulder measurements alone had gone from a hefty forty-eight inches to a whopping seventy-two, disqualifying him from fighter training. He was simply too massive to fit in a cockpit. And he had too much pride to make a place for himself anywhere other than at the pinnacle of the Air Force.

That was the thing: He had to be at the top. His sense of self demanded it. It was almost by accident that he drifted from the Air Force to the CIA. But it was no accident that, once at Langley, he'd gravitated to the independent work-group Acrobat: Another pinnacle, where only raw ability counted for anything.

Russell Orr rolled over in bed and deftly sped through the file cabinet of issues on his mind, his mental fingers flipping through all the files as if checking to see that they were all being handled and were currently up to date.

"Russell is undecided."

The thought just popped into his head like an ink bomb,

blotting out everything else. *Russell is undecided.*

Why did I say that, why did I say that, he thought to himself, those stupid, piddly little words droning on and on through his skull: "*Russell is undecided—Russell is undecided—Russell is undecided . . . ,*" each repetition making him feel more and more embarrassed—foolish—stupid.

Why do I keep saying stupid shit like that?

He'd been an idiot lately, no question about it. Where once he'd been careful and thoughtful, now he'd turned over-cautious, indecisive. And the absolutely dumbest things kept popping out of his mouth!

What the fuck is going on? he thought to himself, unnerved and panicked even as he began to doze off, wishing he could turn to Ljubica and shake her awake.

But he couldn't do that. Not anymore.

In that perfectly lucid moment you have just before you fall asleep, Russell suddenly realized that there wasn't just a single love of your life—there were many. There were perhaps hundreds of people you could fall in love with, perhaps thousands. Perhaps millions. And each of these people could bring out a different version of yourself. Just like different colors bring out different moods, different loves bring out different renderings of yourself.

Ljubica lay beside him, sleeping, her long limbs and body curled up, her straight hair spread out across the pillow. Russell had excellent night vision, and in the darkness, he could see her body rising and falling with every breath she took. He loved her, no question. He loved her, and because of that love, because of that desire to hold her interest, he had turned himself into a man that he despised. This version of himself, brought out by love, wasn't thoughtful, wasn't cautious: It was weak and indecisive, smart-alecky (*Russell is undecided*), niggardly, and petty. It was a version that felt itself at once superior to others and at the same time terrified that he was not quite good enough.

Ljubica too hated this person he had become: She hated it—despised it—and the funny thing was, she'd had a hand in its creation.

So thinking, Russell Orr fell asleep. He wouldn't remember any of this the next morning. All he would remember was that he had discovered something important about himself—something essential. But not something important enough not to be lost.

Amid thick fog, an abandoned Chevy Suburban sat in the middle of a field of green in the eastern Pennsylvania countryside, a field surrounded by thick, bushy trees that gave cover from the two-lane road nearby. As it was, the truck was being worked over by a swarm of technicians, all of them wearing blue windbreakers with yellow FBI lettering on their backs and white latex gloves on their hands. Two men in cheap brown suits stood nearby, watching the progress of the technicians and chatting with each other as they were all slowly drenched by the fog that had settled in overnight.

Presently, a small rental car pulled up onto the field and slowly drove toward the truck, stopping some twenty yards from it, its tires wet from the morning dew. The two agents turned and watched as the driver's side door opened.

Out of the car stepped Amalia, in a suit as severe as the one she had been wearing yesterday in New York.

She paused, looking at the Chevy Suburban for a moment, then closed her car door and walked across the field to who she guessed were the two lead FBI men.

"Felicity Matthews, Bureau of Alcohol, Tobacco and Firearms," said Amalia, pulling out the fake ID Matthew Wilson had made for her just before the chase for Acrobat began. For some reason Wilson always thought it was better to produce fake IDs with the names of television characters, as a mnemonic device; a technique lost on Amalia, she didn't watch television.

The two FBI men didn't seem too big on TV either, because neither of them remarked on Amalia's odd alias, nor did they bother checking her ID, assuming she was whom she said she was. They simply greeted her with open hands.

"George Karvakolis," said one as he shook Amalia's hand.

"This is Ben Urbine. Our office got the call from the local sheriff's office about an hour ago."

Unlike Denton, Amalia knew nothing of finesse. "What do you know exactly about this truck?" she asked both men.

They looked at each other, both of them so similar in their clothes, manner, hair, and features that they could have been brothers.

"We-e-ell," said Urbine, "we know this vehicle was stolen from the parking lot in the train station at Stroudsburg. Stroudsburg's on a straight line from New York, so-o-o . . ."

"Why do you think the bank robbery suspects stole this vehicle?" asked Amalia, without bothering to inflect her question.

"We-ell Ms. Matthe-e-ews," said Urbine, walking toward the Suburban, Karvakolis and Amalia walking with him, "we found bloodstains, apparently from two individuals. Let me show you."

One look was enough for Amalia. The Suburban had three rows of seats, the middle one drenched in blood—light-colored blood, like from an extremity. The Suburban had tan upholstery, so it was easy to tell that someone with a wounded leg had lain across the middle row, trying to get comfortable.

"Pretty bad-looking, huh," said Karvakolis. "If I had to guess, I'd guess a leg wound. From what's been coming down the line, one of those New York bank robbers got shot in the leg."

"Mmm-hmm," said Amalia, as she looked at the stains, thinking, *Greene, Ljubica Sarah.*

"And here in the front," Karvakolis continued, motioning to the front passenger seat, "there's this little stain, u-u-uh . . . the-e-ere we go, right there," he said, pointing to a few droplets on the seat and middle armrest.

Amalia impassively looked at the dime-sized stains, thinking, *Idaho, Jerome Duncan.*

"Fingerprints," she asked, again without any inflection in her voice.

"Jerry," said Karvakolis, speaking to one of the technicians who was finishing up, "how many prints?"

A thin, balding, bespectacled man with a slight stoop said, "Twenty-three sets, but eight of them are children's, so fifteen possibles. I'm gonna send them all down to Washington right now."

"You get good prints?" asked Urbine.

Jerry only nodded as he finished closing up a suitcase of gear.

"Fifteen possible," said Urbine to Amalia. "That's pretty good."

Amalia only nodded, looking inside the cab of the Suburban. An FBI photographer was taking pictures of the interior, the flash momentarily blinding in the blue morning glow.

"Did they leave anything behind," she asked the two agents, without looking at them.

"Nothing aside from cigarette butts," said Urbine. "We think we can get some DNA off the saliva."

"Have you looked for stolen cars in and around the area," she asked.

"We got a couple of men over at the sheriff's office right now looking into that," said Urbine. "Bu-u-ut . . . it's too soon. If they stole a car, it might not be reported for a while, maybe even a few days if the owner doesn't notice it's gone. And if they had a car waiting for them, or if somebody was helping them, we-e-ell . . . then we're never gonna know what they're driving."

"Mmm-hmm," said Amalia as she took out two small blank cards and noted down her cell phone number and her current alias on each of them.

The two agents watched as she wrote, glancing at each other in curiosity, wondering why the ATF was looking into this bank robbery—properly the FBI's jurisdiction.

"If you find out anything about a stolen car, please call me at this number," Amalia was saying, handing them each a card. As they took her cards, she gingerly extended her hand and said, "Thank you for your assistance."

Karvakolis couldn't stand the suspense anymore. "Say," he said as he took and held on to Amalia's hand, smothering it in both his own. "Why's the Treasury Department, of all people, so interested in a bunch of bank robbers?" he asked with a smile, trying to charm her.

Amalia wasn't charmed. Amalia was horrified as she looked at Karvakolis's hand, staring at it as if it were a monster's claw. "Please let go of my hand," she said quietly.

"Are these guys gunrunners or something?" asked Karvakolis. "Is there a little more to their story?"

"Let go of my hand now," Amalia said quietly, looking up at Karvakolis in the eye, an inch away from pulling out her firearm and killing the man where he stood.

Karvakolis was looking down at her; and when she looked back at him, he dropped her hand and took a step back, feeling adrenaline pumping through him for no obvious reason, his legs going weak and rubbery, as if a demon had taken a sudden, damning interest in him. *This woman is gonna kill me,* he thought clearly and without any doubts.

"Why, uh, why did you come here?" he asked again, quietly, afraid of her. "What did these people do?"

Amalia looked back at him with blank, saucer eyes.

"They're criminals," she said.

Then she walked toward her rental car, got in, and drove away.

Nicholas Denton's office was a large and elegant, wood-paneled affair that had belonged to his predecessor, Keith Lehrer. The walls were dark and smoky, the furniture comfortable overstuffed leather couches and armchairs, the office giving the impression of being some gentleman's clubroom where its lone member could sit and think in peace.

But whereas Lehrer—in keeping with that men's club motif—had hung portraits of hunters and birds, Denton's taste in art ran to the abstract and the rather bold. He had an original Rothko on one side of his office, a gift of his parents for his fifteenth wedding anniversary; an interesting chess set made of brass, the pieces of which could be fit together into a cube, the set meticulously placed on a small table all its own in a corner of the office; an odd-looking abstract painting in yellows and reds, dominated in the center by a black sphere shot through with streaks of blue-green; and behind his desk, an ever-changing gallery of fiercely abstract watercolors done by his four-year-old daughter, Claire.

This morning, the day after his briefing of the President, while Amalia was checking up on Acrobat's Suburban, Denton sat alone, thinking. He was smoking a cigarette, slouched in his leather chair, his suit jacket draped over its back. He was drinking coffee from a mug that said I'M SO HAPPY I COULD SHIT, a Father's Day present from his oldest son, nine-year-old Nicky Junior.

"Do you know what your mother would say if she saw this?" he had asked his son when he had unwrapped the gift about a year ago.

Nicky Junior had smiled his mother's shy smile, nearly breaking Denton's heart. "You won't tell Mommy, will you?"

"It'll be our secret," he had nodded solemnly at his son.

After sitting there for a few minutes, thinking, Denton abruptly leaned forward and pressed the intercom.

"Send him in," he said to his secretary.

In came Bart Michaelus, all 250 pounds of him, furious at having been made to wait twenty minutes.

"Hi Bart," said Nicholas, thrilled at the sight of a man as desperate as Michaelus. "How's it goin'?"

Michaelus didn't answer the question. He was a short, squat man with hardly any neck at all, and a chest that was thick and massive as a barrel. He scared people around Langley. Whatever accidents had made his personality had turned him into a volcano of raw, explosive energy, energy that made him work harder than anyone else, but energy that led to periodic explosions that were devastating to all who were unlucky enough to be around when they happened.

But though Michaelus might explode with other people, he never exploded around Denton, his supposed colleague. Because Bart Michaelus, the Deputy Director of the Operations Directorate, the man who ran all the covert CIA programs, knew enough not to mess with Denton.

"What do you think you're doing?" he asked, as soon as he came in.

Denton smiled. "What's wrong, Bart?"

"You kn——," he said, then stopped, controlling his temper. He stood there, looking at Denton, wrestling with his temper as if it were an alligator. When he was cool, he said, "Your Acrobat people have really screwed the pooch this time."

Denton smiled wider still. "What do you mean, 'my people'? They're your people now, Bart."

"No, that's not true," said Michaelus, as reasonably as he could. "*You* put them together; they're *your* responsibility—"

"Wait-wait-wait-wait a second," said Denton, holding up his hand. "I run Counter Intelligence; you run the Operations Directorate. When Acrobat was doing CI work, they reported to me."

"Yes, like they still do—"

"But-but-*but:* When they started doing operational work, you insisted that they ought to report to you, remember?" said Denton, looking at Michaelus. "Remember that meeting we had? The one you invited yourself to? We had a big discussion about who Acrobat should report to—you, me, and Tom Carr, may he rest in peace. You practically had a fit because you said that if any Counter Intelligence work-group started doing field work, then they ought to report to you."

"I know what I said," said Michaelus, looking at Denton and suddenly realizing what was going on. "You knew this was going to happen."

"Bart, Jesus—"

"You *knew* this was going to happen—I am not gonna stand still for this butt-fuck, Nicholas, these are *your* people—"

"They're your people now," said Nicholas Denton, now deadly serious. "And I have the memos to prove it. I put Acrobat together, sure, but when they started producing results, you and Tom Carr *insisted* they ought to work for you instead of me. So—over my objections—Acrobat was transferred to your Directorate. And now that they're screwing up, you're trying to get me to take them back? I don't think so, Bart.

Acrobat is now on your report card, not mine."

"You *wanted* me to take them over."

Denton blinked. "What?"

"You were the one who called that meeting," said Michaelus—accurately. "You were the one who brought up the jurisdiction problem; you *made* me take them over."

Denton scoffed through his smile. "You give me too much credit."

"You motherfucker," said Michaelus, distinctly spacing his words, finally understanding. "You knew all along that they were gonna blow up; you wanted me to take them over so that the blame would fall on me!"

"Bart, please, enough with the insults, hmm?"

"I'm the only guy who's putting some brakes on you; you've been scheming to get me out of the way—"

"What are you talking about, I—"

"—and you're using Acrobat to do it."

Nicholas Denton looked at Michaelus. "I have a lot of work to do, Bart."

"You're not getting rid of me that easily," Michaelus said.

"I'm not trying to get rid of you!" said Denton, with about as much conviction as a five-dollar hooker faking an orgasm. "I'm trying to help you. I've already liaisoned with the—"

"By cutting me out of that briefing with the Presi——"

"Bart, Bart, Bart," said Denton, holding up his hand with a smile.

Michaelus stopped, looking down at Denton across his massive desk.

"You know how this game is played," said Denton reasonably enough. "When you produce results, you get steak and potatoes every day. But when things go south, they serve you that piping hot shit-sandwich fresh off the grill. You wanted Acrobat; you got 'em. So now it's time you scoot up your chair and get ready to take a big bite. But, so sorry, I won't be joining you for that meal."

Michaelus said nothing, the blood draining out of him, making his legs weak and rubbery.

"You motherfuc——"

"You can go now," said Denton, suddenly not smiling any-more.

With a quick, uncontrollable thrash, Michaelus swiped a leather pencil holder off Denton's desk, spilling pencils across the Persian rug.

Then Michaelus left the office.

"Mother . . . *fucker!*" he shouted when he got to the elevator.

Bart Michaelus would have happily killed Denton if he could've gotten away with it. Of *course* the word had gone out about Acrobat—Denton had made sure of that. Only a handful of people knew about Acrobat and the specifics, but the general vibe had filtered out: Acrobat was now radioactive, and anyone involved with them was gonna get the worst kind of cancer—the career-ending kind. As Michaelus walked down the halls at Langley, he could feel people withdrawing from him—even the secretaries and clerks were pulling away from him—even the fucking *analysts* were avoiding him—and never mind the other deputy directors, who would wave nervously as they passed him by, calling out, "Late for a meeting!" over their shoulders, scurrying away like rats off a sinking ship. Fucking turds.

"Messages," he barked at his secretary as he got to his suite of offices.

His secretary, a severe old maid with a face so pinched she looked as if she were sucking down a peeled lemon through a quarter-inch straw, handed him a sheaf of white-and-blue message slips. One look at her and he could tell: Even she knew he was in freefall.

"What are you looking at," he growled, making the old biddy squirm and wriggle and hide behind her computer as he stomped into his office and slammed the door shut behind him.

The only thing that would save him was the Acrobat work-group—alive. He needed them alive, he needed them talking—he needed them the way he'd need a gun in an Old West–style shoot-out.

They were no use to him dead.

• • •

They were driving down a Pennsylvania highway on their way to Washington.

Duncan Idaho and Monika Summers were sitting in the front seats, Duncan at the wheel, the two of them looking like any average young couple. Tobey Jansen was sitting in the back seat, watching the scenery slide by as he absently twirled his spiked goatee. They couldn't all go to Washington in a single car, so Acrobat had split up, Duncan, Monika, and Tobey taking the Toyota Camry, Russell and Ljubica taking the pick-up truck.

"We'll meet up tomorrow at Pentagon City," Ljubica had suggested, referring to a large shopping mall just outside of Washington proper. "At the food court, at noon."

"Okay," said Monika, everyone somehow resigned as they split up their gear, loaded them into the cars, gave each other directions, and then said their casual good-byes.

Duncan, Monika, and Tobey had gotten in the Camry, Duncan pulling out of the motel's parking lot and signaling to turn into the flow of traffic.

As they waited to join the flow of traffic, Tobey Jansen had happened to look through the rear window, looking at Russell and Ljubica as they got into the pick-up truck. He flashed them a V-for-Victory sign.

Russell didn't see him, but Ljubica did. She smiled thinly, flashing a V of her own, her face drawn, her black hair lank and straight, as if it were too tired to do anything but lie there.

That was the moment when Tobey realized that Acrobat was over. It was a realization that struck him cleanly, like a binary switch that had suddenly been thrown.

Acrobat was over.

Then Duncan had accelerated, the Camry pulling away from the motel's parking lot, Russell and Ljubica disappearing.

Now, looking around at the scenery they were passing, Tobey drank in the sights—the tan upholstery of the car; the view from the back seat of Duncan driving and Monika looking at the map as she retied her blonde hair with her purple scrunchie; the color of the road; the sight of the occasional cars passing by. Tobey had a whole collection of final memories, little mental snapshots of places he'd lived in and things he'd seen, snapshots taken at the moment just before they ended. The more he thought about it, the more the image of Russell and Ljubica struck him—Russell putting the gear in the back of the pick-up truck, already turning away, already on his own separate destiny, Ljubica flashing her V-for-victory sign at Tobey as they drove away. Even though they'd meet at Pentagon City in just a day, Tobey knew from experience that Acrobat was over, the Russell-atom and the Ljubica-atom already split off from the rest of the Acrobat block.

Duncan drove on, but slowly, cautiously, with the cruise control set firmly at sixty-five-miles an hour. The road started ebbing along, the day turning into afternoon, and then the afternoon into evening.

Tobey Jansen said nothing. He sat, still as a stone, his eyes fixed forward, looking to the south as they slowly closed the distance between themselves and their future. Thinking about what waited for them in Washington, he thought how fluid things were, like mercury or water. And for some reason, that made him think of hydrogen—properties of, reaction of said to other elements, even the odd fact that, under the right set of circumstances, hydrogen could be made to behave like a metal. It was something that always surprised him, and on its face it sounded absurd—how hydrogen, a diffuse, flammable gas at the heart of the sun, could be turned into a metal. But it was true—with enough pressure, hydrogen could be made to conduct electricity without resistance. This odd fact also proved that a diffuse and gaseous planet, no matter how scattershot and buoyant, was, at its core, solid, and impenetrable.

PART II

The Gang's All Here

In a corporation, or a bureaucracy, people are interchangeable. The specifics of who you are don't matter—it's what you can do for the system that counts. And I don't begrudge that. After all, I'm not asking any corporation—or any agency—for friendship or love, just employment.

Monika popped the tab on her soft drink and drank some, a natural pause to think a bit more carefully before she spoke again.

That corporate mentality is seeping into our daily lives, she said. We're treating each other like replaceable cogs. Our lives are becoming machines of existence, with no one to believe in—or to love—but ourselves.

I don't like this situation. But I'm a practical person. I work with what I've been given. I don't pretend things are different from what they are. I know when I've been beat.

CHAPTER 3

Soldiers & Drifters

So what the hell do people *do* at CIA—that's what everybody wants to know.

If you tell some Ivy-educated, liberal-minded moron that CIA collects and analyzes intelligence data, chances are he'll laugh in your face. "What about foreign assassinations and overthrowing governments?" he'll ask you with some stupidly knowing look, pissing the hell out of you. It'll piss the hell out of you because you know better—you know that you really *do* collect and analyze intelligence data, and you know that it's boring as all hell. If only you really did assassinate foreign scumbags and overthrow shady governments—at least then you might be having some fun.

But you don't have any fun. Instead, you slog your way through the poop, like Tobey Jansen was doing just before he joined Acrobat.

Up until the fall of '99, Tobey had been marking time before heading off to graduate school. He'd been working as the, quote-unquote, "Chief Financial Analyst, International Trade, China Desk," which sounds exotic as all hell, and very grown-up, too. But don't be fooled; it was a shit job. All Tobey had to do was measure the total commercial transactions going on between the United States and the People's Republic of China. Then, every month, he'd write up a report about it. Why did he do this? Because the Treasury Department needed an independent verification of its own balance-of-trade figures . . .

and because Tobey needed a sexy résumé-builder before heading off to business school.

How sensitive was this work? Not very. How dangerous was this work? Guess.

By the way, that's the sort of thing 95 percent of the people at Langley are involved in on a daily basis—analyze data, and then write up innocuous little reports. It's even simpler than that, because what you're doing at CIA is, in effect, *regurgitating* data. No trick to it: You read reports, statistical bulletins, newspapers, you watch foreign TV, maybe get a sneak peek at some *outside poop,* which is information gathered by roadrunners. Then, once you have all your little poop sheets assembled, you turn around and write up your own reports and memos and little missives that get filed somewhere and never read.

That's your life at Langley. You're stuck in a little cubicle, reading through a pile of poop and not getting enough sunlight. You're cursing your boss behind his back. You're worrying about your wife and the hunky gardener, or your hubby and the hunky gardener, as the case may be. You're nervous about that boil you discovered that's growing right in your armpit, gently touching it and wondering, *What the hell is that goddamned thing?* as you sit there at five o'clock rush hour, stuck on the Beltway, the asphalt practically boiling as the inside of your two-and-a-half-year-old leased sport utility vehicle that you knew you were overpaying for even as you signed the stupid lease papers slowly turns into a naugahyde coffin on wheels, the rubber tires seeming to melt into the black asphalt, the heat of Washington too damned hot, the traffic too damned slow, your life too damned miserable for words—

Basically, your life sucks.

Of course, the outside world doesn't *know* that your life sucks. You tell them you work for CIA, most real people figure you're in league with the Prince of Darkness himself, with your very own pitchfork and everything.

So—quick! Do you admit the truth and tell people you're

just a bureaucrat, with a bureaucrat's petty nightmares and impossible dreams?

No! You don't tell the *truth*—you lie! You lie your ass off, and instead of telling the awful, humiliating truth, you play I Spy.

Not the children's playground pastime, I Spy is that simple, sickeningly addictive CIA game that adults of all ages and insecurities can play, a game Tobey Jansen played all the time.

Listen:

Tobey Jansen was sitting in a crowded Georgetown bar in the fall of '99. Unlike in his later incarnation a few months hence, in this lifetime, Tobey didn't look like some punk rocker. Far from it: Tonight he was dressed in a navy blue sports jacket and pleated khakis, his blondish brown hair short and neatly coiffed, his loafers tasseled and ready to boogie. He was wearing contact lenses that made his eyes occasionally blink and water, nursing a beer as he sat at the bar, careful to be inconspicuous as he looked at the pretty girls all around.

The bar was a hang-out for sleek young men and women who were just starting out on the Hill and in the media— research assistants, segment line coordinators, congressional liaisons, people like that: Junior members of the chattering classes. They were people who didn't look at the press and the government as if they were some higher calling, but rather as if they were symbiotic businesses, only a revolving door separating the two; and they thought themselves quite clever for being so sophisticated. They dreamed of growing up to become Andrea Mitchell and Alan Greenspan.

Tobey wasn't too sure what he was doing here. He didn't *look* out of place—he looked like just another preppy-geek. But still, he felt out of place. What's a boy to do.

He was looking around, craning his neck far and wide, when all of a sudden—

Bingo! Lookee here, at the end of the bar, we've got ourselves an attractive *girl!* The female kind and everything! She's looking to be around Tobey's age, standing there oh so lonesome, smiling shyly and trying to find a way that she too can plug into what's going on around her here at this junior-sophisticated bar. She's quite attractive in that brainy, head-screwed-on-straight kind of way, a fairly common sight in Rivercity—fine-boned and sharp of eye, feeling happy now that she is a bona fide adult and finally past all that high-school/college-age bullshit, finally coming fully into her own, a butterfly of a girl who's just *begging* to be noticed now that she is finally emerging from that pupa of nerves and insecurities that has held her wrapped in its claustrophobic death grip for so long.

Tobey gulps his beer like an ostrich swallowing and makes his move.

"Hi," he says to the woman as he sidles up to her, extending his hand. "I'm Tobey Jansen."

"Hi Tobey," says the woman, looking him over with a smile. "I'm Katrina Wopat."

"Can I, uh, get you a drink? . . . oh you—oh you have one," he says, noticing her working on a beer.

"I surely do," she says.

"Uh—this is an amazing place, isn't it?"

"Yeah," she says with a smile. "I had no idea people partied in Washington so much."

"Yeah they do," says Tobey. "So where do you work?" he asks.

"On the Hill," she says. "I'm an assistant to House Speaker Dennis Hastert," she adds crisply, proud of where she works, waiting for him to ask her more.

"Wow," says Tobey—

—and *here*, exactly *here*, is where those carefully educated IQ points Tobey possesses in such abundance begin leaking right out of his ear.

Instead of drawing out Miss Katrina Wopat with the tried-and-true method used since the dawn of the species (*id est,* fake compliments, empty flattery, and pretended interest), what does Tobey Jansen do? *He tries to trump her!* Yes indeedy, instead of trying to make little Miss Katrina Wopat feel all good and clever about herself (and therefore susceptible to Tobey's not-inconsiderable geeky charms), Tobey decides to play I Spy at full blast, working that CIA trump card for all it's worth.

"I work at CIA," he declares, as if he knows the answer to a tough question.

Poor little Miss Katrina Wopat doesn't know what to say to that one: Either Tobey is lying (and therefore a potential weirdo/stalker/creepy nut), or he is telling the truth, which in a way is worse. Either way, Miss Wopat deflates like a popped balloon as she says, "Oh, that's, uh, that's very interesting."

"It can be," Tobey agrees, with a pregnant lilt.

"Uh—so what do you do there?" she askes gamely.

Tobey shrugs. "This and that," he says cryptically, "but I really shouldn't talk about it."

"Oh," she says, feeling squashed, picking up her glass of beer and mentally pulling away from Tobey as surely as the tide.

He can feel it, so he tries his best to recover. "I do a lot of balance of trade stuff," he says, trying to salvage the situation, wondering where he's played it wrong. "I do a lot of work for the Treasury Department, corroborating their trade figures— what about you?" he asks, with a squeak in his voice. "What do *you* do?"

Too late! Too late!

"I work on homeowner insurance policy," she begins, giving him a practiced, automatic spiel as her eyes drift away, looking around the bar, her smile now fake whenever their eyes meet.

When she is done describing what she does in words that sound a lot like a résumé, they stand there looking embarrassed, not much left to say to one another. Soon enough, someone else comes jostling through the crowd, a young man more like this Katrina Wopat. In clothes and looks and demeanor, this new man—who isn't much different from Tobey, except maybe in that he wears glasses instead of contacts— seems to be what this young woman is looking for, because she begins talking to him at about a thousand miles an hour, telling him all about her work and her new apartment and her cat and her life, ignoring Tobey as he stands there beside them.

Give him this: He doesn't walk away, at least not at first. As best he can, he tries to make a place for himself, talking to the woman and to the man, trying to hold their attention. But soon enough, Tobey knows he just doesn't belong here anymore. He's finessed his way right out of the conversation.

He circulates a bit, half-heartedly looking for another chance to connect. But when nobody throws their arms around his shoulders and calls him a long-lost friend, he finally gives up and walks out of the bar just as the crowd really gets going.

He drives on home through black, rain-slick streets, little-boy-lost depressed about his stupidity in handling Katrina Wopat, wondering when it would be that he, too, would fit in.

He sure didn't seem to fit in at CIA.

Every day, at exactly 12:30, the entire Langley campus reshuffled itself with terrifying efficiency as everyone headed off to the main cafeteria, which was a huge room full of tables and chairs, just two degrees dressier than a high-school mess hall. And it was during lunch that all the little cliques at CIA came together, the little cliques as distinct from each other as animals at a zoo.

There were the secretaries, of course—the most obvious group. Plump, occasionally overweight, middle-aged women in suits, a brooch at their lapels, their hair frosted, their legs short and stout, their ankles swollen as their feet were fit into low-heeled pumps that seemed to overflow with fatty flesh. They were all divorced, with two or three teenaged children and irregular alimonies they constantly squawked about like walruses on a beach.

Then there were the tech guys, who goofed around together in their splendid isolation. Some were big and bearded and slow in their movements, just like bears, while others were skinny and gawky and awkward, just like giraffes. But they were all geeks. And though they might think that they had more brainpan power than the next guy, they knew full well that they were geeks. Perversely, they reveled in their social ineptitude, behaving in ways that would guarantee their isolation. But then again, they weren't isolated—they hung out with people such as themselves. Acne was still a problem among this set, as were body odors, but they didn't seem to care. What they cared about was computers. They cared about a technological future. They were spellbound by the beauty of computer code, and they derived enormous satisfaction from solving a knotty technical problem. And though attractive people frightened them, though they were sometimes ashamed that they'd allowed themselves to become as odd as they were, they didn't care, because they were confident that they were the Chosen People—the inheritors of this brave new technological planet.

Political analysts, in contrast, perched together as nervous and tense as birds. There were a lot more women here than among the tech guys, though they were just as intellectually arrogant: They knew languages, they knew history—as a matter of fact, they knew just about everything except how *not* to come across as a pompous asshole. They tended to be theory-weenies, political analysts having no trouble pounding a square fact until it fit a round theoretical hole, the consequences be damned. Truth to tell, getting the facts to fit the theory was a point of pride among the analysts, and it was probably why CIA tended to fuck it up when it came time to making predictions. Theory got in the way.

Sort of above the tech guys and political analysts were the ferrety administration people, who poked their snouts all over the place but who were really only interested in each other. Their smiles were swift and easy when they sucked up to their superiors, their rubbery lips hiding snapping chops that could tear a subordinate to pieces without compunction. They pretty much gave you the creeps.

Finance types, like Tobey, were a much smaller group at the Langley mess hall, neatly divisible into two discrete cliques.

On the one hand, there was the Pocket-Protector Set—accountant-types who wore short-sleeved, button-down shirts and clipped hair and glasses, time-warped people from the 1950s who were busily mooing their way up to middle-management. They were usually from fly-over states—you know: Nebraska, Iowa, Kansas—cow country like that, and they were just as unsophisticated and boring as one would expect. They tended to marry fat, slatternly women who spent their days eating chocolates in front of the television.

Opposing them were the Ivy Bankers, haughty men and women who wore tailored suits and always had a hyena smile on their lips. You would think that it would be easy to confuse them with the administration types. But in fact, they were as different as night and gray-flannel. Ivy Bankers were swathed in money—most of them came from money, and all of them came from the coasts. Nicholas Denton, for instance, was an Ivy Banker, only of course amplified and refined. He—like any other self-respecting Ivy Banker type—would have scoffed at being confused with the administration people. Administration types were more hardscrabble, more arriviste— they had no grace or class or breeding: They weren't PLU.

This was the mess hall at Langley: A whole cornucopia of social divisions, each sector as separate as armies from different nations. Only the naive or the oafish would think that race played any part in these divisions—it was all about interests and temperament and class.

Among all these divisions and groups, Tobey Jansen was a drifter, falling somewhere between the Ivy Bankers and the Pocket-Protector Set. He stuttered insecurely, yet he wore nice suits and ties. He was a Phillips Andover/Dartmouth College boy, but with roots lost in divorced lower-middle-class obscurity. He was not quite one, not quite the other.

He had lunch with both cliques, though—what the hell else was he supposed to do, eat alone? But even as he hung out and got to know elements of both groups, Tobey belonged to neither, listening in from the periphery as they set up weekend get-togethers that he was not invited to. It wasn't that the Ivy Bankers or the Pocket Protectors were *mean*—neither group invited him because they simply assumed he belonged to the other group. They simply assumed he belonged elsewhere.

Tobey got to his apartment building in Alexandria, parked his car, went up to his place, and turned on the television, even though it was late.

He was drifting. That was the thing. He was a Drifter,

among all these Soldiers. He'd occasionally noticed other people like him in that regard—attached to no group, drifting along in the social tide, with no place where they could belong.

This drifting isolation seemed to perpetuate itself. Weeks went by when Tobey hardly said a word to anyone outside of work. And even at Langley, he didn't talk to many people. He had no reason to, sitting in his cubicle, working away on his reports, watching his computer screen as his fingers tick-tick-ticked away on his keyboard, a whispery cascade of fingertips that was all the sound he heard.

The more he tried to connect, the more desperate he became, making him do either stupid things like playing I Spy or else scaring people away with his intensity, his need to unload all this-this-this *stuff* off his mind. Books he had read from cover to cover filled his shelves; ticket stubs to all the movies and museums he had gone to piled up in his dresser drawer; used airplane boarding passes to weekend getaways he took alone gathered dust on his kitchen counter—all these things accumulated in his apartment, the physical debris of everything crowding the attic of his mind, an attic that was bursting with experiences and thoughts and conclusions that had no means of expression in the life he led. If the world was a collection of Soldiers from different armies, then Tobey was a Drifter looking in on a locked world.

He'd always thought that one day he would find happiness. He'd catch it, the way a dog would catch a bunny. After all, that was the explicit promise held out by this country—life, liberty, and all the rest of it. Somewhere at the end of that pursuit, happiness would be waiting like a cool pillow at the end of a long hard day.

Next weekend, he promised himself as he fitfully turned off the television and got ready to go to sleep. *Next weekend it'll be better.*

Of course, he knew that was a lie. It was only now, at twenty-five, that Tobey Jansen was beginning to acknowledge that simple, sickening truth:

Tomorrow would be pretty much the same as today.

• • •

They say all good things come to those who wait. Bullshit. More of the same comes to those who wait. But sometimes, you get caught in forces at work. That's what happened to Tobey Jansen.

It started off inconspicuously enough. One day in September 1999, his boss at PRC Finance came over to his desk and told him that Tom Carr, the head of Asian Counter Intelligence—three rungs of the ladder above him—wanted to speak with him right away.

Off he went.

When he got to Tom Carr's office, Tobey was surprised to find him laughing uproariously as he sat chatting with his own boss, Nicholas Denton, the head of CI.

"He said that?" Tom Carr was saying. "He actually said that?"

Nicholas Denton nodded with a smile, fastidiously brushing away a flake of cigarette ash off his pants leg before taking another drag on his coffin nail. "Can you believe it?"

"Fucking asshole," said Tom Carr with a laugh, before noticing Tobey's presence. "What do you want?"

Tobey looked from Denton to Carr, both of whom were staring back at him with casual, assured patience.

"Uh, hi, uh, I'm Tobey Jansen? From over at PRC Finance?"

Tom Carr only shook his head as he stared at Tobey Jansen. "And you want what?"

"You called me?" he said nervously. "You told John Seebert that you wanted to see me right away? Uh—hi Mr. Denton," he said, nodding at Denton and generally feeling nervous and miserable.

"Tobey Jansen?" Tom Carr asked, turning to Denton.

"Do I know you?" Denton asked, confused.

Tobey Jansen couldn't help himself. In a skitter-shatter voice that was too high and too nervous, he said, "Yeah, I, uh, I worked at your office? As an intern? When I was in college? For like nine months?"

"If you say so," said Denton, lost.

But Tom Carr had remembered him. "Oh, yeah, right, right," he said, making the mental connection. "John Seebert says you're not a total idiot," he said, looking at Tobey Jansen. "Is this true?"

"Uh—nosir," he said.

"Oh, so you *are* an idiot?"

"Nosir," said Tobey quickly, "I meant—"

Tom Carr smiled and shook his head at Denton as he held up a silencing hand at Tobey. Then he looked at him and pointed out his office door. "Go find Monika Summers—she's the blonde girl with the Smurfette doll on top of her computer. She'll get you squared away in your cubicle and whatnot."

Tobey, confused, blinked and shoved his glasses up the bridge of his nose with his middle finger.

Denton and Tom Carr frowned at the bird-flipping.

"But I work at PRC Finance," said Tobey.

"Not anymore you don't," said Tom Carr as he turned back to his visiting boss.

Tom Carr looked at Denton for a second, expecting Tobey Jansen to leave. But when he didn't, he turned to him with a deeper frown. "And you are waiting for what, my permission?—my blessing?—my absolution? Chop-chop, Mr. Jansen—Monika Summers is waiting. Go to it."

Glancing at Nicholas Denton, Tobey Jansen mumbled, "Yessir," and wandered off, looking for a Smurfette doll atop a computer.

It wasn't hard to find. Down a hallway, the cubicles of Tom Carr's work-group were all squeezed together in the middle of a big, windowless room, the dividing walls barely shoulder high. Peeking above these walls, Tobey Jansen spotted the Smurfette doll saucily posing as she looked out onto the world, Tobey's lighthouse as he walked across the foamy blue, sound-sucking carpet.

But when he walked around the cubicles and got to Monika Summers's desk, Tobey realized that, even though it was mid-morning, there was no one around, not even Monika.

Not really daring to go back to Tom Carr's office, Tobey stood there and waited.

He waited for a while. But then all of a sudden, a goofily handsome blond man bounded down the hallway, wearing a leather biker's jacket and carrying a motorcycle helmet looped through his arm, walking around with a crazy sort of charisma—something about him made you absolutely positive that he was nuts.

"Hey!" he said with a smile. "Who are you?"

"I'm Tobey—Tobey Jansen," he said, standing there, unsure what to do.

"Tobey-Tobey Jansen, huh?" he said.

"Just, just Tobey—one 'Tobey,' " he said. "Mr. Carr told me to come over here and talk to Monika Summers?"

The blond man rubbed his chin, thinking. "You're the accountant, right?"

"Uh—actually, I'm a financial analyst?"

"I bet," he said, putting out his hand. "I'm Duncan Idaho."

Tobey shook it. "Nice to meet you; I'm Tobey Jansen."

"Yeah, I know."

"Right, right."

With a smile, Duncan put his flat hand at eye level. "Okay, this is you," he said, referring to his horizontal hand, which then drifted a whole foot down. "And this is where you want to be," he added.

"Right, right."

Duncan Idaho cracked a smile and tagged him on the arm. "You'll fit right in, we need a revved-up guy like you around here," said Duncan with a shrewd, playful look to him. Before Tobey could say anything to that, Duncan instantly switched gears. "Come on," he said. "I gotta go do something and I need an extra set o' hands."

With that, Duncan Idaho took off, Tobey falling in step behind him. Duncan walked so fast, Tobey had to skip a bit to keep up.

"Oh man, if I hadn't found you, I dunno what I woulda done," said Duncan as they passed offices and cubicles along the way to the elevator, Duncan waving and smiling as he passed people he knew.

They got into an elevator and went all the way down to the underground parking level.

"Where are we going?" asked Tobey, as they walked toward a lone motorcycle parked under the fluorescents of the parking lot.

"I gotta go do this thing," said Duncan vaguely, putting on his helmet and straddling the bike. "Hop on."

"I don't have a helmet," said Tobey nervously, as Duncan started up the crotch-rocket with a silky *vroom!*

"Dude, I only wear a helmet 'cause I can't afford another ticket," he said. "If we wipe out, we'll be killed instantly, with or without a helmet, so relax, hop on."

Tobey wasn't relaxed exactly, but he did hop onboard, Duncan throttling his Kawasaki to 4,000 rpm as he scooted them out of the parking lot and up into the daylight.

Duncan Idaho drove like a nut. Even with Tobey Jansen, who had never ridden a motorcycle before, Duncan Idaho had no problem taking turns at close to forty miles an hour, allowing his 1,100-cc Kawasaki to lean over 'til their knees were almost brushing the pavement. At a stoplight, he told the terrified Tobey Jansen, "On a bike, 'defensive driving' means riding faster than anyone else on the road—you're outrunning your obstacles."

Uh-huh, was all Tobey was able to even *think* before Duncan hit the gas, tearing quick as a whip into D.C. proper.

When they got to Adams Morgan, Duncan zig-zagged his way to a liquor store, pulling up right on the sidewalk, pedestrians be damned.

"Come on," he said, walking into the liquor store, the buckles on his boots jangling and tinkling, Tobey dazed from the ride as he followed right behind, wondering all the while what the hell they were doing here.

Behind the counter, a middle-aged fat man in a tweed sports jacket was reading the paper. He looked over his rimless reading glasses as Duncan waltzed in. "Hello Duncan my friend," he said with a vaguely foreign accent. "How goes the spying business."

"I'm on to you, Vlad," said Duncan, shaking the man's hand. "I'm onto you, and that agent of yours, Vanna White," he said, the two of them laughing. "They come in?" asked Duncan.

"All three of them," said the store owner, making his way around the counter and walking to the back. "That's two-ten."

Duncan sighed. "Okay—say, Tobey is it?" he asked casually, turning to Jansen. "You got any money on you?"

"Uh, no, not really."

"But you got a credit card, right?"

"Yes . . . ," Tobey said suspiciously, debating how wise it would be to lend money to this crazy man—or how wise it would be to *not* lend money to a coworker on his first day on the job.

"Great, can you pay for this?"

"Pay for what?"

Duncan blinked, nonplussed. "For the beer," he said.

Twenty minutes later, Tobey and Duncan were pulling three kegs of Guinness out of a taxicab they'd flagged down and into Duncan's house in Adams Morgan.

"Christ, these weigh a ton," said Tobey.

"Don't roll 'em," said Duncan with a worried/nervous frown. "It bruises the beer, and you can't bruise Guinness, dude—these were imported from like, straight from fucking Ireland."

Tobey wasn't too sure if it was even possible to bruise beer, but he didn't argue the point, too struck by Duncan Idaho as they manhandled the kegs into his house.

He was a big kid, at bottom—a twenty-eight-year-old ten-year-old. Duncan's Adams Morgan house looked like a college fraternity franchise—dirty laundry was piled four feet high in a corner, the furniture was cheap and worn down, and there were odd knick-knacks scattered all over the place. There was also a vintage Wurlitzer, lovingly buffed to a psychedelic sheen, with all the lights working fine, as well as two fully functioning video arcade games from the early eighties, Tempest and Battlezone, in mint condition. When they walked into the apartment, Duncan punched the buttons on the Wurlitzer, the Gap Band's "Burn Rubber" coming on like a long bong hit—phat and happy, much appreciated.

"Fuck that rap shit, huh Tobey?"

"Sure," said Tobey, who liked hip-hop but was too blown away by Duncan to say different.

"Check it out, let me show you something," said Duncan, as he walked over to his bedroom.

From under the unmade futon in his bedroom, Duncan pulled out a firearm—what looked like a GLOCK 9-mm automatic, though it seemed a little too round and flimsy, and too shiny, as if it had been melted a bit.

"Whoa," said Tobey nervously.

"Neat, huh? It's made of porcelain," said Duncan, eyeing the weapon and showing it off as he checked the hard plastic magazine and the safety. "Can beat any metal detector on earth. I'm bringing it along for a test run. Cool, huh?"

"Uh, yeah, I guess," said Tobey, looking hypnotized by the firearm. Just because he worked at CIA didn't mean he had ever even seen a weapon before in his life, let alone something as exotic as a porcelain firearm.

"Besides the bullets, it doesn't have a single metal part; and it's a lot sturdier than composite too," said Duncan.

"Uh—what exactly do you do at Tom Carr's office?"

"You mean Acrobat," Duncan corrected, checking the porcelain GLOCK as he walked over to his closet and pulled out a one-piece jumpsuit.

"What's the difference?" wondered Tobey out loud as Duncan tossed the gun and the jumpsuit on his open futon and began to undress.

"Dude," said Duncan, "Tommy's into all sorts of funky dung—he's a real roadrunner. But Acrobat, we're a hard-core field work-group. We do real spying and shit."

Tobey shook his head, confused. "The Operations Directorate does the field work, right?"

"Yeah, so?"

Tobey scratched his brow. "Well, if Acrobat is part of

Counter Intelligence, then it's not supposed to do any operational work at all, is it?"

"Yeah, but things tend to get kind of blurry sometimes," said Duncan, straightening out the jumpsuit.

"And-and Counter Intelligence—isn't CI supposed to refer anything they find to the FBI?"

"You *know* the Pope's Jewish, don't you?" asked Duncan as he lit a cigarette, the whole James-Dean-with-a-porcelain-gun thing going for him big time even as he started putting on the dweeby-looking jumpsuit, comically hopping around the room, trying to get his legs all the way in.

Just as Duncan was zipping up, Tobey asked, "Are we . . . are we going on some sort of intelligence gathering mission?"

Duncan's eyes suddenly bulged out of their sockets as he started going into convulsions, his cigarette jittering at his lips, his hands grabbing onto the sides of his head and holding on for dear life. "Too many questions! Too many questions!" Duncan yelled, as if in the grip of a terrifying seizure.

Tobey only looked at him, feeling very small. But then Duncan stopped mocking him and gave him a smile, tagging him on the arm.

"Well, yeah, we're going on an intelligence-gathering mission, but we don't call it 'an intelligence-gathering mission'—we call it scoring. This, right now, this is a lay-up with no defenders, an easy two-pointer. C'mon, it'll be fun."

But then, Duncan stopped and looked Tobey up and down.

"You wanna change later?"

"Well, why?"

"No offense, but you got that whole working stiff/working dweeb look to you, and I'm not so sure you want to come across that way tonight."

"What's going on tonight?"

"What do you think I got the Guinness for?" asked Duncan. "For the party."

"I'm invited?" asked Tobey.

Duncan sighed. "No, we need cheap laughs and someone who can clean up the ashtrays—of *course* you're invited to tonight's thing: You're in with Acrobat. If you're nice to me,

I'll even set you up with some really hot paralegals from Wilmer, Cutler & Pickering."

"Uh, I'll change later," he said.

"Suitcher self."

Out the room Duncan went, and Tobey followed.

They hopped on the Kawasaki and tore ass to Alexandria, where there was a big FedEx van sitting on one of the side streets, as if abandoned.

The FedEx van looked huge and scary, like it might be rigged with explosives or something. Looking around to make sure that no one was watching them, Duncan Idaho approached it and reached into the well of its front right wheel.

"Ljubica Greene set this up," said Duncan, as he found the keys taped to the inside of the fender. "She's great with gear, just finds it all over the place. Born to be a shopper, I'm telling you. Hop in, dude."

Duncan got in the driver's seat and Tobey got in on the passenger side, the two of them sitting there.

"Now we wait," said Duncan.

"Okay," said Tobey.

Duncan sat staring straight ahead, a bored look to his face, his hands loosely on the wheel. He checked his pack of cigarettes, as if to light one, but then hesitated, replacing the pack in his jumpsuit without taking any.

Tobey looked at Duncan, then away, not sure if he ought to ask what they were waiting for, nervous about asking anymore questions.

Duncan suddenly perked up. Quietly at first, he began making noises: Car noises. Acceleration noises: "Rrrrrrrrrr-RRRRRHHRrrrrrrrrrrRRRRRHHRrrrrrrrrrRRRRRHH."

Tobey looked at Duncan, who was turning the steering wheel this way and that, completely concentrated even though the van wasn't moving, Duncan now making noises as if they were going unbelievably fast: "Rrrrr *rrrrRRRRRHH*-Rrrrrr *rrrrRRRRRHH*-Rrrrrrrr *rrrr-EEEEHH!!!—NO!!!*—KER-BLANG!!!" he yelled as he threw his arms over his face, as if trying to protect himself from a head-on collision.

Tobey just looked at him.

Duncan took a quick peek over his elbows, as if trying to ascertain the damages—then looked surprised that there were none.

"Whew!—That was close!" he said, turning an amazed look on Tobey.

Tobey just shook his head, unable to keep from smiling, Duncan grinning back at him.

Tobey faced forward, seeing cars passing by on the street crossing this alleyway as in his mind's eye, he saw a giant space station fast approaching.

"Space Station *Explorer*," said Tobey, his voice gone remarkably deep and sonorous. "This is the *Odyssey* coming in for our approach."

Duncan instantly started pretend-driving again as he covered his mouth and said in a thick West Virginia drawl, "*Odyssey,* you're-ah, clear for your approach on-ah, vector niner-sixer-tango-kilo, over."

Tobey said calmly, "Roger that, *Explorer,* our approach vector is niner-sixer-tango-kilo, relative speed is fifty-two hundred feet per second—firing retro-boosters in five, four, three, two, one, fire retro-boosters."

Duncan—now the copilot—said calmly, "Firing retro-boosters," as he flipped the windshield wiper lever of the van.

Then he jerked in his seat, flipping the windshield wiper switch off and on, as if it weren't working. He turned horrified eyes on Tobey.

"Retro-boosters not firing!"

"*What!?*"

"They're not working, Captain!"

"Go to back-up retro-boosters."

"Back-ups are dead!"

"Oh, for God's *sake!*—Turn!-*Turn!-Turn!*" Tobey yelled.

"I *can't,* she's *frozen up!*"

"Velocity *increasing* to eight thousand feet per second!"

"*Noooooooooo!!!!*"

"*Ahhhhhhhhh!!!—Kah-FLUEY!!!!*" shouted Tobey, making exploding sounds in the back of his throat.

Duncan and Tobey laughed like hell.

"This is stupid," said Duncan, shaking his head and grinning, offering his pack of cigarettes to Tobey (who declined) before lighting one himself.

"So what are we waiting for?" asked Tobey.

"Agh!" said Duncan. "The others. They always say that I'm the one who's always late; but when it comes down to brass tacks, they're all slouches."

"The others?"

"Yeah, the others in Acrobat—"

Just then, there was a banging noise at the back of the van. *"Jesus!"* Tobey jumped.

Duncan smiled as he exhaled smoke. "High-strung, are we?" he said as he got out of the driver's seat and went to the back of the van.

"Who *is* it?" Duncan asked in a sing-song voice.

"It's me," said a woman's dark, smoky voice.

"Me who?"

"It's me-me," said the woman, getting irritated.

" 'It's me-me'?" said Duncan, winking at Tobey. "That's not the right pass-phrase."

"Quit screwing around, Duncan," said the woman, clearly pissed.

"That's the right pass-phrase," said Duncan, opening the back of the van.

A tall, elegantly beautiful woman with straight black hair—Ljubica Greene—stood there, shaking her head. "You can be so annoying," she said. Then she hopped into the van, Duncan helping her up.

"Who are you?" she said.

Duncan said, "This is Tobey Jansen—the new guy."

"Oh. Hi," she said, nodding at Tobey as she stood there in the back of the van, amid neat racks of boxes. She took out a pad and looked at it as she and Duncan conferred.

"I have this van for two and a half hours," said Ljubica, all business. "It has to be back here no later than one P.M. or else the FedEx people will realize it's missing."

"Okay, no sweat, what else?" said Duncan easily.

Ljubica picked up a clipboard hanging from a hook on the inside of the van and flipped through the pages. "The package is coded . . . right here, AZ23548," she said, pointing the entry out to Duncan, then pointing to a package in one of the racks. "That's the package. The delivery counts; there may or may not be a pick-up today, but don't count on it."

"Okay, what else?"

Ljubica wrote in her pad some, studiously ignoring Duncan. Then she turned and looked him in the eye. "This is a clean score," she said. "Hand it over."

"What?" said Duncan, sighing innocence.

"Your firearm," said Ljubica.

"I'm not carrying a firearm," he said casually, without any heat that would give him away.

"Duncan, please: Hand it over," she said. "This is sensitive. The nightmare will never end if you get pinched."

Duncan turned to Tobey. "You saw me strip and get into this stupid getup," he said. "Am I carrying a firearm?"

"No," Tobey said simply.

Ljubica blinked, Duncan impressed. Tobey was a remarkably good liar.

Just then, there was another banging on the door.

"Open it up," said Ljubica irritatedly, hooking her thumb at the door as she looked at her pad.

Duncan opened the door and in stepped a huge bald black man with narrow features and gold-rimmed glasses, wearing a sports jacket and a white dress shirt with no tie—Russell Orr.

"Hello, campers," he said. "Ready for another merit badge?"

"Hey, Russ," said Duncan.

Ljubica said nothing, looking up from her pad with a glowing smile on her face and kissing Russell on the lips.

"Hey," said Russell, noticing Tobey Jansen. "Who's the suit?"

"Tobey-Tobey Jansen," said Duncan. "He's the new guy—the accountant we asked for—though he *claims* he's actually a financial analyst."

"Right," Russell said. "Nice threads. I'm Russell Orr."

Tobey shook his hand, amazed at Russell, who was the biggest black man he had ever seen.

"Hi," said Tobey—and then it simply popped out of his mouth: "How come you're wearing glasses with no prescription?"

Russell eyed him coolly. "Because I'm in disguise," he said with a mockingly dangerous tone of voice.

Duncan laughed and Yuvi smiled as she shook her head, Tobey going all red in the face and already feeling he was on a slide with these people.

"So where's the other jumpsuit?" said Russell, switching gears as he began to take off his jacket, as if he were about to change.

"Under the seat," said Ljubica.

"Wait a second," said Duncan, looking confused. "I thought Monika was going to back me up."

"She couldn't make it," said Ljubica. "Russell can back you up."

"I'm in disguise," Russell deadpanned.

But Duncan looked away, clearly pissed.

"What?" said Ljubica.

"Why isn't Monika coming?" Duncan asked.

Yuvi shrugged. "I don't know."

Duncan shook his head. "The hell with it," he said. "I'm really not gonna need any back-up—you guys go on back to the ranch; I'll deal with this delivery myself."

"What?" said Russell.

"Jesus, *Duncan* . . . ," said Ljubica.

Russell opened the back of the van and hopped out. "Shit, I had other things to do you know," he said, pissed as he fixed the lapels of his sports jacket.

"Well, sorry," said Duncan.

Ljubica closed her pad and replaced it in her purse. "Duncan, we're all here. We'll back you up—"

"I don't need any back-up."

Ljubica looked at him. "You need back-up. You *are* going with back-up."

Duncan thought a bit, then made a snap decision. "Fuck it, I'll bring along the new guy instead," he said.

Ljubica and Russell both scoffed, Yuvi motioning for help getting down off the back of the delivery van. Russell easily picked her up and set her gently down.

Then she turned on Duncan. "Our morning was ruined because you don't have the nerve to ask Monika out on a date," she said. "That's not fair."

"Yeah, well, life sucks, get a helmet," said Duncan, leaning out and pulling the delivery van's rear door shut.

"Asshole," he and Tobey both heard Ljubica mutter.

"She seems sort of upset," Tobey said as Duncan went to the front of the van and got in the driver's seat.

"She'll get over it," he said moodily, turning the engine on the van and pulling out of the alleyway.

They tore out of Alexandria and into Washington proper, driving to Embassy Row.

Once there, they turned into the embassy of the People's Republic of China, stopping just outside the main entrance.

Duncan didn't look at Tobey as he eyed the security people manning the entrance to the embassy, only hooking his thumb over his shoulder. "You know that clipboard back there?" he said, clearly all business. "Go find it, and the box Yuvi pointed out."

"Okay," said Tobey, getting out of his seat and going to the back of the van, finding the clipboard and the box.

"What do I do with them?" Tobey called out as the van came to a stop.

"Bring 'em up front," said Duncan casually as he opened the door of the van and got out.

The two of them walked into the Chinese Embassy, carrying the box.

"He's my supervisor," said Duncan, casually explaining away Tobey's suit and tie as they waited to get past the security checkpoint at the entrance to the embassy. They not only had to surrender their keys before they crossed the metal detector, the keys were in fact checked by one of the guards.

"Arms up, legs played," said the uniformed Chinese security man in a weird rhythm, as if he'd memorized the words but didn't quite know what they meant.

" 'Legs played?' " asked Tobey, catching Duncan's eye, who smiled, Tobey suddenly getting what the security guard had said: Legs *splayed*.

"Legs *played*," the security guard said again, toeing Tobey's shoes.

Duncan and Tobey spread their arms and *splayed* their legs as the security man ran a metal-detecting wand over their bodies.

Tobey normally would have been sweating bullets. He was the kind of guy who got nervous at airport security checklines, who worried that his Visa card would be declined at the supermarket checkout, who was forever anxious that one day the IRS would come knocking on his door demanding an audit. You could say that authority intimidated Tobey to no end.

But as he stood there at the checkpoint, he suddenly felt no fear, only a weird kind of getting-away-with-it-ness that was positively intoxicating.

The security guard waved the magic metal-detecting wand over him and let him go.

I beat The Man, thought Tobey, dropping his arms and taking a step forward. *I beat* THE MAN—

—*EEEuh-EEEuh-EEEEE!!!!!* squawked the metal detector.

Tobey whirled on Duncan, the Chinese security man suddenly very tense.

The gun!—arrested!—deported!—Chinese concentration camp!—forty years—!

So ran Tobey's thinking as he panicked in place, his eyes going wide.

Duncan didn't even flinch. In fact, Duncan looked downright sleepy as he looked at the security man, shook his head, then remembered, pulling out a Zippo lighter and a pack of cigarettes.

The Chinese security man was all over both items, handling them and checking them, even going so far as to remove the cigarettes from the pack and checking them individually. Finally, the stern young man looked at Duncan.

"You get these back when you leave, yes?"

"It's just the aluminum wrapping paper—

"You get these back when you leave, yes?" said the guard more fiercely.

"Whatever," said Duncan. "Can we go now?"

"Go—quick!" said the Chinese security man.

The package they were bringing had gone through the X-ray machine, and it was sitting there, waiting for them as Duncan picked it up. Then the two of them walked to the elevator of the embassy.

As they waited for the elevator, Duncan began to mumble morosely, "I shouldn't't've snapped at Yuvi like that; she pegged me right as rain. Shit. I'll make it up to her tonight."

Tobey didn't even hear him. "God," was all he croaked while they waited.

Duncan turned on him and smiled, playfully tagging him on the arm. "Tobey, you *worry* too much," he said. "You think they're gonna catch us?"

Tobey turned eyes big as pancakes on Duncan. "Uh-huh," he muttered.

"Okay," said Duncan, humoring him. "If they catch us, what do you think they're gonna do, huh?"

"Strip search us, rape us, deport us to a concentration camp in the heart of China for a gazillion years," said Tobey instantly.

"Oh man, you don't know shit from shinola," said Duncan. "If they catch us, we get arrested and then turned over to the DCPD, who then turns us over to the Secret Service, who *then* turns us over to Tommy. Tommy yells at us then sends us to compromise some other embassy—it's a round robin, dude."

"Are you sure?" asked Tobey, surprised.

"Course I'm sure!" said Duncan with a laugh, deciding that he liked this dweeby, nervous guy who hadn't lost his lunch when others would have. "Look," he said calmly, "scoring in D.C. is like, no worries. The worst that can happen to you is that you get blown so many times, you get stuck behind a desk back at the ranch. So relax; have some fun."

The elevator doors opened and they walked in.

—strip search, rape, deportation, Chinese concentration camp, life over, everything over—

The elevator doors closed.

"You took him on a scoring run!?!" Tom Carr screamed when they got back. *"Are you out of your fucking mind?!?"*

"C'mon Tommy! It was fun, and he did great!" said Duncan, still wearing his delivery boy jumpsuit as he slouched in one of the chairs, casually smoking a cigarette as he sat through Tom Carr's rant. "We made the delivery and then picked up the product no sweat, and—"

"I don't care!" Tom Carr shouted, standing over his desk as he harangued Duncan and Tobey. "He has no clearance, no field-work protocol—"

"I don't have field-work protocol either!" Duncan shouted right back, unable to keep from laughing at the irony. "And I go out all the time!"

"You wipe that grin off your face, mister, or I'm gonna kick it off."

"Aw, man . . ."

"You were supposed to go with back-up!—*real* back-up, not with the walking stupid here!—and by the way," said Tom Carr, turning on Tobey, "What on *earth* made you go along with him? What, you said to yourself, 'Oooh, sure, break into an embassy the first day on the job, why not?' Was there a sign in the heavens?—did the little green men tell you to do it?—are you secretly a moron who doesn't know shit?"

Tobey, sure that his first day on Acrobat would be his last, said meekly, "I guess I'm a moron who doesn't know shit."

Tom Carr stopped, jolted out of his anger by the scared sweetness of the kid. So he said, "Yeah, goddamned right, a fucking moron is what you are! Now get out of my office and go find Monika Summers like I told you to this morning!—get that paperwork done!—start doing your job!—*move! move! move!*"

Tobey dashed out of the office, stunned that he hadn't been canned.

"Aw man, Tommy, why'd you scare him like that?"

"You shut up, asshole, I'm not done with you."

Over at the cubicles where Acrobat worked, everyone was goofing around as they listened to Tom Carr scream his head off. He had been shouting so loudly, it was impossible not to hear him. So when Tobey Jansen burst in on them, they all clapped.

"Hey!!" said a pretty, blonde young woman. "You busted your cherry!"

"Way to go, what's your name again?" asked the big black man—Russell Orr—who stood up and shook Tobey's hand.

"Tobey, Tobey Jansen," he said, looking at Ljubica, Russell, and the blonde woman smiling at him, surprised by the warmth he was feeling.

"I'm Monika Summers," said the pretty blonde, dressed from head to toe in conservative office black.

"Hi," said Tobey, smiling nervously.

Monika looked at him more closely. "Do you know what you just did?—He doesn't know what he just did," said Monika, turning to Ljubica Greene. "Isn't that cute?" she said.

"Charming," said Ljubica, but with a smile for Tobey.

"What did I do?"

"You busted your cherry!" said Monika with shining eyes and a happy smile, completely ignoring Tom Carr's hollering, which was indistinct but vaguely terrifying.

"Uh, is it normal for him to get that mad?" Tobey asked.

"Don't worry about it," said Monika. "Tommy's a screamer; it doesn't mean a thing."

Tobey looked in the general direction of Tom Carr's office, then back at Monika and Russell and Ljubica, completely unnerved.

Russell listened, sighed, then checked his watch. "This is gonna take forever, and I'm hungry."

"This isn't that bad," said Monika. "Remember when he broke into the UN? That was bad."

"That was *stupid*," said Russell.

"Duncan broke into the United Nations?" asked Tobey.

"Duncan's broken in *everywhere*," said Monika.

"I'm really hungry," Russell repeated.

Ljubica, her arms crossed, leaned over and extended a finger out from under her elbow, poking Russell's belly with a smile.

They heard the door to Tom Carr's office open. "Hey guys!" Duncan called out. "This is gonna take awhile—I'll see ya at the cafeteria."

"Shut that fucking door," shouted Tom Carr. "I'm not done with you by a long sight!"

They heard the door slam shut.

"He's like a cartoon," said Russell.

Tobey, Monika, Ljubica, and Russell all trooped down to the Langley mess hall, casually chatting away as they took the stairs instead of the elevator. At the entrance to the cafeteria, each of them picked up a dark green fiberglass tray and slid it down the lunch-line, which was packed with analysts and supervisors and secretaries of all ages.

The special was penne pasta salad.

Tobey got a cheeseburger at the grill, so he was the last one of the Acrobat group to make it through the cash registers. Once through, he squinted as he looked around, holding his hunter-green tray and trying to find all his newfound coworkers. Still looking, he walked into the dining area until he was standing dead-center in the middle of it, looking around as the murmur of people talking and the gentle surf of Muzak filled the air.

But for the life of him he couldn't see anyone from Acrobat.

After a few seconds, in that tired, resigned way, he started looking for a spot to sit by himself—maybe near the old Pocket-Protector Set from Finance or maybe close to the Ivy Bankers, if he could find a seat that wasn't too conspicuous. He turned to the right, with that feeling of resignation, spotting the Ivy Bankers, who looked sleek and intimidating, and took a step in their direc——

"Hey," said Monika Summers, touching his elbow.

"Hmm?" said Tobey, turning to face her, surprised to see her.

"We're over here," she said, tossing her head in the direction of a far-off table, on the very edges of the main dining area; she'd left her tray at the table to come look for him. "C'mon," she said.

"Oh! Okay."

Tobey walked over, Monika leading the way. She and Russell and Ljubica were sitting facing each other, an empty spot plainly reserved for him.

Tobey sat down in the spot.

"The man of the hour," said Russell ironically.

"Tell us about it," Monika demanded once she'd sat down.

"About what?" he asked.

"Your scoring run!" said Monika.

So Tobey told, even though he hadn't done much, telling them everything except the stuff about the spaceship make-believing.

The whole affair had been pretty inconspicuous: He'd just watched as Duncan took the package to some official deep inside the Chinese Embassy, who had casually signed for it without even bothering to catch Duncan's eye. It had all looked perfectly normal, and positively loaded with meaning.

"Like something—like something was *happening,* you know?" said Tobey.

The others around the table nodded.

"Wow, your first scoring run!" said Monika with a happy-camper grin. "Most people have to train for at least a *year* before they get to go out. You're like a prodigy already!"

"Really?"

"Yeah, I can't believe Duncan took you."

"Duncan's crazy," Ljubica pointed out.

"Well, yeah, that too," said Monika.

"Was he carrying a firearm?" Ljubica asked again, still not sure.

"I didn't see him with one," said Tobey. "And we went through a metal detector and everything."

"I'd bet he had one on him," said Monika.

In an ironic monotone, Russell said, "He loves the nightlife; he's got to boogie."

"No kidding," said Ljubica.

Tobey ate some of his cheeseburger, then drank some of his soda and asked, "You been working here long?"

Ljubica and Russell shrugged.

"About a year," said Monika. "Yuvi and I started together, back when Tom first formed Acrobat. Then Russell came onboard seven months ago?" she asked, looking at Russell, who nodded. "Then Duncan came aboard, about, oh, four months ago I guess," Monika went on. "He came over from the Operations Directorate."

"So Duncan's an operations guy?" Tobey asked.

"A true roadrunner," said Monika. "He used to work for Tom from before. Tommy was the one who recruited him," she added.

Back in Tom Carr's office, Tommy harangued Duncan Idaho for a while even as he was clearly thinking about something else, the insults and recriminations just a spiel as he organized his head.

"So," said Tommy, finally getting down to brass tacks. "Tell me about the kid."

"What, you ream me out because I take him scoring, and now you want the 411?" asked Duncan as he took out his cigarettes and lit one.

"Shut up and gimme one of those fucking things," said Tommy, ripping the smokes out of Duncan's hand. He leaned on the edge of his desk, lit a cigarette, blew a smoke ring, and finally settled down.

"Talk to me, Duncan," said Tommy.

"He could be good," said Duncan simply. "He didn't lose his lunch, he kept an even keel the whole time, even when some things were clearly wigging him out. All-in-all a trooper.

And he can really keep his mouth shut too, when he wants to."

Duncan paused, thinking.

"What?" asked Tommy, puffing away even though he had technically quit.

"He liked it," said Duncan. "I mean, he *really* liked it. He could develop a real taste for it."

"How could you tell?" said Tommy.

"The little things, nothing you could pinpoint, but, yeah."

Tom Carr picked bits of tobacco off the tip of his tongue, thinking.

"So who is he?" asked Duncan.

Tom Carr shook his head. "Just a finance drone," he said. "He's done some serious number crunching around the fourth floor, but he's out of the loop—everybody's figured him as a future B-school boy. You noticed those clothes he was wearing? He just wants to be here long enough to develop a solid résumé before he goes to Sloan or Tuck or Wharton or whatever. He's not interested in Langley long term, which is good—he doesn't owe allegiance to anybody. The only thing that concerns me is that he interned for Denton awhile back."

"I worked for Denton for a whole year," Duncan pointed out. "And sure as shit, I was *not* an intern."

"I'd forgotten about that," said Tom Carr. "Anyway, let's stick with the original intent: Rotate him among Acrobat; get everyone to learn all the finance stuff that he knows. From what John Seebert was telling me, the kid's an idiot savant with the numbers—and everyone in Acrobat needs to know numbers but bad."

"Okay," said Duncan without getting out of his chair, thinking as he smoked his cigarette. "You know," he said, "a little reciprocity wouldn't be a bad thing here. I think we ought to train him."

Tom Carr was already getting into his suit jacket, getting ready to go to lunch. " 'Reciprocity'? Idaho, what did the doctor say about sneaking peeks at the dictionary, hmm?"

"Come on, Tommy, I'm serious," said Duncan, staying in

his chair so he could get Tommy to concentrate on the problem. "I think we ought to train him."

"For Skunk Works?" asked Tom Carr, playing for time.

Duncan Idaho shrugged. "Yeah, maybe."

Tom Carr scoffed. "Bringing a virgin in on that little orgy; I don't think that's such a good idea," he said, shaking his head as he stood with his hand on the doorknob of his office.

Duncan slowly got out of his chair and went over to Tom's desk, looking for his cigarettes amid the mess. "Tommy, you don't have to sell me on scoring Skunk Works. That shit sells itself, and I'm sold. Hell, I joined this outfit so I could pull crazy shit like that. But *tactically* we can't do it. Acrobat is just four people. Four people is just not enough to score a location like Skunk Works. I'm not making this stuff up, Tommy. We need a fifth; and if you're not up for doing it yourself, then we need to bring someone else in."

Tom Carr nodded and let go of the doorknob, thinking about this problem, knowing Duncan Idaho was right.

Duncan snuffed out his cigarette and immediately lit another as he said to his boss, "You want us to score Skunk Works in April, right?"

Tom Carr stood there with his arms crossed, looking at the ground, fully concentrated. "Yes," he said. "Late April would be ideal."

"Okay, that's eight months from now," said Duncan. "I can train someone in four months, easy. But we need to be looking for a fifth member of the Acrobat work-group *now,* or else it'll be no joy on Skunk Works."

Tom Carr took a deep breath and sighed, making up his mind. "Give the kid a whirl; see how he does. Let's have a sit down about the kid in two weeks. If he's a wash, then we see about recruiting someone else; and if he's alright, then we take it from there."

"Okey-dokey," said Duncan, the meeting now definitely over.

"But no more sensitive shit like today's scoring run. Duncan? Duncan look at me: No more scoring without my say-so."

"Relax Tommy, I got it all under control," said Duncan Idaho with a killer smile.

"And that's supposed to make me feel what? Happy? Or horrified?"

The party at Duncan's that night was fantastic.

CHAPTER 4

Zapping the Bank

Over the next few weeks, the work-group Acrobat did its job.

Tobey taught them numbers—how to spot money movements, how to sniff out dummy accounts, how to break through the corporate shield and figure out who was really in control of assets and monies. He taught them all this through a combination of highly sophisticated accounting techniques, and some good old-fashioned computer burglary.

"The information superhighway? *The* best thing that ever happened," he told Ljubica Greene. "Now that cash is totally on the outs? With enough time and patience, you can track any money."

"Why is cash 'totally on the outs'?" Yuvi asked, lighting a cigarette; there was a no-smoking rule at Langley, a rule everyone in Acrobat ignored.

"Nothing's wrong with cash," Tobey admitted, "except people don't use it much anymore, which is sort of like a shame. See if you do electronic transactions? Bank transfers and so on? There's always a paper trail, even if it's really well hidden. But with a cash transaction? With no receipts? Once the money moves—*wheet!* It's gone. The money vanishes. All you gotta do is launder it."

"I thought laundering money was quite difficult," she said.

Tobey gave her a look. "Unh-uh!" he said.

Then he showed her how easily it could be done.

For her part Ljubica taught Tobey how to shop. She didn't

talk much about how to do it, but she showed him plenty, taking him along throughout Washington, putting him in touch with all sorts of people Tobey had only read about in pulp fiction—forgers, computer hackers, illegal weapons dealers, electronics specialists: A whole subculture that ranged from the serious and staid to the out-and-out nutty.

"Some of these people are weird," he said at one point.

Ljubica only nodded.

"But if we work for CIA," Tobey asked, "then why do we have to deal with these people? Can't we just, like, go to the CIA store and get all these goodies that we might want?"

"I take it you know what we do at Counter Intelligence," she said.

"Yeah," said Tobey, "I guess."

"At Counter Intelligence," said Yuvi with inscrutable logic, "we track foreign intelligence assets operating within our borders. We also police the Central Intelligence Agency itself for moles, sell-outs, and traitors."

"Yeah, track foreigners and police the Agency. So?" said Tobey.

But Ljubica didn't say anything more, letting Tobey draw his own conclusions. Tobey wasn't sure whether to scratch his watch or wind his butt.

Acrobat was involved in all sorts of odd schemes that didn't make much sense on the surface—for instance, Acrobat went to illegal outside sources for equipment; they were maintaining careful surveillance on a couple of key Chinese Embassy people, without actually registering the activity, like they were supposed to; they were compiling detailed dossiers about all sorts of people no Counter Intelligence work-group ought to even concern itself with. In short, they were doing all sorts of weird stuff, all rather confusing, but not so terribly illegal as to make anyone sit up and pay attention.

But little by little, Tobey began to realize what the work-group Acrobat was really doing: Acrobat was looking for someone inside of Langley. Acrobat was looking for a sell-out.

Tobey figured it out one day early in October, when he was giving Big Russell Orr his tutorial.

It started with a hypothetical. Russell asked him, "Say you wanted to track a payment of about sixty million dollars made by a foreign government to someone here in the United States: How would you do it?"

Tobey leaned back in the chair of his cubicle, thinking about the problem. "Okay, you'd have to get a lot more specific." he said. "Do you have the name of the person? The name of the country? And was it one payment or multiple payments?"

Russell frowned a bit, rubbing the huge dome of his skull, the knuckles of his hands as big as walnuts. "One payment. Let's say you have the name of the suspects and the name of the country," he added, just as Tom Carr waddled up to Tobey's cubicle. "Could you track this payment?"

"Uh—hello sir," said Tobey, nearly falling out of his chair on seeing his boss. That whole authority thing again.

"Don't mind me," said Tommy, so short he barely cleared the dividing wall of Tobey's cubicle. "What are you talking about?"

"A hypothetical," said Russell, who—seated—was almost as tall as Tommy. "How would you trace a sixty-million-dollar payment."

Tom Carr looked at Russell; then he looked at Tobey. "Well?" he asked, "how would you track a payment of sixty million dollars?"

"Okay," said Tobey, trying to think clearly under the stress of supervision. "Uh—If you knew the name of the country that was making the disbursement? And had the name of the suspect? You could probably make an evidentiary bridge; prove that the suspect received a payment, yeah, sure. But it wouldn't stand up in a court of law, 'cause you'd probably have to *break* the law to get at this information?"

"Courts aren't important; I just want to know how you would do it."

Tobey bobbed his head, thinking. "Well, you'd investigate the targets, first of all," he said conversatonally. "You'd scrutinize all their assets—and there are lots of ways to do that."

"What if the targets set up off-shore accounts?" asked Russell.

Tobey scoffed, remarkably secure and confident when it came to his job. "If you don't care about getting evidence that'll stand up in court, then off-shore accounts don't matter. Some people think that they're like magic bullets? But they're not—they're easy to spot if you know what to look for. In a weird way, sometimes it's easier to scrutinize off-shore accounts and corporations, 'cause see, the target of that sort of scrutiny? He's not gonna realize he's being probed. So you look at the target's assets—off-shore and domestic—and if it's a big enough payment with no justification to it, you'll pretty much know that the target's guilty."

"What about cash?" asked Tom Carr. "Yuvi told me cash is a lot harder to trace."

Tobey nodded his head. "Yeah, I told her that. Cash *is* the best—but it's not just hard to trace, it's *impossible* to trace. That's why the government doesn't convict big-time drug lords that often. Drug money is all cash, the money *physically* transferred from person to person and from place to place."

"So cash is best 'cause it's easy and it's untraceable," said Russell, Tom Carr following the conversation like a tennis match.

"Untraceable, yeah, but easy? Hell no," said Tobey. "You ever thought how *big* sixty million dollars is?" asked Tobey.

"It might fill up a big suitcase," said Russell casually.

Tom Carr guessed unobtrusively, "I'm guessing it'll fill three suitcases."

Tobey shook his head as he picked up his calculator. "Sixty million dollars works out to six hundred thousand one-hundred-dollar bills, right? Now a bundle of a hundred bills? That weighs about half a pound, so you're looking at . . . three thousand pounds of money. That's like, a car."

Russell whistled, Tom Carr raising his eyebrows, neither of them ever having thought of that practical aspect before.

"*Moving* three thousand pounds of money is like, a nightmare?" said Tobey. "I mean you're doing it illegally, so you can't just hire Brinks Security to move that kind of cash—any reputable firm has to register any cash amount it's carrying over ten thousand dollars with the IRS. To move that kind of money, you'd need a brilliant disguise—and lots of manpower to protect it. And anyway, assembling sixty million in cash? Like in the movies they do it all the time, but in real life it's *real* hard. That's why you don't ever use cash to transfer that kind of money. You do it electronically."

"If you did that, you'd have a paper trail, which might be traced," said Russell.

"Yeah, and so that's the core problem," said Tobey. "Do you want to deal with moving three thousand pounds of money, or do you risk a paper trail?"

Tom Carr considered the problem. "Good question."

"I'd risk the paper trail," said Russell.

Tobey shook his head. "Paper always leaves a trail. Smart people, they do illegal payments like that in cash or some other sort of legal tender. So then that means that, if you figure somebody imported sixty million bucks in cash? Then you gotta look for an item weighing in at three thousand pounds. That'll be the money."

Russell glanced at Tom Carr, who was leaning against the cubicle dividing walls. He nodded and stood up straight, slapping his belly. "Interesting," he told Tobey. "Keep it up." Then he waddled away.

Tobey watched him leave, then frowned as he turned back to Russell. "Uh, Russ? You're talking about sixty million dollars—that's a pretty specific figure, isn't it?"

"No it isn't," said Russell. "Fifty-eight million, seven hundred thousand dollars: *That's* a pretty specific figure."

Tobey blinked and frowned. *Fifty-eight million, seven hundred thousand—?* Tobey leaned forward. "Is Acrobat targeting someone? Someone who got sixty million bucks?"

Russell looked at Tobey very carefully from behind his non-prescription glasses. "Yep," he said.

"Is this target . . . here at Langley?"

Russell looked Tobey right in the eye. "You're growing a goatee," he said. "I hadn't noticed."

Tobey frowned, touched his chin, then looked at Russell as he leaned back in his chair. And then it was Tobey's turn to whistle.

Duncan too was supposed to get a "Tobey Tutorial," as they started calling the number-crunching sessions. But whenever they got around to it, somehow they always wound up at the firing range, with all kinds of weapons spread out before them.

"You know numbers, right?" Duncan asked. "So that means *I* don't need to know numbers. I know other stuff."

What Duncan knew was firearms—handguns, rifles, assault rifles, machine guns—and he taught Tobey all there was to know about these weapons: The various makes, the various models, the different calibers, even the different kinds of bullets.

But more than just the mechanics of firearms, he taught Tobey their uses.

"You think this is a dangerous weapon?" Duncan said, holding up a nickel-plated .45 Colt revolver, a hand cannon as big as his head.

"Yeah," said Tobey, the two of them standing in the booth of a firing lane.

"You think this is like a Dirty Harry Doomsday gun, right?"

"Yeah!" said Tobey, hypnotized by the shiny weapon.

"Hit that target," said Duncan, setting the weapon down on the ledge and stepping out of the way, a paper target hanging at a range of barely forty feet.

Tobey stepped forward and handled the weapon. Like Duncan had taught him, he was quite careful, loading it and checking it while pointing it in a safe direction. Duncan never worried about Tobey's weapon's safety protocol before he fired a weapon—it was the after part when Tobey got sloppy.

Tobey squared up in a policeman's stance, like Duncan had taught him, with his right hand on the gun, his left hand holding the butt of the weapon, knees bent slightly, back straight, and shoulders thrown back. Then he waited.

"Fire whenever you're ready," said Duncan.

Tobey aimed at the target and fired a single shot—and missed.

"God!—it kicked," said Tobey. "The recoil was just *huge!*"

"That's okay," said Duncan. He pressed the button that controlled the distance of the paper target, bringing it in closer. "Try it again."

Tobey looked at the target, now barely twenty feet away. He'd been practicing steadily for a month now; there was no way he would miss. So again he squared up in his policeman's stance. Again he aimed carefully. Again he fired. Again he missed.

Tobey looked over at Duncan, who just shrugged and motioned for him to try it again.

Aiming as carefully as he could, Tobey went through the remaining four bullets, and not once did he hit the target.

"Damn!" said Tobey, his arms too weak and shaky for him to be really embarrassed, looking at the unblemished paper target.

"Yeah, you pretty much sucked canal water," said Duncan as he took the .45 from Tobey.

"But I did everything right!" he said.

"No shame, Tobe; the gun's just too big for you, is all," said Duncan casually, squinting cigarette smoke out of his eyes. Pressing the control button to the left of the rest ledge, Duncan moved the paper target to a range of over sixty feet. Then he prepped another weapon, checking and loading a fresh magazine. "Try this one," he said, motioning to this new weapon, a little .22 automatic.

Tobey picked up the gun and got in a stance again. Even with sore wrists and sore arms, with the .22, Tobey hit the target dead-bang between the eyes on his first shot.

"Hey!"

"A regular Wyatt Earp," said Duncan, relieving Tobey of the gun, which he was waving around without realizing it. "Weapon's safety," he repeated.

"I know, I know," said Tobey.

"Okay: The lesson," said Duncan, holding up the .45 revolver and looking at Tobey. "This weapon's scary, but it's

useless," he said. "Great for crowd control or bullying people."
Then he picked up the puny little .22. "This one kills 'em."

"Cool," said Tobey.

They practiced a couple-three times a week, usually spending an hour or two at the firing range. Duncan knew everybody, including the owner, John Mead, an old retired DCPD
sergeant who was an army veteran just like Duncan, only of
course, a whole generation earlier. John and Duncan always
got around to talking about Vietnam while Tobey mowed
down paper targets, talking about strategy and tactics and
about what McNamara and Johnson and Westmoreland *should*
have done to win the war. Lots of times, perfect strangers
would come up to them and join in on these bull sessions as
if everyone was a buddy.

That was the thing about Duncan Idaho. He had a magic
about him: He made friends easy. Sometimes, he'd simply
decide to go make a friend, which always blew Tobey's
mind—how Duncan would suddenly get up and say, "I'm
gonna go make a friend." Two hours later, he'd be hanging
out with someone he'd never seen before in his life, talking
to him like he was a long-lost buddy.

That ability made him irresistible to people, making it all
even more ironic that Duncan could not deal with Monika
Summers. Monika was the same—but different.

Whereas Duncan Idaho was a hale-fellow-well-met kind of
friend, making few demands and giving his friends a lot of
space, Monika Summers built complex, intricate relationships,
the kind that formed a latticework of emotions. She was the
sort of friend you'd tell your darkest secrets to, the kind of
friend who'd help you figure out who you were, maybe because *she* was figuring out who she was through *you*. If you
could say that Duncan defined himself by the crazy shit he
pulled (and you could easily say that), then you could say that
Monika Summers defined herself by way of her friendships:
They were who she was.

"So I was going through Hell Week at my frat at Dartmouth?" Tobey told her one time, the two of them in the
snackroom, monotonously devouring mini-bags of chips one

after the other. "You're supposed to do something really outrageous for Hell Week, something memorable. So I broke into Kiewit—uh, the computer system on campus? And I changed my frat brothers' grades to straight As!"

"But then you got caught," Monika guessed.

Tobey's shy smile collapsed into a droopy sad-face, as if surprised by the inevitability of what had happened. "But then I got caught," he agreed. "They suspended me for a whole year. But I got an internship here at Langley, so I guess all's well that ends well."

"And your frat brothers . . . ?"

Almost comically sad about it, Tobey said, "The college told them to depledge me, or else."

"All 'cause you wanted to fit in," said Monika thoughtfully, mulling over everything she knew about Tobey.

"Mmm," said Tobey, confused by his own life.

"You think all that moving around you did growing up made you shy and insecure?" Monika asked.

"Well, yeah," he said. "My mom, she just, like, chased guys. So whenever she changed a guy, she changed a city. So then having to be the new kid in a new school all the time? Boy."

"But didn't it make you good at adapting to new places and situations?"

Tobey considered that. "Well maybe, I guess," he said. "I'd never really thought of it that way."

Monika held up her hands and swallowed her chips. "Okay, reality snapshot: You were working as a financial analyst; then you've been plucked out of there to come work here with us. On the first day, you scored; and now two weeks into this new gig, you're like a pea in a pod, with zero friction. Everyone here likes you."

"Thanks," said Tobey modestly.

Monika looked at Tobey and frowned, a deep vertical line cutting through the middle of her forehead. "You think I'm being generous," she said abruptly. "You think I'm telling you pleasing lies. You don't believe people can really like you. But *I* like you, Tobey. So do Russell and Duncan, and even

Tom. Even *Yuvi*—even though she doesn't show it—thinks you're great. But, Tobey, *I* like you—and I don't have to lie to you. So don't go pulling crazy stunts for my benefit. If I didn't like you, we wouldn't be talking."

Tobey was so struck by what she said, he couldn't talk, standing there by the vending machine with his mouth literally open, feeling tears welling up as if he were watching a sad and manipulative commercial—only this was *real,* which made it all the more intense.

As if sensing his mood and not wanting to embarrass him, Monika looked at the nearly empty potato chip bag she had in hand and ate the last of them, mumbling, "I'm going straight to work-out hell for these." Then she gave him a smile like a morning sunrise.

Tobey thought Monika was the prettiest, nicest girl he'd ever known, which was why he decided—without debate— that there was no way she'd ever be interested in someone like him. But she might be interested in *Duncan.* After all, Duncan sure was interested in her, and Duncan was Tobey's friend.

"She mention me?" he'd ask casually when they were at the range, shooting some assault rifles.

"Yeah, lots of times," Tobey reported loyally. "She told me that you broke into the UN and bugged the place—is that true?"

Duncan tsked. "No big deal," he said modestly. "We had to find out about some Security Council vote. Monika thought that was cool?"

"Yeah, she did," said Tobey. "She told me all about it."

Duncan nodded to himself.

"Yeah," Tobey agreed again, "you should ask her out—she really thinks you're cool."

"Mmm," said Duncan, thinking, getting ready to fire an AK-74 he'd rustled up from a friend. "I'm gonna let it marinate a little before I make my move—firing," he said.

"Firing," Tobey repeated, slipping on his ear protectors.

Duncan went through a whole clip on full automatic, zipping through the magazine in about four seconds, every one of his bullets finding the head of the target.

"Nice grouping," said Tom Carr, suddenly just *there*.

"*Jesus!*" Tobey yelped.

"Fuck, you startled me," said Duncan, looking like he hadn't even blinked.

"So are you two talking about Monika or talking about guns?" Tom Carr asked them.

Tobey and Duncan exchanged a look.

That was Tom Carr's ability—he could magically appear anywhere, sliding right into the middle of a conversation, usually with a pretty fair idea of what the talk was about and where it was going.

Like for instance: Around Halloween, Tobey was explaining to Monika and Ljubica how to run a general asset search on a target. For the exercise, Tobey had picked someone they were actually about to start investigating as a possible conduit for pay-off monies—a man named Wu Wey, who was a consular official of the People's Republic of China in San Francisco.

"How long will it take?" asked Ljubica as she wrote in her pad, the two women camping out in his cubicle as they got their Tobey Tutorial.

"A couple of days," he said. "Maybe three?"

Ljubica looked up. "Then instead of Wu Wey, we should target Gordon Chen, that lawyer in Chicago."

Monika tsked. "We've looked him up like three times, and he's always clean," she said.

"That doesn't mean he's innocent," said Ljubica.

"He's low priority—Wu Wey is a player," Monika insisted.

"Wu is new to the consular mission; he doesn't know his way around San Francisco yet. He's probably busy tapping into his inheritance," said Yuvi. (An "inheritance" is what you call the assets and contacts an Intelligence officer inherits from his predecessor.)

"Unh-uh," said Monika, shaking her head as she tied her hair up in a scrunchie. "Word is, Wu Wey is bad manna from China—we should check him out first. Gordon Chen isn't going anywhere."

"I disagree."

"Hello ladies," said Tom Carr just as Tobey felt the air temperature between the two women begin to climb. "What's going on?"

They explained the problem, Tommy dealing with it with nearly Solomonic elegance. "Gordon Chen isn't that important, so why not use him as a guinea pig?" he suggested. "Tobey can run the investigation on Chen, both of you ladies watching and learning how to crunch the numbers like a champ. Then when that's done, you both work together on Wu Wey," he said. "Gordon Chen is probably clean," he told Monika, "but now with Tobey, we'll find out for sure," he told Ljubica. "Okay?"

"Fine," said Yuvi.

"Okay," said Monika.

Tom Carr smiled and watched them for a while, the three of them turning their undivided attention to Mr. Gordon Chen of Chicago until they didn't realize that Tom Carr had drifted away.

That was Tom Carr: Always floating around, walking the fourth floor at Langley as if he had a radar screen pinging their exact locations in his head. It wasn't as if he watched them all the time. Not at all, sometimes Tom Carr would up and vanish for days, sometimes even for longer, leaving Acrobat to their own devices.

Where he'd go he'd never say; but whenever he came back, he always brought along some poop—solid poop, too. Poop that could shine.

Like for Thanksgiving, for instance. One Tuesday morning, in mid-November of '99, Tom Carr spoke on the phone for nearly an hour. When he was done, he stood up, put on his suit jacket, and looked around his office, thinking.

Tobey Jansen happened to be passing by. "Hi Tom," he said casually, now far more relaxed around his boss. "You okay?"

"Hmm?—Fine kiddo, fine," said Tom Carr, staring off into space. "I'm gonna go to uh-h-h . . ."

"Go where?" asked Tobey.

"I'm gonna go," said Tom Carr, snapping out of it, suddenly decisive; straightening his tie and brushing his charcoal gray chalk-stripe suit. "How do I look?" he asked.

"Like a man to be reckoned with, sir," said Tobey.

Tom Carr smiled and clapped Tobey on the shoulder. "Thanks kid, I needed that," he said. "Your goatee's coming along great."

"Thanks," said Tobey, touching his inch-long goatee as he watched Tom Carr walk away.

That was Tuesday morning. No one saw or heard from Tom Carr during Wednesday, Thursday, or Friday—

—which was a problem: Friday was D-day—delivery day. And though Acrobat had prepped the package, they needed Tom for the authorization to go drop it off.

Every Friday before lunch, a member of Acrobat and a back-up would go to the Chinese Embassy and make the usual delivery, like the one Tobey had first gone on when he met Duncan Idaho. In the six weeks since he'd joined Acrobat, Tobey had gone on all six runs, always as the back-up, never as the primary, always with Tom Carr's explicit though qualified approval. Tom didn't really trust Tobey not to screw things up, but at the same time Tom Carr knew how much the others hated the boredom of pulling back-up duty.

This time, now that Tom was gone, Duncan—God help us all—had an idea:

"Hey Tobey, why don't you be primary?"

Tobey jerked a happily surprised look at Duncan, clearly all for it.

But Russell Orr immediately shot the idea down: "No no no no no no," he said quietly, shaking his head.

"Why not, O Learnèd Voice of Reason?" said Duncan.

Ignoring the jibe, Russell raised one massive hand and began counting off the reasons without hesitation: "No experience, no training, not his specialty, and not adequately briefed on the full extent of the mission. Plus the fact that he probably doesn't want to do it to begin with. Now that's five reasons," said Russell, holding up his open hand. "In most states in the continental United States, five good reasons qualifies as a winner."

Tobey deflated, knowing what Russell was saying was true.

But Duncan wasn't so sure. "I think Tobey should be the one to decide if he's up for it or not. Why should you or me be the judge of whether he's ready or not?"

Russell looked at Duncan, unhappily smirking a bit. Then he turned to Tobey. "Tobey, you think you're ready to go on a scoring run as primary?"

Duncan turned to Tobey. "Come on sport, what do you say?"

Russell said, "Don't let him push you around. Answer honestly."

Tobey glanced at Duncan, but then looked downcast at Russell. "No, I guess I probably shouldn't go as primary," he said, without much good grace.

"There you go," said Russell, problem solved. "You can go as Duncan's back-up. But Duncan's primary."

But Duncan Idaho could not let that sit. On the drive over, he said, "Russell's wrong—much as I respect him, Russell's wrong."

"What do you mean?" asked Tobey nervously, no longer liking the idea of going as primary so much. Primary meant it would be his responsibility to make the delivery—and his head if he screwed it up.

"You should be primary," Duncan declared, looking over at Tobey.

Tobey shrugged. "Maybe Russell's right," he said cautiously. "I don't have any training; and besides, I'm an accountant, not field personnel."

"Come on, there's no trick to this shit; you've seen me and Monika and Ljubica do this, what, half a dozen times," Duncan said. "You could probably do this in your sleep."

"Yeah, but—"

"Come on Tobe, don't pussy out on me," Duncan said. "Do you need permission to take out the garbage?"

"No," said Tobey, trapped and not liking it. "But I need permission from Tom to go on a run. I shouldn't even be going as a back-up on this one."

Duncan sighed. "It's one thing for Russell to get all cautious and careful about stuff," he said. "He's the Voice of Reason, that's why he's on Acrobat. But you want to be careful, Tobey. You want to guard against becoming too conservative. Next thing you know, you become paralyzed."

Tobey looked at his friend and then at the oncoming road, not liking the place where he was at.

It took awhile; quite awhile. Longer than Duncan would have expected, in fact. But in the end, he needled Tobey into being primary on that week's delivery.

They didn't hear from Tom Carr when they got back from the embassy scoring run. Nor did they hear anything on Saturday. But then on Sunday night, a little after eight o'clock, all the members of Acrobat got a short, cryptic call from him: "Meet me at the ranch—now," was all Tom Carr told each of them before hanging up.

Thirty minutes later, the Acrobat work-group was sitting in his office, staring at their boss.

Tom Carr looked bad enough to stare at. His suit—the same one he'd had on when he'd left on Tuesday morning—looked almost slimed, it was that dirty. He hadn't shaved, his tie was gone, and the collar of his shirt had a thick brown ring of grime; it was almost black.

"Dude, you smell," said Duncan Idaho.

He wasn't kidding, but Tom Carr didn't even hear him, nervously lighting a cigarette. "Is everyone here—where's Monika?"

"Here," said Monika breathlessly, arriving in full athletic gear, sweating heavily as she plopped down in one of the chairs of Tom's office. Then she really looked at Tom Carr. "Are you okay?" she asked, amazed.

"I'm fine," he lied, his eyes red-rimmed and glassy—he hadn't slept, and he was clearly on something to keep him awake and alert; probably amphetamines from the look of him.

"Aw, man," said Duncan Idaho, happy as a clam to see Monika outside office hours, but happier still that Tommy looked like he'd been road-running. "You brought back some poop, didn't you? Where you been at?"

"Around," said Tom Carr, hunting through his desk drawer for something. "Anyone seen my aspirin?"

"No," said Ljubica Greene queerly.

Duncan turned to Yuvi and Russell.

Russell looked sort of okay, but Ljubica's hair didn't have its normal straight and slack look—her hair looked a little mussed up, as did her clothes, which looked as if she'd rolled around in them—

—and then suddenly everyone in the room realized that it was coitus interruptus for Russ and Yuvi, both of them looking and acting weird and off-kilter and kind of low-grade crazy in a smoldering sort of way.

"What's up with you two?" Tom Carr asked them thoughtlessly as he found his bottle of aspirin.

They all looked at him for a moment, and then Monika and Duncan burst out laughing as Russell turned a chocolate red and Ljubica looked at her lap.

"Nothing," said Russell, his voice strangled in his throat.

"Uh—sorry," said Tom Carr, parentally embarrassed, concentrating on opening the aspirin bottle instead.

"I don't get it," said Tobey.

"How many *times* did you do 'nothing,' huh?" asked Duncan, Monika whooping beside him.

"Oh I get it," said Tobey, shriveling up in his chair from embarrassment and touching his growing goatee.

"Shut up Duncan!" said Russell, pulling out a pack of cigarettes and absently lighting one.

Duncan turned to Monika and said, "Yep, that's right: After good lovin', a smoke."

Yuvi cringed, and Monika burst out giggling so hard she started to cry, rolling in her chair, her feet kicking up in the air. "I gotta—I gotta—I gotta go *pee!*" she said, bolting out of Tom Carr's office.

Russell hissed after Monika, "*Pss-sss-sss-sss-sss-sss-sss!*" Duncan and Tobey and even *Tom* joining in on the chorus of hissing.

"Who's childish now?" Ljubica asked Russell, who shrugged and smiled, standing behind her as he rubbed her shoulders.

"Okay *enough* already," said Tom Carr, everyone finally settling down as he nervously puffed on his cigarette. Everyone was smoking, actually, except for Tobey, who didn't yet know how—but he was learning. Duncan was teaching him.

Tom said, "First of all: A bird told me Tobey did primary on the Friday delivery. Is that true?"

Duncan winced and Tobey squirmed as Russell smirked and nodded to himself.

Duncan began, "Yeah, but—"

Tommy just held up a hand. "Save it," he said. "I know you guys don't like doing the weekly delivery—it's boring and it's time-consuming, I agree. So, this is how it's going to be: From now on, Tobey sets up the logistics and does primary on all future deliveries."

"Awright!" said Duncan, clapping his hands and pounding Tobey on the back.

"But, Duncan," Tom Carr went on, "is his back-*up—forever.*"

Duncan's face fell, and Russell laughed a foghorn in his face: "Ha, ha." Duncan flipped him the bird in answer.

Ljubica, quite casually, asked Russell, "You told Tobey not to be primary?"

Russell just nodded as Monika walked back into the room, distracting the others from what Ljubica then said:

"You should have let him be primary," she said, her upswept almond eyes rising to catch his own eyes, then turning to look away.

No one heard what his girlfriend said. They were all distracted by Monika, as she laughed at what Duncan had brought on himself. But Russell heard her. He heard what Ljubica was saying.

Feeling like he'd lost a round, Russell decided to change the subject. "So where were you?" he asked Tom Carr as Monika finished laughing.

"I was out, Dad," said Tom Carr, making the others laugh

at Russell. "But now I've got a problem. And you're gonna solve it for me, so shut up and listen.

"In lower Manhattan," Tom began, "there is a bank, a Chase Manhattan Bank. In that bank, there's a safety deposit box. In that safety deposit box, there is a complete PCB board. Tomorrow, first thing in the morning, our favorite friend, the Chinese cultural attaché, the Right Honorable Xiao Hsün, is going to walk into that bank, open that safety deposit box, and get that PCB board."

"Oh shit," said Monika Summers. No one was laughing anymore.

"What's a PCB board?" asked Tobey innocently.

"It's sort of like the brains of the next-generation spy satellites," said Ljubica, combing a strand of her black hair over her ear. "It's an incredibly expensive piece of equipment, incredibly classified," she added with cool, professional knowledge.

"Xiao Hsün . . . ," said Russell, unconsciously leaning on his girlfriend so hard that Ljubica winced, touching his hands with her own; Russell instantly relaxed his grip.

"So this thing, this PCB board—it's in Manhattan?" said Tobey Jansen. "How d'ya know that?"

Tom Carr frowned at him. " 'Cause the tooth fairy told me, a'right? We met up for drinks, shot the shit, then she told me all about it before we got down and dirty."

Duncan tsked. "The way you're looking? I don't think so," he said.

Everyone laughed, sort of, but not really, thinking over the bomb Tom had just dropped in their laps.

Monika Summers leaned forward, her windpants whispering nylon. "Are you sure it's Xiao Hsün?"

"Pretty much," said Tom Carr, his eyes on deep focus. "Sneaky little bastard . . ."

Tobey looked around from friend to friend. "Okay: I gotta ask," he said. "Who's Xiao Hsün?"

"Xiao Hsün's with Denton," said Ljubica, without emphasis.

Everyone winced and turned away, as if they didn't want to look at an accident, or at an execution.

Confused, Tobey looked at Yuvi then at the others. But before he could figure it all out, Tom Carr sat up, scratching his three-day beard with the jerky ticishness of a speed high, and said, "Fuck that, what matters is, Xiao Hsün is going to Manhattan to pick up the PCB board first thing tomorrow morning. So the question becomes, How are you guys going to get it before *he* does?"

Everyone looked at Tom Carr.

"That's a good question," said Russell, distractedly rubbing Ljubica's shoulders again as he stood there behind her. "We could make it easy on ourselves and use law enforcement."

Tom Carr nodded. "Call up the FBI," he said.

"An anonymous tip would probably be enough," Russell went on. "We wouldn't have to tell them how we know the PCB board is in this bank."

Duncan Idaho snorted.

"What," said Russell.

"An anonymous tip? To the Federated Butthole Idiots? You can't be serious," said Duncan.

"Hey cowboy," said Russell, "that's what the FBI is there for—they're there to arrest people. Let the Feebles deal with this PCB board. They get paid enough."

"Russell's right," said Tom Carr. "It's the FBI's jurisdiction."

"Okay, let's play it your way," said Duncan Idaho, leaning forward and intensely aware that Monika Summers was watching him. "Say we call up the FBI and tell them about the PCB board in Manhattan—what do you think is gonna happen?"

Tom Carr, studiously looking at his half-smoked cigarette, shook his head like he didn't know; Russell Orr just stared at Duncan.

Duncan Idaho smiled on the kill. "They won't move without some bona fides. And the only bona fide we have," he said, motioning in Tom Carr's direction, "we can't give up. If they don't have bona fides, the Feebles won't have Probable Cause. Without Probable Cause, no judge will ever give them a search warrant for the bank. No search warrant means there's nothing to stop Xiao Hsün from picking up the PCB board and creating a whole nightmare for us. And do we want that?" Duncan asked them all.

"Obviously not," said Tom Carr, turning from Duncan Idaho to Russell Orr. "So what do we do to keep that from happening?"

"Put pressure on the Bureau," said Russell Orr, running his hand over his shaved skull. "They can get a search warrant if they want one. We can make it clear to them that even though this material's anonymous, it's coming from Langley—the very fact that someone from CIA is telling them that the PCB board is at the bank is enough Probable Cause for any judge."

Duncan just shook his head. "It'd be better if we scored the bank ourselves."

"Score a bank?" said Russell, again leaning on Ljubica's shoulders.

"Russell," she said.

"Sorry," he said, taking his hands off her shoulders as if they were hot. Then he looked at Duncan Idaho. "Cowboy, you can't just score a bank like you're knocking off a 7-Eleven."

"Sure you can!" said Duncan, a whip-smart smile on his face. "And see, this would also be a great way to see what we look like for the Skunk Works score."

Tobey felt everyone in the room shift uncomfortably when Duncan spoke, so he couldn't help asking, "What's that? What's Skunk Works?"

Duncan caught Tom Carr's eye, who nodded back at him. So Duncan turned to Tobey. "It's nothing—in a few months' time we might be pulling a pretty complicated scoring run. But for now, don't worry about it, pardner: When the time comes, we'll talk about it in a whole lot more detail."

Tobey Jansen looked at Duncan and Tom, dying to know. But he just said "Okay" instead.

Duncan turned to the others. "Scoring this bank could be like a tryout—we could use this opportunity to really gauge where we're at."

Russell almost said something, then stopped, thinking. "On the prowl or strong?" he asked.

"Dude, whatever," said Duncan, leaning back in his armchair and leaning closer to Monika. "Hey how come it's always the cultural attaché who turns out to be the Mr. Meanie, huh?" he asked her quietly.

Monika frowned as she thought about it. "You know, you're right," she wondered thoughtfully, turned on by the idea of scoring the bank—turned on by Duncan. "Why is that?"

"Hey," said Russell sharply, sharp enough to get everyone to snap their heads at him as he stood looking at Duncan Idaho. "This is some serious shit you're talking about. You want to score a real place; that's not something—"

"Russell, dude, get off the fence and stop being a pussy about what we do around here," said Duncan casually.

Russell's face went blank. "Whoa, cowboy," he said very quietly, everyone suddenly and simultaneously very aware of just how big Russell Orr really was. "You'd best back off just a bit."

Duncan Idaho turned toward Russell Orr, ready for anything—

—but Tom Carr cut in. "Shut up, the both of you," he said, puffing away on his smoke, his fat hands too big for the scrawny cigarette. "Our problem is, we cannot allow Xiao Hsün to get that PCB board tomorrow. So you guys tell me— let's have some instant democracy here: Is it gonna be FBI, or is it gonna be a scoring run?"

"FBI," said Russell. "It's easier for us, and they're prepared for this sort of thing."

"So are we," said Duncan Idaho. "We are an operational work-group—"

"We're not," Russell interrupted. "We are a Counter Intelligence task force that's been doing operational work. And we could get into a shit-load of trouble for pulling an operational stunt like this."

Tom Carr gave Russell a little wave. "Don't worry about

the law so much on this one; with something this serious, results are going to be all that matter."

Russell shook his head.

Duncan said, "We can do this, no problem—we've been scoring around Rivercity long enough that we've got it all down. The Manhattan bank's a cinch."

Russell, catching the glance Duncan Idaho shot to Monika Summers, found an opening. "Just because you want to look cool for the babes," he said to Duncan, "doesn't mean I'm going to follow you off a cliff."

Duncan, leaning back in his chair, suddenly blinked and turned hard, his casual grin now not-so-casually rigid.

"What are you talking about?" said Duncan.

"You know what I'm talking about, cowboy," said Russell. "Or do you want me to embarrass you right here and now?"

"What?" said Monika Summers, looking between both men, clueless that Russell and Duncan were referring to her.

Duncan said, "A big man with a big mouth, but I'm not sure—"

"What about the rest of you?" said Tom Carr, deftly cutting off Duncan and Russell, his attention on Monika and Ljubica. "What do you think we ought to do?"

Tobey Jansen looked at Tom Carr. "What do *you* think, sir?" he asked innocently.

Tom Carr smiled at Tobey Jansen as he stood up and patted the pockets of his suit jacket. "I think you guys are grown-ups who can make up your own minds," he said, taking Russell's cigarettes and lighting one. "So what's it gonna be?"

"Scoring run," said Duncan Idaho instantly. "We're primed for it. That's what we should do," he added, looking from Tom Carr to Monika Summers. "Monika?" he asked her.

Monika began to slowly nod and smile at the same time. "Yeah," she said simply. "Yeah," she said again, warming up to the idea.

Tobey looked serious, but a sloppy grin kept trying to break out of his face. "Scoring might be the most . . . efficient way to go about this situation," he said, over-enunciating his words, as if they lent his decision more intellectual heft.

Russell shrugged and looked down, massaging Ljubica's shoulders, Ljubica patting his hands with both her own, relieved she hadn't had to spell out where she stood: Ljubica was with the others.

"Three to two," said Russell, mistaking Ljubica's silence.

"It's settled, majority rules," said Tom Carr as he walked to the door of his office. "How you score this bank is up to you, but remember: No residue and *no* casualties.

"It is . . . ," Tom Carr continued as he checked his watch, "nine-thirty in the pee-em. This PCB board is in Manhattan. So! I'm going home, watch the tape of the Redskins—"

"They lost," said Tobey helpfully, "thirty-seven to twenty-one."

Tom Carr looked at him. "Thank you for that information, Tobey. Now I don't have to waste my time actually *watching* the game, you little shit."

Unconsciously, Tobey pushed his glasses up the bridge of his nose with his middle finger, gulping and blushing. "Sorry, sir," he mumbled.

"I'm going home, I'll get something to eat, then I'll get some sleep," said Tom Carr. "Work this problem—work it as a team. Don't let the problem work you."

"Yes sir," they all said.

"And Tobey?" said Tom Carr as he stood at the threshold of his office.

"Yes sir?" said Tobey.

"You flip me the bird one more time, and I'm gonna chop that finger *off,*" he said pleasantly. "Understand?"

"Yessir."

Tom Carr walked out of his office, leaving the Acrobat work-group alone.

Tobey shuddered, his glasses slipping down his nose again. He pushed them up with his middle finger again.

Duncan laughed as he stood up. "Dude, we gotta work on you," he said.

About twelve hours later, shortly before nine in the morning, a long black limousine with tinted windows and white-walled

tires sat idling in front of a Chase Manhattan Bank. The branch
was in the New Amsterdam district, the oldest part of New
York City at the very tip of Manhattan Island, where all the
streets have short, percussive names that sound like the slap
of a hand on a horse's flank: Broad Street, State Street, Wall
Street, Stone Street.

Russell Orr was at the wheel of the shiny black limo, wearing a chauffeur's cap, a black suit, white shirt, and thin black
tie, staring at the front façade of the bank. Through the brilliantly reflecting glass and the gauzy tan curtains, he could
barely make out the bank employees inside going about their
morning routine, getting ready to open their doors for business, having no idea what was about to happen to them in just
under four minutes and twenty seconds.

"Gimme an extra clip, just in case."

In the back of the limo, the other members of the work-
group Acrobat sat around a large, open suitcase neatly filled
with automatic weapons and ammunition.

Though they were all wearing dark, conservative suits,
Monika and Ljubica both wore bright white sneakers and
sports socks, in keeping with a weird habit of New York working women—comfort above all on the morning walk to work.
Tobey, dressed just a shade more conservatively than he usually was, looked icy and avant-garde with his growing goatee
and his round glasses. Duncan, the biker slob, was the most
startlingly transformed: Shaved and showered and all dressed
up, he was almost unrecognizable; a Master of the Universe.

Each of them were checking their firearms, M-16s with
their serial numbers filed off.

"Untraceable," Ljubica assured them as she checked the
contents of a smallish carry-on case she would be bringing
along.

Out of a plastic grocery bag, Monika Summers pulled out
four baseball caps with wide brims, tossing one to each of the
others. "Keep your brims low for the surveillance cameras,"
she said.

They all put on the caps, all of them ready. Russell, in the front, looked in his rearview mirror, casually noticing that the team logos of their caps were all different, but all from teams from the American League East.

In the bank, the employees were ready to open for business.

In the limo, Acrobat was ready to go for a strong-arm score.

Out on the sidewalk, standing beside their limo, a civilian in a tan barn jacket and an orange baseball cap was cleaning up some poop from a medium-sized black puppy.

"Come on, Claire—no pulling!" said the man as his dog pulled hard on the leash just as he was picking up the shit. *"No pulling!"*

The dog stopped and sighed, waiting for her master to clean up after her.

"A lot of mushrooms," said Russell quietly, the man in the barn jacket walking off with his dog.

"There won't be that many in the bank," said Duncan, leaning against the partition between driver and passengers.

Russell flinched his eyes in agreement, checking the clock in his car: 8:54 A.M. "You good to go?"

"Uh-huh," said Duncan, clapping Russell's shoulder and sitting back in the limo.

The main pedestrian entrance to the bank was a revolving glass door. It had a small sign perched on the inside that said CLOSED. Russell decided that that sign would be his mark.

"I'll give you ninety seconds after your mark, then I'll pull up right at this same spot," said Russell, looking at his watch. "How far should I get?" he asked Ljubica, looking at her.

"At least a hundred yards," she said. "It'll be hot and hard. We'll be clear at eighty seconds."

"Okay, at eighty seconds, I'll be at a hundred yards," said Russell. "Ten seconds later, I'll be in this exact same position. Good enough?"

Ljubica nodded tensely to herself. "Yeah."

"Literally the nick of time," said Duncan, watching as a woman inside the bank walked to the revolving glass doors, kneeling to unlock them.

"Stand by for your mark," said Russell, watching the

woman unlock the doors. "Any second now," he said.

Duncan, Tobey, Ljubica, and Monika all looked at each other, their M-16s tight in their hands.

Oh-boy-oh-boy-oh-boy-oh-boy-oh-boy-oh-boy, thought Tobey.

Russell looked at Ljubica in the rearview mirror; he blew her a little kiss and a wink.

"Right back at ya," she said.

"Be careful," he said, as he eyed the bank.

Ljubica answered with her posture.

Duncan looked at Monika. "We're gonna rock," he told her.

"I know," she said, retying her blonde ponytail with her black scrunchie as her firearm lay patiently across her lap.

Duncan smiled and looked away.

Ljubica winked at Tobey.

—oh-boy-oh-boy-oh-boy-oh-boy-oh-boy-oh-b——

"Breathe, Tobey," said Duncan. "Don't forget to breathe, okay, pardner?"

Tobey took a breath and smiled. "Okay, cowboy."

"Stand by," said Russell, watching as the woman inside the bank stood up and reached forward to flip the OPEN-CLOSED sign.

Russell said, "Ninety seconds on my mark, and . . ."

The woman flipped the sign.

"Mark."

Ljubica, Monika, Tobey, and Duncan got out of the back of the limo, a quartet of Wall Streeters no different from any others except for their dark sunglasses, their brightly colored baseball caps, and their eggshell-white latex gloves. They walked with a clear line and purpose straight toward the bank, the air with the crackling crispness of fall in New York, their breath fogging as they looked up and down the sidewalk, each of them keeping their M-16s close under their dark overcoats, only Ljubica carrying anything besides her weapon—she wheeled the carry-on case behind her, loaded with all the gear they'd need for this score. All of them tried and succeeded in looking inconspicuous as they crossed the ten-yard-wide sidewalk and got to the revolving glass door of the bank. Duncan, the last one out of the limo, slammed the car door shut, the limousine smoothly pulling away from the curb as he followed the others toward the revolving glass door.

"Hah-ha-ha!" said Monika with a winning smile, glancing back at Duncan.

"I got point, I got point, ooh!-ooh! me-me-me-me-me," said Duncan eagerly, as he skipped a bit to get in front of the others, letting his black overcoat fall off his shoulders and to the ground, suddenly the M-16 in his hands, Duncan the first one through the door—

"Nobody move, this is a robbery!" he shouted.

"Everyone!—*Everyone!*—Hands in the air!" Monika shouted even louder, her M-16 aimed level as she moved hard on the real people standing around the lobby, all of whom were bank employees, all of whom were too stunned to do a thing. "I wanna see those hands! I wanna see your hands up in the air!-*Now!-Now!-Now!-Now!*"

Tobey and Ljubica, the last ones through the door, flipped the OPEN-CLOSED sign back, Ljubica taking a small truss-rod and jamming the revolving glass doors shut.

"We're shut down!" Ljubica called out.

"Shut down, check!" said Monika.

"What the fuck are you looking at, fat man?" said Duncan to a security guard.

The security guard, frozen-like, suddenly found the butt of Duncan Idaho's automatic rifle rammed into his enormous belly, the man going down like a sack o' potatoes.

"Augh!" said the guard, lying on the floor in a fetal crouch as Duncan relieved him of his handgun and used his own handcuffs to shackle the man's hands behind his back.

"Nice and quiet, fat man," said Duncan, looking around and surprised to see there was only one guard for the lobby area. "Stay down and out of the way."

Calmly but quickly, Monika walked over to the bank officers sitting in their little cubicles, aiming her weapon at them all.

Oh lookee-lookee here at all the pretty little mushrooms! she thought to herself with a smile, looking at all the real people staring at her with a total loss of bearing.

"All you people, on your feet, hands in the air—*on your feet, hands in the air!-Now!-Now!-Now!-Now!*

"You, you, you, and you," she said, aiming her firearm at each of the civilians she singled out. "Get over there to the corner right now—MOVE!" she shouted, all of them getting up with their hands to their heads and racing over to the corner Monika was herding them toward—the corner farthest away from the exit of the bank.

Meanwhile, Ljubica and Tobey ran around a corner of the bank's lobby to the vault area in the rear, weapons drawn. A wide opening in the hallway, and they were in the antechamber of the vault itself, Tobey the first one in.

"Don't fucking move!!!" Tobey screamed at the two security guards manning a simple table in the antechamber of the vault, aiming his M-16 at both of them.

One of the security guards looked at the M-16 and raised his hands as he said, "Hey—"

Tobey screamed, *"Shut the fuck up motherfucker—hands in the air!—get up on your feet!—move and I'll blow your fucking heads off, motherfucker!!!"*

Both security guards freaked, jumping into the air with their hands trying to touch the sky.

"Okay," said Tobey, rather surprised that the two security men had actually done what he wanted them to do. "Okay," he repeated, looking at Ljubica, as if wondering, *What next?*

Ljubica Greene couldn't *believe* what was going on with Tobey: Because of the coldness outside and the warmth and relative humidity of the bank inside, his glasses were fogging up.

"Can you see through those things?" she asked.

"Yeah, sort of," he said brightly, his glasses now gone completely white.

So, trying to hide a smile, Ljubica looked away from Tobey as she went around the table in the vault antechamber and relieved the security guards of their guns and handcuffs, shackling them one at a time as Tobey covered them with his useless M-16.

—ohboyohboyohboyohboyohboyohboyohboy—

One of the security guards said to Tobey, "Wha——"

"Did I give you permission to talk? Are you allowed to talk? How'd you like to get a mouthful of lead, you cheap cocksucking motherfucking shit-for-brains!?!? You want that?—You want that?-huh?-huh?-huh?"

In the lobby of the bank, Duncan and Monika shot each other a look.

A mouthful of lead? Monika mouthed silently.

Duncan shook his head. "Kids," he mumbled.

Don't look at him, Ljubica thought to herself, nearly dizzy she had to laugh so bad. *Don't look at Tobey or you'll pee yourself.*

"Come on," she said quietly to the security guards, taking them each by the arm and leading them out.

In the lobby, Monika was there to greet them, loaded M-16 pointed at their faces.

"Move pigs, go join the others in the corner," she said, shepherding both men to where the other civilians were rounded up, but not before she gave Yuvi a look.

"What was that all about?" she asked Ljubica quietly.

Ljubica only shook her head, trying to keep from laughing as she turned and ran back to the vault's antechamber, yelling, "Time!" over her shoulder.

"Fifteen seconds," said Duncan, keeping track of the time they'd been at the bank as he swept the lobby with his rifle and his eyes.

Oh-kay, thought Duncan. *Time for the speech.*

"Listen up!" he said loudly, getting all the mushrooms' undivided attention. "I said listen *up!*" Duncan shouted calmly, putting his foot on the ass of one of the downed security guards, all three of whom lay there like trussed turkeys.

"We're not interested in you people," he said. "Don't make me be the bad guy. Don't make me make you dead. If I have to shoot you in the face, if I have to shoot you in the head, I'm gonna feel real bad about it. But I'll get over it. You won't. So sit tight, do what you're told; in ninety seconds we'll be on our way."

Duncan sounded so confident and self-assured that even Monika got relaxed, sweeping her weapon and making sure no one in the lobby was doing anything foolish.

"How we doin'?" said Duncan, sweeping the lobby, simply just *knowing* that this was going to go smooth.

"We're good," said Monika, catching Duncan's eye, excited by the decisiveness and surety of the hit.

In the vault's antechamber, Ljubica opened the carry-on case and took out its contents, one item at a time, setting each item on the ground beside her.

One of the items was a thick extension cord neatly bundled up. Tobey grabbed it and hunted around the vault antechamber for a wall socket, which he found underneath the desk the two guards had been manning. He plugged in the extension cord, then began running it toward the vault door.

"You don't have to shout," Ljubica said as she checked that everything was there in the carry-on case, speaking to Tobey.

"What?" Tobey croacked, his throat on fire.

"At the guards," said Ljubica, looking up and smiling at Tobey like an older, wiser sister. "A simple 'Don't move' is enough," she added with quiet sensibility.

"I know, I know," said Tobey, wishing he hadn't screamed so loud; his throat already felt peeled raw.

"Help me," she said.

Both Tobey and Ljubica each picked up a lock-punch, a device very similar to a hydraulic nail gun. They went to each of the two locks on the vault door proper and inserted the tips of their lock-punches into the two locks.

"Ready?" asked Ljubica. "On the beat after three."

Tobey nodded, holding the lock-punch steady.

"One-two-three."

Crang! went the vault's lock, Tobey and Ljubica immediately pulling the door open.

"Time!" Ljubica called out as she strained against the weight of the bank vault door, which swiveled slowly but effortlessly.

"Twenty-five seconds!" Duncan shouted back, covering the

lobby, his back to the tellers' windows. The tellers behind the bullet-proof glass were gone—probably already calling the cops from the back offices of the bank, which was fine with Acrobat. They'd be gone before the police arrived.

"Nice little 'shrooms," said Monika, sweeping her firearm from side to side, her eyes wide open.

Suddenly, a balding, skinny man in a French-blue shirt, cowering with the others in the lobby of the bank, got up on his knees and shouted out, "There's no money here!"

Monika turned on him, her weapon aimed right at his guts. "What did you say?" she asked quietly. "What the fuck did you say?"

"There's no money here!" said the bald, skinny man.

"Who the fuck are you?" said Monika.

"I'm Potter Scheisskopf, the ba-ba-ba*hhNNn*nnk—the bank manager—oh please don't shoot me, plea-please *please*—"

"What do you mean there's no fucking money here!" Monika shouted, Duncan realizing she was pretend-shouting: Monika was two tickles short of cracking up.

"Off the capitalist, blood-sucking pig!" Duncan suddenly shouted out, laughing as he paid attention to the entire lobby and not just to the bank manager, all the while sweeping the lobby with his eyes and the barrel of his weapon. "Piggies to the slaughter! Off the pig!"

"Don't tempt me, please, do not tempt me," said Monika, her weapon and her eyes dismissing the bank manager, looking around the lobby of the bank, only her voice paying attention to the pathetic little man. "It'd do the world some good to off a capitalist pig like you."

"Please please *please* don't shoot me! Please-please-please don't-don't-don't-shoot-me-don't-shoot-me-don't-shoot-me-don't-shoot-me—"

"Shut up already," said Monika, already bored as she swept the lobby, making sure all the other civilians were good and passive.

Monika wasn't even looking at the bank manager—she was completely ignoring him. But he still blabbered on hysterically.

"Please don't shoot me, I'm so sorry, please don't shoot me—!"

"Shut *up*," said Monika.

"I'm-sorry-I'm-sorry-I'm-sorry-I'm-sorry-I'm-sorry—"

Monika sighed and looked at the man—she'd had enough.

With a vicious snarl, Monika turned, took three decisive steps toward the man, and aimed her rifle right at the man's blabbering face, screaming, *"Get ready to DIE, you fucking capitalist PIG!—DIE!—DIE!—DIE!—DIE!—DIE!"*

"No!"

And then—the long-sought-for *presto!* The bank manager peed himself as all the other cowering bank employees groaned in sympathy and revulsion.

"Score!" Monika yelled out triumphantly as she glanced at the bank manager's soiled trousers. "I win!" she cried, catching Duncan's eye, her own bright and sparkling, like a lake's swelling surface on a sunset.

Duncan caught her eye then looked away, not laughing nearly so hard now as he felt a warm rush go through his body. He felt so giddy, he had to consciously bring himself back down to earth, reminding himself exactly what it was that he was doing here.

I am in the middle of scoring—I am not club-stalking.

Monika caught Duncan's eye again, this time her own eyes shining wickedly—like she knew what was going through his head. As if she knew exactly what effect she was having on him.

"Time!" shouted Ljubica from the vault area.

"Thirty-eight seconds!" Duncan shouted back, suddenly, deliciously afraid of what he might give away if Monika caught his eye again.

In the vault antechamber, the vault door was wide open, Ljubica kneeling in the middle of it, opening a slim object that looked much like a portable computer, while Tobey ran the extension cord all the way to it. The extension cord had about two yards to spare, which Tobey left bundled up on the floor as he took the female end of the extension cord and plugged it into the side of Ljubica's device.

As expected, there was nothing inside the vault except three walls of safety deposit box doors, all closed tight. In one of those safety deposit boxes was the PC board, but Ljubica paid the doors no mind as she concentrated on the device on the floor in front of her.

"This was a good idea, Tobey," said Ljubica.

"Thanks," he said.

"No, I mean it," Ljubica said again. "Simple, elegant: A very good idea."

"Thanks, Yuvi," he said, feeling very happy.

It had been Tobey's idea to do what they were about to do. It had been Tobey's idea to *not* retrieve the PCB board.

Rather, they were there to destroy it.

"Come over here," said Ljubica calmly as she worked on the device. "You ought to learn how this thing works."

"Okay," said Tobey, walking into the vault and squatting beside Ljubica, looking down at the open device.

It looked like a laptop computer, and in fact it had a small alphanumeric keypad as well as a screen. It was about eighteen inches wide and twelve inches tall, barely four inches thick, made of hard black plastic with a smooth, matte finish, just like a laptop.

But it was no computer. It was actually a bomb—a very sophisticated, very specialized sort of bomb.

"First you type in the sequence code to get it operational, see? Like that . . . ," said Ljubica, tutoring Tobey on the job, as it were.

Electronic circuitry do not take microwaves well. One harsh blast of microwaves and sayonara to anything electronic. From this basic principle, years ago, CIA, in conjunction with the Department of Defense and the Raytheon Company, created something very exotic. They created a microwave bomb.

"See when the green light turns red?"

"Yeah? Is it gonna go off?"

"Not yet—now it's just armed," said Ljubica. "Now you have to set the blast radius . . ."

There was really no trick to building a microwave bomb. For all intents and purposes, it was a microwave oven turned inside out—instead of bombarding microwaves inward, the bomb just sprayed microwaves outward, frying everything within whatever radius one wanted, a radius determined by the power of the blast.

"What kind of radius should we go for?" Ljubica asked Tobey, unconsciously giving him an on-the-job seminar.

"Uh—twelve feet?" Tobey asked.

"Ordinarily, yes, a twelve-foot radius would be enough," said Ljubica. "But these walls might have some sort of built-in shielding," she said, rapping her knuckles on a wall of safety deposit boxes. "And we really want to get this job done."

"Right, so . . . maximum setting?"

"That would be a hard burst of seven hundred and forty-five watts," she said dolefully. "Everything within a hundred-yard radius would get fried."

"Too much?" Tobey asked.

Ljubica frowned thoughtfully. "Better safe than sorry," she said.

"Less is less, but more is better?" said Tobey.

Ljubica looked at him with a smile. "Exactly—Time!"

"Forty-nine seconds!" Duncan called out, looking around the lobby, all of a sudden getting major heebie-jeebies.

For the last fifteen seconds, something had been off with Duncan—some internal sensor was ringing out a five-alarm fire.

Something's off, something's wrong, something-something-something-what-what-what-what-what-what—

(How come there was just one guard in the lobby?)

Bingo!

Just then, the answer to Duncan's question came waltzing into the bank's lobby.

"We got company," Duncan shouted before he'd seen or heard a thing.

At the end of the lobby, diagonally opposite the revolving door entrance, there was a short hallway that led to the public toilets. Just as Duncan turned to look in that general direction, who should step out of the bathroom but the second security guard manning the lobby.

"Oh no," said Monika.

The security guard was black, maybe about fifty, with a salt-and-pepper moustache and a receding hairline. He wasn't tall, maybe only five feet eight, but he looked trim and in shape.

He so casually walked out of the bathroom that he didn't seem to realize what was going on, walking a good four or five yards back into the lobby before slowing down and stopping, looking around him, and suddenly realizing Duncan Idaho was directly in front of him, pointing an M-16 right at his face.

"Don't move!" Duncan shouted clearly. *"Do not—fucking—move!"*

At that moment, in surprise, the security guard hitched a step, automatically crouching a bit, clearly getting ready to go into a policeman's firing stance.

Monika—as surprised as anyone—froze.

But the security guard didn't reach for his gun. His hands just floated there, over his hips, as if he were *about* to go for his weapon. But he wasn't going for it.

"Get down!—Get down!—Get on your fucking knees now!" shouted Duncan Idaho, his assault rifle pointed right at the security guard's face.

The security guard didn't move. The security guard just stood there, staring right at Duncan Idaho. Unlike Monika, he wasn't staring like someone frozen in surprise. The security guard looked like he was trying to get an angle, trying to get a bead on the situation and see if maybe he could do something about it.

Oh fuck, thought Duncan Idaho, recognizing that look.

With his thumb, for the first time, Duncan turned the selector switch on his assault rifle from "safety" to "full automatic."

"Don't be a fucker," said Duncan quietly, looking right at the man. "Come on—don't be a fucker."

"Why don't you set that rifle down, son," said the security guard with a quiet determination.

The security guard looked like a kind man—like a brave man. His black face weathered, his belly trim at his belt, all of a sudden Duncan just knew he was a veteran—probably Marines. He didn't know why, but he would have bet anything that this man had been a Marine.

"Come on, Greenie," Duncan mumbled against the stock of his firearm. "Get on your knees and let me go about my business. Don't be a fucker—don't make me zip you. Just gimme sixty seconds and we'll be on our way."

Duncan was aiming right at the security guard's face. There was no way Duncan would miss if he fired.

No no no no no no no no no, thought Monika, still completely frozen, looking at Duncan and the security guard.

Duncan said nothing, unable to look at his watch as he and the security guard stood there staring at each other.

"Mister," said the security guard. "Why don't you put that weapon on the deck and we'll just—"

"Get on your goddamn fucking knees!" Duncan suddenly shouted at the security guard, trying hard to rattle him.

But the security guard just would not get rattled. He just would not get down on his knees, his eyes roving as he tried to get an angle on the situation, Duncan having no doubt whatsoever that this man had not only been a Marine, but a Marine who had seen live-fire combat.

In the bank vault, Tobey stood up to go help Duncan, his M-16 in hand.

"No," said Ljubica instantly, grabbing Tobey's arm and stopping him cold.

"But Dunc——"

"Duncan's a big boy," said Ljubica. "He can take care of himself. You do your job; you let him do his job. Understood?"

Tobey looked at Ljubica, torn.

"Focus, Tobey," said Ljubica. "Duncan doesn't need you— he's got Monika. You're here to back me. Focus, Tobey. Let Duncan do his job; you do yours."

Tobey stood there, then knelt back down and continued helping Ljubica.

O-kay, thought Duncan in the bank lobby, his rifle aimed at the security guard's face, realizing how he was going to handle this situation.

"Hey partner," Duncan called out to Monika.

Monika didn't respond, thinking Duncan was speaking to the security guard.

"Hey! Little Miss Merry Sunshine!" said Duncan, a little peeved. "Quit staring and come on over here, I need a little muscle," he said loudly, not taking his eyes off the security guard.

Monika blinked and suddenly blushed crimson, realizing she'd frozen up. "Right," she said tightly, humiliated as she ran around the lobby and got in position behind the security guard, pressing the barrel of her M-16 right up against the base of his skull.

As soon as she was set, the security guard relented, relaxing and raising his hands into the air.

"If he moves, blow his head off," said Duncan.

"Absolutely," said Monika, furious with herself for freezing up so bad.

Duncan stepped forward and took the security guard's gun out of its holster, pocketing it before resetting the selector switch of his M-16 to "safety."

"Gosh dang it," said the security guard.

Monika poked the back of the security guard's head with the barrel of her rifle. "Shut up," she barked.

Duncan took the security guard's handcuffs off him as he eyed Monika. "Go cover those mushrooms," he said to her. "I got it covered here."

Monika gave him a curt nod, then turned to the civilians.

"Gosh . . . *dang* it," said the guard, with real feeling as Duncan handcuffed the man behind his back.

"Why you'd risk your life for a stranger's money, I'll never know," Duncan said.

"I need this job," said the security guard.

Duncan stared at the back of the security guard's balding

skull, making sure that the handcuffs were snug but not tight.

"I'm gonna lose this job," said the security guard, without bitchiness, just a statement of fact.

Duncan looked at the man and then nodded, looking at the ground. He walked around to face the security guard.

"What?" said the guard quizically.

Duncan looked at the man, glanced at his M-16, then grabbed hold of it by the stock and barrel.

Then he smashed the butt of his rifle to the security guard's face.

"Gosh *dang* it!" said the security guard, stunned and taking an involuntary step back.

Blood flew everywhere, the man's nose streaming bright red, a cut in his eyebrow splitting open and dumping even more blood down his face, soaking his shirt.

But he didn't fall, and he certainly didn't lose consciousness. He didn't fall or lose consciousness because Duncan simply hadn't hit the man that hard.

"Dang it, that *hurt*," said the guard, his voice suddenly very nasal.

"Time!" Ljubica shouted.

"Sixty seconds!" Duncan shouted back. Then to the security guard, he said, "Get ready, here it comes again."

And again, Duncan swung the butt of his rifle to the guard's face, this time going for his jaw.

"*Gosh* DARN *it!*" said the security guard, wobbling on his feet but still not stumbling or falling, his hands firmly clasped behind his back as his lip split open and poured even more blood down his shirt.

"Don't move," said Duncan, grabbing hold of the man's chin in his right hand and quickly examining where he'd hit him, his latex gloves getting all bloody.

The security guard's face *looked* like mush, but face cuts are deceptive. Duncan saw that he'd probably broken the man's nose, as well as split his lip and one of his eyebrows— nothing really serious, maybe a half-dozen stitches at most.

But it looked spectacular.

"You'll live," said Duncan quietly, letting him go and

reaiming his rifle at him. "Now on your knees, brother."

"You broke the crown on my tooth!—Why'd you do that for!" said the guard indignantly, trying to sniff the blood out of his nose as he knelt to the floor. "And I think you broke my nose, too," he said, sounding even more nasal as he spoke. "Why—"

"Who gives a shit," said Duncan quietly, quietly enough that only the guard and Monika could hear him. "No one's gonna call you a pussy now, you know what I'm saying?"

The security guard, on his knees now and about to say something else, suddenly snapped his mouth shut with an audible *click!* looking up at Duncan.

Monika too looked at him. She looked at him, then looked away, for the first time really and truly surprised by Duncan Idaho.

"See what happens to fuckers who get wise with me?" Duncan yelled out loud as he swept the lobby of the bank. "You get your face turned to hamburger, that's what happens. Next wise guy here is gonna get turned into *dead meat*—are we clear?"

In the vault, Ljubica was all set. The bomb was lying open in the middle of the vault, Ljubica done with the keypad, about to press the "return" button, which would set off the three-second timer.

"Hey Tobey?" she called out quietly.

"Yeah?" he said hoarsely, rubbing his throat.

"Wanna set it off?"

Tobey's eyes went sort of wide, then back to normal, as if trying to rein in the excitement. "Sure," he said eager-beaverly.

Ljubica smiled. "Okay, on my signal," she said as she walked out of the vault and stood by the bare desk in the antechamber, looking right at Tobey as he knelt by the bomb. "Ready?"

Tobey nodded, too excited to speak.

"Everyone!" Ljubica shouted, "CLEAR!"

"Clear!" Monika and Duncan shouted back.

"Go," said Ljubica, pointing to Tobey.

Tobey pressed the keypad and bolted out of the vault.

Three seconds later, there was a soft *click!* like the sound of an automatic camera taking a picture—no flash of light, no explosion: Just that soft *click!* But suddenly all the lights and every single one of the computers in the bank lobby winked off, as if some main circuit cable had been hacked with an ax.

"That's it," said Ljubica.

"The PCB board?" asked Tobey.

Ljubica looked at Tobey with a smile. "Toast," she said.

"Oh boy!"

Ljubica ran into the vault and retrieved the bomb, checking it and closing it as Tobey grabbed the extension cord and quickly cinched it up, the two of them putting everything back into the carry-on case.

"We're done!" Ljubica called out.

"Eighty-five seconds!" Duncan called out.

Monika was already moving toward the door as she covered all the real people in the bank, pulling the truss rod out of the revolving door.

Tobey ran out of the vault area, giggling as he ran with flapping limbs across the lobby, looking like a schoolkid who needed to go pee. Ljubica walked quickly but calmly behind him, and she called out to him when he got to the revolving door.

"Stop," she said, Tobey stopping and turning and unable to stop *giggling* of all things as Yuvi, Monika, and Duncan smiled at him and shook their heads.

Ljubica gave Tobey a once-over, fixing his overcoat's lapel and checking his baseball cap, then looking outside.

"Okay," said Ljubica as she walked out, Tobey with her, Monika following them out onto the sidewalk.

Duncan waited until they were all gone, then glanced at the bleeding security guard. "So long, brother," said Duncan, catching his eye before stepping out of the bank at a fast walk.

Once he'd dropped off the Acrobat work-group, Russell Orr had quickly driven the limo around the block, pulling up in front of One New York Plaza on Water Street—a building whose façade looked like a giant silver waffle stood on end. He kept the car there, idling, double-parked, waiting for the microwave bomb to go off.

He wasn't liking any of this.

From where he was double-parked, Russell could see all the way down Water Street, the buildings on either side turning the street into the riverbed of some immense canyon, a canyon of red and gray and brown concrete, and of silver-, steel-, and green-colored glass. The Chase Manhattan Bank branch Acrobat was scoring was two hundred yards away in a straight line.

Should've called the FBI, Russell was thinking, looking around and checking his watch, waiting as the seconds ticked away.

Sixty seconds.

Should've put the screws on the Fee-Bees to crack this bank—washed our hands of this whole mess.

Seventy seconds.

No business pulling this kind of stunt—this isn't Counter Intelligence work, this is operational, we've crossed that bright dividing line—Yuvi wanted it too, didn't she?—yeah she did, she wanted to go score with the others—it's smart to score it, we've got the flexibility; but it's not our place to score, what we're doing is illegal—

—I should have said no—

Eighty seconds.

An amazing thing happened: All of a sudden, all the cars passing by in front of the Chase Manhattan Bank fell dead, some of them stopping immediately, others just gliding along, as if their drivers hadn't yet realized what had happened to their automobiles.

¿áΩßÕ‡$%°°!mmm mmm . . . , thought Russell Orr, an emotion between surprise and relief and approval and objection, a hot flash that happened while he accelerated the limousine, leaving his doubts behind along with the pedestrians, passing the streetlight at Broad Street without stopping, a streetlight that had also suddenly died.

Russell pulled up by the fire hydrant and waited, looking

through the passenger-side window at the bank beyond. Through the window, without looking, Russell could *feel* the change in the air—a deathly stillness, as if some deep-seated electric-soul had been robbed from its circuit-body by death. People were walking to and fro, but they all seemed a little shaken, a little quizzical, as if there was something wrong with the picture, but something which—for the life of them—they could not put their finger on.

Russell was about to mumble, "Hurry up," when just then, Ljubica and Tobey came out of the bank, Tobey carrying the carry-on case, Ljubica carrying both of their rifles. None of the pedestrians even noticed them as they dove into the back of the limo, the people out on the street distracted by the change in the air.

"We fried it!" said Tobey as he got in.

"Yeah, I know," said Russell flatly, watching through the passenger-side window as first Monika, then Duncan came out of the bank, both of them getting in.

"Go go go!"

Before he heard the door close, Russell hit the gas, driving up to the next broken stoplight and turning left onto William Street, and then driving up to Wall Street proper.

"*Yeeee*-hah!" shouted Duncan.

"If it was in there, it got fried," said Monika.

"It was in there," said Ljubica, already sitting right behind Russell, suddenly a distance between them that hadn't been there before.

"What was *that* all about?" Monika asked Tobey in the back of the limo.

"What was what?" Tobey croaked, knowing what she was referring to.

"Oh how'd it go?" Monika asked Duncan.

Duncan mimicked a gangster from the thirties, " 'How'd ya like to get a mouthfula lead, ya lousy cocksucking, mother-fucking, shit-eating copper you!' "

"Yeah—what a mouth!" said Monika.

" 'I'm gonna pump ya full a lead, ya lousy—' "

"*Okay already,*" said Tobey, feeling embarrassed, swallowing, and then feeling how raw his throat was.

"Man, you shouted yourself hoarse!" said Duncan.

"Oh, and you?" said Tobey, his voice going even more hoarse as he spoke. "You got all like a wussie in there," he said, then mimicking in a cruel falsetto tone, " 'Don't make me be the bad guy—please, I don't wanna be the bad guy— *please, please!*—I wanna be a *good* guy! Please-please-please!' "

"Shut the fuck up you little piece of shit!" said Duncan, lunging at Tobey and tackling him to the floor of the limo.

"Get off me you asshole!" Tobey shouted, Monika laughing as Duncan and Tobey wrestled, Tobey suddenly pivoting and now on top of *Duncan* for a change.

"Ya like it?—Huh?—Ya like it?" yelled Tobey, pounding Duncan's arm with his fist.

"*Ow!*—you fucking little piece of shit, that *hurt!*" Duncan yelled, Monika laughing and laughing as the limousine drove across the Queensborough Bridge.

Ljubica looked back at the others, then forward at Russell as he drove back to LaGuardia Airport.

"You okay?" Russell asked quietly.

"Russell you should have *been there!*" she said, for the first time ever faking it with her lover, "it went so *smooth*—and it felt so *right!*—this *fit!*"

"I bet," said Russell Orr, driving along toward LaGuardia Airport.

CHAPTER 5

Thanksgiving 1999 (Victory Lap)

"My my my, we've been busy, haven't we," said Nicholas Denton the next day, the Tuesday before Thanksgiving. He dropped a manila file folder on his mahogany desk as he sat down, a smile on his face. But smile or no smile, the other two in the room knew he was furious. He was furious because he was in serious trouble.

Tom Carr sat in the armchair facing his boss, his hands folded over his potbelly, his feet tucked under his chair. He said nothing, watching Denton.

"Very busy," Denton added with a sigh.

"I'll say," said Bart Michaelus, the other person in the room.

Denton turned to him. "I don't recall inviting you to this meeting," he said pleasantly.

Bart Michaelus shrugged. "Tom figured I ought to come."

Nicholas Denton looked at Michaelus and winced almost imperceptibly, even as he smiled.

"Fair enough," he said, then sat up in his chair, opening the manila file folder as he spoke.

"So!" he began. "We've talked about this before, but I'll say it again: It is not the responsibility of the Acrobat workgroup to decide to go off and pull an operational task like this," Denton said. "Tom, I think it's time we reconsidered the role of Acrobat within Counter Intelligence. And maybe your own role as well."

Tom Carr looked at his boss. "What do you mean?" he asked cautiously.

"When I authorized you to create the Acrobat work-group, I gave you specific limits as to how far you could go," said Denton. "I wanted aggressive Counter Intelligence work against the Chinese, but no covert ops, and certainly not within U.S. borders. CIA has no charter to carry out covert operations within the United States."

"Oh get off your high horse, Nicky," said Bart Michaelus, happily goosing Denton, knowing how much he hated being called by his diminutive. "Acrobat pulled off a coup. You should be happy Acrobat came through the way they did. Though I don't know how you're gonna explain this all to the Senate Intelligence Committee . . . ," he added fake-casually, Bart Michaelus being an exceptionally bad actor, especially when he was gloating.

Denton fixed a frozen smile on Michaelus, hating his guts as he kept mute.

"I don't know, Nicky. Those senators are gonna be mighty pissed."

That was the problem, of course. Denton, as the Deputy Director of Counter Intelligence, couldn't have a work-group pulling covert operations, no matter how sensitive or vital they might be. One thing was picking up and delivering poop on the sly, or maybe putting a hard-target surveillance on a foreign embassy official. An aggressive, active, covert op was something else. And as far as pulling such a monster scoring run within U.S. borders . . . Denton was in serious trouble with the Senate Intelligence Committee, and everyone in this office knew it. After all, Acrobat worked for him—they were his responsibility.

Denton gave a doleful smile to Tom Carr, ignoring Bart Michaelus. "I gave you specific limits, Tom," he said, getting ready to lower the boom on Acrobat. "If you can't work within those limits, then maybe it's time we reconsidered Acrobat's continued existence within the Counter Intelligence Directorate."

"Acrobat could always work inside the Operations Directorate," said Bart Michaelus casually.

Denton whipped his head at Michaelus, staring at him.

Michaelus pretended not to notice as he spoke to Tom Carr. "You and your Acrobat work-group could be reshuffled administratively," he said. "That way, you, Nicholas, wouldn't have to supervise Acrobat. And Acrobat could go about its business."

"I don't think so," said Denton.

"Why not?" said Michaelus.

"Your office is in charge of a lot of work-groups and operations," said Denton. "I think that maybe adding another might be burdening you and your office with a superfluous, eh, a superfluous group of people—"

"Fiddlesticks," interrupted Michaelus, Denton's eyes flashing at being interrupted in his own office—

(. . . even as in the back of his mind, a voice was saying, *I can't* BELIEVE *he just said "fiddlesticks."*)

"Acrobat began by doing Counter Intelligence work," Michaelus was saying, "but they've moved on to bigger and better. They've turned pro—they're doing operational assignments. Well, it so happens that operational assignments are *my* bailiwick," he said, pausing for the punch line.

"I should have direct control of the Acrobat work-group."

The oxygen in the room was suddenly sucked out, instant depressurization happening with that single sentence.

Give credit where it's due, Denton recovered fast. "I see," he said, smiling, his gears clearly spinning in overdrive. "I'm aware that you run the Operations Directorate, Bart, but transferring Acrobat would set a dangerous precedent—"

"Clearly Acrobat is necessary," said Michaelus, loving to watch Denton in a box. The first time he ever had, as a matter of fact. "But since we have this leakage of material out of Skunk Works—Tom, you said this PCB board came from Skunk Works, am I right?"

"It looks like it," said Tom Carr, silently watching his two superiors slug it out.

"Well, with this leakage, we can't organize another work-group this late in the game," said Michaelus. "We have to take advantage of Acrobat's experience. They've gotten their feet wet. It's time they moved over to my Directorate."

If he'd had a cigar, he would've blown smoke in Denton's face right about now.

Nicholas Denton sat at his desk, staring at Michaelus. "Acrobat put lives at risk with this little stunt," he said quietly.

"Spare us, Nicky," said Michaelus. "Your humanitarianism is duly noted."

But Denton continued, visibly losing his temper with every word he said. "They put lives at risk, they broke Federal law—they effectively staged a bank robbery, and on top of *that*, if that weren't bad enough, they set off a microwave *bomb* in downtown Manhattan!" Denton finished, clearly furious, wincing at his own loss of cool.

Tom Carr looked at his hands folded on his potbelly, while Bart Michaelus only smiled.

"Are you through?" Michaelus asked.

Denton didn't say a thing, staring at his counterpart.

"Acrobat got the job done," said Michaelus, shooting a look at Tom before turning a smirk on Denton. "The PCB board got fried, and it got the FBI up off their asses and working for a change."

"Bart, at Counter Intelligence—"

"Ah-ah-ah," said Michaelus, holding up a patronizing hand. "Results matter, not excuses."

Denton looked at Michaelus. "Well," he said, "if you both feel that way, then maybe it would be best to transfer Tom and his Acrobat group to your Directorate," he said, speaking as if it were his idea, the other two knowing he was boxed in.

"I think that would be for the best," said Michaelus, relishing this victory.

He stood up and paced around Denton's office. "I'll send you a memo about the Acrobat work-group later in the day. We'll do the formal transfer work-up after Thanksgiving. Come on, Tom, let's go."

Tom Carr got out of his chair, his eyes fixed on Denton. Then he turned and walked out of the office.

At the door, Michaelus turned to Denton. "By the way," he said. "I think that maybe—for safety's sake—you should check up on your other work-groups. Maybe get the Senate Intelligence Committee to set up an independent review of your Directorate?"

"No, Bart," said Denton, "I don't think that that's really necessary."

"Oh I think it is."

As soon as he and Tom Carr got out of Denton's office, Michaelus marched straight back to his own, every few feet checking to make sure Tom was following behind.

When they got to Michaelus's spare, modernistic office, Michaelus shut the door and turned on Tom Carr.

"What the fuck is going on?" Michaelus said. "You score some bank in fucking Manhattan? Are you outta your fucking mind?"

"I had good reasons—"

"I don't give a flying fuck if the Poon-Hound-in-Chief gave you your marching papers, I wanna know *exactly* what the fuck you think you're doing, 'cause I'm not going to have you do whatever the fuck you feel like doing on any given day."

Tom Carr stood there, looking up at his new boss. When Tommy screamed, there was something about it that made you realize it was an act—there was no meanness behind his rants.

Bart Michaelus, though, was a mean bastard. As the two men stood there, Michaelus was using his five-inch height advantage to physically intimidate Tom Carr, standing over him, making him have to look up at his new boss.

Lie with dogs, you wake up with fleas, thought Tom Carr.

"The raid on the PCB board was part of a larger effort," he began, stepping away from his new boss. "An investigation," he added, "with a specific target."

Michaelus didn't get it at first. "Great, you're doing your fucking job, shit, you're *supposed* to investig——Who are you targeting?" said Michaelus, interrupting himself as he realized what was going on. "Denton? You're targeting *Denton?*" he nearly squealed, thrilled by this new discovery.

Tom Carr grinned ruefully and bobbed his head, holding up both hands as if trying to hold back a tide. "We're looking at things; things are pretty compli——"

"*Augh!* Christ Almighty!" said Michaelus. "Tell me everything!"

"It's too soon—"

"Fuck *that*—tell me," said Michaelus, smiling at Tom Carr, but with a hungry edge to his eye, like a bratty child wanting his toys *now*.

Tom Carr sighed, a little overwhelmed by Michaelus's size, but now more than anything else overwhelmed by Michaelus's intensity. "Bart," he said, trying to calm the horses, "let's take our time. I still work for him—"

"That'll be fixed by the end of the day—so tell me the hard poop, tell me."

Tom Carr considered what he was about to say, then blurted out, "I can't tell you—not yet."

Michaelus gave a start, his eyes going wide. "Why the hell not—?"

"Bart, listen, this is sensitive," he said.

Michaelus almost interrupted, then held himself in check. "Continue," he said tightly.

Tom Carr went on. "We're not sure what's going on. We've got . . . hints. The PCB board was a hint. Some other stuff—numbers, meetings: More hints. We don't have anything solid. The PCB board was the most solid thing we've had in months. Beyond that . . . it's like smoke."

Michaelus by this time had walked around his desk, standing in front of it. Now he sat down in his chair and looked at Tom Carr. "I see," he said, clearly underwhelmed.

Tom Carr looked at his new boss, trying to figure out what would keep him happy in the interim.

"So is Denton alone on this?" asked Michaelus, using the space between them and the tone of his voice to convey lordly cordiality.

"Logistically, several people would have to be involved,"

said Tom Carr, deciding it would be best not to sit down, gauging his new boss.

"So who else are you targeting?" Michaelus asked. "People close to Denton?"

Tom Carr shrugged.

Michaelus narrowed his eyes. "The Ombudsman, Phyllis Strathmore. Denton's conveniently close to that fucking bitch, that's for sure."

Tom Carr said nothing, looking down his chest as he buttoned his suit jacket.

Michaelus's eyes narrowed even further as he stood up and walked from behind his desk over to Tom Carr. "No shit," he said.

"Who else is he close to," asked Tom Carr.

"Makepeace Oates, but he's in Europe right now," said Michaelus, now a foot from Tom Carr.

"Not Oates. Who else."

Michaelus now looked down at Tom Carr like a giant little boy who's just met Santa. "Kurt Wenger?"

"Who—else."

"Mother of God—Arthur Atmajian? *Atta-boy* is involved in this thing?"

Tom Carr unbuttoned his jacket, then rebuttoned it, as if unable to decide which way he liked his jacket best.

Bart Michaelus got so excited, he grabbed Tom Carr's shoulders and shook him back and forth. "Atmajian and Wenger and Strathmore, holy *fuck!*" he said, as he started to prowl around his office, his back to Tom Carr, his head full of ideas. "All of them in this thing together!"

"Maybe," said Tom Carr.

"Maybe?" said Michaelus, whipping his head at Tom Carr. "What do you mean 'maybe'?"

Tom Carr sighed. "This is . . . —delicate," he said. "It's so sensitive, my own kids aren't too clear as to where we're going. I'm giving them goals and targets, but I'm not letting the cat out of the bag, not even with them."

Michaelus scoffed. "I'm not some fucking teenager, Tom," he said.

"I know, sir," he said. "But if you want me to succeed, I can't have anyone else rocking the boat."

"What do you mean?"

"I need latitude, and I need support, and more than anything I need quiet," said Tom Carr. "If Denton gets wind of this thing, he'll shut down ... I think he suspects—but I'm not sure."

Michaelus considered this, knowing what Tom Carr was saying was true, but hating to have to let him wander off on his own—hating to be the one whose hand wasn't holding the poker.

"I'll want periodic reports," he said finally.

"No problem," said Tom Carr.

"Once a week," said Michaelus.

Tom Carr shrugged. "A lot of times we're slogging our way through an awful lot of poop—sometimes there's nothing to report in a week."

"Once a week every week," Michaelus repeated. "And something else—you do *not* score domestically. That stunt in Manhattan? That thing alone might be enough to sink Denton, but I'm not gonna have that happen to me. The little prick was right: We have no mandate to score within U.S. borders. You or your Acrobat kids pull a stunt like that again, I'll fry your balls with a side of bacon. Got it?"

Tom Carr nodded.

Michaelus nodded in return, satisfied. "Now, just to show you I'm not a bad guy or a hard boss: Don't worry about support; you just keep on doing what you're doing. Put all the pieces together until they're a hard, stiff dick of poop. I won't interfere. But I want something rock hard that I can pound up Denton's fucking ass. Understand?"

Tom Carr looked at his new boss. "Okay," he said.

"He outsmarted me—as simple as that," said Denton.

Arthur Atmajian, Denton's best friend, said nothing, working away on Denton's Mercedes 380SL convertible, the clicking sound of a socket wrench filling the hollow space of the garage at Atta-boy's house: *Crrr!* (pause), *Crrr!* (pause), *Crrr!* (pause).

The Atmajian house was huge and built for kids, Atta-boy being the proud papa of eight children, the oldest a twenty-year-old senior at Swarthmore College, the youngest a toddler of three. Inside the house, the kids and their neighborhood friends were all running around making a cheerful racket that grew louder and then faded as they ran near and far.

Denton paced around the garage, scuffing the soles of his shoes on the pale gray concrete. Outside, through the open garage door, it was quite dark, already past seven o'clock. But inside, the two meager lightbulbs hanging above the three cars gave off a cozy light as the two men spoke alone.

"When was the last time you changed the spark plugs on this thing?" asked Arthur, his voice sounding hollow as it ricocheted inside the engine.

"I don't know. I didn't know you were supposed to change them that often."

"Well, you are," said Arthur, standing up and looking at a spark plug he'd extracted. He examined it, blowing gunk off of it.

Atta-boy was a huge, balding fat man with a thick black beard and wide, thick features. He looked like a pirate—all he needed were red silk pants, a cutlass, and an eyepatch.

In theory, Arthur Atmajian was head of Langley's Physical Plant Security, known as PhysPlanSec (pronounced *"fizz-plan seck"*). PhysPlanSec was the office charged with maintaining the integrity of the Langley compound—making sure no one tried to break into Central Intelligence, either physically or via computer connections. But the PhysPlanSec job—though it was a real job, and a job he attended to every day—was just a cover.

"Look at this," said Atta-boy. "Look at this—see all this gunk? You can't have this," he said, irritated. "Nicholas, you gotta change the plugs on your car—and you gotta check the points, too."

"Okay, Mr. Goodwrench."

Atta-boy scoffed and turned his attention to the engine again.

What Atta-boy *really* did was manage the half-dozen wet-boys CIA kept handy. Sometimes wet-boys are called Tin Men. Other times they are called Dog Soldiers; you know, the whole Cherokee/mystical-warrior thing. But Arthur Atmajian—a straightforward, no-nonsense kind of guy—was rather impatient with the cute monikers. He believed in calling a spade a fucking shovel. If anyone had asked him what he really did at CIA, he would have told the truth: Arthur Atmajian was in charge of CIA's assassins.

He and Denton went way back.

"Tom Carr just plain outsmarted me," Denton repeated. "Using his own people to score the PCB board—simply brilliant. He nixes the PCB board exchange, gets *me* into trouble, and accelerates his transfer to the Operations Directorate," he said, shaking his head. "He could've used the Feebles to do it," he said, referring to the FBI. "But instead, he plays it so tight, nobody knows shit about what's really going on. Smart little bastard."

"Nobody's said otherwise," said Atta-boy as he unwrapped a new spark plug and examined it before diving back into the engine well. "What about Michaelus?" he asked.

"You know him," said Denton, shaking his head. "Michaelus thought he was being all clever, but I could see him coming a mile away. It was Tom Carr who really surprised the shit out of me. With that one move he finessed his way right out of my Directorate, lickety-split."

From deep inside the well of the engine, Atta-boy stopped turning the wrench and said, "But you'll still be able to keep an eye on Carr and his kids, right?"

"Arthur: Think," said Denton, taking a swig of his beer and a drag on his cigarette, his tie loose and the sleeves of his snow-white shirt rolled halfway up his forearms. "With all of them cuddling up to Michaelus over at the Operations Directorate? I don't think so."

Atta-boy popped out of the engine well and turned on Denton. "So then why did you let him do that?" he asked, clearly upset. "You didn't *need* to. You could have just insisted that they stay in your Directorate."

"What the hell was I supposed to do," said Denton casually. "Say no? Make a scene? Make Tom Carr even more suspicious than he already is?"

"But Nicky, c'mon—"

"Hey," said Denton. "We're really far along. We're not there yet, but we're close enough to see the shore. All we need is a little patience."

"Well, yeah," said Atta-boy reluctantly, looking at the tool in his hand and thinking things over. Then he turned back to the engine well. "At least your source inside Acrobat is still working."

Denton sighed. "The source didn't warn me about the bank thing."

Atta-boy stopped turning the wrench again, again coming up for air and looking at his friend. "I thought you told me you were working the source."

"Oh I am," said Denton, sighing and puffing away on his cancer stick. "The way I'm massaging it, I could open up my own parlor. But the source didn't give me a head's up until after they'd scored the bank."

"Shit," said Atmajian, "this is getting too complicated, maybe—"

"No, we're doing fine," Denton interrupted, recovering some equilibrium as he sighed. "We were close," he said. "We'll get close again."

"Close don't count," said Atta-boy, then turning his attention to the used spark plug, blowing more gunk off of it, examining it carefully. It kept him from examining Denton.

At rest, Nicholas Denton looked spent—bags under his eyes, shoulders slouched. At the office, after getting the news of the scoring run on the bank in Manhattan, Denton had suddenly realized he had nervous sweat streaming down his arm-pits—even though he changed shirts, he'd had to go through the rest of the day wearing his jacket, water literally dripping off of him.

Now, in the garage, Denton leaned against Atta-boy's Volvo and sighed.

"Hmm?" asked Atmajian, instinctively feeling Denton was about to say something.

Denton frowned for an instant. "How's it going?" he asked casually but carefully, referring to Arthur's domestic drama—a devoted, clinging, needy wife and eight children in this household; an expensive, cheating mistress who gave him no peace of mind in a Georgetown condo that Atta-boy paid for.

"How's what? Oh—that. Fine," said Atta-boy, not wanting to talk about it.

"You sure?"

"Yes of course I'm sure," Atmajian mumbled.

"Okay," said Denton, sounding resigned. He and the Ombudsman, Phyllis Strathmore, another close friend from their early days at Langley, worried a great deal about Arthur and his dangerously messy—not to mention criminally expensive—domestic drama.

"Hey," said Atta-boy, giving his friend a knowing little look. "Don't change the fucking subject."

Denton rolled his eyes and smirked.

"What happens when the source stops feeding you any poop?" asked Atta-boy studiously.

Denton didn't say a thing, smoking and staring off into space.

Atmajian's shoulders relaxed, drooping. He looked at the used spark plug in his hands and said, "If Tom Carr and these Acrobat kids of his make a hard move—and they will, eventually, unless you put them away—then it'll turn ugly. And then I'll be forced to make *my* move."

"I don't want it to get to that tenor."

"Neither do I—*but* . . . ," said Arthur, looking at Denton. "If you can't maintain the source, then we're gonna be blind."

Denton bit his lip, nodding.

Arthur Atmajian looked at him carefully. "If the source fades completely," he said, "then no more clever stuff, Nicholas. We're playing with fire here when we don't need to. If things keep on going the way they're going, we're going to have to find a permanent solution to the Acrobat problem. That's what I deal in, that's what I like: Permanent solutions."

Denton nodded at what his friend was saying. Then he looked Atta-boy in the eye. "If the source shuts down completely, I'll be speed dialing your number."

Thanksgiving weekend came and went, but none of the members of the work-group Acrobat left town for the holiday. None of them had anyone or anyplace worth going to.

On Monday, at lunchtime, the five members of Acrobat made their way through the sea of people to their regular table on the periphery of the mess hall. From the Muzak speakers came a sanitized version of the Stones's "Ruby Tuesday" covered by Ray Conniff–type vocals; nonsense music that wafted out across the mess hall, threading its way through the murmur of people chatting away their lunch hour.

Everyone seemed to be minding their own business, but Tobey could almost feel it: All eyes were on Acrobat. No one *stared,* exactly, but everyone seemed aware of them, calling out not-quite-casual hellos to them as they all walked to their favorite table.

"Are people staring at us?" Tobey asked Ljubica, who was walking beside him.

"Mm-hmm," she said, looking straight ahead.

"Why?" he asked.

Ljubica almost didn't say, but then she said cryptically, "What did we do last Monday? What are people just beginning to find out?"

Tobey started looking around, smiling in amazement as they made their way to their table.

Duncan, looking over his shoulder, spotted Tobey's look, then turned to Monika beside him. "Don't it feel good to turn a victory lap?" he asked her.

"It surely does, cowboy," said Monika Summers, her blonde ponytail flopping along as she walked to their table, staring straight ahead with a small, toothless smile on her lips.

There was a vibe between Duncan and Monika that was

unmistakable: Though they didn't look or sound any different, there was like a weird force field going on between them, invisible but totally obvious to Tobey, Russell, and Ljubica, who all exchanged a look as they followed them to the table.

The Acrobat work-group sat down at their regular table, pointedly minding their own business—but all of them sitting on the side of the table that faced the rest of the dining area. Tobey found himself sitting between Yuvi and Monika, in the exact middle of the Acrobat group.

There were lots of work-groups, of course, but only a few designated ones like Acrobat—work-groups with very specialized, very sensitive taskings. They too sat on the peripheries, something Tobey had never noticed until he'd joined Acrobat. Now, these other work-groups were the ones who started drifting over, passing them by on their way to their tables, trying to pump the members of Acrobat for information.

There was Annie Roth and Dexter Carson, from the Paradise work-group, which usually had lunch clear on the other side of the cafeteria. Yet they wandered all the way around to the Acrobat table to not-so-casually shoot the shit and pump them for the poop.

"I heard you guys've been bad," Dexter Carson finally said.

"Oh we were *good*," said Duncan Idaho, the other members of Acrobat guffawing as Dexter and Annie shook their heads and wandered off.

And so it went during the rest of lunch. Nobody knew specifics—nobody even knew the generalities—but the key people at the Langley mess hall just *knew* that Acrobat had made the quantum leap. The quantum leap to *where,* well, that was pretty hazy too. But clearly Acrobat had accumulated a big batch of brownie points, and so everyone was suddenly curious.

Ljubica was cool, minding her salad as acquaintances of hers would stop by and ask her questions she only answered with monosyllables, the reigning monosyllables being "No" and "This and that."

Tobey giggled a lot.

Monika just nodded with a big, sloppy grin on her face, every so often turning to Duncan beside her as she spoke vague pleasantries to her circle of friends.

Duncan smiled a lot as he kept on squeezing Monika's hand. At one point he suddenly leaned over and kissed Monika's cheek for no apparent reason, and rather awkwardly at that. Yuvi, Russell, and even Tobey didn't say a word.

Of course, the masses in the middle had no clue what was going on. The geeky tech guys and the bird-like analysts, the Ivy Bankers and the Pocket-Protector Set—they had no idea who Acrobat was. Tobey, looking out across the cafeteria at where he used to sit, realized he never would have spotted Acrobat either if he'd been back out there.

At one point, Georgie McNamara, a buddy of Duncan's who usually manned the kegs of Guinness whenever he threw a party, stopped by Acrobat's table. "Hey, Dunc, guys," he said,

"Hey Georgie," said Duncan as McNamara sat down in front of him, leaning forward across the table.

"Is it true you guys pulled a monster op just before Thanksgiving?" he asked quietly.

Tobey let loose a giggle—he couldn't help it—as he stared at his food, pretending he was eating.

Georgie McNamara glanced at Tobey, then at Duncan. "I think I just got my answer."

"Georgie," said Duncan, crossing his arms and leaning forward across the table, "can you keep a secret?"

Georgie McNamara smirked as he leaned back before he got up. "Yeah I can keep a secret, and I bet you can too, asshole."

"Absolutely goddamned right—*hey!*" said Duncan, giving the Black Power salute. Tobey began laughing outright, trying to hold it in.

"Fuckers," said Georgie with a smile, connecting his closed fist with Duncan's. "Later," he said as he walked off to his regular table.

Duncan and Ljubica watched him go as Tobey giggled into his food and Monika simply held Duncan's hand.

"You're sad," said Russell to Tobey, who kept on giggling, finally bringing himself under control.

"I'm gonna go get another cheeseburger," Tobey said, getting up and shaking the giggles out of his head.

Tobey walked back to the cafeteria grill and ordered his food. While he waited, a guy he knew vaguely as one of the ferrety Administration types sauntered over casual-like, as if he just happened to be passing by.

"Tobey! Tobey Jansen, how the hell are ya?" said the guy, an oily little shit Tobey had seen around by the name of Ray Hamway. Hamway clearly didn't remember (or was pretending it had never happened), but he'd been the biggest dick with Tobey awhile back . . . and yet here he was, sucking up like a champ.

"Hi, uh . . . hi," said Tobey, blanking on the guy's name.

"Ray," said Ray. "Ray Hamway—where there's a will, there's a Hamway," said the little prick.

"Yeah, right," said Tobey warily.

"So," said Hamway, waiting him out.

Tobey didn't say a thing.

"I heard you're hanging out with some Operations people, huh?" said Hamway. "What, you're too good for Counter Intelligence?" he added with a laugh.

Tobey couldn't help smiling. He'd never actually been on the receiving end of a suck-up—yet here it was, and my my my my did it feel good.

"Yeah, I'm over at the Operations Directorate," he said. "What about you? Still in Administration?"

"That's right," said the prick, holding on to a plastic smile.

Ljubica happened to glide back into the cafeteria, picking up a bottle of tea and sliding over to where Tobey was. "Hey," she said, in her husky, sexy way, even though she was all business. "I've been meaning to ask you: What did you do with the work-up we did on consular personnel?"

"Cowboy's got it," said Tobey. "I gave it to him awhile back."

Ljubica frowned. "Why does he have it?"

Tobey sort of shrugged and scoffed at the same time. "He

borrowed it from Mon, back when he was dropping in on her cubicle all the time."

"Ah," said Ljubica, cracking open her bottle of tea and drinking some.

Tobey thought a bit, then said, "I'm glad they're finally together."

Ljubica nodded.

"It's makes me really happy, as if *I* had hooked up with someone," he added. "Is that weird of me to say?"

"No," said Yuvi, looking carefully at Tobey, wistfully envious of him: Envious of the simplicity of his heart, a simplicity that was a kind of elegance. "That's not weird at all. Just the opposite."

"And who might you be?" Hamway butted in, speaking to Ljubica.

Ljubica frowned then blinked, looking over her shoulder and then back at Hamway as if she couldn't believe he was talking to her. Then she looked at Tobey. "Is he a friend of yours?"

Tobey blinked. "Not really, no," he said.

"One cheeseburger, loaded," said the guy manning the grill.

"Thanks, Greg," said Tobey as he took the burger and walked off with Ljubica, leaving Ray Hamway behind.

At the Acrobat table, Monika and Duncan were holding hands and talking into each other's ear as Russell Orr sat there, done with his food and looking out across the mess hall. Ljubica and Tobey were walking back, both of them stopping to talk to people along the way. Russell, who could read lips, saw Tobey speak to someone about a football pool. Ljubica was standing there beside him, not saying anything but peacock proud nonetheless.

Just like high school, Russell thought, unnerved. Scoring the bank had been a huge chance; but more to the point, it had been unnecessary. But they'd done it anyway, as if on a dare. Between Tommy and Duncan, the whole work-group had been maneuvered and manipulated into doing something crazy-foolish and now, instead of counting their lucky stars, everyone felt cocky as hell, invincible—bullet-proof. Checking out Monika and Duncan all lovey-dovey beside him, Russell realized it was no accident that Duncan had finally made his move only after they'd scored the bank.

We're gonna wind up driving off a cliff if we're not careful, thought Russell, leaning back in his chair and coolly eyeing the other members of the work-group Acrobat.

Flash forward five months:

On Saturday, April 29, 2000, around 7:20 in the morning, Tobey Jansen was driving like a maniac to Duncan Idaho's house in Adams Morgan.

Please please PLEASE *be there,* he thought over and over again as he drove as fast as he dared through the streets of D.C., which were empty and quiet and sleepily happy on this pretty spring morning.

Tobey was very different now. His blondish brown hair was shaved clean off, and his fashionable oval-framed glasses had been replaced with small, round, industrial granny glasses with flat lenses. His goatee, once just a tuft of hair, was now a gelled, platinum-blond spike sticking six inches out of his chin, and on his left shoulder blade he had a tattoo: A tumbling acrobat dressed in a baggy red outfit and yellow piping, wearing a blue hat with droopy ends.

When he got to Adams Morgan, Tobey didn't turn into Duncan's street. Instead, he passed it, driving down to the back alley behind Duncan's apartment house, turning into the alley, and slowly meandering along until he found the right back door.

Though he was desperate, six months with Acrobat had taught him not to lose his cool. Tobey deliberately left the engine of his car idling as he got out and looked around. Seeing nobody, he went to the wooden door to the backyard and tried to open it, but the door was locked from the inside, with no latchstring. So after a few rattles, Tobey scrambled over it and dropped down into the backyard, running across the lawn, longish and in need of a mow, and up the rickety wooden steps, banging on the kitchen door as he whispered, "Duncan! *Duncan!*"

No answer.

Tobey took off his gray, zip-up sweatshirt, wrapped it around his arm as best he could, and then smashed his elbow into one of the panes of glass of the door.

The glass tinkled as he brushed it aside with his cushioned elbow. Taking his sweatshirt off his arm, Tobey reached in through the curtain of the door, trying to unlock it.

Then a hand grabbed his wrist.

"Agh!" yelled Tobey in surprise.

Duncan recognized his voice.

"Tobey?" he asked sleepily, as he let go of Tobey's wrist and began to unlock the door. "What are you *doing?*"

"Open up, quick, Duncan, open up!" he whispered.

Duncan opened the door, standing there in just boxer shorts and tousled hair as he blinked the sleep out of his eyes. "What are you *doing* here?" he asked again.

Tobey didn't answer, pulling Duncan out the kitchen door and down the rickety wooden steps in his bare feet.

"Come on, we gotta go, we gotta go now."

Halfway down the steps, Duncan stopped him. "What the fuck—"

"It's coming down," said Tobey quickly, looking up at him. "It's going down this morning, maybe right now, so we—"

"Wha-what-what's going down?" asked Duncan, confused.

"Denton," said Tobey, looking at his friend. "Denton is coming for us—he's gonna have Acrobat arrested and charged with conspiracy, treason—"

"What?—What are you talking about—?"

"Denton is gonna nail us," said Tobey, grabbing Duncan by the arms. "He's gonna have us arrested today, and he's gonna lay a whole truckload of stuff at our feet—conspiracy to commit treason, treason—"

"We—holy, holy shit," said Duncan.

"Duncan man," said Tobey, almost crying, "we gotta go— *now.*"

"Hold on, hold on—how do you know this?" said Duncan, no longer sleepy or cold in the morning air.

"I know—it's too complicated, it was an accident that I found out, I went down to Langley to check up on some work stuff—they'd *sealed our offices*—I'm telling you, it's coming down right now, we gotta move *now,* there's no more time for—"

"They sealed our offices? Who did?"

Tobey gulped. "PhysPlanSec's Internal Security. You know what *that* means? It means *Dog Soldiers* are coming for us—Duncan, Duncan, I heard Arthur Atmajian *himself* is gonna come look for us," Tobey squealed, terrified of the head of the Dog Soldiers—with good reason.

"Atmajian and Dog Soldiers, holy shit," said Duncan, unaware that he'd gone all goose-bumpy.

"Please please *please,* we gotta go right now."

"Okay, calm down, I'm going—did you get in touch with anyone else?"

"No, I—"

"Monika's with me; I'll get in touch with Russ—"

"There's no time to go running around, they're probably right outside your front door right this very second—Duncan, *please,* let's run *now,* now while—"

"You get in touch with Tommy, I'll deal with Russell and Ljubica, we'll rendezvous—"

"We can't—"

"Gimme a minute," said Duncan Idaho, going back into his apartment.

"We don't—"

"Gimme a *minute,*" he said over his shoulder, taking the steps up to the kitchen three at a time.

In the bedroom, Monika was naked under the covers, sleepily rubbing her face.

"What was that?" she asked, muffled through her hands.

"Get dressed," said Duncan, throwing Monika her blouse and jeans as he got into some pants and rummaged under the futon, pulling out his porcelain gun. Checking that it was loaded and good to go, he shoved it into the small of his back, then grabbed a sweatshirt and pulled it on over him.

When she saw the gun, Monika quit dithering, getting dressed as quick as she could, without bothering with underwear or socks as she pulled on her gray Ked sneakers.

"Where's my purse—"

Duncan threw it at her from across the room as he looked through the bureau for his wallet and more magazines for his gun. Grabbing a handful from underneath his clothes, he yanked them out and headed for the kitchen, Monika slinging her purse over her shoulder and following him out the door.

In the living room, she saw Duncan going to the kitchen, but she thought he was getting something. So she walked to the front door, about to open it—

"*Hey,*" he called out, a short, flat sound as he stood by the back kitchen door, his hand on the doorknob, looking at her across the apartment with the oddest expression on his face.

Monika looked at him, frowning.

He shook his head exactly once: Left: Right.

That was when Monika knew what was happening.

Oh no, she thought as they stared at each other. She turned to the front door, looking at the brass doorknob as if it were lethal, then turned to Duncan and quickly crossed over to the kitchen, the two of them bursting out the kitchen door into the bright spring morning, the air tangy and clean.

The wooden backyard door was open, Tobey Jansen already behind the wheel of his car. When Duncan and Monika got in, Tobey said, "Get down, don't let them see you."

Duncan slid into the back seat, Monika into the front, both of them lying down as Tobey slowly pulled away, in no rush as he yanked his baseball cap down over his face, trying to look inconspicuous.

He pulled out of the back alleyway, then turned right, down the cross-street. Casual as any Saturday morning driver, he slowed down at the corner without actually stopping, looking in both directions before crossing the street and driving away—but not before he saw the back of a nondescript American sedan with two men in suits sitting in the front, in a spot invisible from the windows or porch of Duncan's apartment house. The car, the two men, their suits, Saturday morning—they practically screamed "surveillance" to the world: Surveillance, or worse.

"They're there," said Tobey, already past them and driving to Connecticut Avenue.

"Don't drive too fast," said Duncan from the back.

"I won't," said Tobey.

"Tell Monika what happened—tell her everything you told me," said Duncan.

So Tobey told. By the time they were out of Duncan's neighborhood, Duncan and Monika were sitting up in the car, everyone up to speed.

Duncan said, "Get us to a phone, we'll call Tommy and Russell and Yuvi—"

"If they're coming down, the phones are probably bugged," said Tobey. "That's why I came instead of called."

"You're right, you're right," said Duncan, thinking.

Monika said, "We have to get in touch with the others, we just *have* to."

"Pull up at a Metro station," said Duncan. "The first one you see."

"But—"

"Tobey, please, just do it," said Duncan from the back.

Tobey was silent as he drove around, looking for a Kiss & Ride of a Metro station.

"Monika, you take Tobey's car, get in touch with Tommy; Tobey and me'll find Russ and Yuvi," said Duncan. "We'll all meet up in a few days."

"Where?" Tobey asked.

"Uh—"

"New York," said Monika in a flash. "We'll all meet up again in New York."

"Where and what time?" asked Duncan.

Monika counted the days. "Today's Saturday? Sunday-Monday—Tuesday, at ten in the morning, in Times Square."

"Times Square is too big," said Tobey. "*Where* in Times Square."

"Not out in the open," said Duncan.

She thought for a second. "Okay, make it the Red Line subway—the downtown Number Two line," she told them both. "Times Square, Red Line subway platform—you can't miss it."

"The Red Line platform, Times Square, Tuesday at ten in the morning," Tobey repeated, memorizing it. "Red Line, Red Line, red, red like Fred."

"That's it," said Monika in a rush. "We'll meet up there, and by that time, we'll have transportation all set up."

Tobey found a Kiss & Ride, smoothly pulling in and stopping the car, leaving the engine idling.

"You got Tommy's address?" asked Duncan.

"Yeah, I think," said Monika. "Saint Andrew's Drive?"

"Go down Fairfax Drive, it's right across the street from Fairfax—"

"—from Fairfax High School, I know, I know, I remember now," she said.

"Tobey, scoot out," said Duncan, the three of them getting out of the car.

By the driver's side door, Tobey took a step back and turned away as Duncan and Monika kissed their good-byes, hugging each other tight in the middle of the Kiss & Ride.

"Be careful," Duncan whispered. "Maybe I should go get Tommy."

"I can manage, and anyway, if there's anyone waiting outside from SD, they'll recognize you. I'll take care of Tom," she said.

Duncan looked over his shoulder at Tobey, then leaned close to Monika. "When you get Tommy, at the first chance you get, split away from him."

Monika looked at Duncan, not understanding. "Why would I do—"

"Just do it," Duncan repeated. "Because they're after Tommy, not you. You'll both be better off if you split away from him. Tommy'll understand. You can both run easier, and you'll be safer. Okay?"

"Okay."

"Okay," he said. "So, ten A.M., Tuesday, Red Line, Times Square—be there or be square."

"You betcha," she said, kissing him.

Tobey was standing there, looking away, when he got a tap on the shoulder. He turned around and got a big hug from Monika, tight enough that it crushed his spiked goatee.

"Oooh!" said Monika.

"S'okay," said Tobey, smiling at her as he straightened his goatee. "Just don't crash my car."

"I won't," she said with a smile.

Monika pecked his cheek again, then turned and gave Duncan a fumbling last kiss. Then she got in the car and drove away.

Duncan and Tobey watched until the car had disappeared.

"I shoulda gone get Tommy," said Duncan.

"Well, let's go get Russell and Yuvi," said Tobey.

"No," said Duncan, still looking after the vanished car.

"What?"

"No, I'll go get 'em—you go underground," he told Tobey without looking at him.

"But what about Russ and Yuvi—"

"Tobey, no, look," he said, as he turned to face him, "this isn't like a regular scoring run; this is real."

Tobey looked at him, pained, and Duncan misinterpreted the look, sighing in response and putting his hand on his thin shoulder.

"Look, you've got the balls of a tiger," he told Tobey, "but you don't have the mileage, as simple as that. Nothing to be ashamed about; you've done awesome. But it'll be easier if we split up now. I'll deal with Russell and Ljubica, and Monika can handle Tommy. You go on your own; it'll be less conspicuous that way. Then we'll meet up at the rendezvous point."

"I can go with you, I can help you," said Tobey.

Duncan smiled at Tobey and grabbed him by the back of the neck, pulling him close.

"You did great, Champ, a clean touchdown," said Duncan. "But this is the deep end of the pool. Nobody's gonna be looking for you, so you'll be safe. Go underground. Don't use credit cards, don't use your passport. You got any cash?"

"Just a couple of bucks."

"Okay, so go get some cash *now*—get as much cash as you can out of a bank machine right this second. Then put as much distance between yourself and that bank machine as you can. Okay? Don't go get anymore cash after that, they'll pin you within a half hour. Go straight to New York, find an out-of-the-way spot where you can hunker down for a few days. In a worst-case scenario, sleep in a park. Sit tight. Pay cash and don't use your real name. On Tuesday we'll have transportation set, and we'll have all we need to sink Denton. Okay?"

"Okay," said Tobey, feeling miserable.

"Chin up, you did good," said Duncan, giving him a quick, fierce hug. "Now go."

Tobey didn't move—it was Duncan Idaho who walked away, going down the electric escalator of the Metro, leaving Tobey Jansen alone.

Tobey took off his baseball cap, running his hand over his scalp before he reset his cap, wondering what would happen next. Wondering if he had done good.

On Tuesday, May 2, 2000, the work-group Acrobat met up at the Red Line platform of the Times Square subway station in New York City.

Nicholas Denton pounced, Tom Carr was killed, and Acrobat was on the run.

PART III

You Won't Be The First
(But You Could Be The Next)

Once, I couldn't get enough of him. Now he makes my skin crawl. It's not that he judges me. It's that he doesn't.

I know how sometimes, the more you understand, the less you forgive. But perhaps that's what's needed—less acceptance, more judgment. Because I know I've done cruel and evil things, things I'm so ashamed of. Maybe being judged by the one I most love—risking the love I most need—is the only way to expiate the wrongs I have done, and so leave them behind.

But instead of risking our love, instead of choosing sides and calling things by their name, we agreed to this sophisticated, mature moral calculus; a mask for cowardice. He called it tolerance. Acceptance. Space. Like a fool, I called it good.

This is where it's brought us.

CHAPTER 6

Getting the FBI to Wax Acrobat

On Thursday morning, May 4, 2000, two days after he had "chatted" with the dying Tom Carr at the Times Square subway station, Nicholas Denton was sitting in the sun-drenched breakfast nook of his McLean home, having a cup of coffee as his three children ate their breakfast.

They were very quiet children. Nine-year-old Nicky Junior (actually, the fourth Nicholas Andrew Denton) was slurping his cereal, which was soggy and pasty, the way he liked it. Seven-year-old Artie was staring off into space, his yogurt untouched, a child naturally stoned on some powerful, hypnotic drug. And four-and-a-half-year-old Claire was waiting for the housekeeper, Jane, to give her her eggs and toast, her little hands folded on her little lap, looking a little bit like a miniature Joan of Arc, preparing herself for the consuming fires of day care.

Carefully watching everything from his favorite spot by Denton's feet was Sinatra, the Denton family dog. Sinatra was a smart old Labrador with a dazzlingly expressive face who'd been with them since he'd been a nine-week-old puppy. He was eleven years old now, and though he could still play a mean game of Frisbee-catch, over the last year he'd become more and more insecure about the world as he slowly but inexorably went blind. Poor guy: Glaucoma. His blindness had made him a bit ornery as of late, though he was still a puppy when he was around his master.

Denton himself was buried deep in a copy of the *Washington Post*. The journalist I. F. Stone once remarked that the *Post* was a great newspaper because you never knew on what page the page-one story was going to be on. It took Denton two passes through the entire paper before he came across any mention of that Thursday's page-one story, the Acrobat story.

A-ha! thought Denton when he spied the article. Instinctively, he sat up.

Buried deep in the back pages of the national news, the piece was brief: Two paragraphs recapitulating Tuesday's "bank robbery," blah-blah blaah, blah-blah blaah, the old lady who got shot in the arm, blah-blah blaah, blah-blah blaah, blah-blah blaah, released from the hospital last night in care of her sonny-boy, how sweet, blah-blah blaah, blah-blah blaah, blah-blah blaah, no leads, no clues, blah-blah blaah, statewide investigation, and . . . —nothing new. Not really. There was no mention of Tom Carr by name, much less any mention of where he had worked. The way it was written, Denton could tell an inexperienced writer had put the follow-up piece together, which meant the editor didn't plan on spending any more inches on the story.

God I was a bad man, thought Denton, smiling happily to himself as he remembered his little chat with the dying Tom Carr. *A bad, bad man—I'm gonna go straight to hell for that one.*

Then he laughed.

"What's funny, Dad?" asked Nicky Junior.

"Nothing, kiddo," said Denton. "Just something funny that happened at the office. Hey, and don't slurp your cereal; you know better," he said without looking up from the paper, still smiling but coming back down to earth, thinking about what he was going to do with the remaining members of Acrobat.

"Why?" asked Nicky Junior.

"Why what?" said Denton, forgetting about Acrobat for the moment.

"Why can't I slurp my cereal?"

"Because it's bad manners."

"So?"

"So you have to have good manners," said Denton sensibly.

"But why?" asked his son, slurping a spoonful extra loudly, just to be annoying.

"Because if you don't have good manners," said Denton, without missing a beat or looking up from the paper, "your mother and I will be forced to give you away to the circus."

Nicky Junior stopped slurping his cereal. He stared at his father, as did Claire. Even Artie snapped out of his morning daze.

Denton continued, as if he didn't notice his three children staring bug-eyed at him. "We had to do it with the other Nicky Junior, the one we had to get rid of before you were born? He was a good boy, a very good little boy, but *he* slurped his cereal, *too*. So-o-o-o . . . the circus came? And they took him away. We never heard from him again—*ever*."

The three children stared at their daddy in horrified awe. Only the sound of Jane casually frying eggs interrupted the silence wreaked by this hideous new revelation: Another Nicky Junior! Sent to the circus (the *circus,* is there anyplace scarier than the *circus?*) for slurping his cereal! Dad in on it (of course he was in on it, he had to be the mastermind behind it!), but Mommy in on it *too!* And any one of us might be *next!*

"Hymc!" squeaked Claire, clapping her hands to her mouth.

Denton nodded ruefully without looking away from the paper.

Artie leaned forward, touching his daddy's arm. "Really?" he whispered cautiously.

Denton looked at his middle, most-loved son, a smooth smile on his lips, his eyes narrowed and deadly.

"No," he said.

Artie sighed, as if he'd just dodged the biggest bullet in the world.

"You be*lieved* him, you *dope!*" yelped Nicky Junior, cackling and, in his frightened, relieved excitement, dribbling Cheerios all down his chin.

"Wow," said Artie, holding his enormous seven-year-old

head with his tiny seven-year-old hands, "the circus."

"Oh-h-h-h!!!" wailed Claire, making angry little fists and looking up at the ceiling, as if asking God to give her strength.

"You are such a *dope!*" said Nicky Junior, laughing at his dreamy younger brother.

"Shut up," said Artie, annoyed and promptly deciding to go back to his daydreaming.

Claire stood up on the nook bench and walked behind her brothers to her daddy, throwing her arms around his neck like a little Miss Faust bargaining with a minor Devil.

"Why do you have to lie to us all the time?" she asked seriously, rubbing her smooth cheek against his sandpaper one.

"Because the three of you are so gullible," said Denton, thinking about Acrobat as he unconsciously put an arm around Claire's little body. "You three are *so* gullible," he repeated.

"Yeah," said Claire, nodding in agreement. Then she perked up. "What's that mean?" she asked brightly.

" 'Gullible'?" asked Denton, glancing at Claire as he turned a page of the paper. "It's when someone believes everything they're told, without question. Like you guys," he said, looking at his sons as Claire clung to his neck. "You are so gullible."

"I didn't believe you," said Nicky Junior, shaking his head wisely, nine years old and proud of it.

"I believed you," said Artie, a startlingly frank and honest little boy.

"Gulliver," said Claire, trying to remember the word.

"Gullible," Denton corrected, picking up his coffee cup and taking a sip.

He suddenly realized that if he let them go, the Acrobat work-group would try to kill him if they had half a chance.

"Claire, your eggs," said Jane, the housekeeper, a fortyish black woman from Martinique. A little sheepishly, Denton had had the Personnel Office at Langley compile a dossier on her before they'd hired her, just before Claire had been born; she'd checked out.

Claire wandered over to her place at the table, passing behind Artie and Nicky Junior before sitting down. Quickly, she began gobbling up her fried eggs that were almost raw, they were so runny.

"Comment peut-elle bouffer çà, je ne comprend pas," said Jane.

"Elle a l'estomac en béton," groused Denton, making Jane laugh. Denton had an ulcerous stomach and an insipid diet to match.

"Hmm?" asked Claire, feeling herself watched.

"How can you eat that?" Denton asked her as he leaned on the table and stared at his daughter, thinking how easy it would be for Acrobat to get at her.

Claire hunched her shoulders as she munched on her eggs and a sliver of toast, having no idea why she liked her eggs runny but knowing that she did.

Denton nodded thoughtfully in return, calm, all sorts of images coming into his head: Images of his children killed because of revenge.

Abruptly, Denton suddenly decided that it would be best to get his family as far away from him as he could, until the whole Acrobat thing blew over.

"Claire, eat with your mouth closed, hmm baby?" said Denton automatically, picking up the paper once again and feeling much more at ease now that he had made up his mind.

"Okay Daddy," said Claire, chewing with her mouth closed for two bites before forgetting her resolve.

The three Denton children sat quietly eating at the breakfast nook as Jane made them their lunches. Idly, Denton began to watch them over the top edge of the newspaper.

Nicky Junior was his mother, without question—a big, jocky, happy little boy. From his looks to his personality, he was his mother, through and through.

Artie, though, was an odd, worrisome hybrid: Artie had his father's looks but his paternal grandfather's disposition—soft and gentle, dreamy and impractical, yet kind and thoughtful. Denton could see that, like his own father, Artie would be a weak man—a man who would inspire great love in all the people around him, but weak.

Claire, however, wouldn't be weak. Even though she

wasn't quite five years old, Denton could tell. Claire looked like her mother on the outside, but on the inside, she was just like him. She could walk and talk and chew gum at the same time. She could take care of herself.

Thinking about his parents, Denton suddenly had an idea to get rid of his family.

"How would you guys like to go see Gramma and Grandpa in Maine this weekend?" Denton suddenly asked his children.

They all looked at him in stunned, comical surprise, not sure if he was teasing or really serious.

"No fooling," he told them. "The real deal."

"Yeah!!" they all said.

"Can we take Sinatra with us—?"

"Can we go in the lake—?"

"Can I bring Missy—?"

Suddenly, like a tornado, Denton's wife appeared—Karen.

"Aren't you all ready? I'm ready, how come you're not done with your breakfast? Jane, why aren't they done with their breakfast, I have a million things to do, and I can't have you guys being late *again,* understand? Artie quit dawdling and finish up your breakfast, Nicholas, why aren't you ready for the office—where's your jacket?—are you gonna wear *that* tie?—it's too bright; you look like a pimp!—"

"What's a pimp?" asked Claire.

"When you're older," said Karen.

"A pimp's a guy who sells crack," said Nicky Junior knowledgeably.

"Nicky, be quiet—Am I the *only* one who's ready?—Janey, where's my coffee?"

"Here it is, Mrs. Denton," said Jane, handing her a mug of coffee as she and Denton and the kids threw out a net of looks between them.

"Thanks Janey, you're my hero," said Karen as she drank the coffee without bothering to blow it cool, oblivious to the looks passing between the others.

"Mommy's crazy!" Artie whispered to his dad.

Denton nodded like it was a lamentable fact he'd grown used to, then turned back to the paper.

Karen was a very tall woman. In fact, she was taller than her husband by about an inch or so, and if truth be told, she weighed somewhat more than Denton did too. But she wasn't fat, just very, very big, with a shapely figure and long, thick, auburn hair that she wore loose and free. In college, she had captained the field hockey team for three years, until her senior year, when she'd switched to squash so she could be nearer to the casually cruel young man who was now sitting in her kitchen, reading the morning paper.

"Gimme a kiss," she told her husband suddenly and possessively, quickly walking toward him and leaning down.

Denton looked up from the paper and obliged, Karen nipping on his lower lip just a bit.

Denton frowned, then looked back at the paper.

"Daddy says we can go to Maine this weekend!" said Claire in her piping little voice, Denton glancing at his daughter and, in that glance, suddenly seeing her little body made black and blue, pale from death, her eyes open and pleading as she lay on a morgue's table.

Acrobat, thought Denton.

"What?" yelled Karen, looking at her husband. *"Maine?"*

"I'm swamped with work. Why don't you guys all fly up for the weekend?" said Denton without looking up. "Even Jane could go along, if she wants to."

"I'd love to," said Jane, in her lilting Caribbean accent.

"Are you crazy?" Karen asked loud as hell, her booming voice filling the kitchen. "We can't go this weekend, we have *plans,* for God's sake, or did you forget? Saturday? The barbecue at the McIntoshes? We have blown them off *twice* already!"

"So we'll blow them off again," said Denton casually. "I can't make it anyway; I've got a mess at the office."

"Rh-*Rh!*" Karen growled, drinking her coffee as she stomped around the kitchen.

"How about it if you guys went up this afternoon, hmm?" said Denton easily, in his mind's eye seeing Karen's face split in two—one side perfect, the other side ripped apart by a bullet hole.

"Are you crazy!" she shouted, flapping her free arm over her husband and children, her coffee sloshing in its mug and nearly spilling over, outraged. "We can't go today! They'd miss school tomorrow!"

"Yeay!!" said the three kids in unison.

"You be quiet," she told the kids.

Denton smiled, closing the paper and imagining his family all dead, each of them lying on a brushed-steel slab in some morgue as he stood over each of them in turn, looking down at them as he identified their bodies one by one.

I've got to put the tag on Acrobat, he thought, nodding to himself.

"We can't go today, or even tomorrow," Karen was saying. "They'll all miss a day of school and then they'll have to make it up, and on top of *that,* we have *plans* for the weekend, Nicholas! We can't just run off like we live on a permanent vacation, we have to . . ."

Amalia shouldn't deal with Acrobat, Denton thought as he nodded and smiled at his wife. *She could be traced to me,* he thought, mentally wincing at this inevitable corollary. *And Atta-boy's people are as subtle as a stampede.*

". . . it's not as if somebody else can do our chores for us," Karen was saying, speaking to the kids as much as to Denton, trying to convince this unruly band of revolutionaries to stick with the program.

"Awww*wwwWWW*, Mo-*om!*" the guerrillas began to groan.

"No!" said Karen—then suddenly turning on Denton himself. "Nicholas, are you listening to me?" she asked.

"Yes of course I'm listening," he said automatically, thoughtfully frowning as a vague image from his past strained to surface in his mind—something important.

Karen looked at him and the kids suspiciously. "I want you all to understand why we're not going to Maine today—it's a good idea, it sounds like fun, but we have a lot of responsibilities we have to take care of. Life isn't all fun and games!"

"Yes of course," said Denton, nodding as he thought to himself, *Maybe I should just leave it all up to Atta-boy, you know he's good, you know he won't stop until he's put them down, but what's this idea that's bubbling up here? What's this . . . ?*

Suddenly Denton remembered an old T-shirt he'd had in college, a T-shirt with a simple, clever little motto:

DON'T DO IT!!!
(GET SOMEBODY ELSE TO DO IT FOR YOU!)

Denton blinked and frowned and then suddenly smiled.

DON'T TAG ACROBAT!!! . . . *Get the* FBI *to do it for you!*

"Nicholas!"

"Mmm?" said Denton, stoned on his own idea . . . and seven-year-old Artie looked at him with a kindred nod, his father's son.

"I'm trying to be the adult here," Karen was saying. "Help me!"

Denton looked at his wife, those big brown doubtful eyes staring back at him, her face open to anyone who'd care to read it: Listen to me, listen to me, won't you please please listen to me?

Denton winked and blew her a kiss.

Karen blushed, feeling literally weak at the knees, as if she'd been struck on the head with a hammer.

Denton patted his thighs and reached for Karen, pulling her toward him until she was forced to sit on his lap.

"Nichola-a-as . . . ," she whined, everyone in the kitchen knowing she was about to lose.

"Maine's beautiful right now," said Denton softly, looking up at his wife with a calculating eye as he held her around her waist. "I'm swamped at the office, but I think it would be a terrific idea if you all went."

"It's a *rotten* idea," said Karen, trying to recover.

"No it isn't," he said.

And then—ruthlessly and without mercy—he used her love for him to get her to do what he wanted.

Bart Michaelus was sitting in his office, alone, doing administrivia.

If someone had been watching him, they would have been struck by how Michaelus attacked the paperwork he was doing, almost as if the pages of documents were slippery little beasts he had to attack and decimate. His pen flashed over the material, paragraphs crossed out, writings in the margins, signatures dashed off in hurried, almost spastic motions. His face, grim and set, glared down at the documents as if he found this paper-butchery distasteful but necessary, and queerly attractive in a sickening sort of way. His thick arms rubbed the edges of his glass desk, his foot kept tap-tap-tapping like a Morse code operator's signaling stylus, his gold fountain pen restlessly flashed sparks of sunlight as it left a trail of blue ink.

Bart Michaelus was deep into the long slide.

No one was coming into his office today. Ever since Acrobat had gone underground, Michaelus's office had been mausoleum-quiet, the phones as inanimate as rocks, the E-mail mostly spam and flyers. Out in the hallways around Langley, it was no better, to the point where even the CIA Director, Christopher Farnham, the fucking toad, kept smiling and walking away whenever they ran into each other, tossing off a hurried "I gotta run!" grin as he practically bolted away. Denton's whisper campaign had gotten to the point where Michaelus was too afraid to eat in the executive mess hall at Langley—afraid he'd wind up sitting and eating alone. And he would have, too. Even when he got out of his car this morning and walked to the elevator, even as he stepped in along with all the other people arriving to work, he could feel it—people giving him a wide berth as they let him slide.

The long slide out. O-U-T: Out.

Michaelus finished with one set of papers, then turned to another, furiously scribbling and scratching away at the snow-white documents, waiting for his phone to ring, waiting for Roy Livre at the FBI to call.

It wasn't as if Acrobat was common knowledge. Maybe eight or ten people were in the know, if that. But somehow, this core group—Farnham, Denton, Atmajian, Phyllis Strathmore, Kurt Wenger, a couple of others—had all let it be known around Langley that Bart Michaelus was sliding. Just this one little group, this one little circle that truly ran CIA—a group Michaelus himself had belonged to: This handful of people had arbitrarily decided to let him go.

And so he was out.

Oh how Michaelus would have loved to have his people go out there and grab Acrobat. Bart Michaelus ran the Operations Directorate, the operational arm of Central Intelligence—he wasn't some little daisy, crouched paralyzed and petrified as the tornado bore down on him: No sir. Bart Michaelus had power, real power, power that counted—he had the power to make changes in the physical world. Under his direct supervision, he had 120 covert operatives around the world—the scary kind of covert operatives; the kind that didn't fuck around. Michaelus would have given *anything* to cut his people loose on this problem, have them out there strewn across the country, looking for Acrobat.

Only problem was, Bart Michaelus didn't dare order any of his people to so much as fart. With all eyes on him, if he crossed the line even a little bit, he'd be in Fort Leavenworth by sundown.

"Fucking . . . mother*fucking*—cocksuckers!" Bart Michaelus mumbled, ripping through more paperwork, waiting for Roy Livre's call, the nib of his pen writing on the papers so hard that his glass desk made tinkling sounds like a drumstick rapping on a bell jar.

Roy Livre at the FBI was all he had left. Yesterday, after Denton (motherfucking *Denton*) had told him it was time to take a bite out of that shit sandwich, Michaelus had called FBI Director Roy Livre. CIA does not call FBI, not if they can help it, but everyone at Langley was turning away from him, so what the hell else was he gonna do? Call Santa Claus?

So he called Roy Livre.

And what had happened? The motherfucker wouldn't take his call! The motherfucking Feebie fuck had his secretary take a message!

So—seething—*furious*—wanting above all else to rip Livre's head off his scrawny little shoulders and shit down his *neck!*— . . . Michaelus had politely left a fucking message.

Then this morning—against all his better judgment—he couldn't help it—he had called Roy Livre again. . . .

. . . and again he hadn't been there, according to his secretary. Again Livre had been avoiding his call. Again Michaelus had made a fool of himself.

Michaelus wasn't a dummy; he'd been around. How many times had he seen someone slide out. How many times had he seen people thrash and yell and go berserk, trying to stop the slide. Michaelus *knew* that the harder you tried to stop the slide, the faster you slid. He *knew* it—and yet still, he couldn't help himself. He still couldn't stop convulsing, even as he knew that that would just accelerate his fall.

"Mother*fucker!*" Michaelus shouted out loud, grabbing his gold fountain pen and throwing it point first onto his glass desk, the nib snapping off and expelling blue ink all over the place, almost as if the desk with all these administrivia papers had been shot and were now bleeding royal blue blood.

"Fuck!" he shouted out loud, stopped stunned as he watched the blue ink roll across all his papers.

Then he reacted, getting up and going to his private bathroom, grabbing a roll of paper towels and returning to sop up all the blue ink. Except for his grunted, mumbled curses and the squeak of glass as he cleaned the desk, there wasn't a sound in his cavernous office.

More or less around the time Bart Michaelus was making his glass desk bleed blue, Nicholas Denton was in *his* office, playing The Game.

". . . I can't tell you that, just trust me, I know; Means & Methods and all that—I could tell you, but then I'd have to kill you, ha ha ha ha ha, just kidding, Margaret, just kidding . . ."

He paced around his conservative office with no particular direction, a telephone headset strapped to his skull, a gray sponge-covered microphone an inch from his lips. His suit jacket was off, his shirt eerily white, his tie (not the pimp tie; a different one) loose. In the background, the first movement of Smetana's *The Moldau* was playing, program music mimicking the flow of the Moldau River through the forests of Hungary.

"Okay . . . Okay . . . No, I can't tell you that, but I'm telling you: These bank-robbing creeps you're after . . . Okay . . . Okay . . ."

There was a gentle knock at the door, and then it opened a crack. Matthew Wilson, one of Denton's closest people, peeked his head inside. Denton waved him in as he continued talking.

"No, look, I'm not going to have this discussion: The poop is accurate, and that ought to be fair enough. . . ." Denton sighed. "Margaret, do you really think I'd send you on some goose chase?"

Wilson sat down in one of the armchairs in Denton's office, a couple of manila folders in his hands. Though dressed cautiously enough, Wilson looked like a twenty-something mass murderer: He was huge, and his sideburns were just a bit too long, too white-trashy, too felony-convict-out-on-bail-before-he-starts-his-twenty-five-years-to-life sentence. But looks deceived: For all his bad-ass aura, Goldilocks could've beat him up.

But then again, Wilson wasn't around for any kind of strong-arm goon stuff. Wilson was Denton's pooper-scooper—a guy who could hack his way to any information.

". . . Okay? Okay . . . Alright . . . That's right . . . I'll be rooting for you, Margaret. Good-bye."

Denton pressed the "hold" button on his telephone system, which was sitting on his desk beside three huge Rolodex spindles.

". . . Hey, you there? Sorry, someone I had to touch base with. So anyway, I can't *believe* the motherfucker had the balls to go do it, but he left me no choice, so what's a dirty white boy like me supposed to do . . . ?"

As he spoke Wilson raised the manila folders he had in hand to get his boss's attention. But Denton shook his head as he started flipping through one of the three Rolodex spindles, each spindle easily holding five hundred cards, perhaps even more. Denton looked through the cards in no rush, bullshitting away all the while.

". . . Oh you know it, my brother, you know it—! Hang on I got another call, hang on hang on hang on."

Denton hit the "hold" button and started dialing a new number.

"Denton here. . . . Hey, yeah, I wanted to talk to you about that. . . . No no no no, yeah, I know it sounds like that, but no, Acrobat's all coming down to D.C., for sure. . . . Do I know? Of course I know, what do you take me for. . . . Okay. . . . Okay. . . . Okay, good, g'bye."

Denton's fingers found another address card in another one of the spindles. He was looking at the address card even as he pressed the "hold" button on his phone system.

"Melissa? I'm yapping with Arthur about some pressing administrivia, mind holding on for just a couple more? You're a doll."

Denton hit the "hold" button then pressed the other line button.

"Johnny-boy: This dirty white boy's got to boogie on down the highway. . . . A'right. Give my love to your wife and my kids. . . . Ha! Ha! Ha! Ha! That's a good one. Later, goon."

Denton hit the line button.

"Melissa, dahling . . . Oh hush, you know that you'll only end up doing what I want. . . . No. . . . No. . . . No . . . ," Denton tsked. "You're so sexy when you're angry. . . . *Me!* Oh that is so *not* true. . . . That— . . . *Oooohhh!* I'm gonna tell Karen on you, I swear!—hang on a second, hang on, I've got another call."

Denton hit the "hold" button and began dialing another number.

"Is this FBI Director Livre's office? It's Nicholas Denton from Central Intelligence calling . . ."

Matthew Wilson blinked, wondering what his boss was doing, calling up the FBI.

Denton caught the look and just smiled and shook his head, as if to say, "Na-a-a-ahhhh . . ."

"Director Livre? Hi, it's Nicholas Denton. . . . Yes, I know that. . . . I see. . . . I wouldn't exactly call it an electronic *bomb*. . . . I can imagine the havoc it caused, but you're bark—er, bawling out the wrong guy. Acrobat's activities were under Michaelus's supervision: He's the one responsible for all this. . . . I see. . . . I see. . . . Well, yes, they *did* break into Skunk Works, and you're right: They *have* run amok. That's why I'm calling you. I have some information you might find useful: Acrobat will be at the Pentagon City food court today at noon."

Matthew Wilson's jaw dropped. *Wha?* was all his mind could get around to spelling out, Wilson completely blown away by his boss's casual knowledge.

Denton, seeing his subordinate's surprise, grinned and winked.

"I can't tell you how I know, I just do. . . . I just got off the phone with Margaret Chisholm—she's the point person for this manhunt, am I right . . . ? No. . . . No of course not. . . . Roy, I don't mean to be rude, but think: Would I be fool enough to pass along information I wasn't a hundred percent on? Make myself look like Peter crying 'Wolf'?"

Denton began flipping through one of his spindles, looking at cards, getting to the one he wanted with all the leisurely grace of a royal making tea.

". . . How do I know? I bought this wickedly good crystal ball—I'm working it as we speak. I'm about to ask it for this week's lotto numbers."

Denton winked at Wilson.

"I'm being flip, I'm sorry, but Director Livre, look: You put me in an impossible situation. I know where Acrobat is going to be, so I've told you and your special-agent-in-charge. If you ask me *how* I know this information, I will *not* tell you. I will not and cannot compromise my sources. If you think I'm giving you bullshit poop, fine, so be it. Tomorrow we'll get a D.C. judge to subpoena the security tapes at the Pentagon City shopping center. If Acrobat isn't on the tapes, then you can call me liar-liar-pants-on-fire to my face. But if Acrobat *is* on those tapes, then, well, I'm not going to be looking so foolish, now am I?"

Wilson sat very still in his armchair, watching his boss as he spoke on the phone, Denton staring off into space as he paced around his office.

"Yes. . . . Yes of course. . . . So Margaret Chisholm will arrest the Acrobat people . . . ? Good, excellent, I . . . Yes, well, good, thanks, fine, I'm glad you see it that way. . . . Okay. . . . Yes, I'd enjoy that, I'll see you then. . . . Looking forward to it. Good-bye."

Denton hit the "hold" button, motioned Wilson for the documents he had in hand, and continued talking as he flipped through the manila folders.

"Melissa, you still there? Oh honey-bunny, you're the sweetest, the most patient woman I know—when are you and me gonna have a torrid affair, huh . . . ?"

Denton talked to four other people by the time he got through signing the papers Wilson had brought him. All the while, Wilson just sat there, staring at his boss with wide-eyed awe. *A Zen fucking master,* he was thinking. *A black belt in the art of babble.*

Smetana's *Moldau* continued to play, music with a sound like the inevitability of a destined end.

FBI Special Agent-in-Charge Margaret Chisholm was on the third floor of the Pentagon City shopping mall, looking down at the food court below. She stood five feet, seven inches in her low-heeled sandals, casually dressed in a saffron blouse and matching tan jacket and slacks that complemented her long, curly, fiery red hair. She stood leaning over the guardrail, casually looking around, and by her clothes, her look, and her demeanor, she came across as a forty-year-old suburban housewife, busy killing her morning at the modern-day amusement park known as the mall. . . .

She checked her watch and looked over the food court below, spotting the nine men and women of her arrest team. Her long and curly red hair was loose and thick, cascading down to her shoulders, perfectly concealing her ear-piece receiver, the wire of which slithered down the back of her blouse to the radio pack strapped to her waist. Right next to the radio pack was a huge 45-caliber revolver, also strapped to her waist, both items hidden under the long and loose linen jacket she wore. Unlike Tobey Jansen, Margaret Chisholm always hit what she aimed for with that revolver.

She was half an hour away from putting Acrobat down.

"Red Girl here," she said softly into her transmitter, tucked by her throat, inside her blouse. "Gimme a comm check."

"Position one, check."

"Position two, check."

"Position three, check . . ."

From the word go, she knew this arrest was a mistake. Chisholm had worked at the FBI for close to fifteen years—six of them as Deputy Director Mario Rivera's in-house troubleshooter. She knew better than anybody how tough it was to arrest more than one person in a crowd. One lone suspect was no problem, really—surround, contain, arrest. But five suspects? Five *armed* suspects? Five armed *bank-robbery* suspects—in the middle of a cloud of civilians? Awful things could happen.

But even arresting five bank robbers wasn't enough to make Margaret Chisholm think twice. What was giving her major heebie-jeebies was the thought that she was about to arrest five people involved in CIA shit. And she knew it was CIA shit. She knew it because her old pal Nicholas Denton had told her so in his own inimitably subtle/blatant style.

"Hello Margaret, how long has it been!" he had said when she picked up the phone in her office earlier this morning.

"Uh-oh," she answered when she recognized his voice, having no idea what he wanted but automatically knowing it would probably be bad.

Margaret and Denton went way back, but that didn't mean they liked each other. Or perhaps it would be fairer to say that Chisholm knew that Denton liked her very much, but Margaret also knew that if she ever got in his way, Denton would not hesitate to turn her into a grease spot on the road.

"How are you? How's Robert?" he asked pleasantly.

"What do you want," she answered right back, staring at her desk, trying to contain the mild disgust she felt when Denton mentioned her son's name, queerly identifying his happy tone with the bright and shiny voice of a friendly neighborhood pederast.

"You're heading the task force looking to get those bankrobbing creeps, is that right?"

Oh no, don't tell me this is your gig, she wanted to say, suddenly just *knowing* that the New York bank robbers she'd been assigned to as a priority effort were no bank robbers at all, but some CIA screw up. Why else would he call, if it wasn't a CIA screw up?

Why is he calling me? she suddenly wondered.

" 'Bank-robbing creeps,' I should've known," she baited him, hoping to draw him out. "You've got a band of your people out without a hall pass, huh?"

But Nicholas Denton was an old hand at ignoring the inconvenient. "Guess what?" he had said. "They'll be at the Pentagon City mall today, at noon, down by the food court. One of them, a woman, is wounded; she might not be there. But all of the others will. If you're lucky, you might just catch them in time."

Right after that, he'd hung up, and right after *that*, Roy Livre, the FBI Director himself, had called and told her in no uncertain terms to get her ass down to Pentagon City and arrest the "bank robbers" on sight.

"But I want them *arrested*, Agent Chisholm," Roy Livre had said. "No shoot-outs, no *High Noon* heroics. Arrested and in custody in one piece."

"Yes sir," she'd said.

So ninety minutes later, here she was, watching over a whole phalanx of Bureau agents as they waited for the "bank robbers" to show up.

It was no accident that Livre had emphasized the arrest-and-custody stuff. A few months ago, the Disciplinary Review Board had flagged her jacket because someone had happened to notice that, of all her attempts at arresting suspects in the past six years, only 40 percent had actually been taken into custody.

That did not mean that the other 60 percent had gotten away from her. It meant that the other 60 percent had been shot by her.

"Do the best you can, Maggie," her boss, Mario Rivera, told her. "These guys we're dealing with: Armed to the teeth, for sure—but we need to crack their skulls open. We need them in one piece."

"This is like a whole CIA thing, isn't it?" Margaret said dimly.

Mario—her boss but also a close friend—sighed and looked away before turning back to Margaret with a pained look on his face. "Watch yourself, Maggie," was all he said.

Margaret Chisholm looked up at her mountain of a boss. "Is this a CIA operations group?" she asked.

Mario didn't answer.

"Is it?"

Mario blinked like a nodded yes.

"Jesus Christ," said Chisholm.

"One of them used to be Special Forces."

Margaret scoffed. "*Jee*-sus . . ."

"I think another one of them is an accountant, though," Mario said vaguely.

"What about the others?" Margaret asked. "Are they accountants or SF?"

"The others might be tough," Rivera admitted.

Margaret Chisholm winced and shook her head as she turned away, furious at what she'd just been handed.

"Maggie, you've handled worse," said Rivera. "Put them down as best you can. Handle this with just Bureau people— no cops running around, screwing things up. No more Times Squares. Go down there; get them back alive."

"I'll try," Margaret had mumbled.

"Try hard," Mario had warned her.

Margaret Chisholm wasn't too happy about how quickly this was happening. Her people were good, but they hadn't had the time to plan out exactly how they were going to take down the "bank robbers."

She had no doubt that they would show up, though. One thing about Denton, he would never embarrass himself with inaccurate poop. The only question was, exactly how did Nicholas Denton, of all people, fit into this whole thing?

And why had he called?

To warn you, silly—to warn you what to expect, she suddenly realized, knowing that Roy Livre would never have told her how dangerous and resourceful these people could turn out to be. Nor would Mario Rivera, for that matter.

Margaret Chisholm let her thumbs fiddle with each other as she looked down at the food court below, leaning her elbows on the gleaming brass railing, spotting her people.

The architecture of Pentagon City was rather interesting. Rather than being simply a long, rectangular mall, Pentagon City was shaped like a fat *L*, upscale department stores anchoring the building on either end, large skylights letting in the sun from the ceiling. What with the sunlight and the white marble floor and the tall ceilings, the shopping center had a heightened sense of space, the hallways vast and open enough for a half-dozen suburban moms behind strollers to walk abreast.

At the vertice of the *L* of the shopping center, though, all the upper floors gave way to balcony halls that wrapped around the ground-floor space below. On that ground-floor space, there was a food court, lined with different fast-food restaurants that had been gussied up to look a little better than a typical fast-food outlet, Pentagon City being one of those more upscale shopping centers, where the crowd was white and Asian and Jewish and suburban and young enough to need all sorts of things that really weren't all that necessary for a happy life. In a way, Pentagon City was a crackhouse of consumer goods, happy addicts crawling all over the place looking for another comfy fix.

As she looked down on the food court below, Margaret was surprised at the late-morning Thursday crowd. Not being one to ordinarily visit a mall except on a weekend, it amazed her that there were so many people sitting at the food court, eating their early lunches and chatting together. Looking at the crowd, she spotted no office types, only people dressed casually, in pairs and groupings of three mostly, almost no one walking alone.

She wondered what secrets they each held—what secrets glued them to each other. Looking down at the people flowing like corpuscles through veins and arteries into the single-chamber heart of the mall, she wondered what connective tissue was between these people loitering and shopping away the day. Common interests? Convenience? Simple liking? A desire—or perhaps a *need*—for company? An inability to be alone? Margaret had no idea. In her life, the only connection she had with the people around her was the common purpose of an arrest, or the love she felt for her son. But as all mothers know, a mother's love is as unbalanced and one-sided as a grown-up and a child sitting on either end of a seesaw.

With an arrest, though, there were responsibilities that ran both ways.

Clicking the nails of her fingers against each other, looking down at all her agents scattered throughout the crowd in the food court below, Margaret made up her mind how it was going to be.

"This is Red Girl," she said into her microphone. "Listen up."

The chatter ceased, all her people waiting for what she was about to say, all of them instinctively looking up to where she stood on the balcony.

Margaret sighed.

"If things start to happen," she said carefully, "do not hesitate. Did you all hear what I just said? I'll say it again: Do—not—hesitate. If things look like they could go either way, put them down and put them down hard. Because these people won't think twice."

Her arrest team didn't say a thing to this.

"Any second now," she said. "Look sharp."

Margaret Chisholm turned and walked to the escalator that would take her down.

CHAPTER 7

Thursday Noon at Pentagon City

About twenty minutes later, at 11:50 A.M., Tobey Jansen, Duncan Idaho, and Monika Summers arrived via Metro.

The Washington Metro system has beyond question the spookiest stations around. The roof is a gentle arch of prefabricated concrete slabs in a waffle design, perfect for sucking out the sounds of clattering shoes and approaching trains. The lights don't hang from the roof, but rather, rails of fluorescent light tubes are recessed against the far side of the tracks, casting an indirect light that makes all the stations seem *dark,* even though there is enough light to read by. The platform, covered in red hexagonal tiles, runs between the two tracks, glass and chrome electric escalators connecting the platform to the footbridge above. What with the darkness and the muffled sounds, the train tracks like moats and the curving, gray concrete ceiling that looks as if it were cut out of living rock, every Metro station in Washington looks and feels like a medieval dragon's cave, complete with attendant monsters and goblins lurking in the shadows.

When Tobey, Duncan, and Monika got out of the train, they instinctively looked up and down the platform, looking around. Monika looked to see where the exit was, Tobey to see if he happened to spot Russell and Ljubica, and Duncan to see if there was anyone to worry about.

"Over there," said Monika, the three of them walking to the electric escalator going to the footbridge up above, the station filled with the hollow sound of voices and shoes rebounding on the red hexagonal tiles.

They went up the escalator to the footbridge level, and then through the turnstiles, which gave way to a wide, vaguely circular area that narrowed onto an enormous hallway. The enormous hallway had a ceiling a good forty feet high, the blank gray walls on either side making Tobey feel as if they were part of Moses's gang crossing the Red Sea to safety.

At the end of the enormous hallway, there were a pair of glass doors, the words WELCOME TO PENTAGON CITY! stenciled in green. Just past these double glass doors, there were two short electric escalators running not quite a full floor up. Once through the glass doors and up the electric escalator, they found themselves directly in the Pentagon City shopping center, a smoky and dark-looking sit-down restaurant to their left, a photo film-processing store to their right, the food court in the distance, directly in front of them, about twenty yards away.

They walked the distance in silence, looking around. At the edge of the food court, they stopped, next to an upright map of the shopping center.

"Let's reconnoiter," said Duncan, motioning to Tobey with his chin to take the left side of the food court, Monika and Duncan himself going to the right, the three of them encircling the tables of the food court.

Tobey dawdled a bit as he passed the fast-food restaurants on the left of the food court. None of them had eaten all day, so he couldn't help slowing down and debating whether he should get something quick to go.

He looked to the left, at the various food chains—McDonald's, Sbarro, Panda—then to his right, out over the food court and the potted plants that girdled it on the opposite side—

—and stopped.

Standing beside a potted tree, on the periphery of the food court, a man and a woman were looking at a map, both of them dressed in tourist's uniforms: khaki shorts and Polo shirts. The couple were in their very early thirties, both of them wearing sunglasses to shield their eyes from the glare coming through the skylights directly above.

Something about the pair's look reminded Tobey of Ljubica and Russell—the man was as big and tall as Russell, about six five or so, and the woman was just as thin and pale, with the same straight hair. The only difference was, of course, that Russell was not black, like the khaki shorts man, but rather lighter, café au lait; and Ljubica was much prettier than the khaki shorts woman. So as Tobey's eyes dismissed the Khaki Shorts Couple as tourists who happened to look a lot like Russ and Ljubica, his eyes passed over a thin black man wearing a mall sanitation uniform.

The thin black man had on a single-piece, green jumpsuit with red piping running down the length of it, and he was looking intensely at the Khaki Shorts Couple. The thin black man was mouthing words, as if he were speaking, but there was no one around to hear him. And though the black man in the green jumpsuit was thin, his waist bulged, as if he had something under his uniform, like a tumor, or a weapon.

"Holy shit," said Tobey softly amid the murmur of all the other shoppers, looking at the thin black man as he continued walking.

Saying the words out loud must have made a psychic impression on the thin black man in the green jumpsuit, because all of a sudden he turned and looked directly at Tobey, their eyes locking across the twenty yards and the dozen tables that separated them.

Tobey stood frozen, directly in front of a Sbarro sandwich shop, as conspicuous as a frozen deer.

The thin black man in the green jumpsuit was looking straight at Tobey, and they suddenly both recognized each other.

Go! Tobey screamed at himself. *Go-go-go-go-g—*

Resisting every impulse, Tobey did not turn around and run away. Instead, he faked casual as best he could and looked around him, thinking, looking around and trying to *see*, trying to see the way Duncan had taught him to see.

Where he stood, in front of a Sbarro sandwich shop, people

were patiently waiting to purchase lunch, maybe a half-dozen real people in line. Looking at them, Tobey reached into his sweatshirt's pockets and made a claw with his right hand, bulking up the empty pocket, making it look as if he were grasping something—like a gun. Then he looked directly at the thin, black man in the green jumpsuit.

The thin black man looked like something inside him had clicked. His right hand still holding a broom, with his left, he reached to unzip his jumpsuit, as if he were about to pull out a firearm of his own.

At the sight of that motion, Tobey shook his head almost imperceptibly, left, right: *Don't.* And as he shook his head, he pointed his empty hand at the person directly in front of him in the line, a morbidly fat young woman in an aquamarine shirt that covered her body like a tent.

Except for his lips, the thin black man froze, staring at Tobey as he spoke rapidly to seemingly no one at all.

Forty feet away, on the next floor up, Margaret heard the entire thing over the open channel as she quickly but incon-spicuously made her way to the electric escalator, the thin black man in the green sanitation uniform—Dan Sears, man-ning position two—telling the entire team that Tobey Jansen was armed and threatening a civilian as he stood in line to buy a sandwich at the Sbarro.

"There's too much background—I have no shot if you need back-up," Dan was saying, one of the very best young agents who, like all great FBI men, had a never-ending supply of patience and discipline.

"Maintain visual contact only, I'll handle back-up. Do not approach; do not give other positions away," said Margaret as she walked quickly to the top of the electric escalator leading her down. When she got to the escalator, she slowed down and put on her game face.

The electric escalator led from the second level to the ground floor, depositing its passengers at the very middle of the food court. So as the escalator carried her down, Margaret calmly surveyed the scene spread out in front of her.

To her right, she spotted Dan, at the one o'clock position.

He held a broom in one hand, which he was ineffectually moving around, his eyes shifting from the floor to Tobey Jansen to the couple in the khaki shorts. Tobey Jansen, to Margaret's left, at the ten o'clock position, seemed to have stopped breathing altogether. Looking at his hands in the pockets of his zip-up sweatshirt, they shifted slightly, and Margaret suddenly realized that the kid was bluffing—he had no firearm. *Perfect,* thought Margaret, figuring out how she was going to handle Tobey.

But what disturbed her was the couple—the couple in the khaki shorts and dark sunglasses.

As she floated down on the electric escalator, the man and woman in the khaki shorts and the dark sunglasses were standing just outside the food court proper, at Margaret's two o'clock position, a potted tree giving Dan cover, barely four yards away. The couple were looking at a fold-out map without a care in the world. The woman had a big canvas bag over her shoulder, the bag open, with God knew what inside it, while the man had a heavy banana waistpack that was open too, the flap concealing whatever might be within it.

Margaret decided that the Khaki Shorts Couple was the more imminent threat—once she had them under control, they could deal with Unarmed Goatee Boy.

"Forget about Goatee Boy, he's unarmed—keep focused on the Khaki Shorts Couple."

"Understood," said Dan, watching as Tobey Jansen stood there in line at the Sbarro.

Nearing the bottom of the electric escalator, Margaret said, "Position three and five, move in on the subjects laterally."

As she stepped off the electric escalator, she watched as positions three and five—Sandy Feldsen and Nick Barnes—approached the Khaki Shorts Couple.

Sandy was short, bald, bespectacled, and incredibly strong—on a bet, Margaret had once watched him bench press 385 pounds and not even work up a sweat. Nick, on the other hand, was a short, bearded marksman, hands down the best shot of her nine-man arrest team. Sandy and Nick could handle the Khaki Shorts Couple.

As per the signal, Sandy walked around the tables of the food court, bumping Dan and excusing himself, the signal that he had the ball.

"I got the ball," said Sandy into his transmitter, Dan turning all his attention back to Unarmed Goatee Boy.

Don't screw it up, thought Margaret, watching as Sandy and Nick moved in on the Khaki Shorts Couple.

They were coming at them from either side, both Sandy and Nick a mere three yards away from the Khaki Shorts Couple. All they had to do was—

At that exact moment, Khaki Shorts Couple replaced their map in the woman's bag, turned, and walked toward a store directly behind them, walking like they had a purpose—walking like they knew that Sandy Feldsen and Nick Barnes had been about to take them down.

"Wha-do-we-do, wha-do-we-do?" asked Sandy frantically.

Shit! thought Margaret, knowing they had to be either unbelievably good or unbelievably lucky to walk away at exactly the right moment—Sandy and Nick had to follow the couple into the store, which would expose them.

"Follow them," said Margaret as she stepped off the escalator and loitered by a freestanding map of the mall just to the left of the electric escalators, the exact same spot where Duncan, Monika, and Tobey had decided to split up. "But don't bring them down unless you're clear of background—these people will not hesitate," Margaret added carefully.

"Gotcha, Red Girl," said Sandy, as he and Barnes followed the Khaki Shorts Couple into a shoestore, looking conspicuous as all hell.

Shit, thought Margaret.

Meanwhile, Tobey only had eyes for Dan, the Sanitation Man, the two young men staring at each other like a mongoose and a snake, when it suddenly dawned on Tobey that if there was one, there might be twenty.

Just as he looked away from the thin black man, he noticed the couple of tourists in khaki shorts walking away into a shoestore behind them while two men—a short skinny guy and a short fat guy—followed them in.

¿? thought Tobey, confused and scared as it dawned on him that, for all he knew, everyone in sight might be police—or worse.

He decided he didn't want to wait around to find out.

Turning to his left and scanning the crowd of people milling about at the food court, Tobey spotted Duncan and Monika a good twenty yards away.

"Johnny!" he called out loudly across the food court—loudly, but casually. "Johnny, what do you want?!"

Duncan froze, recognizing Tobey's voice and turning around.

Margaret Chisholm stood next to the stationary map of the shopping center, looking as if she were studying it, the map giving her cover as she spotted a big blond kid, maybe twenty-eight, twenty-nine years old, wearing a leather jacket, standing frozen and looking back at Unarmed Goatee Boy. From experience, she knew that Big Biker Boy was *definitely* armed—he just had that look to him, somewhere between supreme self-confidence and wary knowledge—

(I bet he's the Special Forces guy.)

—a look that actually comforted Margaret. The look told her that Big Biker Boy wouldn't do anything foolish or panicky.

Tobey, meanwhile, oblivious of Margaret, shot another look at Dan, then at Duncan again. "Johnny, come on over, what do you wanna eat?" he called out again, tossing his head in a casual "Come here" gesture, careful not to relax the empty claws in his pockets.

Monika Summers just kept on walking, ignoring Duncan as he double backed over to Tobey, Margaret Chisholm not realizing who Monika was. All Chisholm was looking at was Big Biker Boy, a very, very dangerous subject.

Monika walked through the throng of people, panicking as she wondered what was happening, knowing that something had to be very wrong but not daring to look back at Duncan—not yet anyway.

"Don't go anywhere near Biker Boy," Margaret was saying into her transmitter as she kept an eye on Duncan. "He's all-

American; we don't wanna mess with him in the middle of a crowd."

Duncan walked directly up to Tobey, his face frozen, furious at him; then realizing by the look he was shooting that Tobey had spotted something.

When Duncan got to him, Tobey blurted out, "Don't look now, but there's a cop in a green jumpsuit across from me, directly behind you—green jumpsuit, late twenties, black, with a broom in his hand."

"What are you doing to keep him away?" Duncan asked, looking over Tobey's head and scanning the people milling in line at Sbarro's, his back to Dan Sears.

"I'm a pistolero," he said, making Duncan look down at Tobey's claws in his pockets.

"Good boy," he said.

"He's figuring I'm gonna do something," said Tobey more seriously.

"Even better."

With that, Duncan did a remarkable thing. Even Margaret was surprised. Duncan turned his back on Tobey, turning around and looking directly at Dan, getting his undivided attention. Then Duncan Idaho casually and assuredly reached behind his back, underneath his biker jacket.

Dan Sears nearly lost it. "He's going for—"

"No he's not," said Margaret firmly. "Do not panic, do not move, he's just making it clear he knows who you are."

And she was right. As soon as Duncan had his porcelain gun in his hand behind his back, he pivoted around, facing Tobey and way too close for polite company, his porcelain gun in hand, slipping it into the left-hand pocket of his leather jacket. Then he took a step away from Tobey, half facing both Tobey and Dan, twenty yards away, looking as if he were casually waiting in line with Tobey as he checked out the people in the food court—but Duncan still had his hand in his left pocket, clearly holding onto a gun.

"Are you ready to order?" the woman behind the counter at Sbarro asked them.

"Uh—" said Tobey.

"Two sub sandwiches, to go please," said Duncan without looking away from Dan, scanning around, looking for something—

He spotted her: Amid all the background, almost by pure chance, he spotted a red-haired woman in a tan linen suit, peeking her head out from behind a stand-alone map of the mall a dozen yards away, looking right at them.

"What kind of subs?" asked the teenaged girl behind the counter.

Duncan didn't hear her, so Tobey finally said, "Hero subs."

"Anything to drink with that?"

"Uh—no, just the heroes," said Tobey, so relieved that Duncan was there that he could have cried.

"No, we'll have two Cokes," said Duncan suddenly. "For here. Give it to us on a tray."

"We don't have Coke, only Pepsi," said the woman behind the counter.

"Then Pepsi, then," said Duncan.

"They're trying on penny-loafers," Margaret heard Sandy say into her ear.

What? she thought, then remembering—the Khaki Shorts Couple in the shoestore.

"Stay on them, Position three," she said, looking right back at Duncan Idaho and studying the triangle they made.

Margaret was at one vertice, Duncan and Tobey were at the other, Dan on the third. Between the three of them, about fifty people were sitting at the tables of the food court, everyone having lunch and completely oblivious to what was going on around them—or almost everybody.

She thought over her tactical position: Two of them were in the shoestore, and two of them in front of the Sbarro. The fifth? The second woman? Probably the wounded woman, probably not even here—okay: Margaret decided right then and there that she was going to go for them.

"Positions four and six, spot Biker Boy and Goatee Boy," said Margaret, her tone of voice making it loud and clear that it was going to go down right now.

"Position four here, I got 'em in sight."

"Position six, so do I."

Sandy, in the shoestore, said, "What about ours?"

"How's the background?" Margaret asked.

"We're cool," said Sandy.

"Okay. We'll bring Khaki Shorts Couple down when we've got Goatee Boy and Biker Boy under control, understood?"

"Copy that," said Sandy.

Margaret hid behind the map and took a breath. "Everyone, listen—Goatee Boy is unarmed, but Biker Boy is all-American. Concentrate on Biker Boy," she said, pulling out her own firearm and inconspicuously dropping her hand to her side. The only person who saw her gun was a two-year-old girl in a passing stroller who tried ineffectually to reach out and touch the shiny metal thing as her mother pushed her by. "Position four is point, Position six and Red Girl are back-up, Positions one, two, and nine are second wave. Are we ready?"

"Position one, good to go."

"Position two, good to go."

"Position four, good to go."

Too much background, thought Margaret.

"Position six, good to go."

Too much fucking BACKGROUND.

"Position nine, good to go."

"Move in, Position four," said Margaret.

From one of the tables of the food court, a big, strapping Asian kid—Position four, the point man, Greg Cho—stood up with his tray in one hand and a gun in the other, the gun hidden underneath the tray, which was littered with the detritus of a meal he hadn't eaten and tilted down enough to hide the gun. With his legs, he shoved his chair away and went around his table, walking to the garbage can three feet from Duncan Idaho.

"That'll be four twenty-eight," said the girl behind the counter, sliding a tray with their sandwiches and Pepsis across the counter.

Duncan said to Tobey, with all the casualness in the world, "Mind paying for it? I don't have any cash on me."

Tobey looked at Duncan as if he were from Mars, then reached into his pocket and paid for the meal.

Greg Cho had to stop—a couple of older people stood in his way. He couldn't get past them as they lumbered slow as camels across his path.

Duncan Idaho picked up the tray with his right hand and turned around. The thin black sanitation man, Dan, was looking at the floor, but from his stance he was aware that Duncan was looking at him—and something else: The sanitation guy looked *tight*.

Duncan thought, *It's coming.*

The older people finally cleared his way, Greg having a clear path six yards long, directly toward Duncan Idaho and Tobey Jansen.

Margaret Chisholm didn't make a move yet. Instead, she looked from behind the stand-alone map at Duncan, getting ready to sprint out and cover him.

Duncan Idaho, tray in one hand, one hand on his porcelain gun in his pocket, looked away from Dan and took a step forward into the middle of the food court, looking across the tables as if looking for a place to sit down. Then, deliberately, he turned and looked at Margaret Chisholm, the two of them staring right at each other across the throng of shoppers and their gentle murmur. They held each other's eyes for maybe a second, Margaret's eyes unblinking and, more importantly, unflickering.

Almost . . . , thought Duncan Idaho.

Greg Cho was almost on top of the targets, his thumb checking the safety on his automatic, getting ready—

Now, thought Duncan.

Abruptly breaking the stare, Duncan shot a look at Sanitation Man, spotting him twenty yards away, catching the thin black man's eyes wandering onto a big Asian man coming toward them, the big Asian man with a tray not six feet away.

With his own tray held before him, Duncan barreled forward, crashing into the Asian man, the two soft drinks splashing all over him.

"I'm so *sorry*—!"

Duncan reached under the tray and rabbit-punched the Asian man's groin.

"Yeep—!" squeaked FBI field officer Greg Cho, dropping both his gun and his tray and keeling forward, collapsing on the ground, his forehead actually bashing into the hard marble of the food court's floor, stunning him.

In one motion, Duncan pulled his hand off his porcelain gun, picked up Greg Cho's now-loose gun, and with his other hand picked Greg Cho himself up off the ground.

"Are you *okay?*" he asked, jamming Greg's gun into his gut as he held him steady. "Here, let me help you to your *feet*," he said, as he kneed him in the groin for good measure.

Greg collapsed on the ground again and lay there, almost prone.

"Are you *okay,* George?" Duncan said loudly, with a laugh in his voice, unconsciously clueing all the oblivious mushrooms around that these two were old friends. "George, man, you are *such* a dufus!"

"Back off, back off, back off," said Margaret, not daring to so much as blink away from Duncan Idaho.

Dan too was frozen, looking out across the archipelago of tables, furious with himself as he pushed his broom back and forth, back and forth.

But Position six was still on the move—Greg's partner, a Eurasian woman named Leanne Tetmeyer.

"Leanne, back off," said Margaret, as Leanne Tetmeyer just kept on coming, heading right for Duncan Idaho and Tobey Jansen.

"I'll put a bullet in his brains this second unless you all back off," Duncan whispered to Greg Cho, speaking for the benefit of the assembled spectators.

Margaret felt panic rise like bile as she watched Leanne Tetmeyer walk right toward Biker Boy and his newfound hostage, Greg Cho. "Back off, Leanne, back *off.*"

Leanne Tetmeyer kept on coming . . . and passed by Duncan and Tobey without even glancing at them, not a single yard away, neither of whom realized she was FBI.

"I couldn't back off or they would've spotted me," she

whispered, as she walked away with her back to Duncan and
Tobey, her voice shaking.

"That's okay, that's okay," said Margaret, trying to figure
out what to do next.

Too much background, too much fucking BACK-
GROUND—

The lunchtime crowd was arriving in force, the food court
swarming with people, clogging the lines at all the fast-food
outlets.

Margaret quickly decided to hold on to what she had.
"Sandy, Nick, pull down Khaki Shorts Couple in the shoestore—do it now."

"Okey-dokey," said Sandy.

Margaret heard quiet mumblings, then Sandy saying, loud
and clear over the transmitter, "FBI, do not move—you are
under arrest."

Margaret sighed, concentrating now on the hostage situation in front of her.

Duncan still had Greg's arm as if helping him, Greg on the
floor and slowly sitting up, clutching his groin, Duncan leaning over him, his body concealing the gun he was pointing at
Greg, a pool of soda around them.

This was the worst fucking idea ever, thought Duncan, trying to figure out what to do, knowing that none of this would
have been necessary if they'd just stuck together back in Pennsylvania. *Think think think think think—*

Tobey thought for him.

Duncan felt Tobey suddenly reach into his jacket and pull
out his porcelain gun.

"What are you—?"

"Goatee Boy has a firearm," said Margaret.

And then, with total confidence, Tobey slipped the porcelain GLOCK into his gray sweatshirt pocket and walked away
from Duncan and his hostage—walking straight toward Dan,
the Sanitation Man.

"Excuse me," Tobey said loudly, halfway through the food
court tables, looking straight at Dan, his hand sweating on the
butt of the porcelain gun. He was the only one standing amid

all the luncheon crowd, zero background between him and Dan Sears.

"Excuse me, sir?" said Tobey.

!?! thought Duncan Idaho.

?!? thought Margaret Chisholm.

"He's coming right at me," Dan whispered into his transmitter.

Dan Sears reaches for his weapon, Insane Nervous Goatee Boy firing at him, killing a civilian, reaiming and killing Dan, Big Biker Boy executing Greg then turning on Margaret, everyone falls on the two of them, firefight, background—

"Don't go for your weapon or he'll blow your head off," said Margaret.

"We've had a little accident," Tobey said to Dan, again loudly. "Could you help us clean up?"

With that, Tobey, tossed his shoulder in the direction of Duncan and Greg Cho, the silhouette of Tobey's gun clearly visible, pointed right at Dan.

"Do what he wants," Margaret said, holding on to her firearm very tight. "I'm covering you."

Dan walked away from the garbage can prop he had, walking toward Tobey like a French Royal to the guillotine.

"We spilled some things, could you help us clean it up?" Tobey said, his voice cracking suddenly in the middle of his sentence.

Dan walked ahead of Tobey toward Duncan and Greg. When he got there, Tobey whispered, "Get on your hands and knees and start cleaning up the soda."

"You too," said Duncan to Greg. Then to Tobey he said, "Watch for the redheaded woman behind the map of the mall."

Dan and Greg got down on their hands and knees, and then Duncan dealt with them both.

"Move and I'll shoot," he said as he squatted between both of them, both FBI men kneeling on all fours as Duncan relieved them of their guns and wallets, no one seeming to notice them as the crowd around them surged back and forth.

"Shit," said Duncan as he looked at Greg Cho's open wallet.

"What?" said Tobey, looking around in a semipanic as he stood over the tableaux that was as ordinary as a cotillion on some southern summer's eve.

"They're FBI," said Duncan, looking around the food court.

"Don't go near them," said Margaret. She couldn't believe Nervous Goatee Boy hadn't gone for a shot at Dan—the kid looked that wigged out and terrified.

Duncan Idaho, kneeling between Greg Cho and Dan Sears, looked across the ten yards separating him from Margaret Chisholm, getting her attention.

Margaret caught his eye, quizzical, then going wide. *No*— was all she had time to think.

Duncan Idaho yanked the earpiece receiver and the transmitting pack off Greg Cho, a device disguised to look like a mini personal stereo. And then he slipped the earpiece on, all the while staring at Margaret.

"Game's over for you two," said Duncan Idaho to both Greg and Dan as they knelt there on the floor. "Count yourselves lucky that you're still alive."

With that, Duncan Idaho stood up. "And clean that mess up," he said loudly, spacing his words like a schoolmarm ordering the kiddies about.

Margaret was so furious she could hardly breathe, watching as Duncan Idaho casually took the transmitter and earpiece receiver off Dan too. He pocketed the device and looked around, no longer concerned with Margaret Chisholm.

Margaret was gripping her gun so tight she might have accidentally shot the floor if her finger hadn't been fixed firmly on the trigger guard. With difficulty, her breath hitching in her chest, she said, "They have our frequency—communications are totally compromised."

Their transmitters had no back-up channel.

Duncan Idaho turned to Margaret and nodded, as if he'd heard her.

Margaret looked right at the Biker Boy, enraged—then she got a flash of inspiration.

"I've got your two friends," said Margaret into the transmitter.

Duncan froze, looking at Margaret.

"The big black guy and the white woman?" Margaret said. "Under arrest."

"What's going on?" said Tobey, looking from the two men on their knees on the ground and the suddenly paralyzed Duncan Idaho.

"They've got Ljubica and Russell," said Duncan, still staring at Margaret.

Margaret said into the transmitter, "Put your weapons on the ground, take two steps away from them, and we'll all walk out of this in one piece."

Duncan Idaho looking right at her, slowly shook his head.

Margaret breaks out in a run, going for Biker Boy, her weapon drawn, pointing it at him, the kid shooting covering fire right at her, shattering the glass of the stand-alone map of the mall, killing two people in Margaret's background, Margaret herself firing at Biker Boy, who ducks, her slugs ripping through a fat woman in an aquamarine tent-blouse, Nervous Goatee Boy shooting the prone Greg Cho and Dan Sears, then grabbing a hostage, jamming the gun under the hostage's chin, killing the hostage as he tightens up and accidentally pulls the trigger, Margaret killing Insane Nervous Goatee Boy with a shot in the face, Biker Boy recovering enough to shoot at her, tagging her once—twice—three times in the chest before Margaret plugs the son-of-a-bitch, but not before he kills more people in her background and she kills more people in HIS background, fucking civilians, six-seven-eight dead civilians, two dead agents, two dead "bank robbers," Margaret shot too—

Margaret shook her head.

"I've got your friends, and I know who you are," said Margaret, looking at Duncan Idaho.

Duncan, his hand in his pocket, motioned to the heads of Dan Sears and Greg Cho.

"Yes I know," said Margaret calmly, bright images flashing in her imagination. "You've got my people, but . . . I've got more people, and we won't back off."

Duncan nodded at her—then abruptly walked forward, toward a woman with a stroller, who was standing there, looking around, holding a red plastic tray with food in one hand, shopping bags hanging from her forearm, and the stroller handle in the other hand. Duncan walked right up to the stroller and knelt beside the kid.

"What a pretty baby!" Duncan said to the mother, lightly inflecting his voice to sound homosexual. "How old is he?"

"He's two," said the mother as Duncan made faces at the two-year-old boy, getting him to gurgle and clap his hands, making Duncan smile. Then he stood up and took the woman's tray in one hand, his left hand free to reach for the gun in his pocket.

"Here," he said. "Let me help you find a table."

"Why, thank you! That's very kind of you," said the mother, Duncan escorting the woman into the sea of tables, casually finding a largish table for two, where a solitary accountant-type was eating alone.

"Excuse me, sir?" said Duncan to the accountant-type.

What the fuck are you doing? thought Tobey.

What the fuck is he doing? thought Margaret.

The Accountant looked up in mid-sandwich bite. "Yes?" he asked with his mouth full.

"Would you mind sharing your table with this lady?" said Duncan. "All the tables are full."

The Accountant swallowed hard. "Sure," he said, a little surprised.

Duncan set the tray on the table opposite the Accountant, turning to the mother with the baby stroller. "Here you go," said Duncan to the mother, shooting a look at Margaret, the mother's body between him and Margaret. "Have a nice meal."

"Thanks, I can't thank you enough," said the mother, clearly pooped.

"It was *nothing*," said the flaming-queen Duncan.

As the mother sat down and arranged her shopping bags, Duncan stealthily pulled out his firearm and pointed it at the head of the child in the stroller, behind the mother's back, out of sight of the Accountant, all the while looking at Margaret, who had a clear line of sight on where the gun was pointed.

Tobey saw the whole thing, and he nearly yelped.

Oh no no no no, thought Margaret, nearly vomiting as she saw the sight of the gun barely inches from the back of the young boy's head, Margaret suddenly having no doubt that Biker Boy would shoot the kid—or anyone else—if she made a move.

All Duncan was thinking was whether or not the FBI man he'd taken the gun from had loaded a bullet into the chamber of the gun. The safety, of course, was on, but even so, Duncan felt nauseous at holding a gun on a child's head. He knew a few guys over at the Operations Directorate who would have felt no worries—who wouldn't have hesitated to plug the kid for real, if that's what it took. Duncan thought of himself as a lot of things, but he was no animal. But he had no problem making these FBI think that he was, even if the fear that the gun might accidentally go off made him sick to his stomach.

The mother, now in her seat, half turned around and looked up at Duncan, not seeing the gun in his hand. "Thank you so much," she said.

"My pleasure, anything for a baby as *beautiful* as this one!" said Duncan, his inflection still homosexual and therefore harmless, no matter how biker-bad he might have looked. "You enjoy your meal now—bye!" he said, his gun back in his pocket, his right hand tousling the little kid's hair and then giving him a mini-bye-bye wave. The child clapped his hands and laughed.

The mother turned to her tray, speaking to the Accountant, and Duncan wandered off, his eyes glued to Margaret's.

"If you step on a single mushroom, I'll shoot your friends," said Margaret, using the CIA word, making it clear to Duncan she knew what he was. "I don't give a shit; I'll shoot them both," she added, getting out from behind the map and following Duncan as he tried making his way to the Metro. "They're less than dog shit to me, just like you are."

Duncan raised a noncommittal eyebrow at Margaret as he walked to her right, to where Dan Sears's prop–garbage can stood.

Tobey, meanwhile, watched as Duncan drifted away from him, walking slowly toward the hallway leading back to the Metro station, going around the red-haired woman as if she were the anchor of a compass line he was drawing.

What? thought Tobey, confused by what Duncan was doing.

Duncan was walking slowly around Margaret, looking around him as he kept a constant distance from her, keeping Margaret in sight as he slowly made his way to the maw that led down to the enormous hallway and the Metro station beyond.

Margaret moved away from the map of the mall and came out into the open, her gun at her side, only the background keeping her from raising her weapon and shooting Duncan dead, he had so wigged her out.

"Put your weapon on the ground now, motherfucker, or I *will* shoot your head off," she said quietly into her transmitter.

Duncan finally got to the opening of the enormous hallway that led to the Metro station. He stopped and continued looking around, looking for whoever else was with the red-haired woman. Then he suddenly looked at Tobey and hollered, "Johnny! I think it's time we all went home."

Thirty yards away, Monika Summers was standing by a support column of the mall. She had seen everything that had happened from the moment Duncan walked over to Tobey, and now she saw Duncan standing with a blank look to his face, at the opening to the enormous hallway that led to the Metro station. She could also see Tobey standing there frozen, the two men kneeling beside him on their hands and knees. And from Duncan's body position, she noticed what he was focused on—a woman with fiery red hair . . . who had a gun in her hand, held close to the outside of her thigh, so discreet no one would have seen it unless they had been looking for it.

What's going O-O-ON? Monika thought with a tired, whiny panic that made her want to cry. Her blonde hair, slipping out of her purple scrunchie, made her look even more tired and desperate as she looked away, trying not to stare at the scene that was unfolding among all the oblivious people—so many people who had no idea how close they all were to death.

"Johnny, c'mon!! I wanna go already!" Duncan called out again.

Tobey dithered, looking down at the two FBI men kneeling in front of him, sweat making the handle of the porcelain gun in his pocket slippery. He began moving toward Duncan.

Monika Summers couldn't help a whimper escaping her as she too slowly made her way to Duncan Idaho.

"Put the gun on the ground," Margaret Chisholm was saying, aware that she had pivoted and allowed Goatee Boy to be at her back—but she knew she could handle Goatee Boy: Biker Boy was the real monster she had to take down, no matter what. "Put it on the ground and you'll live."

Duncan slowly shook his head, standing there, all alone and looking right at her, oblivious shoppers passing between them, a very visible shield against Margaret.

"Johnny," Duncan hollered again, his voice casual as a mall rat's call, waving his free hand around for the benefit of any curious civilian, his left hand still in his pocket, holding onto the gun. "I think it's time we got going," he said, all the while looking around him, looking for whoever else was with the red-haired woman.

"You're not going anywhere," said Margaret into the microphone at her throat, looking dead-on at the Biker Boy as she slowly took another step forward, closing the distance between them.

Out of the corner of her eye, she spotted Leanne Tetmeyer, repositioned, looking at a store window, the reflection giving her a perfect vantage point. Next to Leanne was Elise Wein, Position nine, the two women looking like friends shopping together. To Margaret's left, she spotted David Green and Freddy Ricketts, her closest people, the two of them looking like a couple of office slobs hanging out at the mall at lunchtime. . . . Margaret knew she could bring Biker Boy down; she had the people to do it with . . .

. . . it would only take a few deadly seconds.

She took another step forward.

"I'll start zipping mushrooms if you take another step," said Duncan clearly but not particularly loud, Margaret so close she could hear him easily.

"Zipping mushrooms," thought Margaret. *Why, they really are CIA . . .* , she thought dreamily, not really having believed it until this very moment.

They stood there, Margaret facing him as Duncan looked around, trying to figure out who else was with her as real people slithered around and between them, Duncan waiting as Monika and Tobey made their way toward him.

Everyone had been concentrating on the people standing and sitting in and around the food court, a natural impulse. The FBI had been there since eleven A.M., while Duncan and Tobey had assumed that Russell and Ljubica would arrive more or less at the same time as they would, twelve noon.

But Russell and Ljubica had arrived at Pentagon City much earlier—they had arrived around ten in the morning, around the time the mall had opened. And once there, they had gone shopping. In fact, Russell and Ljubica had gone to a Gap store and bought a couple of baseball caps. Now, they were standing inside a music store, a Sam Goody's that faced the food court, pretending to look at a rack of compact discs as they watched the scene going on outside.

They had seen everything, standing directly behind Margaret Chisholm, not ten yards away.

Ljubica, peeking over the top edge of the CD rack, raw and needy fear in her eyes, asked Russell, "What do we do now?"

"Duncan's exposed and so is Tobey," he said to his girlfriend, queerly pleased at the need she had of him at this moment. "I can't tell—"

"I see Monika," said Ljubica excitedly, looking off to her left, "just past those potted plants, over there—you see? You see? You see?—"

"Okay-okay-okay, shh-shh-shh-shh," he said softly, calming Ljubica down. "Can you walk okay?" he asked.

"Yeah, yeah," she said, already feeling like she could bolt as she looked at the back of the red-haired woman.

"Don't run, we'll walk," said Russell. "Let's wait until

Duncan and the others get moving. Then we'll follow them. Okay?"

Ljubica looked at Russell, panicking. Russell was in no better shape, but the thrill of being a different kind of man for Ljubica—tougher, stouter—soothed his nerves. He actually *smiled* at her, a confident smile that made her give him a tiny smile in return.

"It's gonna be okay," said Russell, taking Ljubica's hand in his own, Ljubica not retracting her hand, actually responding to his touch. "It'll be okay, just stay close to me," he said, though he knew that wouldn't be for the best—if they were separate, it would be a lot easier to keep whoever was at the mall at bay.

Monika Summers, in the meantime, finally got to where Duncan was, and she kept on walking, going on to the enormous hallway and the Metro station beyond, not even looking at Duncan as she passed him.

Duncan saw her, and as soon as she was past him, he too started walking, walking backward and slowly scanning the hallway. Tobey too walked on, jogging a bit to get past the red-haired woman, all the while looking at her and looking around, but without Duncan's clinical, discerning eye; Tobey just looked panicked.

Only Monika, up ahead, walked forward without looking around, trying to keep up appearances as shoppers flowed back and forth down the hallway, giving her cover. She got to the top of the escalator that led to the double glass doors and the enormous hallway beyond, and she had to physically keep from looking back as she slowly went down, feeling eyes on her, though she didn't know if they were friendly or not.

You're mine, thought Margaret Chisholm, her eyes glued on Duncan Idaho, knowing that she and her people could bring him down in the station, where it would be less crowded with background.

In the Sam Goody's store, Ljubica and Russell watched as everyone left the food court and started walking toward the adjacent Metro station. "Let's go," said Russell, the two of them walking out of the store, following the others.

Margaret Chisholm, her eyes on Duncan Idaho, made a circle motion with her upturned index finger, then a pointed V at Duncan and Tobey, all her people moving out, following Duncan and Tobey as Margaret herself led this brood.

They're coming, thought Duncan, feeling eyes on him besides Margaret's, catching Tobey's terrified eyes and catching sight of Monika just ahead of them both. *They're coming in force.*

They moved as careful as crabs. Tobey and Duncan took the short electric escalator down, then passed through the double glass doors with the stenciling that read THANKS FOR SHOPPING AT PENTAGON CITY! They kept turning around, looking behind them and glancing forward, trying to keep background between them and whoever else was along with the redheaded woman, having no idea who was who, knowing that at the first sign of motion, both of them would react—one from calculation, the other from panic.

David Green and Freddy Ricketts, the two FBI men dressed up as overweight office slobs, had already moved way ahead of Duncan and Tobey. They were already at the entrance to the Metro station itself, at the end of the enormous hall. They stood there pretending to talk, and when they saw Duncan and Tobey come down the short electric escalator and through the double glass doors, they began walking down the hallway toward the mall.

Margaret Chisholm got to the top of the electric escalators and saw Green and Ricketts moving in on Duncan Idaho from the opposite end of the enormous hallway, but she gave nothing away. Instead, she quickly walked down the electric escalator and got ready to support Green and Ricketts as they started boxing Biker Boy in.

Almost . . . , she thought.

But Monika Summers too saw Ricketts and Green. She had noticed them, the two office slobs, at the shopping center earlier, and she had noticed how they had gone to the Metro station ahead of her . . . and now here they were again, walking away from the Metro station, coming toward her on either side, both men looking toward Duncan behind her.

Green and Ricketts both had their suit jackets slung over their shoulders, approaching Monika on either side of her, ignoring her. From the way they held their jackets, Monika could tell that they had their guns in their hands, underneath the collars of their coats.

Both men passed by on either side of her.

Then Monika reacted.

In her purse, she had a spring-loaded telescopic iron—a foot-long tube of metal with a black release button at its base. Tom Carr had given it to her for the oddest, most endearing reason: He'd been worried Yuvi or Monica might get mugged. When the release button was pressed, the iron telescoped into a three-foot length, as hard and unforgiving as a baseball bat.

Monika turned around and, in one graceful, uninterrupted motion, pulled the retracted iron from her bag, hit the button that extended it, and pulled back, getting ready for a backhanded blow.

Margaret Chisholm, ten yards away, saw the whole thing—and yelled: *"Look out—!"*

Monika Summers swung the iron backhand, as hard as she could, striking the side of Green's head with a hollow *thuck!* sound. Green fell almost instantly, only a brief, surprised *off!* sound coming out of him, falling to the ground motionless. At the end of her swing, Monika turned to Ricketts, who was already turning to face Green, already in the process of pulling out his firearm. Monika, panicking and afraid, whimpered a grunt of effort as she swung forehand with the iron, striking Ricketts once in the face, then again in the throat, accidentally breaking his larynx. Ricketts silently collapsed on the ground, his jaw broken, unconscious from the first blow, asphyxiating to death as his ruptured larynx swelled up and squeezed off his breathing tube. Monika, seeing Ricketts drop his firearm, haphazardly picked it up and dropped it in her purse before turning around and walking on as she had before, only this time a little more quickly, and this time looking around her to make sure no one else was around, whimpering in panic and fear but trying to hold on and not bolt, as she so desperately wanted to.

Down the enormous hallway, Margaret Chisholm nearly screamed, Purple Scrunchie Girl getting swallowed up by a crowd a half-dozen strong that pulled in on the downed Freddy Ricketts and Richie Green. The crowd stood around the downed men, stupidly not turning to look at Purple Scrunchie Girl, who was gone.

Margaret looked around as she jogged quickly forward toward her downed men, catching sight of Big Biker Boy—

—she saw him give her a cruel, satisfied smile just as he passed by the crumpled bodies of her men.

She would have shot him right then and there if not for the crowd of background, standing around her downed men.

"Get out of my way," she said loudly to the people surrounding Green and Ricketts, all of whom were staring.

Margaret knelt and checked to make sure they were okay. Ricketts was out like a light, the pulse at his neck still strong, Margaret not realizing that he wasn't breathing, but Green was coming around, distracting her from Ricketts—

"What happened . . ."

"Don't move, we'll fix you up in a second, sweetie," said Margaret, looking from her downed men and up at the Biker Boy and the Purple Scrunchie Girl through the legs of the dumb civilians gawking.

Margaret stood up and continued after them, slipping between the four or five people standing around, suddenly remembering Nervous Goatee Boy and spying him up ahead, on the right, abreast with Purple Scrunchie Girl, the three of them forming a perfect triangle through which assorted mushrooms passed, like a grid pattern on a radar screen.

I'm gonna put you down, she thought, her firearm still inconspicuously at her side, then realized something—

—aside from Leanne Tetmeyer and Elise Wein, who were both far behind, Margaret Chisholm was completely alone . . .

. . . and she realized that now, finally, she had slipped into the 60 percent side of the solution: Margaret Chisholm was now free to up and shoot Acrobat if she wanted to.

But Acrobat knew it had the upper hand.

Acrobat could see it all. Acrobat saw the red-haired woman

walking away from the two downed men, the redhead holding her gun, clearly ready to shoot at them.

A Eurasian woman and a skinny brunette knelt by both downed men amid all the dumb mushrooms standing around— the red-haired woman was completely alone, completely exposed.

Relaxing their grip on their guns—for the first time truly ready to kill someone—Acrobat slowed down, looking down the enormous hallway at the lone red-haired woman coming up on them.

Margaret too felt it—she was alone and totally exposed, and if she made a move on any of her suspects, she knew the others would kill her. Maybe to hide her fear—maybe because she had nothing to lose—Margaret Chisholm *smiled,* as if she thought this was all fine and dandy.

But Acrobat could see she was afraid.

Margaret regripped her gun and picked up her pace, closing the distance between herself and her end, knowing suddenly that she would not survive, no matter how many of them she took down. Because there would always be more of them than of her.

DOAM!

Margaret suddenly felt as if her teeth had been knocked out of her head.

Staggering forward and turning around, her gun still in hand, she saw that a couple of Them—a man and a woman, Russell and Ljubica—had snuck up behind her, both of them in black leather jackets, both of them wearing baseball caps in subdued colors. The woman—a dark, intense-looking girl with perfectly translucent skin—had hit the back of her head with a telescoping iron, an iron exactly like the one Purple Scrunchie Girl had used on Freddy and Richie. Dark Girl's partner, a big mulatto man in his early thirties, was a couple of yards behind the woman, looking as if he were trying to stop the Dark Girl (*stop the Dark Girl?*) as Margaret raised her gun—

Dark Girl smashed her wrist with the iron, sending her gun

flying off and clattering to the ground. And then the Dark Girl whacked the left side of Margaret's head.

Her legs collapsed like paper stilts, Margaret feeling half her skull light up on fire even as she began to lose consciousness, fading so fast she didn't have time to panic and be afraid.

As Margaret collapsed, Dark Girl raised the iron and whacked her on the left shoulder on the way down, for good measure. But Margaret thought with a dreamy detachment how fruitless that was—she was already going to lose consciousness. The fact that Dark Girl had broken her collarbone with the iron registered with only mild amusement—then a question: *Who are these people?*

As Margaret faded out, just before she struck the ground, she realized as clear as if she were sitting on a park bench: *We arrested the wrong people at the shoestore.* She was going to catch hell for that.

Margaret collapsed on the ground and blacked out.

"You shouldn't have done that," Russell hissed in Ljubica's ear as she walked past the downed red-haired woman and on down the enormous hallway. Ljubica was actually jogging a bit to get closer to the others, her leg killing her as Russell jogged too to keep apace. "You shouldn't have."

Ljubica turned to Russell, genuinely confused. "What are you talking about?" she asked him, turning and looking forward, seeing Duncan and Tobey and Monika about to move on forward to the Metro station. But they were still looking behind, patiently waiting for her, covering her with their eyes, the work-group Acrobat protecting its own.

Yuvi couldn't remember the last time she had felt so happy and safe.

Russell didn't say a thing.

Meanwhile, the skinny, brunette FBI woman who was kneeling by the two men, Elise Wein, broke from her partner and went to Margaret Chisholm—but she knew enough to stay away from Acrobat, giving them all a look, a look Ljubica Greene happened to catch as she looked over her shoulder.

Fear.

That's right, thought Ljubica as she limped along, electric and bullet-proof, feeling her friends around her, watching out for her, protecting her—Duncan, Tobey, Monika: Watching over her and ready and willing to do whatever it took to keep her safe.

Ljubica limped along, getting closer to the others. Duncan Idaho saw that the skinny brunette FBI agent who was kneeling by the downed red- headed woman looked as if she were about to pull out her firearm . . .

. . . but then, what?

"Dream on," said Tobey Jansen, speaking to the skinny brunette, who jerked her head toward him, Duncan and Monika and Ljubica feeling as if Tobey were reading their minds and saying what all of them were thinking: The group mind, the collective hive, the single unity—Acrobat.

The skinny brunette stayed put beside the downed red-haired woman, her whole body seeming to shrivel up as she knelt there on the ground.

"She could have killed you," said Russell in Ljubica's ear.

Ljubica turned to her lover just as they both came abreast of the others, all of them walking through the schools of civilians as if they were a net uninterested in these small-fry.

"She could never have hurt us," said Ljubica, hating Russell, hating his weakness, hating his indecision, hating his doubts about who and what they were, hating him for not understanding what had suddenly happened.

Acrobat had come together.

CHAPTER 8

Defenestration

Then they fell apart.

"They *knew* we were coming—just like in New York, just like in Times Square—they *knew* we'd be there," said Monika Summers furiously, panicked and afraid.

No one else was saying a thing, the five of them in the subway car, everyone's nerves peeled raw as they all came to realize what had almost happened. Monika was so freaked out, she was hanging from the handrail of the Metro car like a nervous blonde monkey going stir-crazy. "How did they know? *How—did—they—know?!?*"

"I don't know, but we'll figure it out later," said Russell, blinking and thinking as one of his massive hands held on to the support rail of the Metro car.

"Not later—*now*, Russell, I wanna know *now*."

"So do I," said Ljubica calmly, as she turned away from the window, her upper lip trembling as if it were slightly spastic.

Russell looked at the floor of the Metro car and massaged his scalp, pulling himself together.

Monika went on. "We agreed to meet here *yesterday*—and all of a sudden they're just there? That's not possible—they couldn't just *know*, they are not fucking *psychic*."

"Who did you guys talk to?" Duncan suddenly blurted out, careening around the Metro car, totally confused by what had just happened.

Russell scoffed. "No one, Duncan—who on earth would we talk to?"

"That thing back there, that was Tommy's doing?" said Monika with a sneer that was too panicked to have any teeth. "Tommy led them straight to us? Not unless Tommy is walking and talking and reading our minds."

"Nobody said anything to anybody!" Russell shouted out loud, making the random tourists and real people on the train stop and turn to look at them. "Do we have a problem?" said Russell, scaring the beejezus out of them with his size and his relative blackness. The mushrooms turned away, having no problem whatsoever.

"Look," said Duncan, trying more than anything to get Monika to calm down. "I don't know how they got there, but they were there, which means that somehow—"

"You don't seem very perturbed," said Russell suddenly.

"What?" said Duncan.

"You don't even seem as if this thing really . . . *surprised* you," said Russell.

Duncan—confused, then understanding—put a cold eye on Russell. "You better be careful there, buddy. Very careful about what you say."

But Russell looked like he had no doubts. "You've always pushed this group into doing crazy stunts, like your ego depended on it—or as if you wanted us all to get blown out of the water," he said.

Duncan blinked. "Wha——?"

"You were the last one to join us, and you worked for *him* before you joined us. You've always said you hated him, but that didn't keep you from working for him for almost two years straight," said Russell.

"You fucking weasel—"

"And you've gone out of your way to wave the red flag—"

"Hey!" said Monika to both of them, "This isn't helping any—"

"*I* was the last one to join up," said Tobey, "and I worked for him too! Does that mean—Russell Russell Russell, *listen* to yourself—"

Russell said, "You know Monika's right—how *did* they know we'd be there? Because Monika, you *are* right—they were just *there*."

"Hey fuck you," said Duncan.

Monika suddenly turned on Ljubica. "You think he's right?" she asked her friend. "You think *Duncan's* the one who fed them where we'd be?"

Ljubica seemed to disappear, the look to her eyes and the expression on her face as detached and far away as some god's across some rainbowed bridge. "I don't know what to think," she said in a normal conversational tone, her voice dark and husky. "We were the only ones who knew where we'd meet— and they found us. We didn't see anyone, we didn't talk to anyone, we paid cash for everything. But they found us."

Oh no no no no no, thought Monika, seeing how it might turn out between them: The two couples at war, each blaming the other—

"I don't know," Yuvi continued without emotion, as detached as a dancing girl at a discothéque, her voice husky and soft. "They were waiting for us. They didn't simply know we would meet at Pentagon City: They knew the time and the specific location," she said with quiet emphasis, looking at Monika. Then she turned to her lover, looking at him full in the face. "How do you explain that, Russell?"

Russell nearly doubled over, as if he'd been kicked in the gut. "I don't," he said. "I don't have to—we didn't talk to anyone. We drove down here, we shacked up in a motel in Alexandria, we've been cooped up until we came down here. We didn't talk to anyone," he said, feeling as the ground suddenly, decisively shifted beneath his feet.

"I think it was really weird how they were just there," Ljubica went on in that same quiet, creepy tone of voice, looking directly at Russell the way a scientist would look at a specimen. "We were supposed to meet at Pentagon City, and when we arrived, there they were," she added, her voice horror-movie creepy precisely because of its very matter-of-factness. "They didn't spot us though. A limping woman, with her six-foot-five, black companion. They didn't spot us—but they spotted Duncan, and Tobey too. What do you think, Russell?" she asked. "Because I don't know what to think."

Everyone stared at Ljubica.

Tobey was the first to recover, filling in the gap—a split-second gap, a nothing in the conversation, as short as a blink and as deep as a canyon—with a fake laugh and a scared playfulness, saying to Ljubica, "Hey, he's one of us. I think we're all getting way too paranoid here; there's a rational explanation for this—"

"Yeah, Tobey's right," said Duncan uncertainly. "I mean all sorts of things might have happened—maybe one of us used an ATM card and forgot about it—hey, let's figure this out later; what's important now is figuring out if the bank is crawling or not."

"Yeah," said Russell, looking at Ljubica as if she were another person—a dark woman he did not know, a woman who was different, yet wearing a Ljubica suit for all the world to see. Looking at her green eyes behind her dark, straight hair, he realized he was one remark away from the end. "Let's go to the bank," said Russell carefully, rehearsing each word a half-dozen times in his head before he said them out loud. "We'll reconn the bank, then we'll talk things over. Okay?" he asked Ljubica.

Ljubica didn't even look up from the floor of the speeding Metro car. "Okay," was all she said.

"What do you mean, 'They got away'?" said Nicholas Denton quietly, quietly furious.

"They got away, Mr. Denton," said FBI Deputy Director Mario Rivera. "Margaret Chisholm: in the hospital, and one of her field agents, Freddy Ricketts: dead."

The two of them were speaking on the telephone, both of them in their respective offices.

Sitting facing Denton were Matthew Wilson and Amalia, both of whom were listening in on extensions in Denton's office. Amalia was impassive as always, but scary Matt Wilson was just shaking his head, one huge scowl across his face.

"They must have known we'd be there to arrest them," Rivera continued. "They couldn't just—"

"Why are you the one telling me this?" Denton suddenly asked. "Why am I speaking to you instead of to Director Livre?"

"Director Livre can't talk right now, Mr. Denton," said Mario Rivera, a wince in his voice.

"I see."

Nicholas Denton sighed and leaned back in his desk chair, putting his feet up on his desk and casually turning to one of the finger-paintings Claire had given him—a painting of a green dog and orange people playing on the surface of what looked like a purple ocean. Denton had mentally dubbed the picture *Waterwalkers*, and looking at it always soothed his nerves.

"Your people didn't arrest anybody?" Denton asked.

"No, like I said, they all got away," said Mario Rivera.

"Was there some kind of shoot-out?" Denton asked.

"No," said Rivera. "It was a hostage situation."

"A hostage situation," said Denton. "Did the Acrobat people take hostages?"

"Not exactly. They were threatening the civilians at the mall—Agent Chisholm decided that she couldn't risk civilian casualties in order to arrest the Acrobat group."

Denton silently shook his head as Mario Rivera went on explaining. FBI Director Livre had sloughed off the responsibility for the botched Acrobat arrest on Mario Rivera—that's why he was the one talking to Denton. And now Rivera was passing the buck on to Margaret Chisholm. Lovely.

Would you have done any different? Denton asked himself.

Then he answered himself: *I wouldn't have fucked it up in the first place.*

"So, let me try to understand this," said Denton. "Acrobat was there, where I said they'd be, but there were too many civilians in the way, which was why you were unable to arrest them."

"Correct."

"Then they hopped on the Metro and managed to get away."

"Correct," said Mario Rivera.

"I see," said Denton, eerily quiet.

Rivera, squirming at the yawning silence—squirming that the FBI had so fucked up what had been essentially easy pickings—began blabbering away, but Denton tuned him out, staring straight ahead, not saying a thing. Wilson was just shaking his head and gesturing with his hands, all the while completely silent so that Rivera wouldn't hear him over the telephone. For her part, Amalia sat still as a statue, looking at her boss.

I shoulda sent Amalia, Denton was thinking, looking at the murderous little woman across from his desk, a woman as small and mousy as a spinster dressmaker.

"I have some information for you," Denton said all of a sudden.

"What is it?" said Rivera, instantly on the alert.

"Acrobat is going to try to get to the Riggs Bank off DuPont Circle," said Denton. "Do you know the branch I'm talking about?"

"Nosir."

"It's the one facing the Circle," said Denton, "on the wedge formed by Massachusetts and Connecticut Avenues. Acrobat will be there, but I don't know when: Maybe in five seconds, maybe in five days. But they *are* going to be there, in a relatively short time frame, ten days on the outside."

"I see," said Rivera. "Why are they going there?"

"I don't have time for questions, Mario," said Denton. "This is what you have to do—send a bunch of your people down to the Riggs Bank at at DuPont Circle: Undercover people, no uniforms. You don't want to scare them away, now do you. When Acrobat gets there—and they *will* get there—arrest them. Do this *now,* Mario—before they get away again."

"Sir, I need to know how you know this information so that I can—"

"Mario? Listen carefully, please," said Denton with a quiet, hard edge. "Tell Roy Livre that I'm going to brief the President on what's happened," said Denton. "I have to. And when I do, I'll be sure to tell him that CIA supplied accurate information to the FBI regarding the whereabouts of the Acrobat work-group not once but twice—"

"Mr. Denton, sir—"

"Listen Mario," said Denton patiently. "I'm not finished. Tell Director Livre that the world's best deodorant is success. I gave you Pentagon City, and you failed. Now I'm giving you DuPont Circle. You can still catch Acrobat, if you make the effort. Are you going to make the effort? Or should I tell the President that you're sitting on your hands while you think about it?"

Mario Rivera was silent for a moment. Then he said, "I'll get right on it."

"Good, great, tell me how it goes," said Denton, hanging up the phone and shaking his head.

Matthew Wilson looked up at his boss. "I talked to a friend of mine at the FBI who was on that arrest team," he said.

"And," said Denton, getting up and lighting a cigarette as he walked to the window of his office.

"She told me the arrest got completely botched 'cause of the crowd," said Wilson. "They accidentally arrested a couple from Alabama, even—the woman they arrested turned out to be a lawyer for the ACLU of all people, so now the FBI's looking at a lawsuit—it's a mess."

Denton said nothing, looking out the window.

Wilson continued. "She also told me it was a woman with a limp who put Margaret Chisholm down."

Denton flinched as he stared, smoking his cigarette. "Good going, Yuvi," he mumbled, knowing all about Ljubica's wounded thigh.

"This friend also told me—"

"Which friend," said Denton.

"Leanne Tetmeyer. She told me Chisholm didn't really go for broke," said Wilson, confused, knowing about Margaret Chisholm and her reputation for being almost reckless in her pursuits.

"She had her orders," said Denton. "Livre wants Acrobat

alive, so he told Chisholm to capture them no matter what. That's why she fucked up—she followed orders instead of her instinct. You don't send Margaret Chisholm to get someone alive."

And Wilson mentally added the corollary: *You send Margaret Chisholm if you want somebody dead.* Wilson nodded, realizing why Denton had maneuvered Chisholm into being in charge of the Feebies's Acrobat manhunt in the first place; he'd been counting on Margaret.

"Tetmeyer told me that Acrobat started threatening civilians—it wigged out all the Feebies, including Chisholm," said Wilson. "I've been monitoring the comm between Livre and Rivera—they're going to replace Chisholm with a guy named Larry Murphy. The rep on him is that he's pretty good, with a very low casualty rate for his arrests, even though he used to be SWAT."

Denton took this in silence, thinking as he looked out the window of his office.

Amalia and Matthew Wilson exchanged a look, Wilson coughing politely before saying, "What do we do now, sir?"

Denton smoked his cigarette, then sighed again. He abruptly sat down at his desk and took a small card and envelope from his top drawer and began to write on it. "First of all, send Margaret Chisholm a big bouquet of flowers. Happy flowers. Daisies or something. Include this card from me," he said, giving the card and envelope to Matthew Wilson, who stood up to take it.

"Yessir," said Wilson.

"Second, keep monitoring the taps on Livre's and Rivera's phones. Tell me if their game plans change."

"Yessir."

"You did good, Matthew. You can go now."

Wilson looked at Denton and then at Amalia. "Yessir," he said, walking out of the office and quietly closing the door behind him.

When he was gone, Denton turned to Amalia.

"I want you to do something for me," he said.

Amalia looked at her boss, waiting for her marching orders.

• • •

Getting from Pentagon City to DuPont Circle was no trick at all. But just to be safe, the work-group Acrobat switched trains a couple-three times, criss-crossing the city, the five of them cooling off as they scanned the platforms and passengers of the stations they passed, looking for anyone who might be following them.

After about an hour of this, around 1:30 in the afternoon, they all got off at DuPont Circle, all of them walking through the eerily dark Metro station like a patrol of weathered travelers, wanderers made nervous not by what surrounded them, but by the proximity of each other.

There are several exits from the DuPont Circle Metro station, but the main one is a set of half a dozen electric escalators that are incredibly long, at least three hundred feet. Acrobat took the escalators up top, amid the flow of lunchtime pedestrians who flooded the station. None of them were worried about being spotted, since DuPont Circle is a busy hub on a weekday, especially a Friday.

Outside, they looked around, a bit dazzled by the strong sunlight and the openness of the city after all the time spent in the dark and cavernous Metro system.

"Down Massachusetts Avenue," said Monika, pointing, instantly all five of them breaking up and wandering toward it on their own.

Except for Duncan and Tobey. They stuck together as they crossed the street, away from the others.

"That cowboy is really getting on my fucking nerves," said Duncan as he strode a bit too quickly for Tobey, who had to jog-skip along to keep up with him.

"Dunc, man, we're all under a lot of pressure—"

"Fuck that," said Duncan. "I think Ljubica's right—I think he's the one selling us out."

"*Don't* say that! It's not true!" said Tobey fiercely.

"Why not?" said Duncan. "Ljubica's saying it. She's his fucking woman, for crying out loud. Your woman doesn't finger you like that unless you're the fucking Antichrist, what the fuck."

"What about me?" said Tobey. "What about Ljubica? Or Monika?"

"Ljubica's cool, you know that. And I had an eye on both you and Monika every second of the way from Pennsylvania down here," said Duncan off-handedly. "I would have spotted you if you'd called anyone at all."

Tobey's voice hitched in his throat in surprise. That Duncan would so casually admit that he didn't trust even Tobey or Monika hurt in a way that Tobey couldn't fathom, or keep from shocking him.

Tobey slowed down to his regular walking speed, letting Duncan pull away.

Duncan, realizing he was walking too fast and leaving Tobey behind, stopped and waited impatiently for Tobey to catch up.

"Hurry up already," said Duncan.

"At the mall . . . ," said Tobey carefully as he came abreast of Duncan, his heart turning cruel as he spoke to his friend. "Duncan, I gotta know—were you gonna zip that kid in the stroller?"

"What?" said Duncan, whipping his head toward Tobey and looking at him with disgust—and panicked surprise, as if called something he'd never entertained before but which he feared might be true. "What do you take me for—what the fuck is going through your head?"

"I need to know," said Tobey calmly, payback for Duncan's distrust.

"Fuck you," said Duncan, meaning it. "Fuck you to death, asshole—zip a little kid, are you outta your fucking mind?"

"I just wanted to know, that's all," said Tobey, not looking at Duncan, unable to help relish Duncan's squirming beside him.

"Fuck you," said Duncan. After a pause—he couldn't stop himself—he repeated: "Fuck *you!*"

Tobey didn't even glance at Duncan, using his quiet like a knife in Duncan's gut.

In sickening silence, Tobey and Duncan got to the end of Massachusetts Avenue, on the corner directly across from both the Circle and the bank, where there was a Starbucks' coffee shop.

It was an ordinary bank, made of brick, on the wedge formed by Connecticut and Massachusetts Avenues, with big windows lined by white sills. It was impossible to see inside, what with the curtains draped over the windows, but it all seemed very ordinary, people coming and going through the glass doors, paying no particular mind to anything going on.

There was a car, though. A mid-nineties American sedan, navy blue with bright chrome trim and rounded bumpers, parked directly in front of the bank. A man was sitting in it, at the wheel, looking as if he were waiting for something or someone.

Duncan stopped and looked. "C'mon," he told Tobey, tapping him on the chest as he walked into the Starbucks'. They got in line for coffee as, through the big windows of the coffeehouse, they had an unobstructed view of the bank and the navy blue sedan.

Duncan was staring at the bank as he saw another sedan, equally anonymous, pull up behind the navy blue car. A couple—clearly Feebies—stepped out of this second car and looked around at all the hundreds of people around the bank and the Circle and the Starbucks and the shops up and down Massachusetts Avenue.

Duncan turned away and faced the counter of the Starbucks, just as his turn came up.

"May I help you?" asked the college-age girl behind the counter.

"Grande latte, no foam," said Duncan automatically.

"Tall Frappuccino," said Tobey, his voice scared and miserable.

"You saw it?" Duncan asked quietly.

Tobey bit his lip and looked at his hand as he came up with the money for the coffees.

When they were served, Tobey and Duncan walked back to

the entrance to the Metro the way they'd come, both of them
smoking cigarettes and silently drinking their designer coffees.

The work-group Acrobat all made it back to the DuPont Circle
Metro station. They stood spread out on the platform, not
speaking, all their gears grinding as they waited for a train
to arrive amid the flood of real people.

When a train pulled up, they all got on board, all of them
taking different seats, none of them looking at the others.

Tobey couldn't take this anymore. Sliding up to Ljubica
Greene as the train smoothly flew down the rails, he nudged
her with his elbow.

"What does that mean?" he asked.

"Think, Tobey," she said, more curt than she meant to be,
her leg aching in synch with her head. Then she sighed and
took Tobey's hand in her own. "I'm sorry," she said.

"How's your leg?"

Ljubica smiled, her leg throbbing. "Better," she said.

Tobey smiled back, then frowned as he thought about
DuPont Circle. "They could have figured out . . . They could
have been there because they figured out we have our IDs at
the bank—they could've figured it out somehow—from be-
fore?" said Tobey, beginning to panic again and trying to hold
it in.

Ljubica smiled softly at Tobey. With her index finger, she
flicked his spiked goatee.

"Don't do that," said Tobey, irritated.

Ljubica flicked his goatee again, smiling naturally.

"Don't do that!" Tobey giggled.

They got to the next station, Farragut North, the two seats
adjacent to Yuvi and Tobey's becoming unoccupied. Duncan,
hanging from a handstrap across from them, walked over and
sat down, spreading out across those two now empty seats. He
turned and waved for Monika to come on over before turning
to Tobey and Ljubica.

"How do you think they found out about it?" Duncan asked

softly, speaking to Tobey, trying to get back into his good graces.

Tobey stiffened and said nothing.

Ljubica frowned at the static between Duncan and Tobey. Duncan blinked at Yuvi and then glanced away with a quick shake of his head.

"Tobey," said Duncan, leaning forward toward Tobey.

"What."

"C'mon."

Tobey nodded without looking at him. "Okay," he said.

"Hey."

"Okay already, what do you want?" said Tobey to Duncan, without looking him in the eye.

Ljubica looked at Duncan, who caught her eye. She turned slightly to Tobey and put her arm around his thin shoulders.

Duncan winced, hating how it was between him and Tobey. He pushed this out of his mind, turning to the easier, more imminent problem of the bank at DuPont Circle. "Did you see those sedans?" he asked Ljubica.

Ljubica nodded.

"So did I," said Monika as she sat down next to Duncan and leaned against him, Duncan automatically putting his arms around her shoulders. "They looked so obvious."

"Mmm," said Ljubica, wincing at the memory.

Russell too made his way over to the others, holding on to the handrail as he stood over them.

None of them looked back at Russell as they reviewed what they had seen at the bank.

Duncan had noticed that the sedans were so American Anonymous they practically screamed "surveillance."

Yeah, Tobey too saw that.

Monika, leaning into Duncan's body, said that she'd gone around the back of the bank, walking on down Connecticut Avenue. There'd been another couple of cars there, also too anonymous to be mushrooms. She'd also spotted a guy walking around the bank who'd looked too, too *static*. Did that make any sense?

"Sure it does," said Russell.

Duncan glanced at Russell as Monika went on talking, talking about how this supposed mushroom looked like a Fed, she didn't know why—something about his hair, something about how put-together he looked.

Ljubica agreed out loud with Monika, not bothering to acknowledge Russell staring at her, Ljubica making no move to connect with him in any way.

Duncan joked about Tobey getting the FBI man in the sanitation uniform back in Pentagon City to clean up the mess he, Duncan, had made, Russell realizing that Duncan was trying to get on Tobey's good side. Something had happened.

Tobey said that *someone* had to think for them, Duncan trying to win his friend back, Tobey making him pay still for his distrust.

"Tobey, that was a smooth play," said Russell.

No one looked at him.

Monika laughed about knocking out the two FBI men, secretly and obviously pleased with how she'd carried herself. Tobey praised her, and Ljubica concurred. Duncan said he needed a bodyguard, and would Monika be willing . . . ? Monika giggled and said she would think about it—but it was gonna cost him! Duncan said he had only his body to trade, and everyone guffawed.

Ljubica smiled at them, sitting there, her arm draped over Tobey's shoulder, Tobey and Ljubica like brother and sister, as intimate in their way as Duncan and Monika in theirs. Ljubica's wounded leg stuck out in front of her, her shod toes almost touching Russell's boots.

"We should check the bandages on your leg," said Russell.

Ljubica didn't even blink, telling Tobey that he should let Monika take care of him.

Duncan laughed, saying how even crippled, she, Ljubica, could still whup some ass.

Ljubica said she got lucky.

Russell didn't say a thing.

None of the others even looked at him, all of them talking about how the red-haired woman looked fit to be tied when Monika had struck her two men, and had she gone suicidal near the end there when she'd blown off her own people to come after them?

"Maybe she had more back-up somewhere," said Russell, without much conviction, his head feeling hollow, the words ricocheting inside of his skull and going out into the world like weak ghosts too tired to haunt.

Again, no one said a thing to Russell.

Duncan said he was hungry, Monika said they should stop somewhere, and Ljubica said nothing as she looked out the black window of the subway car, her arm comfortably around Tobey.

"What is the matter with you people?" said Russell suddenly, fiercely.

Duncan snorted, dusting his jeans as if they had gotten dirty somehow.

"Why, why—what are you doing?" asked Russell. "I didn't talk to anyone—Ljubica, you were with me the whole time; I didn't call *anyone*."

Ljubica looked at him as if he were a stranger as she leaned against Tobey, who was studiously looking at his hands.

"What about Tobey—Tobey worked for him for a fucking *year!*"

Duncan got up, stretching and brushing his pants legs, as if his jeans had some dirt on them. "You fucking turd," he mumbled through a humorless laugh.

Tobey said, "Guys, Russell, Duncan—"

"Tobey," said Ljubica softly, pulling his head closer to her own, silencing him.

Duncan said to Russell, "You know, you say I'm the sellout; then now you're saying it's Tobey—I mean, what the fuck: Denton probably wants to wax his ass the most."

Russell said, "I didn't do a fucking thing, I didn't—"

"You were never on board with us, pal," said Duncan, showing a mean streak a mile wide. "You were always doubtful; you were never a hundred percent with Acrobat. 'Russell is undecided'—fuckit: The story of your life."

"What are you talking about? I sacrificed everything for this work-group."

"Tell that one to the tourists, pal, we're all natives 'round here."

Russell looked at his four friends.

When your friends are no longer your friends, nobody goes to your house and tells you about it. Nobody writes you a memo. When you're out, your phone simply stops ringing. People just don't seem to remember you when it comes time to round up the gang for the picnics at the park or the nights spent drinking out on the town. It's like amnesia—you are no longer remembered. Or maybe it's the opposite of nostalgia—everything good about your past lives together is turned into a photographic negative, a negative reflected in the eyes of the strangers who were once your friends. Good times spent together are seen as hypocrisies, exchanged secrets and confidences begin looking like betrayals. There's no trial, there's only a jury, and there is no appeal. You can complain all you want, but then what? What are you going to do? Sue them? Yell at them? Tell them that they're wrong? You think that'll help? Think that way if you must, but know it won't do you any good—when your friends are no longer your friends, know that there is nothing you can do about it.

"I think you should go now," Monika said quietly, looking at her sneakers, ashamed, but knowing what they had to do with him.

"Go? Go where?" asked Russell.

No one said a thing.

"Where am I supposed to go?" said Russell. "I've got nowhere else to go."

Duncan looked away, smiled, and scoffed. "If you say so."

Russell turned to Duncan and grabbed his upper arm, to make him listen.

"Duncan—"

"Watch yourself, pardner," said Duncan, sloughing off Russell's hand, Tobey unconsciously straightening up, suddenly aware that he had the porcelain gun he'd taken off Duncan earlier at Pentagon City.

"Watch yourself real good," Duncan repeated, looking right at Russell, not fucking around at all, then looking away, catching Tobey's eye. In that look between Tobey and Duncan, the two of them were suddenly five-by-five, A-OK between them, Russell now the bearer of everything fucked up between them both.

Russell took a step back, afraid. He wasn't afraid that any one of the members of Acrobat would shoot him—he was afraid of what was going on. He looked at Ljubica.

Ljubica was looking at Russell, her eyes hard and closed, without saying a thing.

"Why are you doing this to me?" he asked inanely.

Ljubica didn't say a thing.

The Metro began slowing down, approaching a station. Duncan sighed and turned to face Russell, everyone else standing too, as if they were all about to get off.

"I think you should go now," said Duncan, repeating Monika's words in exactly the same tone of voice that she had used—rueful and sad, but inflexible.

"What, you're gonna make me go?" asked Russell.

"Yes," said Duncan.

The train stopped at the Judiciary Square Metro station, the doors to the train opening.

"This is crazy, this is insane, you are all so fucked up it's not even funny, *what are you doing?—what are you thinking?—how far do you think you can go?—I didn't do a goddamned fucking thing!*"

The random civilians on the Metro train looked at Russell as if he were some very dangerous football player–sized weirdo they might have to look out for. Acrobat knew better. Gently—but implacably—Duncan put his hand flat on Russell's chest. Then he slowly pushed Russell backward, out of the train, allowing the tide of people getting off to carry Russell along.

"What are you doing?" he said, frightening the civilians around him, who quickly stepped away from Russell even as he towered above them, looking all of a sudden very big and very black now that he seemed to be losing it.

Russell stared at the friends who were no longer his friends, the four of them perfectly framed by the open doors of the train as he stepped backward, tripping a bit on the edge of the platform, his legs barely able to keep him steady on his feet, legs that had now turned rubbery and unstable.

Duncan pushed him completely out of the train, then stepped back inside, falling in among the others.

The doors closed, locking Russell outside.

"What are you doing?!?"

Too late, he started slapping on the glass of the doors, trying to get them to open, trying to get back inside as the train lurched slightly and began to move, pulling away from him even as he ran after them.

Even as he ran, he could see them looking after him, looking at him through the windows of the train. Monika was crying, Tobey about to, Duncan looking away, and Ljubica appearing as if she were disappearing even faster than the train was taking them away.

Then, as Russell watched, they all turned their backs on him, closing in even tighter as the tunnel of the Metro line sucked them all away.

It was the last time any of them saw Russell Orr alive.

CHAPTER 9

Trying to Get Back into the Fold

Friday morning dawned chilly and gray. What remained of the work-group Acrobat—Duncan Idaho, Monika Summers, Ljubica Greene, and Tobey Jansen—woke up in the two adjacent rooms on the third floor of the International Guest House.

The International Guest House was a three-story bed-and-breakfast run by the Mennonite Church, though it was open to all comers. Located about four miles north of the Mall and just east of Rock Creek Park, it was almost at the corner of Kennedy Avenue and Sixteenth Street, a comfortable house with a nice wide front porch no different from the others up and down the street. A house that looked quiet and kind and out-of-the-way and peaceful.

Russell didn't know about this hostel, of course. It was why they had all moved here.

The IG House was cheaply carpeted, filled with sturdy, bland furniture made of pine and maple, the finish of which was turning vaguely greenish. Since it was a hostel run by the Mennonite Church, the rooms for boarders—fifteen in all, six of them on the third floor—were all decorated in sternly simple yet pleasantly happy colors and cloths: The beds covered in creamy yellow comforters, their dark undersides hidden by frilly valances embroidered by hand, the beds positioned directly beneath Audobon-like prints of bright flowers on white backgrounds, prints that had faded over time and under the sun but which still managed to cheer. On the walls along the upstairs hallways, paint-by-number pictures of country girls were hung in simple frames, the colors of the paintings soft yellows and browns, with dashes of blue and dark pink coming from the dresses of the Holly Hobby girls, who stood in exact profile or in perfect singular composition, the paintings complemented by the two light fixtures hanging from the ceiling, two white frosted glass squares whose corners curled up, hiding the lightbulbs as they let through soft light. The carpeting exuded a soft, homey smell that was vague and unidentifiable but so American-homey, the hardwood floors under the carpeting creaking slightly at the pressure of a footfall.

The stairs creaked most of all, even though they felt heavily wrapped in cushioning and carpeting, the carpeting throughout the hostel an indistinct tan color, the color of pure desert sand.

It was just turning to first light when the four remaining members of the work-group Acrobat made their way downstairs to the dining room. The current Mennonite volunteer who operated the hostel, an older woman named Joyce, was setting out breakfast things for the guests. From her look— her granny glasses, her simple cornflower blue slacks, her nondescript blouse, her short and untinted curly gray hair, and her eyes the color of her unfashionable slacks—you suspected that she was the individual responsible for the decor of the hostel: Its unsophisticated, cheery, and vastly comforting decor. The very naïveté of her aesthetic made you feel so at home and relaxed, you hoped that Joyce herself would be a walking and talking exemplar of this guileless simplicity.

She was.

"Oh, hello there," she said, looking up at them from behind her granny glasses with a smile. "You're all up bright and early."

"Hi Joyce," said Duncan, of the four the most comfortable with the woman.

"My, it's a quarter of six in the morning! You *do* want to get a leg up this morning, don't you?"

"We surely do," said Duncan. "What's for breakfast?" he asked as he looked at the two long, collapsible tables, covered in an embroidered white tablecloth, loaded with stacks of plates and cutlery Joyce had just brought in.

"Well, Craig—I'm so bad with names this early in the morning—you said your name was Craig, was that right?"

"Yes, that's right," said Duncan, wincing a bit at their need to lie to this woman.

"Well, Craig," she said, "breakfast is supposed to start at seven-thirty, but I don't mind getting you all something to eat so long as you don't mind helping me."

"Point the way," said Duncan, following Joyce into the kitchen.

"No, not you, you sit down, dearie," Joyce said to Ljubica, watching her limp into the kitchen with the others. Joyce went around the large dining tables and pulled a chair out for Ljubica to sit in. "You sit down and rest up that leg; we can manage fine," she said, under the impression that Ljubica had pulled a muscle rather badly.

Joyce led the way as Duncan, Monika, and Tobey helped her shuttle food to the table, Ljubica watching as she tried to relax. They all sat down to breakfast, pale blue light coming in through the windows, as Joyce did most of the talking, the members of Acrobat listening in and asking questions, the better so they wouldn't have to talk about what had happened.

Joyce talked about her life in Madison, Wisconsin, where she worked as the administrator of a medium-sized medical practice. She obsessed a bit about her grandkids—about how far away they lived, down in Atlanta, Georgia, and about how she was afraid to fly, so she had to take a bus or train to go see them.

They ate their breakfast quickly, then bid their good-byes to Joyce, Tobey, Ljubica, Monika, and Duncan walking out of the house to confer on the front porch.

"I think this is a bad idea," said Duncan to start off the conversation, the four of them out on the front lawn, all of them smoking cigarettes in the sharp morning air.

"It's a good idea," Monika insisted. "You and Tobey contact Michaelus. Ljubica and I'll stay here—. Are you okay?" she asked Yuvi, rubbing her arm.

Ljubica—noticeably worse for wear—managed only a nod.

"Okay," said Monika. "Get in touch with Michaelus; then once he's secure, we'll go to Langley."

Ljubica sighed. "Why don't we just *go*," she said.

"Aye-aye, here-here," said Duncan. "Second that."

Tobey shook his head. "No, let's try to get back inside," he said.

Duncan bit his lip and looked at the ground, still feeling a little on the outs with Tobey and therefore not really wanting to go full out against him.

"That's right," said Monika. "Call us as soon as you're inside Langley. Michaelus would love to screw Denton over—he knows we can dump a hell of a lot of crap on Denton."

Duncan said, "What we should do is get our stuff from the bank and bug out—"

"How are we gonna do that if it's crawling with FBI or whatever?" said Monika.

Duncan sighed again and shook his head. "If this doesn't work out, the first thing I'm gonna do is put Denton six underground, okay? Just so long as that's clear, I'll go along with this."

"Fine," said Monika tightly. "Get in touch with Michaelus. If he doesn't want to bring us back, then fine, go do whatever you want with Denton. Happy now?"

Duncan scoffed, pissed at himself and powerless to fix the mess he was making with Monika. "Yeah, I'm happy—I'm wearing a huge fucking happy head," he mumbled as he walked off the porch toward their car.

"Shit," said Monika softly, looking after Duncan as he got in the car. She turned to Tobey. "Try the best you can, okay?"

"Okay," said Tobey nervously.

Monika gave him a hug, then Tobey got in their car, the Camry they'd stolen in Pennsylvania not two days ago. As soon as he was in, Duncan drove away, Monika watching them go before she turned to Ljubica and helped her back inside.

"Let's change that field dressing," Monika told her.

As they drove down Sixteenth Street, Duncan said, "We should ditch this car."

"Yeah," said Tobey, thinking. "You really think Russ was with *him?*" he asked.

"Of *course* he was," said Duncan irritably. "He practically confessed as much." Then he scoffed as he drove. "This is a bad, bad idea," said Duncan crossly.

Tobey said, "Why don't we just try? It can't hurt, can it?"

"You'd better believe it can."

"Where the fuck are my car keys," he said quietly before allowing his temper to bloom and explode. "Where, the, *fuck*, are my car keys!" he repeated as he stormed through the house that morning.

Bart Michaelus's home was a lot like Bart Michaelus himself—on the surface neat and orderly, but underneath it all a tension that was downright crystalline, as if this order had been brought about only by the most tremendous pressure and might still just spontaneously shatter anyway, if the right conditions happened to apply.

"Where are my—god—damned—*keys!*" Michaelus shouted as he quickly walked through the living room and dining room and family room, looking for his fucking keys, which was easy—in all of those rooms, there wasn't a single misplaced paper or item, not a single bill or flyer or letter or newspaper lying around. The videos in the family room were arranged alphabetically, and in the living room the assorted decorative knick-knacks—silver spoons from different places, mini abstract sculptures bought at his insistence—were carefully, evenly spaced apart, like soldiers at parade rest.

"Maddy, where are my fucking keys!" he shouted from the family room into the kitchen.

"*I* don't know," said his wife, Madeleine, as she packed their children's lunch boxes in the kitchen.

Their children—both elementary-school age—went through their morning paces, pretending to ignore their father. They'd seen him this way countless times before, raging throughout the house like the Tasmanian Devil, a little mini-cyclone that could not stay put, and neither of these two kids had any intention of interfering with their daddy. Instead, these kids—a girl of twelve and a boy of eight, both beginning to balloon into morbid obesity from sheer nerves—watched their mom pack their lunches as they ate their cereal before the milk had had its chance to turn it soggy.

"I want *two* Ding-Dongs," the boy said quietly, quietly enough so that he wouldn't be heard by his daddy.

"*Where are my fucking* KEYS—? Oh," said Michaelus as he found them, turning into a silent, embarrassed cyclone, which was in a lot of ways worse than a screaming one. "Fucking shit," he fumed. "Always hiding things from me—you're always hiding things from me," he said, leaving the pronoun vague, implicitly blaming everyone but himself in the household.

He was a scary guy. When he was five, some goose pecked him or scared him or did something to him; some goose-thing or whatever. Anyway, five-year-old Michaelus grabbed one of those little gardening shovels and spent a whole afternoon tracking that dumb goose down. And when he found it, he zonked that goose on the head with the shovel, clobbering it to death in a rage of his own making.

"I'm not going to take you to school," he told his kids in the kitchen as he finished tying his tie and watched them contemptuously, hating his own children's fatness and slovenliness and most of all their fear: Their fear of him. That fear made Michaelus want to tear their souls to bits. "I told you to be ready by seven-thirty, and it's already a quarter to eight," he said.

His wife sighed, not bothering to argue as their children looked guiltily between their daddy and their mother. No one mentioned the fact that *Michaelus* was fifteen minutes late, but then it wouldn't have occurred to any of them.

"I'm leaving," he said, not bothering with his breakfast—which he hadn't had time to eat—as he stormed out the kitchen to the garage.

"I want two Ding-Dongs, too," said their daughter to Michaelus's wife.

"OK," she said, dropping another package of Ding-Dongs

into her lunch box, the twelve-year-old girl already fast approaching the hundred-pound mark, with no end in sight.

What for was this? What for? What was the point of breaking one's wife, terrifying one's children, turning one's very self into a psychological pretzel? To succeed at work? Was the work that valuable? Was the work that necessary? Was the work worth turning a life into a crippled, empty thing?

In the garage, Michaelus looked unhappily at his Z3 roadster under its neon-blue canvas covering, suddenly noticing a loose thread at the rear of the covering—two sewn loops were coming apart, about an inch of seam.

"Mother*fucker*," he said to himself, as he examined the loose thread, too late for work to bother going back in and finding out who had done it. Save it for later.

He got into his white Land Rover, which was impeccably clean, down to the tires themselves, which were shiny black from the Armor All. He hit the garage door remote control in his car and waited as it lumbered open.

"Come *on,* come *o-o-on,* shit," he said as he turned on his car.

Michaelus pumped his Land Rover and got it in gear, the tires squealing over the glassy concrete of his garage and rolling off the driveway fast enough that he might have killed somebody, if anybody'd been casually strolling on the sidewalk.

As it was, it was empty, and anyway Bart didn't give a fuck about his neighbors, though he pretended well enough that he did.

He switched gears and hit the gas, all four thousand pounds of the Land Rover leaping forward like a buck mastodon looking to score in the big jungle. He drove to the end of his street and turned left, onto another suburban street that was a couple of hundred feet long, lined with green shrubbery and intersected by the feeder road to the 267.

At the corner, Michaelus signaled to make a right turn, looking to his left to see the oncoming traffic, when suddenly he heard two hollow bangs on the hood of his car.

"What the *fuck*—"

It was Duncan Idaho and Tobey Jansen. They were just standing there in the early morning cold, looking like castaways coming across a rescue ship.

Michaelus rolled down the passenger side window, a huge and friendly smile on his face. "Well hello-o-o there!" he said happily. "Get in," he said, unable to believe what was happening.

Duncan hopped into the front seat and Tobey got in the back.

"All your little fingers and toes inside? Good," said Michaelus, hitting the gas and flowing right into the morning rush-hour traffic.

Holy shit! I got Denton by the balls! he thought gleefully, unable to believe his luck, unable to believe the unbelievability of it all—Duncan Idaho and Tobey Jansen, popping into his car as if a fairy godmother had granted him a big wish.

"God*damn,* you guys startled me," he said with a smile, looking over at Idaho and in his rearview mirror at Jansen. "I thought it was some bum who was gonna hassle me or something!"

Of course there were no bums anywhere *near* Michaelus's house, it being that kind of neighborhood and all, which Michaelus tried to make clear as he glanced at Idaho and Jansen again, trying to punctuate his little joke.

"Sorry," said Jansen a little unsurely, surprised at how unrelieved he suddenly felt. *This is a mistake,* he thought.

"How long have you guys been waiting for me here?" Michaelus asked Idaho, ignoring Jansen altogether.

"About an hour," said Duncan, aware that Michaelus had mentally turned both him and Tobey into objects.

"Just hiding in the bushes there?" Bart Michaelus asked, still stunned and automatically driving straight to Langley.

"Yeah," said Idaho, Michaelus constantly glancing at him—blown away by what he represented.

"So you're Duncan Idaho," he said in his most charming tone of voice, which was very charming indeed, when he wanted it to be.

"Yes," said Idaho, not knowing what to say to that.

"Well, I'm Bart Michaelus," said Bart Michaelus, peacock proud and peachy keen too, talking as though they'd never met before, though in fact they had. "A pleasure to finally meet you. And you, you're? Tobey is it?"

"Yeah, Tobey, Tobey Jansen?"

"That's nice. Before the end of the day, we're gonna have a few things settled," Michaelus said happily, taking over the conversation without really paying attention to the strain between the two of them. In his mind, Michaelus's gears just smoothly shifted through all that he was going to make happen today. "So where are the others?" he asked suddenly, remembering that there were five members of Acrobat. "Russell Orr and Monika Summers and, what's her name? Lejoobicka Greene?"

"'Yu*vitza*,'" Tobey corrected him automatically. "Ljubica's wounded. Monika's taking care of her."

"Too bad," said Michaelus, like he didn't give a shit about her. "What about Orr."

"He's gone," said Duncan.

Michaelus shrugged. "The first thing we're gonna do is debrief the hell out of you at Langley. I want to know *everything*, down to the last detail."

"OK," said Tobey, not relieved at all.

"Then we're gonna go back over it, and then over it again, until we've got it all down."

"But we're gonna get back into the fold, right?" asked Tobey nervously.

"Sure sure sure," said Michaelus, with an easy smile, his lips polishing his words, spit-shining them until they sounded all nice and fake. "You'll be back in the fold in no time."

Duncan turned and looked at Tobey, his eyes trying to say, *See? See where this shit is taking us?* even as he didn't really believe it himself.

Tobey looked away.

"So let's start with last Sunday, when you went underground," Michaelus began as he drove down the Beltway. "Tell me everything that happened since Sunday."

"Well," Tobey began, "we got tipped off? So then we split up and went up to New York . . ."

Michaelus listened with half an ear as he thought through exactly what he was going to do with them. First up of course was wringing them dry and getting the location of the other members of the group. Then, he'd direct the FBI's arrest of Ljubica and Monika before turning Tobey and Duncan over to Livre himself. *Kudos kudos kudos!* Michaelus thought, imaging the face on the Feebie bastard when he turned Acrobat over to him—Michaelus imagining *Denton's* face when he realized who really had him by the balls. Michaelus unconsciously smiled as he thought about how things would be once he'd debriefed and betrayed Acrobat—he'd have all the cards and all the chips.

". . . then when we got away from the FBI at Pentagon City, we went to a bank—"

"—to get some money," Duncan interrupted Tobey. "And uh, that's when we realized that Russell Orr was with Denton."

Tobey looked at Duncan, his face perfectly flat.

"I see, I see," said Michaelus as he drove, missing out on the weird look going on between Tobey and Duncan. "So after you figured Orr was betraying you guys, what did you do."

Duncan said, "We shot him and dumped his body in the Anacostia. Then we found a new place where we could stay, a place Russell didn't know about."

"Smart idea," said Michaelus, happily imagining everyone's faces when he delivered Acrobat, not even fazed at the death of Russell Orr. *A day to debrief, then tomorrow morning I hand them over.*

Michaelus smiled wider as he drove, Duncan and Tobey carefully looking at him as they went on with the edited and fictitious version of where they'd been and what they'd done.

Down the Beltway, they came upon Exit 13, the CIA employees' exit. (Exit 14, down the road a bit, was the tourists' exit; it led down George Washington Parkway along the edge of the river, to the front entrance of Langley, where the gift shop was. Employees never took that exit; way crowded.) Michaelus let his Land Rover drift toward the unmarked Exit 13 just as the Exit 14 sign came on up ahead, the big white-on-green letters spelling it out big as life:

```
            Langley
  Central Intelligence Agency
            Exit 14
           3/4 miles
```

Michaelus took Exit 13, slowing down and signaling for a right-hand turn just as he came to the intersection at the end of the exit ramp.

Turning, he drove down Georgetown Pike, a road that seemed to cut right through the heart of a forested wilderness, going toward the south entrance of the Agency compound. It appeared to their left as the road narrowed into two lanes—big boxy buildings jumbled up and thrown together, Le Corbousier–style buildings. Typical Modernist monstrosities.

Reaching the south gate, the Land Rover turned to the left and into the entrance, which is the only one of the three entrances that leads straight to the privileged underground parking lots. The underground parking lots are privileged because there are few of them, and they are warm and cozy during the wintertime.

At the gate, a lone guard sat sentry in a white wooden checkpoint shack that was vaguely New Englandy in its design. Beside it was the parking card reader, a little slotted box standing at attention atop a four-foot-high metal stick, waiting for Michaelus to feed it his marine-green parking pass.

The three checkpoints around Langley were a bit of a joke, really. They might be good for giving directions to lost tourists, but no way would they know the first thing about stopping a determined band of four year olds from storming the Langley gates. For obvious political reasons, those guards weren't even armed.

But then again, the guards at the checkpoints weren't part of the Langley security perimeter. The real perimeter started just inside the gate, five feet away from where Michaelus had stopped his Land Rover. And that perimeter started underground.

Buried just inside the gate of Langley, there are sensors that detect both aboveground and underground movement. There are also cameras—cunningly concealed in the architecture of the buildings—that monitor the entire perimeter around Langley. Add to that infrared, ultraviolet, along with the fortyman security detail whose sole job was to make sure no one tried to get in by force—well, no one was getting into Langley unless Langley wanted them to.

The guard at the checkpoint was just for show.

As the Land Rover stopped next to the parking card reader, the guard leaned toward the Land Rover's window as Michaelus rolled it down.

"Good morning, Mr. Michaelus," the guard said cheerfully, a very Irish-looking middle-aged man. "How are you today?"

"Fine, thanks," said Michaelus, having no idea who the guard was, even though he saw him every day.

Michaelus already had his parking pass in hand, flashing it at the guard with a smile as he shoved the card into the card reader's slot.

The guard smiled, his eyes casually drifting through the interior of the Land Rover, frowning ever so slightly at the sight of Duncan Idaho and Tobey Jansen, not recognizing them at all.

Don't look at me, thought Duncan Idaho, trying to make himself invisible. Unable to help himself, Duncan Idaho's eyes flashed over the buildings ahead of them, looking for wherever it was those famed cameras were hiding.

Michaelus meanwhile was shoving the parking pass in and out of the card slot, which, as usual in the Virginia humidity, was having a hard time reading the magnetic entry card.

"Fucking shit," Michaelus mumbled as he zipped the card half a dozen times.

The guard, noticing this, was about to say something, but his attention drifted over toward a blue convertible Mustang that had its top down. It was pulling up behind Michaelus's

Land Rover, pulling up too quickly, braking hard but still coming too fast—

KHÖ-*kah!*

A fender bender, the blue Mustang striking the rear of the Land Rover like a too-rough kiss, the inertia lurching everyone forward, as if in the grips of a collective hiccough.

"What the hell?" said Michaelus, his temper suddenly lit, turning to look around him and already unbuckling his seat belt, just as the driver of the blue Mustang stepped out of her car.

The driver of the Mustang was a smallish woman dressed in blue jeans, a white T-shirt, and a black leather jacket, her face obscured by the visor of an off-white yachting cap and a pair of big mirrored Ray•Ban aviator sunglasses, the kind that have those flexible earpieces, guaranteed not to slip off.

The woman—attractive as much by what was seen as what was hidden—was barely five feet two, her skin white and creamy, and what little hair came out from under her cap was straight and field-mouse brown, cut level and even at the nape of her neck. All of her visible or inferred features—her mouth, her breasts, her chin, her hips, her ears—were all slight and minimal, as if her Maker hadn't wanted her to have anything big on her, to hide what she was underneath.

Which was just as well. Because it was Amalia—the next best thing to a living machine.

Michaelus didn't stand a chance.

As he stepped out of his Land Rover with his temper in full flare, Michaelus wasn't worried about making it into Langley with his two stowaways, not anymore—he was worried about how banged up this stupid bitch had left his Discovery. Never mind that his Land Rover was practically made of cast iron, Michaelus—almost as soon as he unbuckled his seat belt—had made up his mind that he was going to let his temper flare like an unsteady sun gone nova. So as he started walking toward the Mustang's driver between the checkpoint shack and the side of his Land Rover, Michaelus was weirdly happy—he finally had a decent reason to blow up: This stupid fucking cunt of a driver had given him his excuse. And there was no reason to hold it in.

Amalia was meantime walking right toward Michaelus, looking right at him, her hands behind her back, not even seeming to care about the damage she had done to her own car. And it was this very aloofness that pushed Michaelus's temper out of the realm of the average temper tantrum and into the realm of the supra-nuclear chew out.

"Can't you see where you're going, you stupid fucking cunt?" Michaelus yelled at the impassive Amalia.

Those were the last words he ever spoke, words Amalia didn't even hear—she was too busy taking advantage of her amazing luck: Her target, Michaelus, was not only right in front of her, he was also walking straight at her, completely surprised, completely unarmed, not even imagining what was about to happen. It was such an amazing piece of luck that Amalia almost hesitated in surprise before taking full advantage of the situation.

Suddenly stopping and spreading her stance, Amalia whipped her hands from behind her back and brought them together around a boxy submachine gun, right hand on the trigger and stock, left hand holding the barrel steady.

Michaelus was too surprised to say another word.

With no hesitation, Amalia sprayed Deputy Director Bart Michaelus right where he stood, shooting him in the head and chest, her boxy-looking submachine gun spitting out bullets like evil sperm—*vvvsh-vvvsh-vvvsh-vvvsh-vvvsh-vvvsh!* while at the same time a continuous stream of spent shell casings popped out of the weapon and pelted the side of the Land Rover with a sound like raining change—*kaching-kaching-kaching-kaching-kaching-kaching!*

Amalia fired at practically point-blank range—barely four feet distant. Blood flew everywhere as Michaelus's body did a jig before collapsing to the ground in a messy pile of suddenly bloody clothes and flesh.

Then, silence.

The security guard's face was splashed with blood and bits of brain matter. His cheek was cut by flying pieces of bone fragment. He was staring in horrified silence at the dead body of Bart Michaelus.

"You," said Amalia, aiming her submachine gun at the security guard, who looked up at her like a spooked orangutan, his eyes wide as Eisenhower dollar coins.

"What?" squeaked the security guard.

"Don't move," said Amalia.

Amalia turned to check on the inside of the Land Rover, her mirrored sunglasses twisting the world as her head moved around and came to bear on the interior of the car.

She was looking to find harmless mushrooms in the Land Rover—she was not expecting to see what she saw: Duncan Idaho and Tobey Jansen, of all people, staring back at her, frozen, paralyzed in surprise.

Amalia blinked. *Duncan Idaho. And Tobey Jansen.*

"Okay," she said to herself, making up her mind how it was going to be.

With her left hand, Amalia reached forward and opened the rear passenger door of the Land Rover.

"*Oh my god oh my god!!*" screamed Tobey Jansen as his door was opened—but still he didn't move, it didn't even *occur* to him to move as Amalia in her off-white yachting cap and black leather jacket calmly reached in and grabbed Tobey by the neck of his Superman T-shirt.

Duncan Idaho recovered, finally, his right hand blindly reaching to grab the door latch as he looked over his left shoulder, reaching into the back seat with his left hand and grabbing Tobey's arm.

"*Come on!*" he shouted, yanking as hard as he could on Tobey's arm, Tobey now turned into the rope of a tug o' war between Amalia and Duncan—

—"No!"—

—but Tobey Jansen's arm slipped through Duncan's fingers. He was Amalia's now.

Amalia yanked Tobey out of the back of the Land Rover like an unwieldy bag of groceries, Tobey falling to the ground at her feet.

"*Let me go, let me go, what are you doing? let me go!*"

Tobey Jansen shouted, still so blown away by what Amalia had done that he made no effort to get away. All he was trying for, physically, was to get on his feet; and even the will for that collapsed in on itself as his eyes locked on Michaelus's corpse, barely a yard away from his face, Michaelus's chest sporting half a dozen holes each the size and shape of cigar burns, his face pockmarked with 9-mm acne, the surprise and shock of it all turning Tobey Jansen into a screaming, splayed mess.

"*Oh-God-oh-God*-OH-GOD!!" he screamed, horrified, the last shreds of his composure completely ripped apart.

"Don't move," said Amalia to Tobey. "And shut *up*," she said quietly, all the while holding on to Tobey Jansen's T-shirt as she turned her attention back to the interior of the Land Rover.

Nicholas Denton had given Amalia her marching orders quite some time ago—shoot Duncan Idaho on sight. Well, she had him in sight alright, Duncan Idaho just sitting there in the front passenger seat, his hands trying to open the door, staring over his left shoulder at Amalia as if waiting to get a bullet between the eyes, looking as surprised as a deer caught in the deadlights.

For a fraction of a second, Amalia contemplated everything and concluded that things were pretty much going her way.

Michaelus had walked clean into her, with no need for a messy chase. Tobey Jansen was so panicked by the sheer speed and decisiveness of the hit that he wasn't putting up any kind of resistance. The unarmed checkpoint guard seemed to be staying put like a good and wise little boy. And she was about to assassinate the panicked Duncan Idaho, with no ugly interference from Langley security, which was staying inside the gate as per procedures.

Indeed, all in all, everything was pretty much going her way.

Good, she thought casually, as she raised her firearm at Duncan and prepared to blow his head off, holding the submachine gun with her right hand, with her left holding on to a fistful of Tobey Jansen's shirt.

In that fraction of a second, things got awfully complicated.

Amalia was counting on Langley security to not make a move on anything going on outside the gate—and on that, Amalia was absolutely right. Orders are, nothing going on outside the gates—absolutely nothing—brings out security, no matter what. Reason? It might be a decoy, designed to draw out forces.

So inside Langley, instead of going out there and stopping her, the PhysPlanSec people simply watched passively, horrified, as Amalia killed Bart Michaelus with total impunity and prepared to kill Duncan.

They *did* call Virginia State Police, sure—they were dialing VSPD before Michaelus even hit the ground. But it would be eons, relatively speaking, before the cops showed up. It would be at least a minute. Long after everything was over. Because from the moment Amalia's blue Mustang whacked Michaelus's Land Rover to the moment she raised her boxy submachine gun to blow Duncan Idaho's head off, less than ten seconds had elapsed.

So as Amalia had calculated, Langley security would just stand pat and watch things unfold, not interfering because of orders.

However, Amalia also assumed that the unarmed security guard, whom she'd cowed with a glare and a look at her weapon's muzzle, would stay put like a good little boy. After all, the security guard was unarmed, while she was strapping a TAC-10 on full automatic, and she'd shown herself more than willing to use it. No one in their right mind would dare mess with her. Amalia had been counting on that normal human reaction to get her past the security guard—after all, unarmed kiddies don't mess with submachine gun-toting grown-ups.

On that, she was dead wrong.

At the exact moment that she raised her TAC-10 to kill Duncan Idaho, the security guard—already standing over Bart Michaelus's body—made a mad dash for the Land Rover, trying to stop Amalia. But he didn't run at *Amalia*—instead, he ran at the rear left door of the Land Rover, smashing into it with his full weight, slamming the door shut right on Amalia's arm and shoulder just as she was about to pull the trigger on Duncan Idaho—*vvvsh-vvvsh-vvvsh-vvvsh!*

Duncan Idaho could *feel* the bullets whiz by his face as the interior of the Land Rover was flooded with the choking smell of hot cordite, the bullets shattering the front windshield of the car, the bullets missing his head by inches, quarter inches, if that—but missing him all the same.

It was a chance he wouldn't get again.

Instantly, he was jumping out the right door of the Land Rover, going straight to the blue Mustang behind the Rover, as he crouched all the way to the convertible.

The security guard, meanwhile, yanked Tobey away from Amalia and screamed, *"GO-GO-GO!"* as he opened the rear door of the Land Rover again and slammed it as hard as he could against Amalia, who was pinned.

Amalia didn't say a word. She'd dropped the TAC-10 when the security guard smacked her with the door of the Land Rover a second time, her entire right arm still in the car and by now completely numb, even though it hadn't taken the brunt of the security guard's hit—it was her right shoulder and breast that had taken the worst of the beating from the left rear door's frame.

And even though the pain was awful, Amalia—looking right at the security guard, who was completely dominating her attention—would not give the fucker the satisfaction of hearing her say a thing. Instead, Amalia decided to deal with him, deal with him good and proper.

The security guard, meanwhile, was staring right at Amalia, his face barely a foot away from hers, totally terrorized and hysterical, screaming uncontrollably as he opened the left rear door again, getting ready to slam it one more time against the young woman-child in the mirrored shades and the off-white yachting cap.

As he pulled open the door, Amalia—though she could have—didn't try to get her arm and shoulder out of the Land Rover and out of the way of the slamming door. Instead, with her now free left hand, she reached behind her back and pulled

out a Beretta, her back-up gun, aiming it for the security
guard's belly, smiling at him just as he saw the gun come out
of nowhere.

PR-RACK! went the unsilenced Beretta.

The security guard—about to leave his wife widowed and
his three teenaged kids in emotional ruins—fell back and away
from the Land Rover though he was still on his feet, his mouth
silent and a big round O of surprise, staring at Amalia, who
was smiling an evil smile at the guard, watching as he fell
backward against the side of the security shack, leaning heavily against the side of the shack but still on his feet.

Inside, the head of the security watch had had enough—he
called on the security detachment to go out there, and fuck
orders about not crossing the perimeter fence.

"Come on!" shouted Duncan Idaho at the stunned Tobey,
already opening the passenger side door of the Mustang and
getting in as he pulled out his gun.

Tobey Jansen, now suddenly ignored in this mêlée, scrambled to the Mustang in a mad crouching dash, but Amalia
didn't see him—Amalia was concentrating on the security
guard.

"You fucking cocksucker," Amalia said calmly to the
guard, as she aimed for his crotch and both of the guy's
kneecaps and blew them out as deliberately as torture—
PR-RACK!—PR-RACK!—PR-RACK!

The guard, feeling as if his legs had been kicked out from
under him, couldn't scream—the pain in his belly, crotch, and
kneecaps was so awful he couldn't even breathe, the guard
thinking hysterically that he would not die from his wounds
but from his inability to breathe, breathe, *breathe*—

Amalia stared at him, smiling, the guard seeing himself
mirrored in her huge sunglasses, Amalia smiling as if she'd
seen this before but was now enjoying a different ending to
the same old story.

Tôh-tôhck! went Duncan Idaho's unsilenced gun, the gun
he'd taken from the FBI agent at Pentagon City, the gun he
was now unsteadily firing at Amalia, getting her attention.

Amalia turned around and saw that she was screwed—her

Bluebird target, Duncan Idaho, was already in the driver's seat of the Mustang, sticking his hand over the rim of the convertible's windshield and shooting random cover fire at her, while her Orange Crush target, Tobey Jansen, was diving into the rear seat of the Mustang.

How cool a killer was Amalia can be measured by this: When she turned around and spotted Duncan Idaho, he again fired cover fire, but this time with a steadier aim—*tôh-tôh-tôhck!*—his third shot so close to Amalia that she could feel it displacing the air around her throat.

Amalia didn't even duck, totally confident that she would achieve her secondary objective, assassinate Duncan Idaho. Nicholas Denton had ordered it, and Amalia had no intention of failing to implement that order.

"Where do you think *you're* going," she said absently, as she raised her Beretta and blew out the windshield of the Mustang—*kreë-AUmm!*—but not before Duncan Idaho had managed to simultaneously duck below the rim of the steering wheel and hit the accelerator on the still-running Mustang.

With a huge squeal of tires, the Mustang backed out of the Langley driveway, smashing hard into another arrival, a Buick LeSabre—*BAH-HACHI*—without even slowing down, Tobey Jansen nearly falling ass-first out of the rear of the car as Amalia calmly walked over to the rear seat of the Land Rover and retrieved her TAC-10.

Turning to the Mustang, Amalia hesitated, afraid of hitting the Orange Crush as she watched the Mustang roar out and away, Duncan Idaho crouching as low as he could behind the steering wheel, Tobey Jansen in the rear seat, his legs comically sticking out of the car like in some silly road movie.

"Mmm," said Amalia, abruptly turning around and looking at the situation.

The security guard was lying on the ground, about to pass out, and Michaelus was of course dead beside his Land Rover.

But the Land Rover was still running.

Casually, Amalia got in the driver's side of the Rover and reversed out of the Langley driveway, hitting the gas at full throttle.

Twenty-five seconds had elapsed from the moment Amalia deliberately smacked her Mustang into Michaelus's Land Rover until the moment she revved that same Land Rover out of the Langley driveway, casually crashing into the Buick LeSabre on her way out.

But even as she got on the road, Amalia knew it was no use—the Mustang was already a hundred yards away from her, and Michaelus's Land Rover, though it was a powerful car, was not built for speed: Even as she floored it, it could not accelerate to catch up with her now-stolen Mustang.

"Mmm," said Amalia, as she realized that she had lost Duncan Idaho and Tobey Jansen.

By the time the security detachment was out of the building, and by the time the Virginia State Police showed up, the very brave but very foolish security guard was dead on the scene, and Amalia and Idaho and Jansen were long gone.

CHAPTER 10

Broken

"Goddamn you!!" Monika shouted in their room at the Mennonite hostel. "God*damn* you, Duncan—*you did this on purpose!!*"

"No, I didn't Monika, I—"

"Shut up!!" she screamed again, the two of them alone in their room. "Shut up shut up shut up!!"

Through the thin walls separating the two rooms on the third floor, Tobey Jansen and Ljubica Greene could hear it all as Monika and Duncan slugged it out.

"Monika, listen-listen—"

"No!" she shouted, stomping around the room, her footfalls sounding like muffled blows.

"Listen," said Duncan, the footfalls suddenly stopping. "We got to Michaelus, we drove up to Langley, we got to the south gate, and then the little woman—the same little woman from New York—she ambushed us at the gate—"

"Bullshit!!" Monika shouted.

"Ask Tobey!!" Duncan shouted back. "He was there! We tried to get back in—we were right there at the *gate,* and she came out at us."

"You don't want to go back," said Monika, crying. "All you wanna do is tag Denton and bug out. That's it. You don't wanna go back, you just—just—just want to run off, go off—"

"Monika, listen—"

"Shut up!!" she screamed again. "Shut up-shut-up-shut-up-shut-up!!"

"Moni—"

All of a sudden, Tobey heard Monika and Duncan tousling, Monika saying "Let go of . . ." as the sound of footfalls rebounded across the third floor. "Stop it . . . ," Duncan was saying, the footfalls continuing, sounding like ballet dancers doing a demonic *pas de deux.*

How did they know? Tobey thought, as he lay there, listening to Monika and Duncan. *How did they know we'd be there with Michaelus?*

Tobey sat up on the bed.

"Don't go," said Ljubica Greene.

Tobey looked at her. Ljubica was lying with her back to him on the other bed, Joyce downstairs under the impression that they were brother and sister; otherwise, she never would have allowed them to bunk together.

"Leave them alone," said Ljubica, turning and looking over her shoulder at him. "You'll only make it worse if you get between them."

Ljubica's eyes were glassy, but otherwise she seemed steady, even though her wounded leg was puffing out like a balloon. Tobey was so naive, it hadn't occurred to him to think that Ljubica might be on something. Of the four of them, she was the one who had taken Michaelus's death most in stride.

But Michaelus's death hadn't even registered with her yet. All she could think about was Russell.

"You need anything?" Tobey asked.

Ljubica stared at him. Then she shook her head and turned back to face the wall, her hands folded under her head, her black straight hair fanning out across the pillow.

How did they know we'd be there with Michaelus—how?—how?—someone must have—

There was a knock at the door.

"Come in," said Tobey automatically.

Monika Summers, looking like she had been crying, walked in, Duncan Idaho lurking behind her in the hallway.

"Hi Tobey," she said, sniffling and wiping her face, her

shoulder-length blonde hair falling forward as she tried out a smile on him.

"Hi," he said.

"Tobey?" she asked tentatively, as if afraid of her voice's timbre. "I, uh . . . I gotta ask you: What happened?"

Tobey sat there on the bed and frowned, looking down at his hands and then up at Monika.

"We tried to get in," he said simply, looking over Monika's shoulder at Duncan, and then back at Monika again. "Into Langley? We were in the car with Michaelus, right there at the gate, like everything was going fine. But then this other car hit us from the back. And that woman? The one from New York? She was driving this other car, and she shot Michaelus right there—like she was assassinating him, because she didn't even talk to Michaelus; she just shot him. Then she tried to kill us? She killed a security guard, too—just shot him," he said, amazed. "And I think she was going to kill me and Duncan if we hadn't been able to get out of there."

Monika nodded through all of this, nodding with growing impatience as if knowing all this already, waiting for the opening. "And you didn't even try to get inside," she said.

"Well, we couldn't," said Tobey. "The woman, she shot Michaelus? He was dead, so how were we gonna get inside without him—"

"And didn't anybody from Langley come out to help you guys?" asked Monika.

Tobey frowned. "No," he said simply.

"They just let this woman try to kill you guys, huh," said Monika, disbelieving.

"Yeah, I guess," said Tobey.

"You guess?"

"It was all so *fast*," said Tobey.

"And didn't it occur to you to run inside?" Monika asked.

"But, Monika," said Tobey sensibly. "It's not just getting inside Langley physically? We can do that right now, right? It's getting back inside Langley, like, *psychologically*? And with Michaelus dead, how were we gonna do that?"

Duncan put his hand on her shoulder and said, "Monika—"

But Monika shrugged him off. "So you weren't there long enough to figure out if they might have helped you or not."

Tobey closed his eyes, trying to sort it all out. "She had this machine gun?"

"An assault rifle," Duncan said. "I think it might've been a TAC—"

"Shut up!" Monika barked furiously, with a visible effort turning on a happy, fake-placid demeanor for Tobey. "Sorry," she said. "You were saying?"

Tobey looked from Monika to Duncan to Monika again. "Monika? If we'd stayed there any longer? She would have killed us both I think."

Monika pounced. "You *think* but you don't *know*—so you didn't stay around long enough to *try* to get back in, Tobey; you didn't *try*—neither one of you tried to get back in—"

"Enough of this shit," said Duncan suddenly, pulling Monika out of Tobey and Ljubica's room.

"Let go of me—"

Clam! went the door, slammed shut by Duncan as he pulled Monika back into their room.

"Let go of me, *let go of me!!*"

"Are you gonna calm down? Are you?"

"I'll do the fuck I want!" Monika shouted out loud.

Silence.

Tobey imagined Duncan had just lit a cigarette, because when he started to speak again, Tobey could only barely hear him, Duncan speaking low and thoughtfully, the way he did when he'd just lit up.

"What did Tobey tell you: We tried to get in but Denton was waiting for us," said Duncan. "So now that we know that, we ought to make a plan for getting our stash from the DuPont Circle bank somehow—"

"You didn't even *try*," said Monika. "You didn't *try* to get back inside, you bastard! You just went through the motions, you didn't *try*—"

"We nearly died trying to get—"

Monika slapped Duncan—hard, hard enough that Tobey could hear it through the wall separating them.

"Jesus fucking *Christ!*" said Duncan.

Suddenly, Tobey decided he'd had enough.

"I'm gonna go," he told Ljubica.

"Okay," said Ljubica. "Where?"

"I don't know," said Tobey, getting up and putting his sneakers back on. He suddenly noticed that there were some flecks of blood on the laces, but whether the blood was from Michaelus or from the security guard Amalia had downed Tobey couldn't tell. He wiped it off as best he could, but the flecks had already dried.

"I'll be back in a couple of hours," he said. "Be sure to tell Duncan and Monika when you see them."

"Okay," said Ljubica, still staring at the wall.

Tobey walked out of their room and closed the door behind him, walking away from the fight as he got to the top of the staircase. Ljubica heard him as he took the stairs down, leaving her to hear Monika and Duncan slugging it out.

She and Russell had never fought like that. They fought with silence. And if and when they had to speak, the words they used were clipped and polite and innocuous. But they knew what the other was thinking. Which was surprising, considering Russell never knew Ljubica's heart.

She grimaced and bit her lip as she stared at the blank wall, seeing the look on Russell's face as they pushed him out of the Metro car. He was so surprised. He had never anticipated that she would reject him, that she would betray him.

Our love wasn't real, she thought suddenly. *He never knew my heart—our love was not real.*

Ljubica cried at the wall, knowing full well that that was true enough: Their love had never been real. *If only he had taken a stand, made up his mind—black or white—green or red—one way or the other,* she thought bitterly, even now refusing to accept the real reason for their counterfeit love: When the moment had come, she had been too afraid. So she kept her heart in check, and demanded that he accept this as good.

And he had.

. . .

Tobey ambled downstairs, and when he got to the first floor, he casually walked past Joyce with a smile and a nod, walking out of the International Guest House and over to Sixteenth Street.

The morning was sunny and beautiful, rush hour just over as he stood on the corner. Tobey looked around, not really sure what he was going to do. A bus happened to be coming down the street, so without any clear sense as to where he was going or what he was going to do, Tobey flagged it down and hopped on board, traipsing to the back of the bus and sitting down directly over the hump of the rear wheel.

The bus drove down Sixteenth Street, Tobey barely noticing where he was going as his thoughts chased each other like slot-cars on a closed circuit.

They knew we were coming, HE *knew we were coming, he* KNEW *we'd be there with Michaelus, he was waiting for us— how?—how?—how did he know we'd be there?—How?*

"Hey mister," said the bus driver, a small, neat black woman with short dreadlocks. "Mister!"

"Who me?" said Tobey, confused as he woke up.

Unbelievably, he had fallen asleep on the bus.

"What happened?" he asked out loud.

"Why, you fell asleep," said the bus driver. "This is Federal Triangle—the end of the route," she went on. "You gots to get off here, unless you wanna go back where you came from."

"Right," said Tobey, getting off the bus without any idea where he was, the words "Federal Triangle" gaining no purchase whatsoever on his brain.

"Thanks!" he called out to the bus driver, who nodded and called out, "Have a nice day!" as she closed the door and pulled the bus away from the curb.

Tobey checked his watch and looked around. It was ten-thirty in the morning, Federal Triangle full of people going about their business. Sunlight streaked overhead like sheets of soft steel, but the buildings on Pennsylvania Avenue cast crisp, hard shadows where Tobey stood, the Capitol Building sitting at an angle down the street, looking almost too real to be true.

Tobey looked around, got his bearings, then began walking down Pennsylvania Avenue, away from the Capitol, toward the White House, looking for a pay phone.

He saw plenty of pay phones on Penn, but no booths, making Tobey wonder where they had all gone. *No privacy,* he thought.

But then he realized that privacy was everywhere. The pay phones up and down Pennsylvania gave no privacy because they didn't need to. Because no one passing by would know who you were, much less care about what you were talking about. Out on the street, everyone was a stranger.

He stopped at the next pay phone he saw, and dialed the operator.

"I'd like to make a collect call, please," he said. "Area code 703, 547-1818."

"Party calling?" said the operator, bored.

"Tobey Jansen."

"One moment," said the operator.

There was a dialing noise, then the sound of someone picking up the phone, a voice saying, "Yes?"

The operator said in a fast, dull tone of voice, "This is a collect call from a Mr. Tobey Jansen. Will you accept the charges."

"Yes," said Nicholas Denton.

"Go ahead," said the operator, clicking off the line.

Neither man said a thing, for a bit.

"Give me your number; I'll call you back on a secure line," said Denton.

"This is secure enough," said Tobey tiredly.

Denton thought to say something, then thought the better of it, waiting Tobey out.

But Tobey said nothing, hanging on the phone as he looked up and down the street. *See?* he thought, as the pedestrians around him passed him by without notice, without so much as a glance in his direction. *I got all the privacy I'll ever need.*

"What's been going on?" Denton asked quietly.

"We've been on the run," said Tobey.

"Yes, I know," he said without a hint of sarcasm, handling Tobey as gingerly as a delicate icicle. "Something like half the world is hunting you down. People think your Acrobat work-group killed Bart Michaelus this morning."

"We didn't kill him, Mr. Denton," said Tobey. "*You* did."

Denton said nothing, waiting on Tobey.

"I guess you decided he had to go," said Tobey.

Again, Nicholas Denton didn't say a thing.

Tobey sighed, a shaky breath coming out of him. But then a stray bit of curiosity got away from him, like a caught fox from a diligent hound, making him naturally perk up and ask, "How did you know we'd be there this morning? With Michaelus?"

"I didn't," said Denton.

Tobey blinked. "So it was just *chance* that we happened to be there when Amalia came for him?"

Denton said nothing.

"I'm not taping this conversation," said Tobey. "Just tell me: Did you know we'd be there?"

"No," said Denton softly. "It was just chance. Tobey, why don't you tell me where you are. I can have a car there in fifteen minutes."

"Oh, yeah, right, and then you'll put me six underground, right?"

"No," said Denton quickly. "Nothing will happen to you—"

"You're so full—"

"I owe you," said Denton. "The fact is, I've been going out of my way to make sure nothing happens to you."

Tobey said nothing, not believing him.

"You don't believe me, okay," said Denton, pausing to think. Then very carefully—careful about being recorded—he began to speak. "When . . . our girl had the opportunity to . . . end things with you, she didn't take it. She . . . had specific orders . . . about you . . . 'Orange Crush.' Do you know what that term means?"

Tobey nodded as if Denton could see him.

"Do you?" Denton repeated.

"Yeah, yeah," said Tobey. "Orange Crush means capture without damage."

"Okay," said Denton. "If I had wanted you out of the picture, our friend could have . . . painted you over this morning. Do you understand me."

"Yes sir," said Tobey.

"I'm letting you go. But I can't give a bye to your friends," said Denton. "They don't deserve it. They don't rate it."

Tobey shook his head. "You got Tom Carr, you got Bart Michaelus. You did everything you wanted to do, why can't you just leave us alone? Huh?"

Denton said nothing.

"Mr. Denton?"

"I'm here."

"Why can't you leave us alone?" Tobey repeated. "Why can't we come ba——"

"*You* can come back, whenever you want to," said Nicholas Denton. "But not your friends."

"You're gonna kill them," he said dully.

Denton sighed, and then, in the same not-quite-paying-attention tone of voice he'd been using throughout this conversation, he asked, "Why do you keep calling?"

"I don't know," said Tobey, honestly confused.

"You keep telling me all about where Acrobat's going to be," said Denton carefully. "But you keep telling me just before it's too late."

It was Tobey's turn to say nothing.

"You warned them that I was coming for them last Sunday morning," said Denton slowly and carefully, "and now you warn them that I'm coming for them just before I manage to get there. That's why Tom Carr died in the dreadful way that he did," said Denton.

"No-no-no," said Tobey, provoked. "You were gonna kill Tommy anyway—"

"Okay, okay, okay—"

"Don't say it was my fault Tom died the way he did, you were gonna kill him anyway, you're a bloodthirsty . . . —

vampire, that's what you are: A smiling, smooth, slick-as-shit *vampire.*"

"Okay, okay."

"So don't you go telling me that it was *my* fault. I didn't send Amalia to waste everyone. I didn't—"

"Remember when you were working for me?" asked Denton quickly.

Tobey stopped talking.

"Remember when you were suspended from college, and then you came to work for me? I took you in, Tobey—"

"Don't-don't—don't," said Tobey. "Don't. That, those days . . ."

"I took you in. Nobody wanted you, except me. Not even your own brother—where is he, out in California?—not even he would take you in. But I did. I brought you in when you were all alone and terrified. At that first interview I had with you, remember? You looked like a refugee. So I brought you in as an intern, and then I helped you get back into college. And then after college, I arranged for your rehiring. I made certain commitments to you, and I kept them. But you? Now? This? Tobey, why? You were just supposed to watch them, that was all. Watch them, and then report what you saw. So why did you join them? Why are you running with them now?"

Tobey didn't answer.

"If you'd brought them in, like you were supposed to," said Denton carefully, "you could have come back into the fold. You could have been back on the inside—with Amalia, with Matt Wilson, with your buddy, Jerry Willard—"

"Jerry Willard quit last year," said Tobey.

"Yes I know he quit last year," said Denton. "He's making a gazillion dollars working as an analyst for Morgan Stanley in Paris. That could be you. You could be back inside, either working here at Langley or at any cushy private-sector job you want. You could be back inside whenever you want."

"You keep saying that," said Tobey.

"I keep saying it because it's true," said Denton.

"It's not true," said Tobey. "It's over. Matt Wilson is in that Discothèque thing you got going—"

"That's—"

"And Jerry's gone, and Kathleen Bigsby's gone too, and Amalia, she's become some sort of monster, you've turned her into a *monster*, Mr. Denton—I can't go back there; there's nothing to go back to."

"You can't go back to Acrobat either," said Denton, his temper slipping a little. "Acrobat is over. It's *over*. Tom Carr is dead, Bart Michaelus is dead. You may think that the five of you can still swing it—"

"It's just four of us now," said Tobey quietly.

"What do you mean," said Denton.

"Russell . . . he's . . ."

"Russell Orr? Is he dead?"

"No," said Tobey. "The others? They thought . . . they thought he was me: They thought he was tipping you off? So he was kicked out of the group. We didn't kill him."

"I see," said Denton. "Tobey, believe me: These things always end badly. I'm giving you a last chance: You can come back into the fold now."

"If I betray Acrobat."

"Forget about Acrobat," said Denton. "I'm going to roll them up, one way or another, with or without your help. I'm not talking about Acrobat—I'm talking about you, Tobey. Come back to Langley now—right this second. If you don't, what are you going to do when this is all over?"

"I don't know, but at least I'm not alone now," he said in a rush. "At least I'm not, I-I-I I have *someone* now, I have people, a place where I can belong *now*. And they depend on me, and they trust me, and-and now I . . . and now I'm talking to you. Fuck."

Tobey fell silent, scratching the keypad of the phone with his fingernail, Denton waiting him out.

"Mr. Denton? I *belong*," said Tobey. "I-I belong—to Acrobat. I-I can't, I can't give that up. I don't have anyplace else where I can belong. I'm standing at a pay phone, and there are all these people around me? And I can never connect to them, no matter how hard I try. I could never connect to any of them. Then, then—you look at any family? They're just marking time before they split apart. You look at any friendship? You know it'll come undone—you know it's transient. And even in a family, even in the best of friendships? They're really not connected because they're missing something; they don't have what I have with Acrobat; they don't have . . . I don't know—secrets maybe? I don't know, but they all just brush up against each other and then drift away. Even blood family: They just . . . float away. They move to different cities, they marry, they get divorced, and they become strangers. You see them at holidays and all the while you just know that they're only putting up with you. They don't want to be with you, they don't much want to talk to you, they don't even *like* you. . . . But it's not like that with Acrobat. I'm bound to them, Mr. Denton—I *belong*. With Acrobat, I *belong*—and I *like* that. I feel safe. Is that so wrong?"

"No," said Denton. "No it's not. But Acrobat is over. And you're right, you can't go back to Amalia and Matthew and Jerry, that's over too. You're right. But you'll find another plane, another set of people—"

"No," said Tobey. "No, I wish I could believe you? But no, you don't find it that easy. After Dartmouth, when I went back to Langley? You said you wanted me to hang loose at PRC Finance. You said that you needed someone you could trust on the inside, for the future. You told me to just hang at PRC Finance and wait, and that when the time was right, you'd bring me back into the fold. So I waited. I waited and waited and waited, and I tried to reach out to the people around me, but it was like, I couldn't *connect*. No matter how hard I tried. And all the while, you're dangling this carrot, that you'd bring me back into the fold when the time was right? *But you didn't*. You didn't pull me back into the fold; you sent me off to Acrobat instead. And they, Mr. Denton, from the first day, from the *first day* they were my friends. From the *first*. They connected with me—they went out of their way to connect with me. And then after six months, out of the blue, you tell me I have to sell them out? You call me and tell me I have to break with them? Mr. Denton, sir, are you really surprised that I wouldn't do that?"

"No, I guess not," said Denton.

"And I can't go back to you—Kathleen's gone, Jerry's gone, Matt's . . .I don't know who Matt is anymore, and *Amalia*—what did you do to Amalia?" Tobey asked. "She's a *monster*. Why did you do that to her?"

"I didn't do it to her," said Denton. "It happened all on its own."

"No, I don't believe you. Amalia—she was *sweet*, she was like a little kid, what did you do to her, *what did you do to her?*"

"I didn't do a thing," said Denton, and by the way he said it, Tobey knew he wasn't lying. "It's a free country, Tobey. She turned into what she is all on her own."

Tobey was silent. Then all of a sudden, he said, "I gotta go. I'm sure you've traced this call already. You probably know exactly where I am, don't you?"

"Yes, I do," said Denton, "just down the street from the Capitol, a block from the White House."

Then he paused.

Tobey waited too, knowing what was coming.

"Where are they?" Denton finally asked.

"I can't—I can't tell you," he said miserably.

"Yes you can, Tobey."

"I can't—I can't—"

"If you couldn't tell me, you wouldn't have called," said Denton patiently.

Tobey rubbed his face with his free hand, crying.

"Tell me," said Denton softly. "You know that I can't let them go. With or without you, I'm going to find them, sooner or later. Tell me. Tell me where they are."

Tobey gritted his teeth, knowing he would tell even as he tried to understand why he was betraying his friends.

"Tobey . . . ," said Denton.

"They're at a Mennonite hostel," he said, hanging up instantly and turning around, running up the street as he cried, running to save the lives of his friends.

• • •

A Mennonite hostel? Nicholas Denton thought quizzically as he held the dead phone. *A Mennonite hostel? That's got to be a first.*

Thoughtfully, he replaced the receiver, then quickly picked it up again and dialed Matthew Wilson's number.

"Yeah."

"Matthew, how would I find out the address of a Mennonite hostel in Washington?" Denton asked without preamble.

Wilson thought for a beat. "Dial up information, get the number of the Mennonite Church in D.C. Then call them up and ask them. You want me to do it?"

"No, I'll handle it myself," said Denton. "Good boy, Matthew," he added as he hung up.

Denton dialed for an outside line, then dialed 202-information. Ninety seconds later, he was talking to a delightful woman at the Mennonite Church in Washington, who gave him all the information he would need about the only Mennonite-run hotel or hostel in the Washington area, the International Guest House.

Twenty-five dollars a night, Denton thought, with an agreeable mental nod, surprised how inexpensive such a place would be.

So thinking, he dialed Amalia's number, the International Guest House's address written out on a piece of paper right in front of him.

Foolishly, Tobey Jansen took a bus back to the International Guest House. It never occurred to him to grab a cab and bolt up Sixteenth Street. He just assumed that taking a bus would get him there soon enough. But Kennedy Avenue was a good four miles from Federal Triangle, and as the bus cantered and crawled up Sixteenth Street, Tobey bounced around, a bundle of nerves, looking out the window and thinking semi-incoherently that he would jump off the bus and grab a cab whenever he saw one pass by.

But there were no cabs once the bus went through the Scott Circle underpass, so Tobey was stuck on the bus, praying—pleading—crying for it to go faster.

"Can't you make it go faster?" he pleaded with the driver, a slightly freckled woman with cornflower blue eyes and short brown hair.

"I'm going as fast as I can—get behind the yellow line!" said the bus driver, whose name Tobey noticed from her clip-on ID was S. Creamer.

"Okay, okay—just hurry up," said Tobey impatiently, as he stepped back behind the yellow line.

"Mister, if you don't calm down, I can order you off this bus," said the driver, needlessly needling Tobey, her flat, sheenless, dark blue uniform and generally mannish manner putting out the butch vibe big-time.

"Okay, alright already, I was just asking, that's all—"

The driver stopped the bus. "Are you gonna go sit down?" she said, turning to look at Tobey; a petty woman with a petty power, happy to wield it now that she had the chance, for no other reason than because she could.

Tobey wanted to scream. "I'm behind the yellow line!"

"I don't care," she said with a corrosive glean to her eye. She had the whippet-thin body of a long-distance runner, and like a whippet—like a ferret—like a *weasel*—she had a personality to match. "I can stay parked here all day if I want to. And I will, too, if you don't shut up and do what I say."

Tobey sat down behind and across from the driver, trying to hold it in.

The bus driver looked at him, reveling in her power. Then, taking her sweet time about it, she got the bus in gear and continued up Sixteenth Street. You could tell she had the makings of a Nazi: You could tell she would suck up to any Grand Philistia, just so long as she was allowed to stomp her jack-booted foot on anything and everything that she found to be against her boobish taste.

The bus route turned off Sixteenth at California Street, so Tobey got off and ran the three remaining blocks up to Kennedy Street, running as fast as he could, the bus driver's parting words ringing in his ears: "Top of the world to ya."

When he rounded the corner at Kennedy Street, he couldn't believe what he saw—Amalia was stepping out of her car.

She had just pulled up directly in front of the International Guest House in an anonymous rental sedan. She had changed into a gray flannel suit, her skirt hemmed boldly above her knees, and she looked calm and in control—then she quickly turned to face Tobey to her left, a gun in her hand, aimed directly at his chest as he ran toward her.

Tobey slowed and stopped in front of her, his feet slapping the pavement as he came within arm's reach of her, Amalia's firearm now aimed at his face as Tobey panted, out of breath.

"Amalia," he said as he gulped air like a fish. "What are you doing here?" he asked, not really seeing the gun she was aiming at him.

"Hello, Tobey," said Amalia, lowering her weapon and checking the safety. "I'm here for Acrobat."

Tobey just looked at her, holding his breath. "Don't," he said.

Amalia stared blankly at her old friend.

"Amalia, please, no—turn around, drive away—"

"No, Tobey," she said, looking at him. "You turn around. You walk away. Surface back at the ranch in a few days. *He's* waiting for you, and he wants you to come back."

Tobey didn't say a thing.

"He specifically told me you were Orange Crush," said Amalia. "I think that's a mistake. If it were up to me, I'd put you six underground, along with your friends."

Amalia stared at Tobey for a second, then looked at the house and then back at her former friend. "How many are in there?"

Tobey hesitated, then said, "Three. They're on the third floor. I think they're all armed."

Amalia nodded. "Tell me what you touched," she said. "I'll make sure to clean it up. You won't be implicated."

"No," said Tobey, standing there, feeling useless.

Amalia stared at him with her hollow, human-machine eyes. " 'No' what?" she asked.

Tobey didn't know what to say, so he said nothing. He simply stared at her.

Amalia looked at him for a beat. Then, dismissing him, she turned her back on him and began walking toward the International Guest House.

Tobey still had the porcelain gun. It was tucked away in the small of his back. Now, he reached behind him, took hold of it, and pulled it out.

Then he shot Amalia three times in the back.

The bullets struck her all in succession, throwing her forward onto the green grass of the front lawn. Her firearm went flying out of her hand, clattering on the sidewalk a few yards away. One of her pumps unaccountably flew off her foot.

For a second, Amalia didn't move. Then she moaned. Then she tried to push herself up back on her feet, managing only to roll over onto her back.

Amalia looked up at Tobey.

"Hi," she said, looking up at him, a bleeding gash on her forehead where she had struck a water sprinkler buried in the lawn.

Tobey looked down at her, holding the gun in his hand, the gun aimed at the gash in her forehead, but drifting—drifting down, then remembering, coming to bear on Amalia again, as behind the gun, Tobey wept, looking down on his friend.

"It hurts so much," she said, dying, blood coming out of her mouth between the words she spoke. "I had no idea."

Tobey didn't know what to say to that, though he wanted to say something. Anything that might comfort her.

Amalia wheezed and began to panic, drowning in her own blood. "I can't *breathe*. Don't let me drown, please, don't let me drown," she said, her voice turning moist with every word she spoke.

Tobey just stood there, knowing what he had to do even as he was unable to.

"Do it," she said suddenly, calming down as she realized how quickly it would all be over. "You know you can. I know you can."

Tobey nodded, taking a breath and steeling himself.

"Go on," she gurgled. "It hurts so much just go *on*."

"I can't," Tobey finally admitted, his gun still trained on Amalia as it drifted, reset, drifted again, and reset again.

Duncan Idaho suddenly opened the front door of the house, his own gun ready. *"Tobey!"* he shouted, bounding off the porch of the International Guest House, looking down at Amalia.

The moment he sensed and heard that Duncan was there, Tobey Jansen had no options.

Amalia looked up at Tobey, gurgling as she tried to speak to him. All she managed to say was, "Tob——"

BLAM! went his gun, blowing half her head off, silencing her before she'd had a chance to call him by name and thereby betray him.

"Oh fuck, oh fuck," Tobey squeaked as Duncan got to him, the two of them standing in the middle of the front lawn of the house, Amalia's body lying across the grass as Tobey waved the loaded porcelain gun around.

"Put the gun down, Tobey," said Duncan Idaho calmly and forcefully, staring at Tobey Jansen as he swayed above Amalia's corpse.

"What?" said Tobey, instinctively turning toward the sound of Duncan Idaho's voice, carelessly waving around the porcelain gun.

"Weapons safety," said Duncan, looking Tobey Jansen in the eye, a hard tack to his voice. He was too far away to tackle Tobey if it came to that.

"Huh?" said Tobey.

"Don't fuck with guns, Tobey—*pay attention!*" said Duncan.

Tobey Jansen stupidly looked at his gun, unable to believe what it had done. He looked down at Amalia's corpse, then looked at the gun again, then looked at Duncan Idaho, his face plain as day: *What did I do?*

Duncan Idaho slowly walked forward, his arms open, his right hand sliding over Tobey's shoulders as with his left hand he took the porcelain gun away. "It's okay," he said quietly, letting his arm slip around Tobey's neck. He pulled him close as he looked down at Amalia, covering her corpse with the porcelain gun, just in case.

But Amalia was gone.

"Shit," said Tobey. Then he looked up at Duncan Idaho. "Did I do good? Huh? Huh? Did I do good?"

"You did great," said Duncan. "Better than I ever could have."

PART IV

Are We Ourselves?

In the summer of '89, I was stationed in West Germany. This was just before the Wall came down, a real scary time. All these refugees were coming out of Eastern Europe, making everybody think that Old Mister Ivan was getting ready for a shooting war. Nobody had quite figured out that those refugees meant the ship was sinking.

Anyway, I was a kid then, nineteen, a spotter on an M1A1 Abrams with a 70-mm cannon. My tank platoon was assigned dawn patrol, so one time I'm sitting up top, alone one morning, drinking my coffee. There's no sun, just gray morning mist rolling like the sea over the little green hills, everything real quiet-like, when all of a sudden it hits me: If the war comes, the first shells are gonna vaporize my position.

This wasn't like a surprise or anything. My tank platoon was on the forward line—I saw the enemy every day, up close, three hills to the east. I knew what would happen when the war came. But that morning was the first time that I understood it. I understood that the life I was living, all the training I'd gone through, it all had a simple purpose: To hold the line.

That's when I understood that my life didn't belong to me. It belonged to people weaker than me, people who couldn't defend themselves. I'd never met any of these people, and they'd never met me. But that didn't make their need any less real, or less urgent.

That was a good time. Maybe the best time, for me. Sometimes I feel like I've drifted a thousand centuries from that morning.

CHAPTER 11

Have Gone to Patagonia

Oedipus wasn't put to death for his terrible crimes. Instead, he was made blind and set to wandering alone into the desert. For his part, when they gave him the choice, Socrates preferred suicide to banishment, consoling and comforting his friends before cheerfully drinking his hemlock. And why shouldn't he have been cheerful? What's death when compared to exile.

In America, though, things are different. Here, people are afraid of death—they're terrified of it. But they're not afraid of exile. It's a meaningless punishment here, because in America, we're all exiles.

Look out across the Mall, that overwide, unbalanced esplanade cutting through the heart of Washington: You'll see. On any spring morning, thousands of American citizens no different from Russell Orr walk back and forth from the Lincoln Memorial to Capitol Hill, passing the national mementos along the way without a single tenderness. Those buildings in the heart of the capital have built no place for themselves in the heart of the people. They're not spaces where the citizenry spends any of their day-to-day living—they're just tourist attractions: Unique curiosities visited once in a lifetime and then crossed off the list of things to do and places to see. Mostly, they're museums, storing the knick-knacks and bric-a-brac of the freest society this world has ever seen, a society so free that its own citizens have no ties to their own capital. Russell

Orr actually lived in Washington, but even to him, the Mall
and the buildings lining it had as much meaning as any other
tourist attraction. And the people he saw as he drifted along
the Mall were just as foreign to him as any crowd of people
from some homely and shy country rarely visited by travelers
seeking adventure and the unknown.

There was no question of going back to his and Yuvi's
townhouse; actually, Ljubica's townhouse. Though Russell
doubted Denton or the Feebles would spend the manpower on
having someone watching the place, there was no reason to
run the risk. Anyway, there wasn't anything important to go
back to: Just objects, picked and paid for by Ljubica's parents.

So instead of going home, he walked right down the middle
of the Mall, a hundred yards of grass on either side of his
path.

People were picnicking, tossing Frisbees, hanging out, the
grass green and thick and luscious as the sky above rolled big
and blue across the horizon, the air pungent with life. He'd
come here after Acrobat had pushed him out of the Metro car;
no other place occurred to him. Besides, he figured it was
probably the safest spot in all of Washington. Only tourists
and civilians ever came to the Mall.

Over his shoulder, the shadow of the Washington Monument followed Russell as he passed the American and Natural
History Museums. Straight ahead was the Capitol Building,
sitting on the hill like a fabled destination. To his left now
was the domed classicism of the National Gallery of Art, and
to his right, facing the National Gallery like an upstart modernistic gunslinger, was the Air and Space Museum, a building
made up of three solid cubes of concrete connected to each
other by two tunnels of glass.

Russell stood there between the museums, looking at them
both. He'd been to the Air and Space Museum before, literally
dozens of times before. After all, Russell was a pilot. Every
time he came, though, he always promised himself that the
next time, he'd first go to the National Gallery and see all the
paintings, for the culture and all that. But every time he came,

he'd stand there between both buildings and think it over for a while, undecided.

"You get that look," Ljubica once mumbled about it, just when things were sliding between them, just a few short weeks after they scored the Manhattan bank.

"What look," he'd asked.

"Like a guilty dog's sneer."

That was meanness talking, but it wasn't far off the mark. Standing between the two museums, trying to make up his mind between them, Russell had that look to his face: A big café au lait man who should've been as decisive as a Roman general, but who instead kept balance on a swing of indecision.

Like Skunk Works.

"I'm not sure this is a good idea," Russell had told Yuvi one night just days before they were supposed to score the compound, the two of them alone in the kitchen of the townhouse they shared, making Nasi Goren, an Indonesian dish.

Yuvi turned away from the chopped onions and green peppers she was frying in a small wok and looked at Russell. "What did you say?" she asked, barely inflecting her voice around her question.

Russell looked down at his feet. "Maybe we're making a mistake," he said gruffly. "Maybe the whole Skunk Works project is wrong."

Ljubica looked at him for a second, the only sound the noise of the frying and the low underlying murmur of flamenco guitar music in the background. Then she turned back to the wok and deliberately went on frying the onions and green peppers, tossing in the chopped carrots she'd boiled in a separate saucepan and pouring a dash of Japanese soy sauce over the concoction she was stir-frying.

"You've had six months to raise any objections," she said, as lawyerly as if they'd been in a courtroom instead of a kitchen.

Russell didn't know what to say, so he said nothing.

"After all this work," she said as she chopped two stalks of celery and tossed them last into the wok, without a glance at Russell. "*Now* you're having second thoughts."

Russell might have said something more, but then Ljubica scoffed. It was a sound as quick and cutting as a piece of chalk slipping across a blackboard. With that sound, Russell shelved his objections to what was looking to be a near-impossible objective.

Scoring Skunk Works wasn't like scoring some embassy. Skunk Works was *hard*. To begin with, just getting into the compound was well-nigh impossible. Every Monday morning, workers at the plant—the machinists and engineers and scientists and such who actually built all the stealth technologies and designed all the computer systems—commuted to John Wayne Airport in Anaheim, where they were checked against a hard-copy manifest and a computer system list. If and only if a worker was properly listed on both, and only if he was carrying the proper identification, then the worker was allowed to board an anonymous 737 commuter jet plane that would take him to Skunk Works. Because the interesting parts of Skunk Works weren't in Anaheim—they were deep in the desert, in the middle of restricted airspace. Not only that, but from photos they'd gathered from various sources, Acrobat knew that there was no way they could drive a Jeep through the desert and break through the outside wall of the place. Skunk Works had ten-foot-high walls of barbed wire, and it didn't take a genius to figure out that the place probably had motion detectors buried in the ground for miles all around for good measure; maybe even a necklace of land mines too, just for the kicks and the thrill of it all. Scoring Skunk Works wasn't any kind of a joke.

In fact, when Tom Carr first brought up the possibility of breaking into the place, it was Russell who'd raised the first objections.

"It cannot be done," he'd said flatly.

But Duncan had disagreed. "There's nothing that can't be done," he'd said with that magnetic cockiness of the truly insane. "We can do this," he'd insisted.

The thing was, Duncan was right: Acrobat did it. They spent the whole winter forging the right documents, breaking into the right computers, creating the fictitious backgrounds necessary to waltz onto that commuter 737 jet plane and make it all the way to Skunk Works. And once there, under cover of being an independent materials team working on an ultra-secret research project, the work-group Acrobat spent a whole week rampaging through the place, looking under every rock in the complex, everything pre-planned back at Langley, gathering up information like fishermen gathering up bulging nets of tuna.

In the Air and Space Museum, an over-thin woman with a dried-out smoker's face asked, "Is that the *real* Apollo capsule? The one that went to the moon?"

"Yes indeedy," said her husband beside her, a squat, neckless man with thick, pepper hair and a thick, pepper beard, wearing a T-shirt and shorts and a Nebraska Cornhuskers baseball cap. "The very one."

The couple stood there and thought about the Apollo 11 capsule. It greeted visitors to the Air and Space Museum like some inscrutable sculpture, the capsule dressed in form-fitting lucite, its butt the color of cigarette ash, twenty feet across.

Even for a weekday, the museum was crowded with visitors, maybe a couple of hundred people milling about the entrance space, looking up at the dangling aircraft that hung from the roof by piano wire. None of these planes were mock-ups— they were the real thing. That there really *was* the Wright Brothers' first plane. This aircraft over here was the actual *Spirit of St. Louis,* no matter how tawdry and flimsy it might look. And that thing over there? That orange-colored, cigar-shaped plane with the little stubby wings? That was Chuck Yeager's very own X-1—*that* was the aircraft Yeager took up past the speed of sound for the very first time.

All these mementos from the history of aviation could bend a pilot's mind like nothing else—whenever he came here, Russell couldn't really believe that what he was seeing was real. The planes he'd read about as a child were right there, surprisingly small and fragile-looking, yet eerily powerful with the iron-hard aura of accomplishment.

He looked around and followed the flow of the crowd,

checking out the space mural on the far wall and then drifting into one of the exhibit rooms showing the development of commercial aviation.

Scoring Skunk Works had been surprisingly anti-climactic. After all, once the commuter 737 landed and they were inside the compound proper, no one questioned their reason for being there. They slept in the rooming facilities provided for the workers, ate at the regular mess hall with everyone else, no one surprised that no one had ever seen Duncan or Monika or Tobey or Ljubica or Russell before because *everyone* at Skunk Works was a stranger. Everyone had their noses to the grindstone and minded their own business.

"The business of America is business. So mind your own."

Acrobat spent the whole week going through everything at the Skunk Works labs. By late Friday afternoon, on the eve before they'd return to Washington, the work-group Acrobat had gathered three cardboard boxes of materials. The five of them sat there looking at the boxes and smoking their cigarettes, everyone surprised that they'd actually done it.

"Wow," said Monika.

"Jesus they're heavy," said Duncan, scratching his head as he eyed the three cardboard boxes crammed with dozens of computer printouts and literally hundreds of ZIP-drive disks. Somehow, none of them had thought of the practical problem of moving all this material once they'd actually acquired it. "How the hell are we going to carry this all the way to D.C.?"

Ljubica said casually, "I'm not carrying any of it."

Monika said, "I'm a girl."

"Mmm," said Duncan, eyeing Tobey, who looked as scrawny as ever, no way able to carry even the lightest of the three boxes for more than a few minutes. Duncan turned to Russell. "Could you carry two of the boxes?"

"Could I or would I?" Russell asked dimly.

Monika said, "Maybe we could put everything into five smaller boxes, one for each."

Everyone shrugged, eyeing the boxes, laziness getting the best of them all.

Tobey began to speak, then stopped, stroking his six-inch

goatee, now fully formed and dyed and gelled. Then, thought-fully, he said, "What if we mail them to ourselves? At Lang-ley?"

Everyone stopped and looked at him.

"Thinkin' dude!" said Duncan, the issue decided.

So they'd taped up the boxes and mailed all the materials to their offices in Langley, using Skunk Works's very own postal service, which, conveniently, was free for all official business.

The next morning, Saturday, the work-group Acrobat boarded the commuter flight back to John Wayne Airport, and from there, they caught the next flight back to Ronald Reagan Airport in D.C., the whole thing over and done with, as real as a movie.

Russell and Yuvi didn't speak for most of the trip, but when the two of them got into a cab to go home, Ljubica said, "Couldn't just help out a little, could you?"

Russell wisely kept quiet as he sat in the back of the cab besides Ljubica. But silence didn't keep them from fighting, the two of them stalking each other through their townhouse that Saturday afternoon, the silent firefight going on even as they went to the supermarket that evening.

Early Sunday morning, things had begun to cool down— they might have made it through another week. But then Dun-can Idaho came looking for them, warning them that Nicholas Denton was onto them—warning them that Denton was com-ing for them.

"Dawg, that *is not* a piece of the moon, man, that be like a model."

"No it ain't, Gee," said the second young black man to his friend, the two of them looking at a thorny piece of gray rock in a small clear plastic case at the Air and Space Museum. "It's a real piece of the moon—read the instructions, dawg," he said, the two young men identically lean and tall, identi-cally dressed in sleeveless basketball shirts and long shorts as big as bloomers, bluish purple with yellow piping on the sides. Their shoes were bulky, white-and-neon-colored basketball sneakers, their snow-white socks a contrast to their smooth, coffee-colored calves. They argued about the piece of moon rock without even bothering to read the discreet placard beside it, their faces contorted like the topography of a flat plain that had suddenly buckled with the force of an earthquake.

The two young men were loud, and they were pushing each other, vaguely making the people around them nervous as Russell Orr passed them by, instinctively and absently understanding the two kids: They weren't fighting; they were playing.

"Aw, you be too stupid to read *anything* 'cept the rate card at the ho house you be livin' at."

"That be yo mama's house you talkin' 'bout, Gee," said the second one, the two kids laughing as they cut each other with practiced panache.

Why aren't they at Freaknik? Russell wondered, as he turned around and watched the two kids giggle and slap each other playfully, the show over, the other museumgoers slowly calming down as the harmless young men went on through the museum. *Isn't it going on about now?* Russell wondered casually.

Freaknik was the spring break celebration in Atlanta, Georgia, where black college kids came together to drink and party and "get freaky," as the saying goes. Russell had been to one himself, in the spring of 1990, when he'd been a sophomore at the Academy, just as the following year he'd gone to Florida for the the white kids' version of Freaknik—spring break at the Redneck Riviera, Panama City.

He'd hated both, but he'd gone to both, again and again, uncomfortable around the rowdy black kids his own age who had danced and catcalled each other up and down the streets, flooding Atlanta with good-natured boisterousness that made Russell uncomfortable with its loudness and its physicality— black limbs and black voices too loud and too full of movement, as if some unarticulated grievance might all of a sudden boil up from the placid crowd and strike out with unexpected, ferocious savagery. That it never did only added to the tension that built up in the front of Russell's skull. He'd been as repelled by those loud black faces almost as much as by the stupefied white faces of Panama City, humorlessly drinking and drinking throughout the hotel rooms and bars and clubs around town, the scary whiteness of the redneck crowd burly and stupefied, a white mob that intimidated Russell even as he towered over all the kids he met. No one would have dared mess with Russell, who was just white enough and just black enough to fit in at either place. When he was at one, he wanted to be at the other, even as he realized how much he'd hate being there, a teeter-totter of indecision as to who and what he was.

Just like everything that had to do with Skunk Works. He'd wanted to score Skunk Works even as he knew that there was no way they could pull it off.

That Sunday morning, once Duncan came to warn them that Acrobat was blown, Duncan, Ljubica, and Russell managed to sneak out of their townhouse, dodging the surveillance car that had been sitting alone out front in their quiet street in Georgetown, sore-thumb obvious.

They split up at the nearest Metro, Duncan on his way, Ljubica and Russell perversely sticking together, even though it might've been better if they'd split apart.

They'd easily stolen a car, then picked up some weapons before driving up to New York City, using one of the fake identities Ljubica had long ago set up for them, just in case something like this happened.

As they drove in silence up the New Jersey Turnpike, Ljubica and Russell both thought about Skunk Works and all the rest of what they'd been doing for the last few months, both of them silently realizing that it was no accident that Denton had moved on them almost as soon as they'd landed back from Skunk Works.

Absently, as he drove, Russell said, "Denton must've been tipped off somehow; I knew it—"

"Don't say a thing—"

"I knew this would happen—"

They turned and looked at each other, and if things hadn't been so far gone between the two of them, they might have laughed. But they didn't.

Russell turned back to face the road. "*You* wanted to do

this, you thought it was a great idea, and now look where we're at."

Ljubica's lazy-shaped eyes looked at him with undisguised hatred. If she could have, she would have killed him. The sun was bright, the air in the car still and warm. Ljubica's eyes bore into him—it almost felt as if her eyes were drilling holes into the side of his head, they hurt so bad.

"Coward," she spit out suddenly.

Russell glanced at Ljubica and then back at the road, ashamed.

Now, Russell stood in one of the exhibits of the Air and Space Museum, an exhibit showing the development of the space suit. Idly, he was staring at a mannequin wearing a pressure suit used by the pilots of the X-15 program, the suits as tiny as the pilots, who all had to be under five feet, eight inches to qualify for the program; the X-15s had been too small to allow for anyone taller than that.

But Russell didn't notice that, or anything else for that matter. All he could see were Ljubica's hateful eyes, looking at him just as they had that night at the motel in Pennsylvania, that night when it had slipped out:

"Russell is undecided."

Acrobat was never undecided—it had no room for the indecisive. Ljubica, Monika, Duncan: Decided, one and all. Even a wimpy little financial geek like Tobey Jansen had more decisiveness than Russell, Tobey all for breaking into Skunk Works, Tobey's eyes shining when he'd suggested mailing the Skunk Works material back to Langley, shining just like when he'd deduced/suggested that Tom must've been followed to the Times Square station, that Tom Carr must've given them away . . .

Tobey betrayed us.

The thought just popped into Russell's head like a hidden jack-in-the-box that he'd somehow always known was there. Of *course* Tobey had betrayed them—the trap at Pentagon City, the Feebles arriving at DuPont Circle, the little woman at the Times Square subway platform. Who but Tobey could have betrayed them?

He should have realized this before. It had been there all along. As he stood there staring down at the little mannequin in its ancient pressure suit, Russell Orr knew he would have spotted Tobey Jansen for what he was if only he'd cast his lot with Acrobat.

But Russell had been undecided.

Maybe Duncan was confused, or maybe he was just tired. Whatever it was, Duncan Idaho was the one who drove Acrobat off the cliff.

"Holy shit," Tobey was saying, staring down at Amalia's corpse. "I sure shot the hell out of her, didn't I? I did good, didn't I? Didn't I do good?"

"You did great, champ. Like a trooper," said Duncan, pulling Tobey away. "Come on, we gotta go," he said urgently, yanking Tobey back up the porch of the International Guest House, just as Monika and Joyce, the caretaker, appeared at the screen door.

"Good Heavens!" said Joyce as she took a step outside. "What's going on out there, what was that loud noise, my goodness what is that, *oh-my-oh-my-oh-my-God-oh-my-God-oh-my-God!*" Joyce screamed as she got a load of Amalia's brains splattered all over the front lawn, freaking out there on the porch of the International Guest House.

"Put some discipline on that woman!" Duncan shouted at Monika.

"What?" said Monika stupidly, staring at Amalia's corpse and turning back to stare at Duncan and Tobey.

"Oh for Chrissake!" said Duncan, walking up to the porch and grabbing hold of the screaming, hysterical Joyce, who had by now been reduced to incoherent whooping wails.

He pulled her back into the house and down the foyer, Joyce wailing hysterically all the while as Duncan locked her inside the small bathroom at the end of the hall.

Then Duncan turned to look out the front door.

Just outside, Monika and Tobey were standing on the porch, looking out over the lawn. From where he stood, Dun-

can couldn't see Amalia's corpse; but he could see Tobey and
Monika. Monika was in shock, but Tobey was wrecked: Crying and down on his knees as he stared at Amalia's corpse,
as if praying for it.

Duncan stood in the foyer as Joyce kept on wailing in the
bathroom. "I'll go get Yuvi," he called out to Tobey and Monika. Then he ran up the stairs.

Out on the porch, Monika looked down at Tobey, kneeling.

"I shot her?" Tobey was saying. "She's dead. I did good,
right? Did I do good?"

"You did great," said Monika as she stared at the body,
lying there in her own blood, the bright spring sunlight hard
and fresh, the gray of Amalia's suit like a hole in the deep
green of the lawn, the sky above blue and humid. There was
no wind and no sound except for the muffled, incoherent wailing of the innocent Joyce.

Even on the third floor, Duncan could hear Joyce as she
wailed away in the first-floor bathroom. When he got to Ljubica's room, he found her getting up and trying to put on her
shoes.

"What's going on?" she asked, sitting on the edge of the
bed.

"No time," said Duncan, automatically realizing that Yuvi
couldn't put on her shoes because of her wounded thigh. He
knelt and helped her with them. "You know that little woman
from New York? Tobey just shot her."

Ljubica was too surprised to say a thing.

"We gotta go, we gotta go *now*," said Duncan, knowing
that if the little woman had showed up, others wouldn't be too
far behind.

With her shoes on, Duncan then simply lifted Yuvi up and
carried her downstairs, running so fast that she was afraid
they'd both go flying head over heels to the bottom of the
staircase.

Joyce was still wailing, and Tobey and Monika were still
on the front porch, staring at Amalia's corpse.

"*Come on!*" hollered Duncan, as he ran with Yuvi out of
the International Guest House, going straight for Amalia's

anonymous, gold-colored sedan, which was conveniently parked out front. Duncan put Ljubica in the back seat, then went to get in the driver's seat.

Monika and Tobey were still there, still staring at Amalia's corpse.

"For God's sake, COME ON!" Duncan shouted.

Monika snapped out of it, jerking her head in Duncan's direction then grabbing hold of Tobey by the arm and hoisting him up.

"Come on," said Monika. *"Come on!"*

Tobey woke up as if from a dream, stumbling haphazardly toward the gold-colored sedan that Amalia had come in, a Ford Taurus. He and Monika got in and Duncan drove away, the suburban morning quiet, without so much as the sound of an approaching car, let alone the wail of an approaching police car. The only sound heard was the muffled crying of Joyce, locked in the first-floor bathroom. Amalia, of course, didn't hear it. Now deaf, now blind, her corpse lay spread out on the grass, her dead eyes staring straight at the sun, as if it were her destination.

They were in a vast, abandoned warehouse in the waterfront section of town, the smell of the Anacostia River like a dash of salt in the air. Hard shafts of sunlight streaked through the rotting roof beams above their heads as they all stood around in silence, no one knowing exactly what to say as they each tried to figure out what to do next.

Ljubica was sitting in the back of the car, the car door open, Yuvi looking straight ahead as if they were still driving somewhere and she was watching the road. Tobey wandered around the warehouse floor, toeing abandoned apple crates that were rotting from the rain. Monika was just standing around without doing much of anything as she waited for Duncan, who had gone out to look around the abandoned warehouse and make sure no one was about.

None of them took note of him when he came back.

"No one's around," he said simply, setting his porcelain

gun on top of a rotting table that was supported by some crates.

Nobody said anything to that, either.

Tobey wiped his face, which was all puffy and red. "So what are we gonna do?" he asked, as Duncan picked up the porcelain gun, checking its action.

"Well," said Duncan cautiously, glancing at Monika to make sure she didn't want to say anything, "I think that maybe we should get our IDs and stuff at the bank and go underground," said Duncan.

"How are we gonna do that with the FBI or whoever crawling all over the place?" said Monika.

Duncan didn't answer that. Instead, he looked over at Ljubica sitting in the back of the car. Her leg looked ready to burst out of her jeans.

Tobey checked his watch. "It's almost noon. So if we go to the bank, we'd better do it now, before the bank closes."

"Even if we get into the bank," Monika added, "our gear might be gone already."

Duncan didn't say a thing, checking the magazine of the porcelain gun and putting in more bullets.

"Duncan?" said Monika, standing with her arms crossed in the middle of the rotting warehouse. "I'm saying our gear might be gone already."

"I heard you the first time," said Duncan. "We're just going to have to take that chance. We have to know, for sure."

Monika opened her mouth to speak then closed it, not knowing what to say. Now that they really couldn't go back to the ranch, the whole world was turning into one very scary place for Monika—a vast, friendless desolation with Duncan the only shelter for miles around. And Duncan was more Joshua tree than a friendly, shady oak.

"Who else could we approach?" Monika asked abruptly.

"What do you mean?" asked Duncan.

"To get back into the ranch," said Monika. "You think someone from Paradise might help us out?"

Duncan scoffed impatiently. "Monika, give it up already,"

he said. "There're just two things left to do: Tag Denton, and get our gear."

"How are we going to get our gear with all those FBI people sitting on the bank?"

Duncan said casually, "We go when they're not there—we could break in at night, on the prowl. It's Friday: We could do it tonight."

Monika scoffed as she winced, turning away from Duncan and walking through the pretty beams of noonday sunlight coming through the rotted roof.

Duncan winced. "Hey—hey—hey wait," he said, skipping to catch up to her, taking her arm.

"Let go of me," she said coldly.

Duncan brushed his tousled blond hair out of his eyes and glanced over his shoulder at Yuvi and Tobey. Then he looked carefully at Monika.

He said, "Monika—"

"I'm sorry," she blurted out, looking at the ground between them. "I'm sorry, I'm just—I'm just so tired."

"I know," said Duncan, taking her in his arms, letting her cry it out against his shoulder.

Monika cried for a while, holding on to him as tight as she could. His body felt so warm and solid; she felt she could have held on to him until it was all over and done for, everything finished and in the past and not worth worrying about anymore.

"I know, I know," he kept saying quietly. "It'll be okay."

Monika just cried, Duncan gently tugging at her, the two of them walking out of the rotting warehouse and out into the bright spring morning.

Seagulls were cawing in the distance, a sound barely heard as a northern breeze washed away the smell of the river, Duncan only smelling Monika's fear underneath her perfume.

"I know we can't go back," she said suddenly. "But I'm so afraid about what might happen to us. I don't *know* what's going to happen to us, and that's what's driving me crazy."

"Don't worry," said Duncan with great kindness in his eyes.

"We'll get our gear at the bank, and then we'll go underground—"

"Duncan, do you have any idea how much that terrifies me?" she asked him.

Duncan blinked. "Why?"

"What are we going to do underground?"

Duncan shrugged, completely nonplussed by this whole line. "I don't know."

Monika smiled crazily and shook her head. "That's the thing! You don't know," she said, her throat so tight the words barely came out. "At Langley I know where I'm going: Work at Acrobat for a while, then go to another Directorate, maybe even go to work at the Ombudsman's Office for a time. These rational steps up the ladder," she said, mimicking with her hand as it went up a discrete set of steps. "It may sound corporate and boring, but Duncan, I'm a corporate girl. And now, this all, this whole thing: It seemed like such a fun idea at first—break out of the rut, go underground, live out our lives without constraints. But now I'm so scared, Duncan. All I can think about is that I'm going to be alone, without any friends, without any of the people I'm used to."

Duncan, the renegade scion of a dirt-poor, trailer-park dynasty, didn't know what to say to this. Once he'd left the Texas of Upshaw County for the basic training of the U.S. Army, he'd always been alone, so he'd never worried about it; never even considered it. It was just the normal state of affairs, the state of nature.

But not for Monika. She said, "I'm so afraid that once we go underground and we've left everyone behind, you'll leave me and I'll be alone."

Duncan nodded, understanding what she wanted. "I won't leave you," he said with a firm, solid voice. "We'll always be together."

"You're not gonna run off to tag Denton?"

"No, I won't run off," he said.

"Promise."

"Promise."

"Okay," said Monika, not sure whether to believe him or

not. "You're all I've got—I'll never forgive you if you leave me," she said.

"I promise I won't," he quietly insisted. "We'll go to the bank, get our gear, then head off underground, you and me, together—I'll be there. It'll be just like being at the ranch, only better, 'cause it'll be me!" he quietly joked.

Monika laughed because he expected it, and because she was tired. But looking at Duncan, she suddenly realized she had no idea if he'd bolt. Or rather, when he'd bolt.

Duncan smiled and hugged her and said, "We'll always be together, okay? We'll break into the bank, get our gear, then catch the first flight to Germany. Have you ever been to Germany?"

Monika shook her head as she wiped her tears.

"You'll love it—it's so pretty and the people there are really nice," he said. "And then we can go to Italy—we can go to Venice and kiss at sunset under the Bridge of Sighs, like they did in *A Little Romance*, remember?"

Monika thought a bit. "Yeah, yeah—oh! *Yes*, the movie about the French boy and the American girl!"

"Exactly," said Duncan, smiling. "Don't you worry about a thing; it'll all work out, you'll see."

A scoring run always puts things in perspective.

"Okay, what are we gonna need to get our gear?" asked Duncan Idaho as they all stood around the worktable at the warehouse.

"Cars," said Monika instantly.

"A high-end combination-breaker," said Ljubica.

"At least one more car," said Monika. "Maybe even two more."

"Something fast, nothing below five hundred megahertz, with parallel processing. And a couple of lock-punches."

"We're gonna need the blueprints to the bank, too," said Monika.

"The blueprints are not as important as the electrical schematics," said Ljubica. "With detailed electricals, I'll be able to deduce what kind of security they used."

"Are we gonna need any guns?" asked Tobey, looking wretched.

"No guns," said Monika forcefully.

"Yes, guns," said Duncan, looking at his girlfriend. "Just a couple," he said. "Just in case."

Monika frowned.

"We might need a portable sonogram machine too," said Ljubica, daintily lighting a cigarette.

"A sonogram machine?" said Monika.

"For the safe door," said Ljubica. "In case the combination-breaker doesn't do the job."

"Well why don't we just blow it up like in the movies?" asked Tobey casually, Monika agreeing with a nod and a "Yeah."

"We can't blow it up," said Ljubica. "First of all, explosives are hard to come by. Second, we're going to need at least three minutes to open the safety deposit box; if we set off an explosion, police will be surrounding the bank before we get what we came for. And third, who here has any experience with explosives?"

Monika and Tobey looked at Duncan. He shook his head, saying, "That was years ago at Fort Benning; I wouldn't trust myself.

"Okay, no explosives," said Monika. "We get a sonogram machine. Where do you get one of those?"

"I know where," said Ljubica.

"Yuvi and me'll get the gear," said Duncan Idaho. "You and Tobey get the floor plans to the bank."

"Fine," said Monika.

"The equipment I'll need," said Ljubica, shaking her head with a sigh, "it won't be cheap."

"How much?" asked Duncan.

"I don't know," said Ljubica. "The combination breaker? Anywhere from five to ten thousand—no more than ten, but no less than five."

"What else?"

"That portable sonogram machine . . . Now that I think about it, we're going to need it, definitely. That's an additional, oh, five thousand?"

"So fifteen?" said Duncan, looking at Monika to make her complicit in the plan; Monika, though, didn't allow herself to catch his eye.

Ljubica said, "What kind of weapons did you have in mind?"

"Assault rifles," said Duncan. "Nothing fancy or hard to come by, something that just gets the job done."

"That will be an additional thousand per firearm," said Ljubica.

Duncan looked away from Monika, letting his eyes fall to the ground as he said casually, "I'm going to need night-vision goggles—really good ones too."

Monika jerked her head at Duncan, but Ljubica didn't notice as she said, "That's another couple of thousand."

Monika said nothing, only looking at him, this time Duncan avoiding her eyes.

"So about . . . how much is all that?" Duncan asked Tobey.

"About twenty thousand, twenty-two thousand," he said.

"Just about," said Ljubica, thinking. "Say twenty-five, just to be safe. It's got to be cash; these people I have in mind won't take credit." She puffed on her cigarette and shifted her weight, wincing a bit. "How much do we have?" she asked Monika.

"Don't worry about it," said Duncan.

Monika said to Ljubica, "We've only got something like fifteen hundred left over."

"That gets us nowhere," said Ljubica.

"Don't worry about money," Duncan repeated. "I know where we can find plenty."

Ljubica and Monika looked at Duncan, then glanced at each other.

"Okay," said Ljubica, Monika frowning a bit but not saying anything.

Ljubica went on, "We're also going to need those plans: The electricals are the important ones really."

"Tobey and I'll get them," said Monika.

"How are we gonna do that?" asked Tobey.

"We're gonna break into the County Registrar's," said Monika, glancing at Duncan, who nodded.

"Okay," said Tobey. "When are we gonna do this?"

"Now," said Monika.

The first order of business was getting another car—no trouble at all.

"That one," said Duncan as they drove down Massachusetts Avenue that bright spring Friday morning, Monika at the wheel as he sat up front beside her.

"Which one?" asked Monika as she prowled down the street.

"That dark blue Audi, the four door," said Duncan, unbuckling his seat belt. "Just drop us off here."

"Okay," said Monika, double-parking next to the Audi sedan, sticking her left hand out the window and waving the car behind her to pass.

"We'll wait for you guys," she said.

Duncan hesitated, then leaned forward, as if to kiss Monika. But she made a quick little jerk with her head—just a little turn of it, if that—forcing Duncan to kiss her cheek instead. He paused, then turned and opened the car door.

Duncan got out of the car and Ljubica followed, and all of a sudden Tobey experienced some major déjà vu: Pennsylvania, at the motel parking lot, Russell loading up the pick-up truck as Ljubica waved a V-for-Victory sign at him. Just like then, Ljubica looked back at Tobey and waved, and Tobey waved back.

That was barely two days ago.

Two days, that's all? Tobey asked himself, surprised. Surprised and, for the first time since Wednesday, really tired. Tired of seeing Amalia looking up at him, gurgling and drowning in her own blood, pleading with him to shoot her.

"Want to sit up front?" asked Monika from the driver's seat.

"Sure," said Tobey, getting out of the car and sitting next to Monika as they waited for Duncan to break into the Audi.

Duncan meanwhile had reached into his pocket for his keyring. Attached to it by a two-inch-long chain, Duncan had an all-purpose lock-picking kit, a little thing that looked a lot like a Swiss Army knife.

With a couple of deft moves, Duncan was in the Audi and turning it on, the car smoothly coming to life. Reaching over, he unlocked the passenger side door for Ljubica, who carefully got in, then he rolled down the driver's side window and looked to his left, to Monika in the other car.

"We'll meet up with you back at the warehouse," said Duncan.

"How long do you think it'll take?" she asked back.

Duncan looked at Ljubica as she carefully buckled up. "Three or four hours," she said offhand.

"Four hours," said Duncan. "Meet you back there at four P.M., okay?"

Monika just nodded.

Then she and Tobey took off, Tobey giving Duncan a tired, casual wave as the Taurus drove off and was lost in the traffic.

Duncan looked after them both, getting some déjà vu of his own: When he'd watched Monika drive off to Tommy's house, exactly five days and one lifetime ago.

"Hey," said Yuvi, touching his shoulder and looking at him quizically.

"I'm okay," he said as he put the Audi in gear and pulled out of the parking space.

Ljubica nodded, then looked forward as they began to eat up road. "Where are we gonna find some cash?" she asked casually.

"Andrews Air Force Base," said Duncan.

Ljubica just looked at him. "I hope you're kidding."

"No I'm not; you'll see," said Duncan.

They took the Beltway, driving around the southeastern edge of the district, smoothly joining the flow of traffic. Ljubica dozed throughout most of the drive until Duncan gently shook her awake.

"Hmm?—Where are we?" she asked, blinking away the sleep.

"We're almost at the base," said Duncan.

Duncan didn't drive into the Air Force base itself. Rather, he drove around it, going up and down the main drags, slowly edging along, looking for something.

"It's gotta be around here somewheres," he mumbled.

"What's around here?" asked Ljubica.

"A Western Union," he said, as he looked around.

Ljubica blinked, wondering silently what Duncan was up to.

They drove around until finally, in a small strip mall that had just gotten a fresh coat of asphalt on its parking lot, Duncan spotted a Western Union, next door to a 7-Eleven convenience store.

He parked the Audi in front of the 7-Eleven and turned to Ljubica.

"How's your leg?" he asked.

"Okay," she said.

"You can walk on it, right?"

"Yes, of course," she said.

"Can you run on it?" he asked.

Ljubica looked at Duncan carefully. "In a pinch," she said. "If I really had to. Why."

"Go into the Western Union," he said. "No rush, take your time; just go in casual-like. Get one of those slips you need to wire money? You know the ones—"

"Yeah, I know," said Ljubica. "Then what."

"Then wait—just pretend that you're filling out the form," said Duncan. "I'll come in in a little bit. You just follow my lead, okay?"

"Okay."

"You have a gun, right?"

"Yeah," said Ljubica. "Will I need it?"

"Just keep it handy, just in case."

Ljubica looked at Duncan. "Okay," she said.

She checked her weapon, one of the guns Duncan had taken from the FBI agents at Pentagon City, then stuck it in the rear waistband of her jeans, underneath her short, black leather jacket. Then, slowly, she got out of the car and limped over to the Western Union.

Duncan kept an eye on the dashboard clock as he checked out the area. With the traffic of the main drag flowing behind him in the rearview mirror, Duncan saw a lot of cars but few pedestrians and almost no one stopping at this small strip mall. Aside from the 7-Eleven and the Western Union, there was only a dry-cleaning shop, and it was closed.

He gave Ljubica two minutes, and when they were up, Duncan took a breath and deliberately exhaled.

Okay, thought Duncan Idaho.

Duncan stepped out of the car with his gun casually and unobtrusively in hand.

Quickly but relaxed, Duncan walked to the glass door of the Western Union and opened it, stepping inside.

The office was a blank and empty room, painted a dingy white, with two teller's windows on the far side, only one of which was on duty. Against the right wall, there was a long counter, chest high, where Ljubica stood, pretending to fill out a wire-transfer slip. She didn't even look up at Duncan as he stepped inside.

A skinny man with a crew cut and glasses was manning the teller's desk, which was behind bullet-proof lucite glass about an inch thick. The teller wasn't paying any attention to either Ljubica or Duncan, working away on some papers, papers that looked to be schoolwork of some sort. Aside from Ljubica and the teller, there was no one else in the office.

Fuckin'-A, let's get it on, thought Duncan with a smile, raising his gun and aiming it at the teller behind the bullet-proof glass.

"Hey!" he yelled. *"Hey!!"*

Ljubica jumped in surprise when she saw Duncan with his gun, looking almost as surprised as the teller behind the glass.

"Open the door!" Duncan yelled, motioning with his gun at the door beside the teller's window, the door leading to the back of the office. *"Open the fucking door!!!"* Duncan yelled, stepping forward, the barrel of his gun barely eight inches from the teller's face.

"I-I-I-I *can't*," said the teller. "I—"

Then—before the teller had the chance to trip the alarm— Duncan fired four times in quick succession, aiming right for the teller's face behind the lucite.

CR-CRACK!—CR-CRACK!

The effect was electric. The teller, completely panicked, jumped out of his chair in surprise and fear as he saw four round stars appear right in front of his face, the teller so panicked that he forgot all about triggering the alarm system. Even Ljubica recoiled in surprise, never expecting Duncan to actually fire, the sound deafening as the room suddenly filled with the smell of cordite.

"*Open the goddamned fucking door! OPEN IT! Or-or-or— or I'm gonna kill her!*" Duncan shouted, grabbing hold of Ljubica by the neck.

Ljubica yelped in genuine surprise, almost ramming her elbow into Duncan's exposed belly—

—but then she stopped.

"*I swear I'll shoot her—I swear I'll splatter her brains all over this office—*"

"*—don't shoot me, don't shoot me, I'm PREGNANT, don't shoot me—*"

"*—I'm gonna shoot her!—I'm gonna shoot her!—I'm gonna shoot her!—*"

"Don't shoot her!" yelled the teller. "*Don't-don't-don't-don't shoot her!*"

"*Fuck you!—she's gonna* DIE*—OPEN THE GOD-DAMNED FUCKING DOOR!!*"

"*Here-here-here!*" yelled the teller, pulling out a keychain from his pocket. "*I'll, let me, I'll let you—*"

The teller opened the door, Duncan immediately letting go of Ljubica and pointing his gun at the teller's face.

"Thank you kindly," said Duncan, in a normal conversational tone of voice, the barrel of his gun pressed right up to the teller's forehead.

"Oh shit," said the teller.

With one glance out the glass windows of the Western Union offices to make sure no one else was coming in, Ljubica slipped into the back offices behind Duncan as he dealt with the teller.

"There's a safe around here somewhere," said Duncan.

"Right," said Ljubica, looking around.

"You're a hostage!" said the teller, looking over Duncan's shoulder at Ljubica.

"Hey hey hey—no-o talk-ing," said Duncan, tapping the teller's forehead with the barrel of his gun on each syllable, as if he were rapping it to see if anyone was home.

"Ow!" said the teller.

"Want it to hurt worse? Then keep on talking," said Duncan.

Ljubica was frowning. "Where's—? Ah," she said, seeing the open safe and making a beeline for it, which was in the very rear of the office, underneath a long table.

Kneeling too fast before it, Ljubica looked in at the safe and then stopped, amazed. "Holy shit," she said.

In the open safe, there were stacks of hundred dollar bills, easily totaling fifty or sixty thousand dollars, maybe even more.

"Is there enough money?" Duncan asked, as he covered the teller.

Ljubica said nothing, wincing at the pain in her thigh. It felt as if someone had taken a knife to it.

Shouldn't have knelt so fast, she thought

"Hey," said Duncan. "Is there enough money?" he asked again.

"Yeah—plenty," she said, pushing the pain away and concentrating on what she was doing.

By the safe, tucked in a cubbyhole, she spotted a canvas bank bag that she picked up and unfurled, filling it with the money in the safe.

"Oh shit, oh *shit,"* said the teller, watching as Ljubica emptied the safe.

"He-*llo*-o-o-o," said Duncan, tapping the teller's forehead again with his gun barrel. "Mr. *Ding*-ba-a-at: A closed mouth catches no bullets—you ever heard that saying?"

The teller, terrified, shook his head.

"Well it's true, take my word for it," said Duncan archly.

Ljubica reached into the safe and grabbed as much money as she could in each hand, cramming most of it into the canvas bank bag in less than ten seconds.

"Let's go," said Ljubica, limping even more than before, but walking as quickly as she could.

"You go first, I'll cover you," said Duncan, watching out of the corner of his eye as Ljubica limped out of the Western Union office with the bank bag full of cash.

He decided to give her some time.

"Oh shit," said the teller, his eyes wandering to the now-empty safe. "Now listen up," said Duncan. "Close your eyes, face the wall, and count to fifty."

"What?"

"No questions now—do it," said Duncan, his gun aimed right at the teller's face. "Just turn around and count, or I shoot your head off. And that would pretty much suck, now wouldn't it?"

"Y-Yes sir, it would," said the teller, reaching up to cover his eyes as he simultaneously turned to face the wall. But before he began to count, he asked, "You won't shoot me in the back, will you?"

Duncan stopped. "No," he said. "If I have to shoot you, you'll know it was me."

"Okay," said the teller. Then he began to count, "One, two, three, four, five . . ."

Duncan silently walked out of the Western Union office as the teller continued to count, his eyes covered tight with the palms of his hands as he stood with his forehead nearly touching the wall.

". . . twelve, thirteen, fourteen, fifteen . . ."

Back at the Audi, Ljubica was already buckled up, so as soon as Duncan was behind the wheel, they took off, casually joining the flow of traffic.

"*Yeeeeee*-haw!!" yelled Duncan, happier than he'd been in a long, long while. "The Acrobat gang ri-i-i-ides again!"

"You're crazy," said Ljubica with a laugh, counting up the money. When she was done, she turned to Duncan: "Sixty-three thousand four hundred dollars?"

"A Western Union, near a military base, on a Friday?" said Duncan. "*Crammed* with cash, believe you me."

"No kidding," said Ljubica.

"Dang tootin', little cowgirl," he said. "So now's as seein' we gots some greenbacks, whadaya say we go get us some shootin' irons, huh?"

"Okay, cowboy," said Ljubica with a laugh, buoyed by Duncan. "Go, uh . . . Get back on the Beltway, and then drive over to Silver Springs," she said. "I've got a couple of contacts up there that'll fit the bill."

While Ljubica and Duncan were driving to Andrews Air Force Base to pull off the first true stick-up job anyone in Acrobat had ever done, Monika and Tobey drove to Georgetown, where Tobey knew of a coffeehouse called the CyberCafé, at the corner of M Street and Eton Court.

"We'll be able to log on from there," said Tobey.

"Okay," said Monika, driving without a word, her blonde hair dirty and unkempt, bags under her eyes from when she'd been crying as she fought with Duncan.

"Tobey?" she asked him suddenly as she drove along. "Tell me the truth. Did you guys *really* try to get back in?"

Tobey shifted uncomfortably in the passenger seat of the car. "Yes," he said. "Ama—That woman? She was tailing us, she had to be? 'Cause as soon as we stopped at the gate at Langley, she started shooting. But I think she'd been tailing *Michaelus?* I think it was just chance we were there when she made her move on him."

"I see," said Monika, patiently driving along Virginia Avenue, then cutting across the Mall at Seventh Street. "Do you think they would have let you in if you'd tried to get in?"

"I don't know?" said Tobey, looking at Monika's profile as, in the distance, the Washington Monument passed by like a distant telephone pole. "She was gonna kill us, so we didn't have time—Monika, did I do good?"

"What do you—you did fine, Tobey," said Monika, glancing at him and taking his hand in her own as she realized what he meant.

"I've never shot anybody before," said Tobey.

Monika squeezed Tobey's hand in sympathy . . .

. . . and then, without even trying to, in her mind's eye, Monika saw Russell wisely taking in all that was going on as he said, "It's all fun and games until someone gets hurt."

He was right, he was right, we never should've gotten mixed up in all this shit—Skunk Works—Tommy's scheme— going up against Denton of all people—fucking around where we had no business being—putting ourselves out there when we really didn't need to—"It's all fun and games until someone gets hurt"—

"You did fine, Tobey," she added, interrupting her own train of thought. "She would've killed us all if you hadn't been there—where had you gone, by the way?" she suddenly asked.

"To the store to get some Pringles chips," Tobey lied instantly, and in the next split second—brilliant liar that he was—he diffused Monika's attention by putting the onus on her: "You guys were fighting? So I didn't—you know."

Monika sighed and squeezed Tobey's hand. "I know; I'm sorry," she said. "And I'm sorry I doubted you before."

For a second, Tobey was confused, but then he realized what Monika meant: She'd doubted he'd tried his best to get back inside Langley this morning. Monika had never doubted that he was one of Acrobat.

They drove along in silence for a while.

"So we'll break into the County Registrar's Office?" said Tobey. "And then we get the schematics and the blueprints. And then when we have those blueprints and schematics, we figure out how to break into the bank."

Listening to the plan—Duncan's plan—Monika nearly started to cry. "Another crazy scheme . . . ," she said as she stepped outside herself and saw how foolish their plan really was—they were running scared.

"You know Duncan," said Tobey with a laugh, missing the panic in Monika's voice. Then he said seriously, "So Monika? Once we break into the bank and get our IDs and stuff . . . uh, then what?" asked Tobey.

"Then we're gonna go underground," said Monika, grimacing at the idea.

Tobey shifted uncomfortably. "Where's that?"

Monika didn't answer as she drove on, Tobey too skittish to repeat his question.

They crossed into Georgetown and started looking for a place to park the car near the CyberCafé. It took longer than they expected.

The CyberCafé was one of those novelty coffeehouses that you suspect will go bankrupt pretty quickly. Expensively decorated in a prime location, it had two rows of high-end computers with which you could log on to the World Wide Web, and an espresso bar down in the back that offered overpriced coffee, yummy pastries, and glacier-paced staffing. Though it was noon on a Friday, it wasn't as crowded as one would have thought.

"Uh—Monika?" asked Tobey, as he sat down in front of one of the computers. "I'll find out where the building plans are, so, uh, could you get me a latté?"

"Sure."

"And a strawberry scone? The kind with the chocolate glazing on top."

"Okay," said Monika, her stomach doing a little nauseous roll at the thought of any food.

She walked to the back of the place and stood in an interminable line, thinking about what they'd gotten themselves into.

Stupid stupid stupid, we should've just let it all slide, stayed put where we were—were we so unhappy staying put?—what's so wrong with staying in one place, dug in and holding on?

By the time the slowpokes behind the counter had filled out her order, Tobey was already coming toward her, with a cheap floppy disk in hand.

"There's no such place as the County Registrar's Office," Tobey said. "It's called the Building Permit Records Office, and it's at 941 North Capitol Street, second floor, between K and H Streets just off Union Square."

"Great," she said, tiredly thinking that now they'd have to get in there to this Building Permit Records Office and somehow get the stupid plans, and what a stupid idea was that. Why didn't they just go back to the ranch and talk to somebody, anybody, somehow get back to the ranch and make it all better—

"Uh, that's not all?" Tobey was saying, as he waved the cheap little yellow floppy disk he had in hand. "The bank was built after 1992? So its blueprints and electrical schematics were submitted electronically? So we got 'em," he said.

"What do you mean we got 'em?" Monika asked.

Tobey waved the floppy disk again. "Right here? All we gotta do is find a large-sized printer—ooh, thanks," he said, taking the coffee and scone off her.

"Tobey," said Monika, "you're a genius!"

Tobey smiled shyly. "It was no biggee," he said modestly, then bit into the scone.

"You're a *super*-genius!"

Tobey blushed and munched.

Fifteen minutes later, they were walking into a Kinko's photocopying store where they'd print up the blueprints and electrical schematics that were on the yellow disk.

"Tell you what," said Monika, reaching into her purse for her wallet. "Here's some money—you do all the printing stuff, okay? I'm gonna go buy some things at the pharmacy," she said, tossing her chin in the direction of a nearby Rite Aid as she counted off sixty dollars.

"What do you need?" Tobey asked innocently.

"Stuff," said Monika.

"What kind of stuff?"

"Girl stuff," she said casually.

"Oh," said Tobey, blushing.

He took the sixty dollars she gave him and walked into Kinko's, Monika watching him through the glass doors as he got in line. Then she turned and walked down M Street toward the Rite Aid pharmacy.

She didn't walk in, though. Instead, she walked up to the public telephones right in front of the store, at the corner there on Potomac Street. She picked up the receiver, pumped in a few quarters, and dialed a Virginia number—a Langley number.

Paradise was another operational work-group at CIA, and during the normal run of things, it usually managed assets out of the Middle Eastern embassies. But this was not the normal run of things—the Clinton administration was getting ready to cut Jonathan Pollard loose. Awhile back, Pollard, a Naval Intelligence analyst, had been convicted fair and square of selling secrets to the Israelis. But through some shrewd manipulations, this traitorous son-of-a-bitch and his lawyers had turned a clean-cut case of espionage into a messy political issue: The Clinton administration was actually thinking about releasing Pollard to the Israelis as a measure of "goodwill" before the end of its term, freaking out everyone in the Intelligence community, with good reason: Pollard still had so many secrets in his head that he was a live wire. No way could the Intelligence community afford to let someone like Pollard slide. So for the last couple of months, instead of doing its regular job, Paradise had been reassigned to build a case explaining to the Senate Intelligence Committee exactly why releasing Pollard was not such a totally groovy idea.

Annie Roth was the *primer inter pares* at Paradise, which was why she happened to be the one who picked up the outside line when it began to ring.

"Paradise," she said casually.

"Annie, thank God, it's Monika Summers."

"Monika?" said Annie Roth, stunned to be hearing from her friend. "Monika, I can't believe it's you—are you okay?" she said as she picked up a pen and threw it across the Paradise work area, hitting her boyfriend, Dexter Carson, squarely on the back of the head.

"Ow!" he said, turning on Annie—

—but seeing her making frantic motions to the phone as she calmly said, "Monika, honey, tell me what's going on—everybody here at the ranch is going nuts—first of all: Are you okay?"

"I'm okay, I'm fine."

Annie Roth sighed, buying time as Dexter sprinted to the other side of the Paradise work area, to the dead key phone.

"Annie, are you there?"

"I'm here, I'm here," she said. "I'm, I'm stunned. The Director, Denton, Atmajian, Strathmore—there's like a total meltdown going on around here. What's going on?"

Dexter Carson picked up the dead key phone, starting the trace-and-record just as Monika said, "They killed Michaelus."

"We know," said Annie Roth. "He was shot and killed at the South Gate this morning—the ranch is crawling with press and police—police-police and PhysPlanSec squads and FBI on top of that. Monika, the word is you guys did it."

"We didn't!" Monika freaked. "We were trying to get back *in!"*

"Okay—"

"That's what I'm trying to do right now—"

"Okay—"

"Get back in."

"Okay, okay, listen, don't worry, we'll get you back in: Where are you?" Annie said quickly.

"I'm—we're—I'm in Georgetown," Monika said, the knot in her mind slowly unraveling as she realized how good this all was, how good it all was going to be. "We left the others just a little while ago—who else is on the line?" she asked as she stood there at the phone booth.

"I'm right here. It's Dexter."

"Dexter-baby!" said Monika, actually beginning to cry as she called him by his nickname.

"Monika, honey!" said Dexter, Monika hearing the smile in his voice as they went through their joshing routine.

"Oh, Dexter, am I glad to hear your voice," she said as she dabbed her eyes.

"So am I, kiddo, so am I," he said with real feeling. "Are you on your own?"

"Yeah—No—Sort of," said Monika. "I'm with Tobey Jansen, you remember him?"

"Sure we do," said Annie. "Super-geek. How's he doing?"

"Not good, not good at all," said Monika, looking around, in case Tobey spotted her and she was found out. "He doesn't know I'm calling, he's-he's doing something right now, and-and-and—oh, God—"

"What happened?" Annie asked.

Monika nearly cried. "I don't know," she said. "It was just—everything just got so screwed up!"

"It's okay, don't worry, everything'll be alright," said Annie soothingly, as she wrote in a pad, tore the sheet off, and gave this note to one of the other members of Paradise, Joey Alvarez.

Alvarez looked at the note and walked/jogged away.

Monika was saying, "It was Duncan's idea, Duncan's and Tom's. They wanted to break into Skunk Works, and then Yuvi was on board too, so then what was I supposed to do?"

Dexter said, "You guys broke into Skunk Works? *Fuck . . .*"

Monika went on, saying, "I didn't really understand what we were getting into until it was all over and we got back on Friday. Then Sunday morning Tom and Duncan made us all go underground."

"Jesus," said Dexter. "So you're not with Duncan anymore?"

Monika didn't even hesitate. "No," she said as she felt a knife slice through the shroud of her conscience. "I just want, I just want to get back to Langley. I want my old life back."

Annie Roth said, "We'll bring you in, honey, don't worry about a thing, just tell us where you are."

"I'm-I'm in Georgetown, at the corner of M and Potomac."

Dexter asked, "Are you on foot or do you have a car?"

"We have a car," said Monika.

Annie Roth said, "Okay, go to the Iwo Jima Memorial at Arlington. Be there in—it's twelve thirty-five: Be there at one. Can you make that?"

"Yeah, yeah, I think I can," said Monika. "I don't know if Tobey will come with me or not."

Annie Roth said, "Don't worry about that, honey, you just go there with or without him, and I'll be there with Dexter, okay, sweetie?"

"Okay."

Dexter Carson said, "We'll see you in a half hour."

"Okay . . . ," said Monika, waiting.

Dexter and Annie both waited, knowing from experience that Monika—like any asset, like any source—couldn't help but spell out her real motivation just before breaking contact.

Monika didn't disappoint. "I can't wait to see you guys again!" she said finally. "I can't wait for it to be the way it used to be, just like old times."

Just then, Joey Alvarez came back to the Paradise offices, leading someone in tow.

"Neither can we," said Annie as she spotted the new arrival. "We'll see you at one, at Iwo Jima, okay sweetie?"

"Okay." said Monika. "Bye girlfriend."

"Bye girlfriend," said Annie Roth, staring directly at the new arrival, Nicholas Denton.

Monika was waiting outside for him when Tobey came out of the Kinko's with the blueprints and electrical schematics of the bank rolled into a blue plastic carrying tube.

"Good to go!" he said, Monika realizing for the first time how cheerful he looked. Ninety minutes ago he'd just shot someone to death, and yet here he was, looking chipper. As if he'd blanked it all out.

He probably has—I would, she thought as she said, "Great. Let's go for a drive."

They got into Amalia's gold-colored Taurus and drove aimlessly around Georgetown, Tobey keeping up a steady, soothing chatter all the while.

"They had the biggest laser printers? I didn't even know that they made them that big—four feet wide, with a never-ending roll of paper? Whew! You could print out like, I don't know, the longest list in the world—you could print out Santa's Naughty-and-Nice list in a single shot!"

"That's something," said Monika, rehearsing the words in her head. "Hey, we've got three hours to kill before meeting up with the others—want to go to Arlington Cemetery?"

"Sure," said Tobey, hugging the blue tube as he watched the road change. "You know, I've never gone?"

"Neither have I—no, I have," said Monika. "One time a few years ago I went with my parents when they came to visit me, back when they could still travel."

"Your folks are that old, huh," asked Tobey.

"Yeah," said Monika as they drove across the Key Bridge. "You didn't know that? My dad's seventy-nine and my mom's seventy-four, almost seventy-five. I'm the baby of six."

"Wow, I had no idea," said Tobey. "Are you close to your brothers and sisters?"

Monika shrugged, then smiled at Tobey, trying to charm him. "Not really," she said as she took the 110 south. "We're all sort of like strangers—my next older brother is ten years older than me, and he's married with kids and he's got a whole different kind of life than me. Sort of like your brother," she added, knowing all about Tobey's screenwriting brother out in California.

"Did you always live in the same place?" asked Tobey.

Monika blinked. "Sure," she said. "My parents still own the house where me and all my brothers and sisters were born."

"You're lucky," said Tobey, fascinated by that stability. "What was it like?"

"It was sort of weird," said Monika. "The house—it's this big, big house up on this little hill, with lots of rooms and cubbyholes. My next oldest brother moved away to college when I was seven or eight, so growing up I had the whole house to myself. Old wooden houses creak like crazy, so at night, I was sure that ghosts were out haunting. My dad retired when I was eleven or twelve, and he and my mom played a lot of golf, so I always had the house to myself—hang on," she said as they neared the Arlington Cemetery exit.

They got off the 110 and drove down King Drive toward the Visitors' Center, by the main parking lot. At the entry booth, Monika took the ticket and drove on through. The parking lot was so full that Monika had to go to the farther edge of the lot to find a place to park, carefully making her way through the hordes of people strolling to and from their cars.

"It was great living in that house," she said suddenly, continuing with her story. "My parents would be away golfing or whatever, so I'd invite all my friends over and we'd have sleepovers and tea parties—little girl stuff. When I wasn't at home with my friends, I was over at their houses. It's weird, I got to be closer to my friends and my friends' parents than to my own family. I guess in a way, you make a family out of your friends, you know?"

"Yeah," said Tobey, clearly agreeing.

"Like the job," she said easily, getting to the hook of her pitch as she looked for a place to park the car. "You're at Langley and it's like your family."

"Yeah," said Tobey, Monika glancing at him and seeing as he turned a little blue, a little down.

"It's so crazy," she said, with a little laugh. "You've got all these stupid secrets you can't tell *anybody*—except other people at Langley."

"Yeah," said Tobey, smiling but still blue, knowing they wouldn't be going back.

"At the ranch, you feel like everyone is, well maybe not a friend; but they're like, in cahoots with you, you know?"

"Yeah."

"That's why I want to go back so bad," said Monika.

"Me too," said Tobey, staring at her, just knowing that something had happened.

Monika parked the car, turned off the engine, and then turned to Tobey. She hesitated, then began, "I got in touch with Annie Roth and Dexter Carson. I'm supposed to meet them in a little bit, over at the Iwo Jima Memorial."

Tobey just looked at her, holding the blue tube with the bank's plans in them, twirling his spiked goatee. Automatically, he looked over his shoulder at the memorial in the dis-

tance, seeing the soldiers raising the flag. Then he turned back
to Monika.

She gave him a small, pleading smile. "Why don't you
come with me?"

Tobey twirled his goatee and looked down, thinking, his
fingers automatically and obsessively manipulating his blond
spike.

Monika gave him a second, then said, "I'm tired, Tobey. I
know Annie and Dexter, they're my friends, especially Annie.
With just a little bit of footwork, just a little shuffling dance,
we could get back inside and forget all about this running
business. We've got so many friends in Langley, people who
like us, who want to help us. All we have to do is ask our
friends for help, and they will."

"Yeah," said Tobey noncommittally.

Monika tugged at his arm. *"Come on,"* she said quietly,
almost in a whisper. "We can blame it all on Tom—I know,
I know, I know," she said, holding up her hand to stop Tobey's
objections. "He was your friend—he was my friend too, and
I miss him like crazy, and I *hate* the way he died. But he's
dead—nothing we say can hurt him. If we just put the blame
all on Tommy, then we'll be able to get back inside. It'll be
like it was before. I don't know about you, but I want that,"
she said, looking at Tobey. "Don't you want that too?" she
added.

Tobey looked at her, then looked out across the sea of
parked cars, at the Iwo Jima Memorial in the distance. It was
very close.

"Yeah, I do, but—," he said, then stopped.

Monika waited. "But what?"

"What about Duncan and Yuvi?"

Monika bit her lower lip and looked out across the parking
lot. She turned to Tobey. "Before we went to Kinko's, you
asked me what'd we do when we went underground, remember? Well, I don't know the answer to that question. I guess
we'd just wander, just drift around like, like, like—I don't
know what drifts forever, but that's what we'd do: We'd never
be able to have any friends, because we'd be afraid they might

turn us in. We'd never be able to get in touch with any of the people who know us. We'd always be looking over our shoulders. We'd never be at peace. Tobey, I, I can't do that. Duncan and Yuvi can, and maybe that makes them better people than me; tougher somehow. I just know that I don't want that," said Monika. "And I don't think you want it either. So let's *go*," she said, pointing with her chin toward the Iwo Jima Memorial, the flag flapping in the perfect blue of the day.

"Let's go home," she said.

Tobey looked at the monument, and then turned to Monika. "Okay," he said.

She blinked, surprised that Tobey had agreed. Then she nodded. "Okay," she said.

They got out of the car.

The statue of the six men planting the flag on Mount Suribachi is overwhelming and almost frightening not because of its size but because of its detail—every last grimace, every last grunt is captured exactly, and with no illusions. If the monument had had even a hint of fancy, even a tiny little dash of romanticism and perfection, it would have forfeited all its power. It would have simply been a big monolith on the edges of a vast cemetery. But the statue is real. The soldiers' gear belts sag at their waists, their helmets are set at cocky, juvenile angles. Their rifles look like they're about to slip off their shoulders and clatter to the ground. When you look at the statue, you can see that the soldiers haven't shaved—and that's what scares you: That ordinary grandeur. The men are giants, and yet they're just like you: So why aren't you more like them?

Annie Roth was sitting on the black marble pedestal of the monument, Dexter Carson standing beside her as the statue rose amid a sea of tourists. The spring day was so pretty, with just a touch of humidity in the air, the sun bright and just warm enough for shorts but not so hot as to make you sweat.

"I don't see them," Annie was saying into the transmitter at her throat, both she and Dexter looking out of place in their severe, conservative work clothes as the tourists all posed around the statue in their baseball caps and T-shirts and snapped away.

"Keep cool," said Arthur Atmajian through their earpiece receivers. "They'll be here soon enough."

Atmajian himself was handling this asset recovery. He was sitting in a parked sport utility vehicle with tinted windows some two hundred yards away, watching it all through binoculars. From his vantage point, he could see Annie Roth and Dexter Carson as well as the three Dog Soldiers he'd brought along—three men who looked like they'd stepped out of their accountancy classes at the local community college. His three men wandered aimlessly through the spring crowd, everyone knowing exactly what Tobey and Monika looked like.

When you handle an Intelligence asset, you walk an interesting line—you're his friend, but you have to keep aloof. You can't be some bountiful lover who gives the whole show away—you have to be a ruthless tease, a stingy flirt: You have to be open and smiling and warm and inviting, but with just enough distance to keep your asset hooked on that delicious anxiety that comes only from uncertainty.

"I see her," said Annie Roth as she got up and smiled and waved and walked through the throng of tourists toward Monika.

Monika looked exhausted. Her clothes looked grubby, her hair unkempt. She was frowning as she looked around, approaching the monument, her eyes scanning the crowd.

The moment she spotted Annie and Dexter, she broke out into a relieved smile, walking straight toward them, picking up her pace, raising her hand to wave—

At that moment, Monika's smile started to fade as she slowed down and finally stopped walking, standing frozen thirty yards away.

Annie Roth was just about her age, twenty-eight, though shorter than Monika, maybe five feet four in her sandals. She was compact and agile, her hair a dark auburn with just a hint of dark red highlights, almost subliminal in their subtlety. Her face was wide and open, but as Monika looked, Annie's face was frozen in a smile—a friendly smile but not a *friend's* smile. It was a calculating look like a salesman's before he gives you a pitch, or before you discover what the fine print really says.

"Wait," said Monika, putting out her hand to hold Tobey back as she looked across the crowd at Annie Roth.

"What's going on?" said Atta-boy, unable to see Monika Summers or Tobey Jansen through the thick crowd in their brightly colored clothing.

Annie kept smiling, looking quizzically at Monika as she continued walking toward her. "Monika," she called out through the crowd, waving at her.

Tobey turned to Monika. "What's wrong?" he asked her.

"Everything," said Monika.

Annie was walking toward her, still frowning slightly as she held on to her smile, Dexter right beside her and glancing around the crowd looking for something—

Looking for who? thought Monika even as she didn't really care. Just looking at Annie was enough. There was that look to her, a look that said she was happy to see Monika, yes of course, happy, yes . . . but not unduly excited. She wasn't thrilled like a friend would be thrilled to discover that someone you care for is safe and free and okay. It was that cool happiness that comes from a professional place, a disinterested look that Monika knew all too well because it was the look she herself had used with assets—

That friendly, disinterested, calculating professionalism you use with asset management.

"Come on," said Monika, quickly turning around and ducking through the crowd, which was thick as a mushroom soup. "Come *on*," she hissed to Tobey, grabbing his wrist and pulling him along as she glanced over her shoulder.

Annie and Dexter both stopped smiling as they lost sight of Monika and Tobey in the crowd.

"I've lost them," Annie said into her transmitter, as she and Dexter started walking quickly forward through the crowd, in the general direction of Tobey and Monika.

Looking around, Annie spotted the Dog Soldiers and shot

out her arms, sending them in different directions. "You go there, you go over to that path, we'll go over to the parking lot," she said into the transmitter at her collar.

Monika and Tobey ducked to the right and walked through a throng of tourists coming down one of the cemetery paths, Monika leading the way and pulling on Tobey's wrist.

Tobey asked, "What's going on?"

"Duck down," she said, pulling at Tobey, whose punk-rocking, spiked-goatee look didn't stick out amid the crowd as much as his six-foot two-inch height did, Monika pulling him down enough so that he slouched down to a height of no more than five ten—average height in the crowd. The tourists all stared at them, though, looking at this odd couple queerly slouching along on their way. But no one pointed them out or gave them away as Tobey and Monika ducked and darted through the crowd, looking for a way out.

"I can't see them," Annie was saying, no longer wearing that professional smile, furiously trying to figure out what had gone wrong even as she scanned the crowd, looking for them.

In the SUV, Atmajian dropped his binoculars and got into the shotgun seat, telling his driver, "Go," the off-white colored sport utility vehicle going up North Meade Street toward the general parking lot of the cemetery.

The Dog Soldiers had broken their cover with their sheer thoroughness, expertly herding the crowd even without them knowing it, the three killers cutting up the crowd around the Iwo Jima monument as they looked for their targets.

Monika and Tobey were out-and-out running through the crowd even as they tried not to *seem* as if they were running, ducking in and out of groups, trying to keep real people between themselves and where they assumed Annie and Dexter were.

Annie and Dexter had meantime split up, both of them heading in the general direction of the main parking lot, knowing that Monika and Tobey had a car—

"They've probably gone back to get it," said Annie.

There were thousands of cars, just thousands—shining boxes of metal and plastic sitting under the sun as people passed to and fro, getting out of their cars or getting in, the parking lot a constant flux of slow-moving cars and even slower moving pedestrians.

"Shit," said Dexter, as he looked around.

"Start looking," Annie ordered him and the Dog Soldiers, the five of them spreading out and going up and down the rows and rows of cars, the occasional tourist bus getting in the way.

Annie Roth angrily looked around the huge parking lot, cars stretching out for hundreds and hundreds of yards, knowing she'd somehow blown it. *"Monika!"* she yelled out, knowing it was no use. *"Monika come back!"*

Atmajian's SUV suddenly stopped beside Annie Roth, Atta-boy rolling down the window. "Anything?"

"No," said Annie simply.

"Let's go," said Atmajian to his driver, the SUV lurching off, cruising through the parking lot, looking for the two members of Acrobat.

Two hundred yards away, the gold-colored Taurus was taking an on ramp onto the George Washington Parkway, Monika Summers crying at the wheel.

Tobey Jansen was looking behind them, craning his neck this way and that. "I don't see them," he was saying, shooting looks at Monika and then looks at the road that was sliding away behind them. "I don't think they're following us?"

Monika just cried as she drove. To their right, the cemetery receded, the pale gray concrete highway taking them away. To their left, a breeze was blowing across the Potomac that made the surface of the river dapple with little waves, water flourishes that looked like small, drowning hands waving good-bye.

CHAPTER 12

Discovering Who and What We Are

At four P.M. sharp, what remained of the Acrobat work-group rendezvoused back at the warehouse, the four of them standing around the worktable, where they'd spread out the building plans of the bank. Shafts of spring sun cut almost vertical beams through the gaps in the roofing, the four of them moving in and out of shadow and light as they talked about what they were going to do tonight.

"This is the bank," said Monika, her voice and her hand shaking ever so slightly as she pointed out the relevant details in the bank's blueprints. "This is the first floor, the entrance, tellers' windows, door to the back offices. Here," she said, again pointing, "is the stairwell down to the basement. That's where the vault is."

She rolled the top sheet away.

"Now this is the basement; this is the stairwell," she said, pointing. "This hallway leads straight to the main vault, here."

"What are these?" asked Duncan, pointing out some rooms off the main hallway.

Monika looked at them, still trembling even two hours after the botched meeting at the Iwo Jima Memorial. Duncan was about to say something when Monika pointed and said, "Privacy rooms for bank clients with safety deposit boxes. Here," she continued, pointing to the entrance of the stairwell down, "is what's important. The stairwell is the only way in or out of the basement. So what they did is, they put a security door on it. When the alarm is tripped, the stairwell door is sealed."

Ljubica, noticeably sweating as she looked at the plans, nodded. "We have to trick out the alarm system anyway," she said. "If we set off the alarm, even if we could somehow keep the stairwell door from locking up, the safe probably has a timed lock. No way we could open it even if we wanted to. Our best shot is to trick out the alarm system first. Then we can have our way with the vault all night."

"An interesting way of putting it," said Duncan with a laugh.

Neither Monika nor Ljubica even smiled as Yuvi wiped her brow and Monika looked at the electrical schematics.

"So about security," said Monika, rolling the top sheet back across the table.

"Let me see," said Ljubica.

The two women went through the bank's plans and electrical schematics for over an hour, Duncan following the conversation and at the same time observing them both.

Neither looked too good.

Ljubica's thigh was clearly infected, even though they'd cleaned and rebandaged her wound every day. But she was a trooper. Along with getting their gear—weapons, the portable sonogram machine, the combination-breaker and all the rest— she'd also scored a hefty stash of drugs: Amphetamines, for the most part, along with a bunch of Valium and some hospital-grade morphine. Surprisingly, they'd been unable to get any antibiotics, which were harder to score out on the street than any illegal drug. "But I'll manage," she'd told Duncan on the drive back to the warehouse. "I'll find a medic when we're underground. I'll *buy* a medic if I have to."

Monika didn't look so good either. Whenever she stopped talking about the mechanics of how they would score the bank at DuPont Circle, she looked like a ghost. Often as not, she'd pause for no reason, a second or two ticking away before she remembered herself and what she was doing.

Duncan was aware of how low the two women were, but he couldn't afford to make it an issue. Instead, he nodded at the blueprints and schematics, and then looked up at Monika.

"You should see some of the stuff me and Ljubica got, I mean the *neatest* damned stuff—come on, I'll show you," he said.

With that, Duncan turned and walked out of the warehouse, Monika automatically following him, almost like a Stepford wife. "The neatest stuff, I swear, and the night-vision goggles are just too cool for cable . . ."

Ljubica, though, stayed by the plans, leaning on the table, exhausted. Even though she'd just wiped her brow, already beads of sweat were forming there again. As he studied her, Tobey noticed that Ljubica was gripping the edge of the work-table until her knuckles were yellow.

"You okay?" asked Tobey.

Ljubica smiled, feeling nauseous. "I'm fine," she said, standing up straight and limping over to a crate, sitting down on it with her wounded leg propped out in front of her.

"I have to change these bandages," she said quietly, looking at her leg, then away at the dirty floor of the warehouse.

"Yeah," said Tobey, suddenly scared at the sight of Ljubica's leg. It looked like a sausage. Even her ankle, peeking out from under the cuff of her jeans, was noticeably swollen.

"I think I might have an infection of some sort," she said, looking up at Tobey. "And I know I tore a muscle just now," she added.

"Now?" asked Tobey.

"Back at the Western Union," she said. "When we were getting money, I knelt down a bit too fast. I think I tore a thigh muscle. And the swelling . . . that's from an infection of some sort."

Tobey looked at her. "Does it . . . smell?" he asked uncomfortably.

"No, not yet," she said. "But it will. That's when I'll be in trouble."

"Hey," said Tobey, kneeling in front of Ljubica. "What if we call it off, hmm? What if we postpone this thing—until you're better."

But Ljubica was already shaking her head. "We have to do this now. We have to get to the vault. We have to get our new identities and our plastic and our stuff. It's our stuff—*ours.*

We have got to get it now or else Denton will. In a couple of days, I'll get real medical attention."

Ljubica stopped and sighed, her lazy almond eyes looking almost as if she were about to fall asleep.

"I'm so tired, Tobey," she said.

Tobey nodded, sitting on the ground in front of her and taking out a pack of cigarettes from his sweatshirt pocket. He lit one, just as Ljubica stubbed out hers.

Ljubica looked up and out of the warehouse, looking after Duncan and Monika. "I just want to be . . . back someplace . . . safe," she said quietly.

"Me too," said Tobey, even more quietly than Ljubica, suddenly speaking in a low, soft mumble, the words skipping through the air as daintily as a skater across thin ice. "You know, I think the last time I felt really safe was when we broke into Skunk Works? When we were all together," he said, catching Ljubica's eye only occasionally, as if afraid of what she might think of what he said. "Ever since we got back from California, I've felt like I've been running, like I've been on the run nonstop. And it was only a week ago! That we got back from Skunk Works! Just a week. I haven't felt peace of mind since then," he said. He took a puff on his cigarette, then looked at Ljubica and then away. "Sometimes I wish I'd never heard about Skunk Works."

"The last time I felt safe," said Ljubica, "was when we waxed that PCB board in New York."

Tobey smiled, remembering. "Yeah," he said. "That was good. I was such a dork!" he said with a laugh.

Ljubica nodded with a smile.

"Ljubica?" he asked her.

"Hmm?"

"What happened with you and Russell?" he asked quietly.

She looked at Tobey. Then she shrugged and looked at her leg, rubbing her thigh around her wound.

"Do you really think he was selling us out?" he asked.

"Do you?" she asked in return.

"No," he said. "Russell . . . Duncan, and especially Monika wanted to believe that someone was selling us out. But Russell, you know . . . I don't, I don't—it wasn't Russell."

"You think no one was selling us out?" she asked him.

Tobey said nothing, looking at Ljubica, then looking at the ground.

"I—"

"I don't think Russell was selling us out," she said quietly. Tobey looked at her. "Then why did you . . ."

Ljubica looked away, as if she were scanning a distant horizon.

"What happened with you and Russell?" Tobey asked again.

Ljubica frowned as she continued to look to that far shore. "I don't know," she said, glancing at Tobey.

Tobey looked unconvinced.

"Sometimes," she said patiently, "there are no reasons, Tobey. No reasons, no explanations. No motives. Sometimes things just are."

Just outside the warehouse, Duncan and Monika were standing over the trunk of the Audi, looking at all the things Ljubica and Duncan had bought.

"Ljubica has the best contacts, I swear," Duncan was saying, trying to cover the surprise he was feeling: Monika was right up against him, holding his hand over her shoulder, trying to get him to take hold of her. "We got all this stuff just like *that*," he said, snapping his fingers. "It was almost like shopping at a mall—look, a combination-breaker, a real-imaging portable sonogram; I mean this stuff's hard to come by even back at the ranch. And weapons, shit, we might as well have been buying lollipops," he said, untangling himself from Monika so he could touch the four AK-74s Ljubica had bought through her contacts.

"Have you taken a good look at her lately?" Monika asked him.

Still looking at the contents of the trunk, his eyes glazing a little, Duncan nodded a bit. "I have," he said.

"Do you think she's got it in her to pull this thing off?"

she said, again trying to make him hold her by taking his hands and deliberately wrapping his arms around her body.

"She'd better," said Duncan with a casual laugh, glancing at Monika and taking a step away. Then he looked in Yuvi's direction and sighed. "I *think* she can pull it off—I'm not a hundred percent on her, but I think she can. At least she's motivated."

"I don't know," said Monika quietly, looking back at the warehouse to make sure they weren't overheard. "Ljubica's out of gas. And Tobey's . . . I don't know about Tobey," she said.

"Tobey's a little hopped up after that thing with the little woman," said Duncan. "That's natural. But Tobey's, Tobey's alright. I think, after a few hours' sleep, you all are gonna make it on this scoring run."

"What about you?" said Monika, stepping into Duncan. "You're going to be on this scoring run too."

Looking her in the eye, Duncan said, " 'Course I am; we talked about it already."

Monika again tried getting Duncan to hold her as she said, "You're not gonna go tag Denton, right? Because we need you for this scoring run."

"I'm not gonna go tag Denton; I'll be there," he said, looking at her then turning back to look at all their gear. "The tough part is gonna be tricking out the alarm system. Once we're through that, it'll be easy pickings," he added, moving ever so slightly away from her.

Monika looked at him, thinking, *What's wrong with him?* Instead, she asked, "Why did you get the uh, the night-vision goggles?"

"Oh, just in case," said Duncan, looking down at the contents of the trunk.

Monika smiled slightly and nodded, not really hearing him as she crossed her arms over her breasts and looked at the ground. "We'll be together, right?" she said suddenly. "When we go underground, we'll be together."

" 'Course we will," said Duncan easily, flinching a bit as he leaned over all the gear in the trunk. He picked up the night-vision goggles and checked their settings. "That's something, how Tobey got all the plans and stuff," he said.

Monika frowned. "What are we going to do tomorrow?" she asked.

Duncan glanced at her. "What do you mean?"

"I mean after we've gotten our stuff," said Monika. "Are we gonna, are we gonna stay in Washington or go someplace you have in mind—what are we gonna do?"

"I don't know," said Duncan casually, checking the AK-74s. "Tomorrow'll take care of tomorrow; right now let's concentrate on tonight. Maybe I should break them all down and check their action," he said, picking up one of the assault rifles.

"But we'll be together, right?" said Monika.

Duncan smiled automatically. "Sure we will," he said as he pulled the bolt on one of the rifles and checked the action, firing the empty rifle: Click.

At four o'clock in the afternoon, just around the time Acrobat was getting back together at the empty warehouse on the other side of town, FBI Special Agent-in-Charge Larry Murphy went to one of the back offices of the DuPont Circle bank and placed a call to his boss, FBI Director Roy Livre.

"Sir, this is Larry Murphy over at the DuPont Circle bank," he began.

"Well?" said Livre.

"Sir, it's closing time here, and it's been no joy. What do I do with my men?"

Livre sighed. "Pull 'em out," he said. "Let's see if something happens Monday morning."

"Yes sir," said Murphy, he and Livre talking about a few other things before hanging up.

At the Bell Atlantic telephone hub, the tap Matthew Wilson and Amalia had set up captured the entire conversation. Using patented IBM voice-recognition technology, the conversation was transcribed in Realtime, then sent via E-mail to Nicholas Denton's desk.

But Denton didn't read the message when it blipped on his computer screen. He was too busy making sure that Bart Michaelus's sudden and tragic death was blamed squarely on Acrobat.

Acrobat slept through the rest of the day, Tobey and Duncan pulling watch, waking each other up every three hours.

At three o'clock in the morning that Friday night, they woke up and split their gear between the two cars. Then they drove to the Riggs Bank on DuPont Circle. The streets of Washington were clear of tourists and natives, some traffic lights turned blinkers like in some small town, the black asphalt of the streets now turned subtly gray by the yellow hue of the streetlights.

Duncan was driving the Audi, Tobey beside him. They were following Ljubica and Monika, who was at the wheel of the gold-colored Taurus that had once been Amalia's.

They drove down Massachusetts Avenue, and when they got to DuPont Circle, they drove around it and continued on down Connecticut Avenue past the Riggs Bank, which they passed to their left. At R Street, they turned left and drove down to Twenty-first Street, where they again turned left onto Q Street. Q was lined with houses, so Acrobat drove slowly, as if they were leaving a party or just coming home.

They slowed down and killed their headlights, for although it was lined with streetlamps, Q had such thick and tall trees that it was remarkably dark once the sun was down, let alone at three in the morning when everyone would be fast asleep, their front porch lights off.

Just before they got to Twentieth Street, they stopped, Monika parking the Taurus sedan on the northwest corner by a fire hydrant, Duncan double-parking directly behind her.

"Aren't you going to find a parking spot?" Tobey asked him.

"This is good enough," said Duncan as they waited.

Both cars sat there quiet except for the ticking sound of dripping oil.

From where they were parked, the huge maw that was the entrance to the DuPont Circle Metro station was catty-corner to them—and just beyond that, to the right, was the rear of the Riggs Bank. Just ahead of them, intersecting Q Street, was Connecticut Avenue, quiet at this hour in the morning, as was everything else around. Not a single car happened to pass by as they waited those few seconds.

"You ready," asked Duncan.

"Yeah," said Tobey with a clean conscience; he hadn't told anyone what they were doing tonight.

"Okay," said Duncan as he opened the door and stepped out of the car.

At the same time, Monika popped the trunk as she got out of her car, everyone but Ljubica crowding around it.

First off, they each put on a slim headset connected by a thin wire to a walkie-talkie, which they each strapped to their hip. They checked their comm link to make sure it was working properly, then turned to the trunk to put on their gear.

Though they were all wearing their normal street clothes (clothes that were now a bit rank after six days without a change), from the trunk of the Taurus they each took out and put on a fisherman's vest, khaki-colored and sleeveless, zipped up the front with lots of big pockets. Instead of tackle, the pockets of these vests were stuffed with the gear they'd need to break into the bank—the portable sonogram machine, the lock-breaker, and the high-speed combination-breaking computers needed to trick out the alarm system, as well as handguns, extra ammunition, and assorted knick-knacks.

Because she was wounded, Ljubica would be the lookout, staying behind the wheel of the Taurus. From her vantage point, she'd have a clear line of sight of Q Street and Twentieth Street, as well as anything coming along Connecticut Avenue. They'd agreed that, once the team was inside, Ljubica would make a short circuit around the block and DuPont Circle every fifteen minutes, checking the front of the bank, which faced Connecticut Avenue and the Circle before heading back to the lookout point at Q and Twentieth. To make sure she stayed awake and wasn't made dull by the pain of her infected thigh, Ljubica was carefully taking amphetamines, enough to keep her edgy and awake, not enough to trip her out. She took a quarter of a tab now as Tobey, Monika, and Duncan rattled around in the back of the car, strapping on their fisherman's vests.

Along with the vests, the three of them each took a 7.62-caliber AK-74 recoilless assault rifle and slung it over their shoulders. They didn't bother putting on latex gloves or anything else that would keep them from being identified. The FBI and everyone back at Langley would know who had scored the bank.

When they were all loaded up, they did another quick comm check. Satisfied, they quietly shut the car trunk, then went around to the driver's side window and gave a thumbs-up sign to Yuvi. She nodded, then watched them as they casually walked toward the rear of the bank, Duncan lugging a huge lock breaker, which was essentially a gigantic pair of pliers that could cut inch-thick pieces of metal, the only item aside from their assault rifles that they carried in hand. From afar, watching them cross the street in their street clothes and assault rifles, to Ljubica they looked like a bunch of campers reconnoitering the wilderness of the city.

There was an eight-foot-high, chain-link fence surrounding the rear parking lot of the bank, which they easily negotiated. Once in the parking lot proper, they unslung their assault rifles and covered each other as they walked over to the small, stout rear door, beside which were what looked to be three electrical relay boxes affixed to the side of the building, each with heavy but discrete locks, each looking to be innocuous and unimportant.

Acrobat knew better. From the electrical schematics, they knew that one of the relay boxes was actually the first hurtle of the bank's security—they would have to trick it out in order to get into the bank.

But before they even did that, they would have to open the relay box without setting off the first line of defense of the bank.

Monika took a small penlight and turned it on, looking at

the edges of the security's electrical box as she ran her fingers along it.

"Right here, this is the one," she whispered, tapping with her fingers a spot on the right edge of the box farthest away from the small, stout door.

Duncan nodded as he took the lock-breaker, Tobey positioning the heavy lock in the jaws of the pliers. Monika held the relay box's door shut, in case it popped open. They held the pose for a second, each of them making sure everything was on track.

Then Duncan squeezed as hard as he could, the lock bending and finally breaking under the pressure of the lock-breaker's jaws.

"We're committed," Monika whispered over the comm link.

She held the relay box's door shut as she removed the ruined lock. Then, she looked at the others to see if they were ready.

Duncan set the lock-breaker on the ground while Tobey pulled out from his vest what looked to be a rather bulky personal data organizer that had thin cables running out of it. The cables, rather than ending in male or female plugs, ended in six electrical pincers, arranged in pairs. This device was an electronic combination-breaker, a dedicated computer that could inductively arrive at the security code used by a security system. Tobey turned on the combination-breaker, put it on top of one of the other relay boxes. From his vest, he took out a pair of wire cutters and put them in his mouth. Then with his now-free hands, he took hold of the three pairs of electrical pincers, ready to go.

Duncan, meanwhile, had a high-speed electric screwdriver in hand, which he triggered a couple of times to make sure it was working fine.

When they were both good to go, Tobey nodded.

Ljubica, who would be keeping time for them, whispered over their radios, *"Five seconds from my mark. . . . Mark."*

Monika opened the electrical relay's cover and shined her penlight on whatever might be inside. At the same time, Ljubica over the radio counted off the seconds they had: *"Five. Four. Three . . ."*

They discovered a simple alphabetic pad no larger than six inches across, with a liquid crystal display that was hard to read by the light of the penlight. They also heard a distinct pinging noise that went off exactly once every half second.

Before Ljubica'd counted to two, Monika began punching in a random series of letters into the keypad, allowing just shy of one second per letter, while Duncan took the electric screwdriver and unscrewed the six small screws that held the front panel in place.

After Monika had punched in seven random digits, the numeric pad let out a single, long electronic bleat—the error signal.

"Seven digits, fifteen seconds, mark," whispered Monika.

Over the radio, Ljubica, running the clock, whispered, *"Fifteen. Fourteen. Thirteen . . ."*

Duncan continued working the screws. Within four more seconds, he had all six of the screws undone, Duncan popping the front face of the security code panel.

Then Tobey went in.

Ljubica implacably kept time: *"Nine. Eight. Seven. Six . . ."*

As quickly as he could, Tobey found the terminals that led out of the numeric keypad and attached the six pincers to three of the wires leading out, leaving an inch-long space between each of the pincers.

"Three. Two. O——"

"Punch it," said Tobey.

While Duncan held the panel in midair, Monika punched another seven random letters into the keypad. Again, there was a lone electronic bleat.

"Ten seconds, mark," whispered Monika into her radio.

"Ten," whispered Ljubica. *"Nine. Eight . . ."*

No one said a thing as Tobey took the wire cutters from his mouth and cut each of the three wires between each pair of pincers. Then he turned to the electronic combination-breaker and cycled it through its first pattern.

"Seven. Six . . ."

"Shine a light on me," he whispered to Monika, the combination-breaker's monitor also being a liquid crystal display, impossible to see in the dark.

"Five. Four—"

"C'mon c'mon c'mon," whispered Tobey, staring at the combination-breaker's monitor, the LCD rippling through digits as if it were trying to find the right code to keep the alarm from tripping.

"Four. Three. Tw——"

The combination-breaker's screen flashed SUCCESSFUL INTERDICTION. *"Got it,"* whispered Tobey, interrupting Ljubica's countdown.

The combination-breaker had tripped up the keypad's alarm, making it think that this was the first time anyone had touched it. Now, every time the combination-breaker tried to electronically enter a new possible security code, the bank's security keypad would assume that this was the first try, and therefore grant a fifteen-second stay of execution before setting off the alarm. Since the combination-breaker would make the keypad recycle every time it tried to find the correct code, effectively the keypad alarm was disarmed. Now, it was only a question of time as the combination-breaker began zipping through every possible seven-digit combination.

"Now's the wait," said Tobey as he dabbed sweat off his forehead and smiled at Monika and Duncan.

Duncan smiled back, Monika only nodding as she kept an eye on the combination-breaker's monitor.

"Seven digits?" Tobey asked in a whisper.

"Uh-huh," said Monika.

"Twenty-six to the power of seven? It'll take us two hours and fifteen minutes to go through all the possible combinations," he whispered in the dark.

Duncan scoffed, *"Two hours?"*

"It's running through one million combinations per second?" said Tobey. *"It can't run any faster."*

"I can't wait two hours," said Duncan.

Monika turned to him. *"What do you mean you can't wait?"* she asked in the dark.

Duncan didn't say anything, shuffling the dust on the ground with his boot.

Monika went ballistic. *"No, we agreed!"* she whispered furiously. *"You said you'd help us."*

Duncan looked around. *"This was the hard part, now it's just mechanical. Once you guys are inside, all you have to do is trick out the numeric pad on the inside. How long will that take?"* he asked Tobey.

"If it's a standard four-digit code? Maybe half a minute, probably less," Tobey said in the dark.

"So you guys don't need me," Duncan insisted. *"You can handle anything else by yourselves."*

"Goddamn you!" Monika whispered furiously.

"Mon—"

"No, goddamn you," Monika hissed again.

Duncan just stood there, unsure of what to do. *"Monika, there's nobody around, not even regular security. You don't need any muscle; you guys got it covered."*

Monika scoffed. *"Go, go—what do I care—go do whatever you want,"* she whispered in the dark. *"You always do anyway."*

"Monika—"

"Guys?" said Tobey. *"I hate to say this, but this isn't like the time or place?"*

Monika and Duncan relented.

Tobey whispered, *"Duncan, you agreed—you'd help out from start to finish. Tagging Denton isn't a priority."*

"Yeah, I know that, but you guys don't need me anymore; you guys can handle this," said Duncan with careful, solicitous logic. *"If it takes two hours, hell, I can do my thing and be back here before you're even inside."*

Tobey was about to say more, *"But Duncan—,"* but then Monika cut him off with a scoff.

"Let him go," she whispered. *"Go, Duncan. Go, what do I care—go play your stupid little games. Go flake out on us when we need you the most."*

Duncan shrugged guiltily, even as he found it all but irresistible—he just had to go. He *had* to, no matter what.

"*I'll be back in ninety minutes,*" he said. "*I'll check up back here, and if you're gone, I'll meet you back at the warehouse.*"

"*Maybe we won't be waiting for you, Duncan,*" whispered Monika. "*Maybe we'll decide to flake out on* YOU." Duncan looked at Monika, trying to catch her eyes in the dark—maybe to see if she was serious or not. But Duncan knew she'd be there for him.

So he clapped Tobey on the shoulder and leaned forward to give Monika a kiss. She dodged him.

"*Ninety minutes,*" Duncan whispered to Tobey. "*But no matter when you're done, if you're done, don't wait for me.*"

Monika whispered, "*We won't,*" just as Duncan turned away and went back to his double-parked car.

"*God*DAMN *him,*" Monika whispered, Tobey watching as her chin shook in the darkness, something liquid about her whispering voice making him sure that she was crying just a little bit.

Ljubica, who'd heard the entire conversation, wasn't a bit surprised. She watched as Duncan clambered over the chain-link fence and came back to where the cars were parked. She rolled down her window as he came up to her.

"*They've got it all pretty tight,*" said Duncan easily. "*So I'm gonna be going.*"

"*I think that might be a mistake,*" was all Ljubica allowed herself to say.

"*Fuckin'-A,*" Monika whispered over the comm line.

"*It's not a mistake,*" said Duncan easily. "*It's something that's gotta get done. Mind if you pop the trunk?*"

Duncan casually walked to the back of the Taurus, Yuvi watching in the rearview mirror as he opened the trunk and took out the night-vision goggles they'd gotten this afternoon from one of her dealers up in Silver Springs. He tossed his fisherman's vest into the trunk but held on to his AK-74. From the trunk, he took out a gun they'd bought that afternoon, attaching a silencer to it and shoving it in the small of his back. Then Duncan quietly latched the trunk door shut and gave Ljubica a little wave which she returned. She watched as he then turned and got behind the wheel of his double-parked Audi, setting his assault rifle in the passenger seat.

Duncan turned on the engine, put the car in gear, and slowly pulled out, the car's engine naturally making only a minimal noise.

At the rear of the bank, waiting for the combination-breaker to match the correct code for the small, stout door, Monika and Tobey watched as the Audi drove a bit down Q Street and got to Connecticut Avenue. Then it turned right and disappeared from view, taking the Circle and going a quarter way around it, taking New Hampshire Avenue south, the sound of its engine fading away faster than either of them would've thought.

"Goddamn him," Monika whispered.

Even as he got into the Audi and drove off, Duncan Idaho really wasn't sure if he was doing right. Truth to tell, Duncan Idaho had never killed anybody before, not even in the heat of the moment, much less in the evening of the mind. And what was coming up would be as dark as any of those evenings ever get.

Fuck that, Duncan thought as he drove to McLean.

A collection of pictures unfurled in Duncan's mind, blossoming like some black and gaudily elegant flower. The center petal was an image of Tom Carr, lying there in the subway station in New York City, his body ground down between the subway train and the subway platform in a cartoonishly awful way. Then next to this petal, another picture appeared: Tobey, squatting next to Tom, trying to get him out of there. Tobey looking so terrified as he tugged on Tom's broken body that it was almost funny, funny in a sickening, horrible sort of way.

There were other picture-petals too: Of Ljubica screaming and passing out as Duncan had bathed her wound in peroxide; of Monika, running down the enormous hallway at Pentagon City, looking so scared it made him want to tear his eyes out; of Tobey, crying over the body of the little woman, Tobey never having shot at anyone before in his life, killing another

human being for the sake of them: For Duncan, Monika, Ljubica, and even Russell.

This flower of pictures and mental snapshots formed a gift
that Nicholas Denton had given Duncan Idaho, a present Duncan fully intended to repay.

He's got it coming, Duncan thought to himself, though
there was no determination behind the thought. All he could
see in his mind's eye was Tommy, dying. Duncan had been
trying to shoot that murderous little woman when some civilian—a construction worker—had tackled her from behind,
sending her down.

In that moment, Duncan had turned to go—and seen Tom
Carr lying there between the station platform and the subway
car. Tommy had been looking right at him, his thin hair all
mussed up; for the first time, Duncan had realized that Tommy
really had no hair on the top of his head, the hair on his sides
combed over so cunningly and seeming-casual that he'd never
noticed before.

The gap between the subway car and the subway platform
couldn't have been more than six inches wide.

Duncan had stared right at Tommy as Tommy shouted,
"Go! Go! Go!" to him. So Duncan had gone, running after the
others through the subway station.

He should've stayed. He should've stayed to talk to his
friend, and comfort him before he died.

Duncan shook his head, trying to rattle that memory out of
his mind. Instead, he picked a different one. He picked the
time when he and Tom Carr had been getting ready to score
Skunk Works.

They'd been in his office, going over the last-minute details
that inevitably pile up, when Tommy had suddenly said,
"Enough."

"What," Duncan had said, but Tommy ignored him, turning
his back to him as he stood up and went to the mini-fridge
built into the cabinetry of his office. Out of the freezer section,
Tommy'd pulled out a bottle of Belvedere vodka, along with
a couple of frosted shot glasses, the moment unexpectedly
turning solemn and serious between them.

Tommy poured the two shot glasses to the brim, and then replaced the bottle in the freezer. He'd picked up his glass and held it aloft.

"To Skunk Works," he said, looking Duncan in the eye.

Duncan picked up his own shot glass and nodded at his boss and friend, gently chiding him, "To *scoring* Skunk Works."

Tommy smiled. "To scoring Skunk Works then."

They'd downed their glasses, and in that moment, when the alcohol hits your belly and your brain anticipates the surge it's going to feel, Duncan closed his eyes and felt as excited as when he'd been a nineteen-year-old kid doing crazy stuff in the Army.

"You'll do fine," Tom Carr said.

"I know," said Duncan. Then for no reason, he said, "My mom was a drunken teenager. She died when she was thirty-five."

Tom Carr knew that already.

Duncan refilled the two shot glasses. "My dad was a petty thief with a big mouth. He got shanked in prison before I was born," he said as he picked up his shot glass. "I kept their certificates, the birth and death ones both. That's all they left on this earth."

Tom Carr knew that, too. He picked up his shot glass and tossed it back.

The next day, Acrobat took off for Skunk Works, scoring the installation as easy as scoring a sandbox. When they'd returned, Duncan and Monika had gone straight back to his house, spending the weekend together and looking forward to Monday, and all that they would be doing—

But then Tobey had came for them, and then they'd been on the run. Duncan had seen Tommy at the Times Square subway station, but now as he drove to Nicholas Denton's house, he realized that he hadn't had a chance to talk to him. He realized all of a sudden that the last time he'd spoken with his friend had been on that last day, when they'd toasted the scoring run and drunk their vodka alone in his office.

As he drove through the dark streets of Washington and on to Nicholas Denton's house, Duncan Idaho didn't feel nervous anymore, or indecisive. He felt, if anything, restful, and at peace.

Over the next half hour, Tobey settled into an oddly boring, horrifically tense and monotonous agony.

The combination-breaker was doing it's job like it was supposed to, going through a million seven-letter permutations per second, tricking out the security system into thinking it was a fresh input each and every time. Only problem was, Tobey couldn't set the combination-breaker on the ground or on top of one of the other relay boxes because the leads going to the security panel weren't long enough, the combination-breaker itself too heavy to leave dangling—it might rip the leads off the cut wires, instantly setting off the alarm. So Tobey had to stand there, next to the small, stout rear door of the bank, holding the combination-breaker in his arms.

If he'd had to guess beforehand, he would have said that he could easily hold the combination-breaker aloft all night. It only weighed four pounds. But after a couple of minutes, his arms started to cramp. After fifteen minutes, he was in agony, his biceps screaming for a rest so the muscles could oxygenate. After half an hour, he would have begged to have an ax murderer chop his arms clean off.

He was too proud to admit this to Yuvi or Monika, though.

For her part, Monika was patroling the area around the bank, especially Connecticut Avenue. Stealthily walking up and down the street, checking every shadow, Monika made sure no one had prepared any kind of ambush. She was carrying her AK-74 on her, but she held it close to her body, the barrel pointed to the ground, making it hard to spot by anyone who might've driven by. Monika was just at the wedge next to the bank's, the wedge formed by Connecticut and Nineteenth Street, where there was a Starbucks. In fact it was the same Starbucks Duncan and Tobey had bought a coffee at as they'd spotted the FBI parked in front of the bank yesterday afternoon, just before they'd expelled Russell from the group—

A lone man was crossing DuPont Circle, walking straight toward the bank.

"Target approaching," Monika suddenly whispered. *"Crossing DuPont Circle, heading for the front of the bank on Connecticut Avenue."*

Oh fuck, thought Tobey on the other side of the bank, unable to see any of what might or might not happen next.

Monika was in the shadow cast by the awning of the Starbucks coffee shop. By chance, a streetlamp was right at that corner, casting such a hard light atop the awning that Monika realized she wouldn't be spotted except for her feet, and then only if she happened to move.

So keeping stock-still, Monika waited for this lone man to approach as she raised her AK-74 under cover of the awning's shadow and flicked the selector switch from "safety" to "single shot." She aimed carefully and deliberately at the approaching man, who sauntered across the Circle without a care in the world.

"Target in sight," she whispered so low Ljubica and Tobey deduced rather than heard what she said.

The man got to the edge of the Circle and crossed the street, not a single car in sight. He was a big and tall man with no neck and thin hair. He had on a long overcoat, which was odd since it hadn't rained recently, nor was it supposed to anytime soon. *Maybe he's got a weapon underneath,* Monika thought to herself as she kept her AK-74 trained on the man.

He got to the sidewalk in front of the entrance to the bank and kept on walking along perpendicular to Monika, not seventy feet away.

"Is he gone?" Tobey asked, the agony of his cramping arms adding to his fear.

Monika ignored him, careful to not so much as blink as she kept her AK-74 trained on the man. She made up her mind that one hesitation and she would put him down.

The man abruptly stopped in the middle of the sidewalk, at Monika's two o'clock position, Monika already squeezing the trigg——

He took out a pack of smokes and fumbled to get one out. He dropped two onto the sidewalk right by the front entrance of the bank on Connecticut Avenue, saying, "Shit," out loud as he did.

Tobey—on the other side of the bank but a mere thirty feet away in a straight line—heard him and froze, the combination-breaker still in his arms but all but forgotten.

Monika watched as the man carefully—overly carefully—bent down to pick up his fallen cigarettes. He stuffed them back into his pack, then carefully lit one, and then he began to—

—suddenly the man vomited on the sidewalk.

Monika winced, thinking, *Grim.*

"What was that?" Tobey squeaked.

The man heaved twice more, the last a dry heave, then spit for a while, spitting the taste out of his mouth. "Fuck," he said to himself, oblivious of anything or anyone around.

He still had the lit cigarette in hand, though, which he suddenly realized with that odd, genuine surprise of the amazingly drunk. He took a couple of puffs, they tasted good, so he continued walking along as before, walking with surprising confidence for someone that hammered.

Monika, though, followed him with her eyes and her assault rifle for two more blocks as he continued down Connecticut Avenue and eventually disappeared from sight.

"Just a drunk," she said into her transmitter when the man was finally gone.

Tobey nearly cried in relief, standing there in the back with the combination-breaker in his arms. He was so relieved that he didn't realize that the combination-breaker had finally defeated the security panel. The monitor was blinking

PASSWORD SECURED:
B-L-U-E-D-O-G

Tobey frowned, wondering if the combination-breaker had developed a mind of its own—then realizing it was the password.

"Hey, guys," said Tobey when he saw the monitor. *"We're in!"*

It took him awhile, what with the darkness and the lack of a moon, but Duncan Idaho finally arrived at Nicholas Denton's house in McLean, Virginia.

The address was on a lonesome road about three miles from the town proper. The houses of the neighborhood, few and far between, were all enormous and tasteful too, each house isolated from every other house by thick brush and tall trees, as if their owners liked their neighbors well enough but not so well that they actually wanted to see any of them. Between the dark and the trees and the distance between each, all the houses were as private as islands, which suited Duncan Idaho just fine.

As he let the Audi crawl down the road, he saw no streetlamps. On any given night, the light cast would have been from the moon and the porch lights of each of the houses. But at almost four o'clock in the morning on a night of a new moon, the houses all looked ghostly as he passed them by, light gray apparitions floating above a darker gray sea of grass.

Just before he turned onto Denton's street, Duncan stopped the Audi and snapped off its headlights. Then he strapped on the night-vision goggles and turned them on, the neighborhood snapping awake with an emerald green glow, as if the whole area had been sunk into some algae-drenched pond. He took a breath, then turned onto Denton's street, letting his Audi drift by the house as he got a good look at it.

Denton's house fit right in with the rest of the neighborhood. The house looked like a colonial barn, with a massive curving driveway leading up to a four-car garage. Two windows above the garage gave the impression of a happy house, the windows like smiling eyes, the garage like a sloppy grin. But at night, now, with the hellishly green tinge of the night-vision goggles, that happy house-face looked surreal to Duncan, insane somehow. As if the house knew what terrible business was about to take place yet remained serenely happy as ever.

Duncan drove on, passing the house by about thirty feet, then carefully parking the car between a couple of trees that separated Denton's house from the next property over.

Duncan Idaho got out of the car.

He was calm now. He was calm, which made him feel all the more uneasy as he quietly opened the trunk of the car. Without bothering to take off the night-vision goggles, Duncan took off his leather jacket and tossed it into the trunk, then stuffed the hem of his T-shirt into his jeans. He checked his boots, making sure there were no trinkets that might make any noise. He emptied the change from his pockets, tossing it all into the trunk haphazardly.

He took out his firearm and checked the action. It was a GLOCK 9-mm that he had gotten with Ljubica this afternoon, the end of the barrel cleanly threaded. He loaded a clip, then attached a silencer. When it was firmly screwed on, Duncan loaded a round into the chamber, then checked the safety. He checked to make sure his little pocket key-pick set was on him, then quietly closed the trunk of the Audi.

Duncan took a breath.

Okay, he thought as he began to walk toward Nicholas Denton's house.

It was clearly a family home, and that thought made Duncan suddenly realize that he had no idea what Denton's family was like, much less how many there'd be inside. He tried not to think of that, but he couldn't help himself, the very family-lyness of the big house driving the point home: Not just one man but a *family* lives here.

Fuckit, thought Duncan Idaho. *Tommy was family, too,* he thought, steeling himself as he walked toward the house.

Walking around the front yard and checking the rims of the windows, Duncan saw that the Dentons had a very simple alarm system, easily defeated. But as he looked the house over, he saw a few things that made him feel a little ill.

Next to the house, on the left side of the property, there

was a large and expensive-looking swing-and-slide set, built out of thick logs, the set obviously custom-made. Boys' toys, and from the look of it, well used. Through one of the windows, Duncan saw a Winnie-the-Pooh night-light; the little orange-colored bear with the bright red T-shirt that could not quite cover his tummy sat there smiling, with a pot of honey on his lap, one of his paws digging in. Something about the night-light made Duncan think Denton probably had a small daughter, no older than six. The thought made Duncan nauseous, as if he had unclean designs on that six year old.

In a way, I guess I do, he thought. Then he continued.

As he walked around the house to the backyard, Duncan happened to look up and notice something—a smallish window that was open on the second floor.

It looked meaningless, but Duncan all of a sudden realized that the alarm system of this house was either not on or not working. If it had been working, it wouldn't have armed with a window left open like that.

Duncan nodded to himself, walking around to the backyard.

When he got there, he came to a pair of sliding glass doors, and an adjacent deck. It was so dark, Duncan would have tripped over the edge of the deck if it hadn't been for his night-vision goggles, goggles that made him look vaguely insect-like, like an alien being walking through the green and ghostly contours of his alien home planet.

With his pocket lock-pick, in no time Duncan was opening the sliding glass doors of Nicholas Denton's house. Stepping inside, Duncan aimed his gun, sweeping what looked to be the family den with his silenced automatic.

There was of course no one in the den, but that didn't mean there was no presence there. Living molecules seemed to fill up the whole space, each and every one of the molecules wondering what Duncan was doing here. On a large, low square coffee-table, there was a stack of coloring books and, neatly stowed underneath the table, even more coloring books, as well as a box of crayons. It took Duncan a second to realize something rather surprising: The Dentons didn't have a television set. *Maybe it's in the bedroom,* he thought absently, but he suspected not. No TV for the Denton kids, though there were plenty of books—books stacked to high heaven. On the floor-to-ceiling shelves that lined all four walls, there were slim children's books, apparently arranged by age; Duncan recognized the gold-bound books of preschoolers, then the slim paperbacks of young adolescents, as well as complete sets of mystery books, all carefully arranged by the numbers tattooed to the spine, all the spines clearly broken by careful reading. There were easily two or three hundred children's books, which surprised Duncan. Growing up, he hadn't known any parents who had read that much to their children.

The den would have made him run. The hominess of it, the sheer gentle kindness of the room. Clearly several children spent a lot of time here, what with the shelves stuffed with cardboard and ice-cream sticks and clear white glue, the upright piano set up against the wall, a very good-looking Ibanez acoustic guitar propped up on an A-stand beside it, and a music stand crammed with sheet music and folders. The furniture was comfortable and sturdy: Two thick couches, a thick and comfortable leather armchair, as well as several collapsible tables, which were open and scattered about. One of the collapsible tables was covered with a plastic model, halfway complete. The model was of a Formula One race car, the chassis all but finished, the engine in pieces beside it. On one of the couches there was a section devoted to dolls, maybe two dozen dolls in all, sitting three or four deep, all carefully waiting there, like an audience at a movie house.

Three boys and a girl, Duncan guessed, sweeping his firearm over everything, feeling ill at the thought of how conscientious the Denton parents were about their parenting duties. *I shouldn't be here,* he thought.

He would have turned back then and there, if it hadn't been for the Le Corbousier chaise.

The Le Corbousier chaise was a shockingly modern piece of furniture to have in this room. With a sleek chrome frame that curved in an arc, it had a long flat cushion made of black leather, and a solid tube of leather that was its headrest. It looked worn, as if whoever used it used it often. Beside it was a small round table, the frame also of chrome, the top of glass, bearing several books that Duncan noticed: *Mao II, Incline Our Hearts, Interpreter of Maladies, Mason and Dixon, For Common Things*. Sophisticated-sounding books Duncan Idaho had never heard of, books he assumed Denton must be reading, which intimidated him more than he would've expected. Duncan wasn't much of a reader.

But it was good too. Feeling intimidated pissed Duncan off, and the Le Corbousier chaise turned Denton into an alien member of his own family, a separate entity. Not so interconnected to people who were innocent.

Just go up there and shoot the son-of-a-bitch, Duncan thought. But still he wouldn't go, dithering in the den.

Imagining it, Duncan Idaho could see how it might go horribly wrong—how Denton's wife might wake up, how she might scream, children rushing in, a whole chaotic mess. He kept on imagining this scene as he struggled to get out of this den.

Then he thought about the black flower in his mind: Tommy, Tommy lying there between the subway train and the subway platform, his body crushed and ruined, using that image as a weapon against this den.

But still the den kept him from doing what he had come here to do. This cozy den, so powerful, kept him pinned down as surely as a machine-gun emplacement.

I won't shoot him in front of his family, Duncan abruptly promised himself. *I won't shoot him in front of any of his family, not even his wife. And no matter what happens, I won't let anything happen to his wife and kids. So can we go now?*

With that promise, Duncan got going, walking around the ground floor of the house, making sure no one was around before he went upstairs.

Tobey was babbling nervously, *"I hate those blue dog paintings? Who painted those awful things anyway, they look ugly as sin."*

"Tell that to Duncan, I'm sure he'd love to go off and kill

him," Monika whispered, as they got ready to break into the bank.

Ljubica tsked over the comm line. *"Monika,"* she whispered.

Monika flushed. *"Shut up and get ready,"* she said.

"Okay," Tobey whispered, abashed.

"We're going in on my mark," Monika whispered to Ljubica.

"Copy," said Yuvi.

Monika turned to Tobey. *"Ready? Mark."*

Tobey input the password. The small, stout door made a sound as if its gears were spinning, then it was silent, Tobey pushing at it. He walked in and found himself in a small antechamber.

The room was about six feet wide and eight feet long, with another security door on the far side, clearly fireproof though nowhere near as secure as the outer door. Besides this second door, there was a numeric keypad with a magnetic card-strip groove beside it and a small LCD display.

Tobey was ready for it. He'd attached a magnetic card to the lead wires coming out of the combination-breaker, a card he slipped halfway into the slot in the wall and held steady.

"Hold it there," he told Monika, who kept the card in position while Tobey turned to the combination-breaker's monitor.

The monitor was saying SEARCHING, while the LCD display on the numeric keypad on the wall was blinking ominously.

Tobey frowned. *"It should have the number already."*

"You don't have to whisper anymore, we're inside," said Monika.

Tobey didn't respond as he stared at the combination-breaker, which was once again going through combinations, only this time of numbers—and disturbingly, the star and pound signs as well. "Twelve characters, what's this?"

"What?" said Monika.

"Ten seconds—What's going on?" Ljubica whispered through their comm link.

Tobey said, "The combination-breaker's using all ten digits

plus the star and pound signs and it's looking for a seven-digit number, not four. What's twelve to the . . . ," he said, trailing off as he blankly looked off into space. "Twelve to the seventh is something like thirty, forty million—*fuckit* we're not gonna make it, let's go—"

"What?" said Monika.

"Fifteen seconds," Ljubica said relentlessly, then began counting away the individual seconds: *"Sixteen. Seventeen. Eighteen . . . "*

Tobey said quickly, "Twelve to the seventh makes more than thirty million combinations, that means we're not gonna make it in less than thirty seconds, we gotta go the alarm is gonna trip we gotta go *now*—"

Monika scoffed. "We're not leaving—oh come on, this is supposed to be the easy part!"

"We're not gonna make it—"

"Twenty seconds—You can make it," Yuvi whispered, *"there are only twenty-two-million combinations—twenty-three. Twenty-four. . . ."*

"Tobey chill out."

"C'mon c'mon oh fuck *oh fuck we gotta go we gotta go*—"

"We are not going anywhere, Tobey," said Monika. "Chill out and stay put, even if the alarm goes off we've got three minutes' response time.

"Twenty-six."

"We're not going to make it—"

"Twenty-seven."

"Tobey, we're not leaving."

"Twen——"

The combination-breaker said, "BEEP!" flashing a code on its screen: 789#987, a mnemonic number.

"Shit!" squeaked Tobey, plugging in the number just as—
"Thirty."

The door in the antechamber clicked, with a fraction of a second to spare.

Tobey just stood there, staring at the numeric keypad and its LCD display, waiting for the wailing sirens to go off and give him a massive coronary. But of course nothing like that happened (or would have happened for that matter—the bank's security had a silent alarm system, which wouldn't have accepted the entry code if it had been input after the alarm had been activated).

"Boy," said Tobey, wrapping his fingers around his goatee spike and twirling it straight.

"What did I tell you," said Ljubica.

Monika rubbed Tobey's shoulders as he sighed, his breath shaking.

"There are almost thirty-six-million combinations of twelve to the seventh power," said Tobey absently, working the math in his head to distract himself from wigging out. "Not twenty-two million like you said."

Yuvi smiled. *"Sue me,"* she whispered, her voice a hazy, sexy thrill. Tobey laughed.

"You did great," said Monika, giving him a peck on the cheek.

Tobey again sighed, his breath still shaky. "If they'd picked eight instead of seven as their first digit, we would've been toast."

"Well we're not," said Monika.

"Get going," said Ljubica over the comm link.

On hearing how impatient and tired Yuvi sounded, Monika and Tobey glanced at each other.

"You okay Yuvi?" Monika asked as she and Tobey opened the antechamber's door.

"Yeah, I'm fine," she whispered morosely. *"Just no more chit-chat."*

"Okay," said Monika just as she stepped into the bank itself.

The keypad outside the door had killed the motion detectors inside the bank—that was the whole point of that line of defense, because although the antechamber's door was thick and strong, it wasn't *that* strong—anyone with a battering ram could've knocked it in. If someone had busted in, the motion detectors would have tripped the alarm. But if someone gave the correct seven-digit password, well, clearly they belonged.

"Now to the vault," said Tobey as he and Monika stepped into the first floor.

Like all banks, the lights were all on, of course: Anyone outside could spot anyone inside the bank—that's why all banks have glass walls: By day, the glare keeps you from seeing in, and by night you can see anyone inside. But to get from the rear entrance to the staircase leading to the basement vault, you had to go through the rear offices, which didn't have windows. Monika and Tobey were safe that way.

The problem was the cameras. Perched on various corners throughout the bank were closed-circuit cameras, all of them on, all of them plainly recording the break-in at a rate of one frame per second. Tobey and Monika paid them no mind, for the same reason they weren't wearing latex gloves.

They made their way through the back office of the first floor to the staircase leading to the vault.

The staircase was curved and completely dark, the first-floor lights illuminating only halfway down the staircase. So first Monika and then Tobey made their careful way down, Monika paranoically holding her AK-74 ready for anything.

When they neared the bottom of the curving staircase, Monika took her penlight and, holding it far from her body, turned it on.

There was nobody down here in the basement. There was just a medium-sized receptionist's table directly in front of the staircase landing. To the right there were two office desks with chairs, everything cream-colored and tasteful, with a wall of camouflaged file drawers, looking like they were part of the wall, with moldings on them and everything. To the other side there were some comfortable couches, clearly waiting-area couches. The entire room was expensively carpeted, a hint of potpourri in the air.

"Wait," said Monika, standing on the last step of the staircase. She looked around the room, then stepped into it, walking around to a hallway behind the staircase, a hallway that led away. Just to the left of this hallway but still in the carpeted area, as if guarding the entrance to the hallway, was a small, high table with a small, high chair, like a one-man bar, clearly the security guard's perch.

Beyond this perch was the dark, uncarpeted hallway, a bank of light switches just inside of it, on the right-hand side. Monika turned the first of the light switches on, hidden fluorescent lights blinking and illuminating the hallway.

It was a white hall, with pure white formica flooring, and it was all spotless. At the end and to the left was the huge door of the vault. To the right were various doors, about a half dozen of them, all of which were closed. The end of the hallway was a dead end, Monika confirming *in situ* what the blueprints Tobey had downloaded had shown—the entire basement of the bank was barely a quarter of the area of the bank above, six inches of poured concrete surrounding the vault itself.

"Skunk Works was tougher than this," said Tobey as he came up behind Monika, scaring the hell out of her.

"Shit Tobey," she said, frowning at him.

Tobey turned on the other lights of the hallway, going straight to the vault and looking at the locks.

"Tobey," said Monika.

"What?" he said.

Monika, still holding the AK-74, waved him to come toward her.

Tobey went over to her and then watched as she checked the six doors that faced the vault—the privacy rooms for the clients. Monika checked them one by one, and of course, no one was there.

"Okay," said Monika, breathing in deep. "Do your thing."

Tobey went over to the vault door and started describing what he saw to Ljubica outside.

"Yuvi, you there?"

"Go ahead," she whispered over the comm link.

"Okay," Tobey began. "The vault is all steel, with like a ship's steering wheel in the center."

"Tell me about the locks . . ."

So Tobey told.

The vault door was pretty much like every vault door, big

and massive as an elephant. It used a hybrid system of one combination lock and two key locks, all mechanical and apparently asynchronous.

"They'd better be asynchronous," said Tobey, getting ready to start on the combination lock first.

"On the electricals there was no power supply to the vault itself, so the locks can't be synchronous. Get started, you'll be fine."

Monika removed the portable sonogram machine from her fisherman's vest and handed it over to Tobey.

The portable sonogram was just like the ones used in hospitals to look at unborn babies, only much smaller. Like the full-sized model, it bombarded ultrasound through a surface and then converted the echos into images it projected onto a monitor. The portable model was the size and weight of a cellular phone, only with a monitor that was half the size of its surface. Its detail was nowhere near a hospital's, but then again it wasn't used for babies but for metal surfaces—like locks and combinations.

Tobey used the portable sonogram first on the combination lock of the vault, the easiest of the three locks to defeat. Setting the portable sonogram around the combination spindle, Tobey moved it around until he spotted the tumblers of the lock, outlined in ghostly blue-grays. Then he simply spun the lock spindle until the tumblers lined up.

"One down," he said.

"Mmm," said Monika, looking around and antsy, her nerves turning into fury at Duncan. *Goddamn him*, she thought as she looked around the basement.

Tobey took the lock-breaker and started on the first of the key locks.

"I'm going up top to reconnoiter," she said, unconsciously using Duncan's word.

" 'Kay," said Tobey, busy talking to Ljubica about the lock system of the vault.

Done checking the ground floor of Denton's house, Duncan Idaho was getting ready to go upstairs.

Just go up there, goddammit, he thought to himself, looking at the wide and long staircase leading up from the entrance foyer to the second floor. *Just go up there and shoot the son-of-a-bitch.*

It was proving impossibly hard. The little things scattered throughout the first floor were worse than land mines, chipping at his will every step of the way. And they were so trivial! Little knick-knacks, stupid little fucking things that sapped the will like torture: A ceramic girl in a sun hat and dress kneeling beside a basket that doubled as a pencil holder; dishes left to dry in the dish rack, most of them made of plastic and covered with cartoons—children's plates; a picture in the kitchen of the most horrible-looking dog Duncan Idaho had ever seen, the frame made of wood and painted by an obviously childish and loving hand. All these little stupid fucking things threatened to drive Duncan Idaho crazy with shame.

But for every little thing that screamed of innocence, there were other objects that were somehow complicit in Tommy's death: A large humidor in the living room, complementing a new carton of cigarettes lying on a kitchen counter; an expensive sound system, designed within an inch of its life until it almost looked like a piece of abstract art; sophisticated, adult paintings hanging from the living room walls; change, a leather-strapped watch, and keys lying on a large glass ashtray on the credenza at the entrance foyer. All these other little things—they so clearly belonged to Denton that they acted like negatives for all the bright and innocent little things in the house.

Think of that couch, thought Duncan, picturing the cruel aesthetic of the Le Corbousier chaise.

Standing by the credenza in the entrance foyer, Duncan Idaho looked up the wide staircase leading to the second floor. Slowly, carefully, he took a step forward, and then another, silently taking the first step up the staircase, his gun aimed up, ready to fire or not fire—afraid of one of the Denton children surprising a shot out of him.

He took each step slowly, carefully testing each footfall;

not worried about minor squeaks but worried about a too sharp one. As he went up the staircase, he had no doubt that Denton was up there, no doubt in his bed, sleeping peacefully. It made Duncan wonder what they had done with Tom Carr's body once they'd pulled it out of the subway track.

Everything glowed green through his night-vision goggles. As he reached the top of the staircase, Duncan flicked the safety of his gun off and turned his goggles up to maximum resolution. The walls practically glowed radioactively as he walked down the upstairs hallway, going to the end of the hall, toward a pair of closed double doors: The doors to the master bedroom, where Nicholas Denton was lying asleep.

They were ordinary doors, with two handles, though to the careful eye it was clear that only one of the handles actually worked, the other purely for symmetry. The handles were shiny brass, the double doors fancy and a bit too romantic— a woman had chosen these doors.

Duncan would have just kicked the doors in and fired, but for his earlier promise. So, carefully, he got ready to open the door that actually worked, mentally seeing himself putting his gun to Denton's temple and putting his hand hard over his mouth, waking him up and then taking him quietly outside, putting a bullet in the back of his head—

There was a noise, a sudden and steady drone, like some primitive and not particularly efficient machine that had been abruptly turned on, a drone that made no sense at all, too loud and too weird to be happening at this hour of the morning.

¿?¿?¿? thought Duncan.

In the bank, everything was quiet on the first floor. Still, Monika decided to check it all out, setting her AK-74 on top of one of the desks in the protected rear office of the first floor and removing her fisherman's vest.

Then, looking now very ordinary in her regular street clothes, Monika did a quickie look around the exposed areas of the first floor, checking that nothing looked out of place.

The walls of windows looking out over DuPont Circle were so big that Monika felt positively naked, and she didn't stay around here long, taking a quick look-see to make sure everything was on the up-and-up.

"First lock down . . . ," Tobey was saying over the comm link.

Monika went to the back offices, set her fisherman's vest in a convenient spot on the ground on the way to the rear door of the bank, then walked back to the staircase.

At the top of the staircase, Monika spotted a camera, aimed down the staircase leading to the vault downstairs. She casually turned and noted it, then turned away—then stopped and looked at it.

Unlike the other cameras, the steady red light under the lens that looked so much like a pimple on a chin was not shining steady. Rather, this one was blinking.

Did that thing move? Monika wondered all of a sudden.

Ljubica sat scrunched down in the car, her eyes just barely looking over the rim of the steering wheel, watching both Connecticut Avenue and Twentieth Street, behind the bank. Tobey had pretty much figured out how to defeat the first key lock on his own, so Ljubica was just monitoring him as he went through his paces.

Around the outside of the bank, streetlights gave off yellow light, the natural undulations of the asphalt taking that light and making shadows out of it as the street curved into the gutters on either side. In the distance, telephone poles, electrical lines, and traffic lights cut up the space, like scaffolding around a building under construction; as if the city itself were being built a little at a time. Far away, Ljubica heard traffic sounds—a car, a honk of a horn, an engine accelerating. But those noises were comfortably far off, the closer sounds around her as natural as they were unremarkable.

She wanted a cigarette. She wanted a cigarette so bad. . . . Ljubica had a whole pack right there in the car, but she wasn't

sure if she dared risk it, even though she was scrunched down
in her seat.

As she sat there thinking about whether or not to light up,
she happened to be looking at the intersection of Q and Twentieth, at a manhole covering almost dead center in the intersection, some thirty feet away.

The manhole cover was moving.

Clearly it had been moving for some time now, because it
was halfway across the diameter of its opening, a set of fingers
in black gloves slowly moving it aside. The covering was awful thin, too—instead of a normal four- or five-inch thickness,
the manhole covering that was all of a sudden in motion
looked paper-thin from this distance. Maybe sturdy enough to
handle the weight of a passing car, but only just barely.

Ljubica didn't even breathe, feeling as if her body was
somehow sinking, the muscles of her arms and belly turning
weak.

The manhole cover stopped moving, as if stuck. The ten
fingers couldn't seem to move it aside—so then another set
of fingers appeared, and between all these twenty fingers, the
manhole covering began moving again, the sound of the heavy
iron against the asphalt low and grating, like the maw of a
cave opening wide.

"Really," said Ljubica, unaware that she'd even said a
thing, watching as the first pair of black gloved hands reached
up onto the street.

A man in a black helmet and black suit poked his head out
of the manhole. He was looking toward the bank as he
emerged, quickly scanning around, wearing night-vision goggles identical to the ones Ljubica had gotten Duncan just this
afternoon.

The man looked directly at Ljubica's car but didn't react,
turning around and looking about before crawling out of the
manhole, a submachine gun strapped to his back.

Ljubica turned and quietly, slowly took hold of her AK-74,
checking that a round was in the chamber and that the safety
was off. Then she set it comfortably beside her and looked
back at the man coming out of the ground.

As soon as he had one knee on the pavement, the man in the black outfit unstrapped his submachine gun and loaded a round in the chamber, crouching as he started to slowly move forward toward the bank.

At the manhole opening, a second man, also in a black helmet and night-vision goggles, peeked out and looked around, another ghoul come to spook in the night. He waited there, only his head out of the manhole, watching his partner.

The first man out was slowly sweeping the street, moving his submachine-gun barrel back and forth and around, checking that there were no surprises. Then he looked back at his partner, looking back in Ljubica's direction, and then made a couple of hand gestures.

The second man began to crawl out of the manhole, the hands of a third man appearing on the lip of the opening.

"*Okay,*" whispered Ljubica. "*You're on,*" she said, then clicked on the comm link.

Standing at the top of the staircase leading down, Monika was staring at the corner surveillance camera with the winking red light.

"We're in!" yelled Tobey from the vault downstairs. "I did it, I did it, we're in!"

Monika looked back at the surveillance camera, slinging her AK-74 over her shoulder as she retied her hair in her purple scrunchie, her chin shoving against her chest, her eyes looking up at the camera.

Now, it was almost imperceptibly more tilted down. As if it were looking at her.

Monika stared right at it, wondering if she was imagining things.

Am I? wondered Monika. *Or is it real?*

Her comm link went staticky, then Ljubica said, "*Monika, we got company, get ready to evacuate through the rear door, confirm: Over.*"

Oh no—

"Tobey, it's a trap," she said, raising and firing her weapon

at the surveillance camera before she turned and ran into the
lobby of the bank.

The sound of Monika's gunfire from inside the bank made
Ljubica Greene make up her mind. As the second man began
to climb out of the manhole and follow his partner up ahead,
Monika's gunfire made both men jerk and hurry.

Ljubica gunned the Taurus and hit the high beams, putting
the car in gear and flooring it.

At the sound of her car behind them, the two men with the
submachine guns coming out of the manhole turned on Ljubica—way too late, the car was already screaming right at
them even as its high-beams blinded both men, Ljubica driving
the car directly over the manhole, her front bumper smashing
the face of the man coming out while at the same time breaking his back as he was bent against the lip of the manhole
opening, Ljubica not stopping even as the first man out of the
manhole, standing with his submachine gun at the ready, fired
right at her.

Frr-rr-rr-rr-rr-rr-rr—

Ljubica's sedan smashed him full at the waist, the right
front wheel catching his feet and legs and pulling him under
the car, his submachine gun flying out of his hands and off
into the air as the Taurus lurched and jumped and ran over his
body.

Then Ljubica slammed the brakes and switched gears, putting the Taurus in reverse and going back to the manhole covering, looking over her shoulder as she turned the car this way
and that, until the Taurus was just to the right of the manhole
covering.

Yuvi came to a screeching halt.

She reached over to the passenger-side seat, took the AK-
74, opened her car door, then aimed her assault rifle directly
into the maw of the manhole that was right beside her, firing
indiscriminately on full automatic—*Frr-rr-rr-rr-rr-rr-rr-rr-rr-
rr-rr-rr-rr-rr-rr-rr-rr-rr-rr-rr-rr-rr-rr-rr-rr-rr-rr-rr-rr-rr!*

She must've hit somebody down there, 'cause she heard screaming.

Ljubica put the Taurus in gear and floored it, even with the Valium and the amphetamines her wounded leg feeling glassy and sickeningly painful. She ignored it as she drove down Q Street to Connecticut, then turned right—

The whole avenue was all of a sudden *crawling* with FBI tacticals, all of them in their black uniforms and their black helmets, their black bullet-proof vests and their black M-16s, like the little suckers were a colony of black bugs that had just materialized right out of the ground—which they evidently had.

Ljubica surprised them as much as they surprised her, all of them—a dozen of them—right out there in the middle of the avenue, all of them on foot, Ljubica driving a Taurus—

She didn't hesitate: Ljubica hit the gas and tried to run them all down.

On hearing the strange mechanical drone coming from downstairs, Duncan Idaho kicked open the double doors of the master bedroom of Denton's house and rushed in with his firearm at the ready, only to find the bedroom empty, the bed neatly made up, the mechanical droning still going on, still droning on directly below him, almost masking the sound of a car coming to life.

The garage door is opening—there's a car in the garage, thought Duncan, quickly running out of the room and down the hall, then down the stairs two at a time, running through the foyer and into the kitchen, looking around, his weapon drawn, knowing without a doubt that Denton was in that car.

Foolishly, Duncan had not reconnoitered well enough, because the first door of the kitchen he opened led to the laundry. On the second try, Duncan Idaho opened the door onto a green Subaru station wagon in the garage, a station wagon that suddenly revved up and peeled colossally loud out of the garage and onto the big driveway.

Duncan almost took a shot, but he didn't dare, frightened

that Nicholas Denton might be using his own family for hostages. So instead, Duncan ran out of the kitchen and through the garage, out onto the driveway, aiming his gun at the Subaru, which was driving backward too fast for Duncan to confidently take a shot.

The Subaru hit the street and then turned around, skidding as it changed from reverse to forward, its tires squealing in the empty night.

Fuckit.

Duncan fired three shots—*Pök!-Pök!-Pök!*—puncturing the side of the green Subaru's cab, but still the station wagon peeled away, racing down the suburban street.

You're not going anywhere, he thought as he ran to his own Audi and jumped in, turning the car's engine and ripping the grass to shreds as he drove back onto the street and chased the Subaru down.

You're mine, thought Duncan Idaho, the wind whipping his hair through the open window.

The green Subaru was two hundred feet ahead as it turned left at a corner.

You're all mine, thought Duncan Idaho as he gave chase.

Maybe a dozen FBI tacticals were strewn out across Connecticut Avenue, rushing the front entrance of the bank just as Ljubica surprised them.

Before they had a chance to react, Yuvi hit the gas on her gold-colored Taurus and went screaming down the avenue in the direction of the Circle, swerving from side to side as she tried to hit as many of the tacticals as she could in this first pass, knowing that she'd never surprise them as good as she had just now.

She struck five of the tacticals—the first one she struck smashing the windshield as he went flying head over feet in the air above her car, Ljubica already turning to hit the next one even before the first one had hit the ground, Yuvi clipping two more at the knees, crippling them, the ones she missed running toward the bank's front door, trying to get out of her way by getting into the bank.

When she got to the end of the avenue, just at the Circle, Yuvi slammed the brakes and switched gears, going backward again at full throttle, this time trying to smash up the FBI tacticals who were trying to get inside the bank.

She clipped four more, grinding them between the hard stone outside wall of the bank and the right side of the Taurus much like the New York subway train had ground Tom Carr to death.

Yuvi had been hearing some random babbling on her headset, words that made absolutely no sense to her through the haze of Valium and amphetamines and the adrenaline rush of fighting off the tacticals. But now, she said—with total assurance and calm—"Get to the rear entrance; I'm there in fifteen seconds."

"You're on," said Monika.

"Don't forget the gear," said Ljubica.

Only a few tacticals had escaped Yuvi's second pass, and they were busy trying to shoot at her as Ljubica kept right on driving backward down Connecticut Avenue, away from the bank, in the direction that the drunken man had gone, heading northwest at forty miles an hour. At R Street, Ljubica braked and turned left, driving farther away from the bank, going east as fast as she could, then turning south at Nineteenth Street, a minor lane just as quiet as Q Street that hit DuPont Circle, which she took, turning on the first right, back onto Connecticut Avenue.

The wounded tacticals weren't expecting this, having heard her car screaming away. The wounded and injured were still lying in the street as Ljubica roared down the stretch of Connecticut Avenue directly in front of the bank for the third time, a couple of the injured FBI tacticals shooting at her as they lay on the ground.

Ljubica just ran them down as she looked for more.

Duncan was driving like a maniac, flooring the Audi as he pushed it and himself as far as they both would go.

The green Subaru station wagon up ahead was about two hundred feet away from him as they raced down the roads of the suburban-side around McLean, the two cars clocking close to a hundred miles an hour.

The Subaru kept fooling Duncan. On the straightaways, Duncan's Audi easily closed the distance between the two cars. But the Subaru kept making sharp, abrupt turns at the last second, forcing Duncan to hit the brakes all-out to catch the corner the Subaru had taken.

Mother FUCKER, thought Duncan as the Subaru took another sudden hard right, Duncan having to hit the brakes so hard the Audi went into a four-point drift, Duncan countersteering to keep control of the car. But even so, the Audi came within inches of catching the gravel shoulder of the road, gravel that might as well been marbles for all the traction they'd give him if he slid off the asphalt of the road.

Come on, you piece of shit, COME ON! he screamed at himself, furiously watching as the Subaru gained another hundred feet on his Audi because of the hard turn.

Duncan had no idea where they were, the small road signs zipping by too quick for Duncan to catch sight of them even if he'd wanted to. But he didn't need to, his sense of direction telling him that the Subaru was heading generally west, into northern Virginia cow country.

There were no houses around here, only roads and woods, and suddenly Duncan knew he'd catch the Subaru sooner or later. Because sooner or later the Subaru would take some long straight road with no intersections—and that's when Duncan would pounce.

"Keep your shit together," Duncan said out loud, driving like a maniac through the black Virginia countryside. "All you gotta be is patient."

"The hell with the stash, Tobey, *come on!!*" Monika yelled from the ground floor down into the basement.

"Give me two minutes!"

"We don't have two minutes—holy *shit!*" she shouted as she looked out the windows of the bank and watched as Ljubica's car mowed down tacticals that had suddenly appeared out of nowhere.

Monika watched her run down four or five more tacticals—then suddenly hit reverse and collide with three or four more, the car scraping and smashing against the front side of the bank, tearing up the small flower gardens around the front door as she smashed some more of the FBI tacticals against the side of the building.

"Holy shit, you just mowed down a truckload of those suckers!" said Monika.

Ljubica answered, "Get to the rear entrance, I'm there in fifteen seconds."

"You're on," answered Monika.

"Don't forget the gear," said Ljubica.

"No joy, we need another two to three minutes," she said, but evidently Yuvi hadn't heard her as Monika watched the gold Taurus disappear.

"Tobey!" she called out, even though they were on the comm link. "Up top, now!"

"Two more minutes!" he called back.

—she would've given him those two minutes if it hadn't been for the second wave of tacticals that hit the front windows of the bank, trying to get in and get away from Ljubica, the men in their bulky black uniforms and heavy assault rifles looking like some *Return of the Living Dead* movie, the tacticals smashing the window of the bank as they tried to get in—

Monika flicked the selector switch on her AK-74 to full automatic and began firing, killing three of the men instantly as more seemed to materialize and try to get in.

A gas-spewing canister came sailing in through the window from outside, filling the bank with smoke, smoke that was—
tear gas

—eating away at Monika's eyes—

—Ljubica came 'round again, only this time from the

south, running over more of the tacticals outside.

"Guys: Get to the back door," Ljubica said calmly.

After her third pass in front of the bank, Ljubica kept driving up Connecticut, to the corner of Q Street, the FBI tacticals' automatic fire following her like fireworks follow the New Year's. Ljubica ignored it as she drove as fast as she could to the chain-link fence Tobey, Monika, and Duncan had climbed over just a couple of hours before.

She skidded across the intersection of Q and Twentieth, by a miracle missing the hole that was left from the uncovered manhole, and drove straight into the chain-link fence, trying to rip through it to get closer to her friends, just as Monika and Tobey appeared at the small and stout rear door with their automatic weapons ready.

It was a weird sight, seeing the gold-colored Taurus trying to break through the chain-link fence, its tires squealing as the fence gave but held, the Taurus reminding Tobey of a tough dog trying to rip through its leash and take a bite out of someone.

Before Monika and Tobey could run and climb over the chain-link fence, more FBI tacticals came running around the corners of the bank from either side, converging on Ljubica and Monika and Tobey, laying down cover fire to keep them pinned as they let loose on Ljubica's car with everything they had.

"Shit," was all Yuvi would allow as her car windows were all blown out by indiscriminate shooting, Ljubica putting the car in reverse and backing off the chain-link fence to give her the space and the time, braking to a halt and picking up her rifle and laying down some cover fire of her own as Monika and Tobey fired in both directions, pinning the FBI tacticals even as a couple of them were cut down.

"Go to the front—and get our stash," said Ljubica, dropping the AK-74 across her lap and spinning the steering wheel left, down Q Street once again and turning right at Connecticut.

• • •

Less than ten blocks away, Russell Orr lay sleeping in Lafa-
yette Park, right across the street from the White House. Ever
so vaguely came the noises of speeding cars and gunshots in
the air, but Russell Orr didn't wake to any of it.

Just as he thought—finally, as the road turned long and wind-
ing and unbroken by any intersections it could duck into, Duncan Idaho started catching up to the green Subaru station
wagon.

Both cars had their headlights off, but Duncan could see
through his night-vision goggles how close the Subaru was—
barely thirty feet, if that, both cars going flat out down the
country road.

Duncan shifted up to fifth gear, the Audi humming along
like a basso sewing machine, the RPM needle not even close
to redlining—the Audi had plenty of gumption left to tap.
Duncan felt almost on fire now that he—

The brake lights on the Subaru came on hard, looking brilliant green to Duncan through his night-vision goggles.

"Oh *shit!*"

Slamming the brakes as hard as he could, even pulling on
the hand brake, Duncan nearly lost control of his Audi as the
Subaru up ahead skidded to a perfectly controlled halt.

Duncan saw the distance evaporating between them, the
rear end of the Subaru coming at him so fast it looked almost
as if it had been shot out of a cannon and right at him. Unable
to do anything else, Duncan shoved the steering wheel of the
Audi hard to the right, scooting around the Subaru on the
narrow country road, the Audi forgiving Duncan the terribly
harsh turn even as its tires screamed across the asphalt road,
the Audi overshooting the Subaru by a good sixty feet before
skidding to a stop.

"Fuck you," said Duncan, looking in his rearview mirror
with his night-vision goggles still on, changing into reverse
and flooring the Audi.

The Subaru—hell, say it when you see it: Denton could fucking drive. Even as Duncan Idaho was skidding past him, the green Subaru was already going in reverse, picking up momentum then twisting around across the road in a perfectly controlled 180-degree spin, already peeling rubber even before the spin was complete, the green Subaru lunging forward as fast as it could go, the tires catching traction and pulling away from Duncan Idaho's reversing Audi.

Duncan didn't know how to pull off a controlled 180 spin, so he did a fast three-point turn—backward turning to the left, then turning forward to the right, scooting back some more to the left, turning and following after the Subaru, which by now had gained easily three hundred yards, the car vanishing amid the curves of the road, only to reappear as Duncan Idaho floored the Audi, this time pushing the car until the RPM needle threatened to go red, both cars still with their headlights off, both cars screaming through the countryside, which was blank and empty, gently hilly and clear of people, only ghostly trees scattered like random sentries waiting for their orders.

"Come-on-come-on-come-on," Duncan Idaho quietly insisted, pushing the Audi as hard as he could control it, eating the distance between the two cars through the hilly road, the gentle undulations throwing the Audi up then pushing it back down, Duncan feeling G-force alternately pulling him up into the air then squashing him down into his bucket seat even as he shifted up to fifth gear, trying to eat up the space between him and the green Subaru station wagon.

The terrain changed suddenly, turning much flatter but far more heavily wooded, as if they were cutting through some thick forest. And though the terrain was flatter, the road became even curvier, zig-zagging through the tall trees that looked like pines, the Subaru up ahead disappearing more frequently, even as the distance between them narrowed from two hundred yards to a hundred, then to fifty.

"Clover," said Duncan, unaware, as he suddenly felt sure that he'd manage to pull up to Nicholas Denton's car and shove it clear off the road. Maybe even send it flying into the trees.

"Clover," he repeated, driving through the Virginia forest, watching as the Subaru disappeared around a sharp curve in the road, knowing that he would soon be catching up.

The bank was a fortress Ljubica was trying to breach as she turned the corner at Q Street and Connecticut Avenue, then raced straight down to the circle without stopping or trying to run over any more of the FBI tacticals.

"Get the stash," she said over her comm link as she turned right at the Circle and drove around it, trying to distract the tacticals who were all on foot, a couple of whom were crazy enough to fire across the total darkness of DuPont Circle, imagining that in a dreamland they might actually tag Ljubica, while in reality only letting go stray bullets that very well might kill some innocent civilian sleeping somewhere in these early morning hours.

"Don't shoot don't shoot!" one of the tacticals had the presence of mind to scream over the din of all the shooting, knowing how dangerous it was to shoot into the night. *"Let that one go, turn on the bank, let's go let's go let's go!"* this officer screamed, redirecting all the FBI's concentration back onto the bank, where Monika Summers was holding down the fort.

Inside the bank, Monika shouted to Tobey, "She's right, go to the vault and get our stash! Box 27-13!" just as the FBI men attacked the bank once again, the lobby by now clogged with the stench of tear gas, Monika squinting as she put down covering fire on the encroaching tacticals—*Frr-rr-rr-rr-rr! Frr-rr-rr! Frr-rr-rr-rr-rr-rr-rr-rr-rr-rr!*

Tobey ran to the back of the bank and back down the curving staircase to the vault, the screaming of dying men and women filling the air as heavy as the cordite and the tear gas, the bank now a whole chaotic mess that, somehow, didn't scare Tobey—like as if it was the right thing. Like they could deal.

You'll manage, he thought to himself as he got to the bottom of the stairs and ran to the vault.

Up top, the tacticals who had made it so far were turning
all of their attention to the bank—and Monika was mowing
'em down one by one, getting cover wherever she could as
she and the FBI tacticals played an all-out game of tag in the
lobby of the bank, Monika bursting out from behind office
desks and tellers' windows and firing and scooting before the
tacticals had had a chance to aim at her. As best she could,
she tried to keep a corridor through the middle of the lobby
open, knowing that once they had the stash, they'd have to
make a run for it right through the middle of the bank's lobby
and into Yuvi's car.

"Where are you, Yuvi?" she called on the comm, as she
crouched under a bank officer's desk, the tacticals confused
and firing on a completely different and innocent desk. *"Yuvi
where are you?"* Monika shouted again, trying to make herself
heard over the spectacular racket and the animal grunts and
roars of the FBI tacticals—several of them were screaming
out war cries, like as if they were in the middle of a last stand
against some mighty badass injuns.

She couldn't help it—Monika laughed. "Yuvi, I got war
cries—*war cries,* Yuvi. You gotta help me out of here, girlfriend."

"I'm there in twenty seconds," said Ljubica over the comm
line.

Monika nodded. Like Tobey, she felt no fear.

After the sharp curve, Duncan Idaho's Audi came upon a huge
dust cloud, as if the green Subaru station wagon had lost control and gone off the road.

Duncan held his breath, slowing down as he hit the forward
edge of the dirt cloud, which billowed green as he saw it
through his night-vision goggles.

The dust cloud enveloped the whole width of the narrow
country road, and it was so thick that Duncan slowed even
harder, afraid of any abrupt curve in the road beyond.

As he slowed, he reached over to the passenger-side seat
and picked up his silenced gun, flicking off the safety as he

looked to his right, at the densest concentration of dust, catching sight of the Subaru's outline. As he drew up to the Subaru station wagon, it turned clearer, its front end off the road and on the shoulder, dipping down with the change in slope, its rear end sticking up.

The Subaru station wagon's driver's-side door was flung wide open.

Duncan lurched his Audi to a complete stop beside the Subaru, looking around with his night-vision goggles, looking to see if he could spot Nicholas Denton.

Abruptly opening the door and getting out, Duncan Idaho listened carefully as he scanned the road up and down, his gun at the ready, waiting for Denton to appear.

Turning around and around, almost like a whirling dervish, Duncan waltzed on over to the Subaru and checked to make sure no one was inside it. No one was. So Duncan, with a quick mental debate, decided not to shoot up the car as he looked around.

As he stood there, the dust began to settle, Duncan moving away from the Subaru, looking dubiously at the trees on either side of the road.

Maybe he ran into the woods, Duncan thought

Ljubica drove east down P Street, looking in her rearview mirror but not seeing anyone behind her, not even regular D.C. Metro cops—

(Where the hell are they?)

—just an empty street behind her; clearly none of the tacticals were chasing her—

Ljubica slammed on the brakes and spun around, flooring it and going back to DuPont Circle.

When she got to it, she went against the flow of traffic if there'd been any traffic at this hour of the early morning, driving clockwise around the Circle and looking at the bank—

—she suddenly saw something she'd never noticed before: The bank was in the shape of a pie wedge, it's narrow end facing the Circle—and that narrow end had big picture win-

dows seven feet high and eight feet wide, easily big enough
for a car to slam right through them and into the very middle
of the lobby of the bank.

"I'm coming," Ljubica said suddenly, twisting the Taurus
onto the Circle itself and flooring it in a straight line, crossing
right down the middle of DuPont Circle as she aimed for the
picture windows that looked like the the opening of a big
cave—

Monika was firing cover fire when all of a sudden she saw
through the big picture windows Yuvi driving across the middle of the Circle, straight toward the bank—
　¿?¿?¿?
Monika suddenly got it.
　*"Tobey! Screw the vault, get up here right now, we're leav-
ing!"* she shouted, just as Ljubica's car smashed right through
the picture windows and deep into the lobby of the bank.

Monika's own shouts warned the FBI tacticals in the bank,
who turned and saw the gold-colored Taurus going right for
them just as it smashed through the picture windows—a few
of them managed to get out of the way, a few more were sent
flying as the Taurus kept on accelerating, getting as deep as it
could into the middle of the bank's lobby.

We're actually gonna make it, Monika thought casually, as
she herself jumped out of the way of Ljubica's Taurus.

As Duncan Idaho turned to face the side of the road opposite
the ditched Subaru station wagon, who should be standing
there but a man Idaho recognized on the spot. Not Nicholas
Denton—no: It was Arthur Atmajian, the dean of CIA's Dog
Soldiers, sporting an assault rifle of his own aimed directly at
Duncan Idaho's face.

Oh shit, thought Duncan as he immediately started to move,
running forward down the road, laterally to Arthur Atmajian's
line of sight as they both fired simultaneously.

Prr-rr-rr-rr-rr-rr-rr-ah!-Rr-ah!-Prr-rr-rr-rr-rr-rr-ah!

Pök! Pök! Pök! Pök!

Arthur Atmajian had on a dark baseball cap and long dark raincoat, his thick black beard full but untrimmed, his head cocked to the left and one eye squinting as he aimed his M-16 directly at Duncan Idaho—he was really aiming to kill, but Duncan Idaho was too fast and it was too dark: Arthur Atmajian shot up the driver's side of the Audi from end to end as his line of fire swept across the car, quarter-sized holes popping open down the length of it—but he didn't manage to tag Duncan, who ran around the Audi's front, shooting cover fire from the hip, with practically no aim, trying to put the front end of the Audi between himself and Arthur Atmajian.

Pök! Pök! Pök! Pök!

Atmajian too started to move, running toward the back end of the Audi as he fired into the car's front end, trying to keep Duncan Idaho pinned down long enough so that he could surprise him from behind.

Prr-rr-rr-rr-rr-rr-ah!

But as Duncan Idaho crouched by the front passenger's side wheel of the Audi he realized what Atmajian was going for—almost as soon as he got to the wheel and started to crouch, Duncan Idaho jumped up onto the hood of the car, sliding across it just as Arthur Atmajian appeared at the rear end of the car and fired.

*Prr-rr-rr-rr-rr-rr-rr-rr-rr-*clink!

His clip's out, thought Duncan.

Diagonally across from each other, the car between them, both of them crouching, Duncan zipped to the driver's-side door and got in, not bothering to close the door as he put the Audi in reverse and floored it, the tires squealing against the black asphalt as Duncan turned to the left, trying to run Arthur Atmajian down.

Atmajian leapt out of the way, the Audi rushing backward past him as he turned to follow it, ejecting the empty magazine from his M-16 as he reached for another one in one of his coat pockets.

Oh fuck oh fuck oh fuck! thought Duncan Idaho as he slammed on the brakes of the Audi and switched gears to first,

Arthur Atmajian directly in front of his car not five yards away.

Arthur Atmajian too realized it was chicken-on-the-freeway time, Atmajian slamming the full mag into his in M-16 just as Duncan Idaho hit the gas on his Audi and roared straight at him.

Atmajian pulled the bolt back and loaded the first round into the chamber, firing even as he jumped out of the way of the Audi, which neatly clipped Atmajian's legs just as he fired.

Prr-rr!-Prr-rr-rr!-Prr-rr-rr-rr-rr-rr-ah!

Duncan would have turned back. The front end of the Audi clipped Arthur Atmajian right on the shins just as he was in mid-air, sending him spinning like a helicopter rotor, Atmajian falling to the ground in a stunned, immobile heap—all Duncan had to do was hit reverse and roll right over Arthur Atmajian and it would be over.

But all that—Denton, Atmajian—they were all secondary to the sudden yellow pain Duncan felt, as if his whole body had been kicked hard by an animal, like a horse maybe, or maybe a mule—some animal with a hard hind leg, an animal that could put all its weight into it, because that's what he felt: A yellow-yellow-yellow pain that went through all of Duncan's body, a pain that somehow managed to reach up into his skull and grab his brains in one fist and shake them good, shake them like dice, shake his brains until they were all confused and messed up, like the yolk of an egg inside its shell, Duncan Idaho flooring the Audi as he tried to get away, not bothering to look behind him at the prone Arthur Atmajian, just *going*, dude—going, going—dude, look!—we've been *shot!*

Ljubica rammed the car deep into the bank, the Taurus demolishing all the desks and potted plants and filing cabinets that were strewn around the lobby, as well as clipping three more of the FBI tacticals—

(Where did all these guys come from?)

—even Monika herself had to jump out of the way of the

Taurus, diving to the ground behind a desk just to the left of
the path of the Taurus's momentum.

The remaining FBI tacticals suddenly found themselves
surrounding the gold-colored Taurus, and they didn't hesitate—
not because they were so professional, but because they were
so surprised: They simply fired their weapons at this new arrival out of delirious panic.

Monika couldn't believe how quickly the Taurus was suddenly riddled with bullet holes, the panicked FBI tacticals actually shooting each other as the crossfire pierced the car
completely and came out the other side to tag two of the tacticals, Ljubica inside changing gears and reversing even before
she'd fully stopped, the FBI tacticals zipping through their
clips on full automatic as the air became so chockful of cordite
and tear gas that it was amazing anyone could breathe—

—Monika felt her calf fall off the rest of her leg, making
her fall to the ground before she'd had a chance to properly
stand up—it didn't hurt that bad—it didn't hurt at *all*—it was
just an annoyance as Monika got up and looked down at her
shot, shredded calf at the same moment that Tobey got to the
top of the curving staircase and began shooting his own
AK-74 in the general direction of the FBI tacticals, everyone
confused and panicked as the air was full of screams and
shouts and the sound of breaking glass—

—Ljubica managed to pull the Taurus completely out of
the bank just as Monika came up to Tobey and accidentally
tackled him to the ground, her broken, ruined calf making it
hard for her to stand—

"Let's go to the vault!" Monika shouted, Tobey getting up
and helping Monika to her feet as all the tacticals ignored them
and fired at the retreating Taurus, the two of them running for
cover down the long curving staircase as up above the tacticals
let loose on the retreating Taurus with absolutely everything
that they had.

Ljubica didn't even know what happened, pillows crashing
into her body and face, sensations that were dull and distant
as she just tried to get out of the bank, accelerating the Taurus,
which crunched and cranked and clambered over the curb and

back onto the street, an FBI tactical firing a grenade launcher and *missing!* for God's sake—the thing going off in the middle of DuPont Circle with a terrific—

PTÖCK!!

—sound as another tactical fired an incendiary grenade at the retreating Taurus, the thing falling right into the now-open trunk of the Taurus and blowing up with a loud *FIZZ!!* as Ljubica drove on and away, without looking back and without stopping, the Taurus somehow still running as it screamed down P Street, only this time heading west and away, west and away, west and away . . .

They were running out of bullets, nothing more complicated than that, Monika and Tobey making their stand in the elegant reception area of the basement, each of them on either side of the curving staircase's landing, ready to start firing at the people up the stairs, trying to keep them at bay.

"Yuvi? Yuvi! What's going on?" Monika kept asking, getting no reply.

The tacticals seemed to be concentrating on Ljubica, but then suddenly a tear gas canister came flying through the air, bouncing on the last couple of steps of the staircase and rolling underneath the receptionist's desk.

Monika limped over to it and picked it up, turning around and throwing the canister right back up the staircase just as it started chugging smoke in earnest.

"*Drop your wea*—(cough! cough!)—*your weapons*— (Argh!)—*and come out with your hands UP!* (cough-cough!)"

"What do we do?" Tobey asked Monika.

She looked at him, then at her leg, bloody where the 9-mm slugs had gouged out her calf muscles.

"*There is only one exit, and we are guarding it—so, so*— (cough-cough!)—*so come out with your hands* UP! *We* WILL *fire upon you if you do not comply!*"

On general principle, Tobey took his AK-74 and fired up the staircase just as the FBI tactical was done with his stupid little speech—but then Tobey's assault rifle tripped emptily: He was out of bullets.

"Shit," he said casually, like it was a no-big-deal inconvenience even though he had no more clips of ammunition. "What do we do now?"

Monika looked at him and winced—not in pain, but as if she were just now realizing something crucial. *He's gone,* she thought, for some reason remembering those times when Tobey's glasses had completely fogged up from the humidity, turning him blind, remembering that it was just this morning that he'd shot the little woman from New York. *He's so smart, but he's so blind, he's gone,* she thought, watching Tobey thoughtfully twirl his spiked goatee, as if he were thinking over some finance problem.

"If we like made like a run for it?" he was saying. "Maybe we could get up top and get going with Yuvi? What do you think?"

Monika looked at him carefully. "I've got an idea," she said suddenly. "Follow my lead, the way we did it in Skunk Works. Just follow my lead."

"Okay."

Monika fired a few more rounds up the staircase, then quickly walked toward the hallway that led to the vault, Tobey close behind.

The vault door was wide open, Monika taking hold of it and making sure she could actually swing it by herself. When she saw that she could, she said to Tobey, "Get in."

"What?"

"No questions, hurry up, get in get in get in," she said, hurrying Tobey enough so that he did what he was told without question, like a good little brainiac.

Monika took her penlight and tossed it at him just as she swung the vault door closed, Tobey looking back at her with the oddest face: As if he'd been found out.

Monika spun the vault locks shut, then limped back to the staircase.

"This is your last chance—"

Monika set the selector switch of her AK-74 on full auto-

matic as she looked up the staircase. It reminded her of when
she'd been nine or ten, her parents off to some cocktail party
of fellow retirees and Monika all alone in the big house after
dark. She'd been scared of the third floor. Standing on the
staircase landing, looking up at the blackness up there, she'd
been positive there were haunts and ghosts of all shapes and
sizes even as part of her knew that there wasn't anything up
there at all, save the goblins of imagination. All she had to do
was run upstairs and hit the lights, and it would all be over.

So that's what Monika did. She ran up the curving staircase, the fire from her assault rifle lighting the way.

Ljubica Greene got away. Unbelievably, amid all those FBI
tacticals, Ljubica managed to get away, finally free of that
golden tether that had kept her in place for so long.

Her beautiful elegance didn't stop her from bleeding. Her
right forearm was shattered where a bullet had gone through
it, and she felt a liquid warmth against her chest, where a bullet
had taken a good half of her right breast. Her entire skull was
on fire—literally: A bullet had taken off half her jaw, the teeth
on the right side of her face gone, her tongue, clearly visible,
singed and blistering from the friction of the bullet's trajectory.
Her right knee and thigh were ruined, three bullets lodged in
them—she was, annoyingly, having to step on the gas with
her left foot, and having to shift with her left hand as well.
The gears grinded down as she was shifting without a clutch,
but she didn't care. All she cared about was that she was on
the run.

I made it I made it I made it! she kept screaming in her
head, trying to say the words out loud but unable to: Her jaw
refused to open, her right eyesight growing blurry where her
right lower eyelid had been blown away, along with her right
cheekbone and her right ear.

She drove down P Street, heading west, driving at maybe
a hundred miles an hour, her car unstoppable, having left
everything and everyone behind. The tail end of the gold-
colored Taurus was on fire, trailing tendrils behind her like a

charioteer. It was only a question of time before the flames from the incendiary grenade licked the gas tank and turned the Taurus into a rolling fireball—

So what? thought Ljubica Greene. *So what, I-made-it-I-made-it-I-made-it-I-made-it-I-made-it-I-made-it-I-made-it . . . ;* she kept on thinking over and over again, a simple, idiot loop of meaning her mind could latch on to and use to stave off the reality going on around her, the smoke from the fire filling the car, her own blood bathing her—

—I-made-it-I-made-it-I-made-it-I-made-it-I-made-it-I-made-it-I-made-it-I-made-it-I-made-it-I-made-it-I-made-it-I-made-it-I-made-it . . .

The Taurus, on fire, roared down P Street, screaming on as it headed west, west, west to a place where one could be free, but really only going nowhere.

Just before crossing the bridge over Rock Creek, Ljubica must have lost consciousness, because the Taurus drifted to the left and slammed head-first into a streetlight. The Taurus's airbags popped open just as the streetlight snapped like a twig, the five-hundred-pound post falling on top of the car, crushing its roof and slowing it down enough for the fire to catch up with the gas tank. And once it did, the Taurus exploded as it rolled on, still revving, still rolling, still trying to go west. Still trying to run, even with its last gasps of life.

Duncan didn't know how long it was before he realized that his car was dying on him, its engine sputtering and fuming, steam coming out of the radiator in the front, the smell of gasoline already filling the cab.

She's gonna blow! Duncan thought disjointedly, the yellow pain in his side making him scream, now that the adrenaline anesthesia was wearing off.

There was a grinding noise coming from the left front wheel, as if some bearing had given, the sound of metal tearing against metal loud enough that it distracted Duncan from the awesome pain he felt in his gut.

"Come on you stupid piece of shit!" he screamed, unaware that he was screaming even as the Audi slowly ground down and stopped in the middle of the road.

"*Come-on-come-on-come-on!*" Duncan screamed, revving the engine, stepping on the gas pedal as far as it would go, redlining the RPM gauge. But the engine only revved—even though the car was in gear, something was broken, something was blown.

"Fucker," Duncan whispered, snapping on the interior light of the car to get a better look at the damage.

With the light on, Duncan saw plain as day that there were a couple of bullet holes in the driver's-side door, and the bottom curve of the steering wheel was shorn clean off. Tufts of upholstery sprouted out of the passenger-side front seat, and the passenger-side window was almost entirely blown out, a few remaining shards of glass hanging from the door frame.

Looking around the interior of the car, Duncan noticed that the radio was off.

The radio's off, he thought, confused, connecting this trivia to the larger problem of his immobile automobile. Duncan tried turning on the radio, thinking that if the radio worked, the car would work, too. But his fingers couldn't discover how to turn the radio on, so finally Duncan gave up, his hands floating in front of his chest, indecisive.

"Holy cow, what's this," he said as he looked down at his body.

Bathed in the yellow interior light, Duncan all of a sudden realized that his stomach and lower chest were drenched in blood.

"I've been shot," he said aloud, amazed. He'd never been shot before.

Dabbing his fingers to the wound, Duncan examined the blood leaking out of him, his fingertips dripping surprisingly thick and viscous droplets of black blood.

"Black blood, oh shit," said Duncan, panicking, remembering how, years ago when he'd been doing his SF med rotation, an army medic had explained to him how black blood was the worst kind. Black blood usually meant that something vital had been wounded.

"Oh shit, oh shit," Duncan mumbled, feeling claustrophobic in the brightly lit interior of the Audi—feeling as if the darkness were closing in, feeling as if he were *drowning*—

Duncan opened the door and haphazardly got out of the car, stumbling, blind with panic, pulling himself out of the car in a daze, his mind scambled and confused.

Out out OUT—

Maybe the air, or maybe standing up—whatever: Results are all that matter, because now that he was out of the car and taking deep breaths of night air, Duncan was thinking a lot more clearly, his momentary panic subsiding even as his whole body felt suddenly far weaker than just a second ago.

"Okay, okay, okay," he said out loud, consciously. "Okay, calm down," he said aloud, feeling dizzy and weak, using his right arm to hold the blood down against his stomach.

The loss of blood, he reasoned with careful, stumbling logic, was what had made him panic. Looking back into the interior of the car, seeing it besplattered with his blood, he reasoned with absolute circular certainty that his panic had also probably contributed to his loss of blood.

Cricket, he thought with random logic, his brain fuzzy and staticky, flooded with mental debris like the calm of an ocean's surface strewn with the wreckage of a downed plane.

This is what it looks like, he thought with an abrupt, cool turn of his mind, standing up and leaning an arm on the roof of the Audi. *This is what it looks like—this is what it feels like. This is what it is: I've been shot, and I may be dying—so can we go on now?*

Duncan nodded then began thinking clearly, pushing back the roar of static that was threatening to engulf his brain.

The first thing: He had to move. Atmajian would be coming for him, so he had to move.

But then a noise under the patient drone of his still-running Audi.

Duncan stopped and stood still, listening.

A car was coming.

It's him, thought Duncan Idaho.

Turning back to the open car, Duncan gulped some air, trying not to vomit as he leaned over and reached in and picked up his assault rifle, which lay on the seat of the passenger side. Casually checking that it was loaded and the safety off, Duncan navigated a broiling sea in his mind, a sea of disjointed and random thoughts, any clear line of reasoning buried underneath the waves of nausea, trivia, and pain.

Pull it together, he suddenly thought clearly, looking around as he stood up and looked around his dead car.

The road he was on was still in the middle of the woods, the forest beginning not five yards from the edge of the asphalt. The light from the interior of the Audi was all the illumination around—Duncan's headlights were still off.

"I should turn off those lights," he said out loud, but knew he couldn't. He'd pass out if he bent his head into the cab of the Audi again.

Turning around, hearing the approaching car, Duncan walked on down the road, thinking that he'd make his way up the road before cutting over to the right and into the woods.

Just then, the green Subaru station wagon appeared from around a curve in the road, behind him, a hundred yards away and closing in fast.

"Fuck you," said Duncan as he turned to face the Subaru. He deliberately checked his AK-74 and put the selector switch on single-shot. Then he raised it to his shoulder, aiming as careful as he could and squinting one eye shut.

Then he began firing.

He shot with discipline, waiting until the Subaru was skidding to a halt twenty yards away, firing three times—*Trr-ah! Trr-ah! Trr-ah!*—blowing out the windshield of the Subaru, which skidded and twisted across the road, directly behind his still-running Audi.

Standing in the middle of the road, completely exposed, Duncan thought with his blurry, scrambled mind that the Audi still gave him cover. That delirious mistake gave him the confidence to continue firing on the green Subaru, each shot careful, as careful as he could make it.

Trr-ah!
Trr-ah!
Trr-ah!

The green Subaru skidded sideways down the road and crashed into the rear of the dead Audi. The crash of the Subaru against its rear end sent the Audi lurching forward and rolling on, even as its engine continued to run.

Duncan stood there and watched as the Audi slowly, implacably rolled toward him, as if it were trying to run him down. Duncan put out his hand and set it on the hood of the Audi, trying to stop it, failing, Duncan skipping backward as the Audi slowly rolled to a stop of its own volition.

The Subaru didn't move, lying across the road eight yards away from Duncan, who stood there with his left arm raised, aiming his firearm at the Subaru.

"Are you still there?" he called out to Arthur Atmajian.

With a lurch, the engine of the Subaru died.

"Hey!" he said again. "Are you still there?"

Only silence from the Subaru. So Duncan stood there and shot it up some more.

Trr-ah!
Trr-ah!
Trr-ah!

Duncan stopped and lowered the AK-74.

"Are you still there?" he called out again.

"Hell yes, dead man," came Atmajian's reply from behind the Subaru's bulk.

"Fuck you," said Duncan, selecting full-automatic on the AK's selector switch and spraying the Subaru good—*Trr-rr-rr-rr-rr-rr-rr-rr-rr-rr-rr-rr*—

TR-CLINK! He'd zipped the clip.

"Fuck," said Duncan, lowering his rifle to look at it as he leaned against the front end of the Audi. He looked up at the Subaru. It was Swiss cheese.

"Are you still there?" he called out again.

Only silence.

"I guess not," mumbled Duncan, relieved but confused, deciding he had to go check to see that Arthur Atmajian was dead. So he shoved off the front end of the Audi and tried to take a couple of steps.

He was succeeding, he was walking, barely, and so he happened to look at his rifle, and that was enough to break his concentration—Duncan's legs buckled and he fell to his knees as he stared at his assault rifle.

"Fuck," said Duncan, realizing he was on the ground, amazed at how quickly it had happened.

He let the rifle fall away from him and clatter to the ground. He bent forward, as if praying to Mecca, his head beside the driver's-side wheel of the Audi, his forehead touching the ground. Then he tried to get to his feet, using all of his strength and concentration, disjointedly thinking, thinking, his mind mush, a droning wash of sound and thoughts, all of them too slippery to grab on to—

Then: *I'll use the Subaru,* he thought with perfect clarity.

"Fuck yeah," he said. "I'll get in that Subaru . . . go warn the others. Then a medic."

Duncan Idaho, got to his feet, his entire body from the chest down covered in his own black blood, gathering his will as he decided what to do: Get to the Subaru. Drive to DuPont Circle. Warn the others. Get to a medic.

"I can do this," Duncan Idaho said aloud.

From behind the green Subaru, Arthur Atmajian stood up too.

"Oh shit," said Duncan, as he began to walk backward away from the Audi and the Subaru, walking backward down the road as he stared at Arthur Atmajian coming toward him.

With a gun in hand, Arthur Atmajian limped around the Subaru station wagon, then over to the driver's side of the Audi. Without looking away from Duncan Idaho, Arthur Atmajian reached in and switched on the Audi's headlights.

Duncan looked at his hands, but they held nothing but the blood he was trying to keep inside of his body, blood that snapped suddenly harsh and deep crimson when the Audi's headlights snapped back on.

Arthur Atmajian's face was completely obscured by the shadow cast by his baseball cap and his thick pirate's beard. His black overcoat whispered as he strode toward Duncan

Idaho, his limp—from where Duncan had clipped his shin—already straightening out.

Arthur Atmajian checked his own gun as he closed the few yards between them.

Duncan looked at where he thought Arthur Atmajian was, completely blinded by the white light coming from the Audi's headlights. "You're not dead yet," he said, squinting, trying to see the man who was coming to kill him.

Arthur Atmajian didn't say a thing. He calmly walked up to Duncan Idaho.

Not like this, thought Duncan, his mind all of a sudden perfectly clear and lucid, falling to his knees again as if in supreme surprise, surprise-surprise. *Not like a dog. Not like something worthless and without meaning. Not like this.*

As Arthur Atmajian came within point-blank range and aimed his firearm down at him, Duncan Idaho looked up and gathered the last of himself.

"How?" he asked simply.

Atta-boy hesitated, surprised that his friend Nicholas Denton had correctly anticipated this final question. "Your boy, Tobey Jansen," said the man come to kill Duncan Idaho. "He belonged to us, like *you* could have belonged to us. But you thought you could make it on your own. You chose to believe in nothing but yourself."

Duncan, confused, dying, said, "I don't understand."

Atta-boy scoffed good-naturedly, shaking the surprise and hesitation out of his head. "It doesn't matter anymore," he said.

Then he fired into Duncan Idaho's face.

The wound in his forehead was small, but the back of his head blew out blood, brains, and skull fragments in the shape of an almost perfect halo, a halo that lasted only an instant before it was gone.

Duncan Idaho fell backward to the ground, his limbs spread out across the road, and he did not move.

The moment Monika closed the vault door on Tobey, the last shreds of light faded out, the only sound the sound of the automatic lock spinning through its cycle, the interior of the vault completely black.

Beyond the door, Tobey heard muffled automatic fire, barely audible through the thick steel—as if it were all happening somewhere far away.

Then it was all silent.

It was pitch-black in the vault, of course; but for the longest time, Tobey didn't turn on the penlight he had in hand—he was afraid that its light would seep out of the vault and give him away.

It took awhile—a good half hour, forty minutes—for Tobey to come to slowly understand that no one outside the vault would see any light coming out of the vault. In all that time—time he had no sense of, the shock of it all making his body feel drowsy and his sense of time turn plastic—Tobey just sat there with his back against the door of the vault, thinking about what they would do when they got their IDs and stuff from the safety deposit box.

After a while Tobey slowly and gradually remembered he still had his headset on. "Hello?" he called out. "Monika? Yuvi?"

Finally, Tobey turned on the penlight.

He shined the light around, then went over to the safety deposit box they'd come for, box number 27-13—the thirteenth box from top to bottom of the twenty-seventh column from left to right. It was actually the biggest box in the vault, about two-and-a-half feet tall and eighteen inches wide.

Tobey tapped the safety deposit box and began thinking again, thinking about how he was going to open the box—

He heard a noise, a sound, like something turning, some gears shifting—not an engine—just gears—

Tobey shone the penlight on the inside of the vault door. It was covered in glass, and through it Tobey saw the locking mechanism of the vault door—the tumblers were turning, someone was unlocking the vault door from the outside—

"Monika? Yuvi?"

"He's in here," he heard a man's voice call out.

Tobey nearly lost his lunch.

As quick as he could, he took the penlight and smashed its butt against the glass covering the locking mechanism of the vault door, shattering the pane with a single blow and cutting the back of his wrist with a shard in the process.

Tobey didn't even notice. Feeling his way through the mechanism of the vault's locks, Tobey found a pair of gears, shoving the penlight between them, the light still on and aimed out into the vault's interior, the only light there was.

He stepped back, looking at the vault door's locking mechanism, stepping on crunching shards of glass as he retreated, the gears turning as whoever it was who was outside started turning the lock of the vault open.

The penlight got stuck between the gears, freezing up the whole mechanism. Whoever was trying to open the vault must've been awful strong, because they began turning the gears so hard that the penlight started to get flattened, its light suddenly snapping off as the batteries inside its casing were smashed and ground to mush.

"Oh shit, oh shit," said Tobey, standing alone in the completely dark vault, stepping on the broken glass now all over the floor.

The fluorescent lights inside the vault suddenly snapped on like a white sheet.

Tobey jumped, looking around, the fluorescent lights flickering and kicking in as if awakening from some slumber.

It was deathly still. Looking around, there were two walls of safety deposit boxes, the bright fluorescent lights turning the vault into a new room, a room Tobey felt as if he had never been in before. The inviting darkness was gone, only a sterility brought about by the white lights above and the white flooring below, the steel walls surrounding him all around.

His earpiece suddenly squawked static, as if it were coming back to life.

Tobey's heart jumped, adrenaline jolting his whole body.

"Yuvi-Monika?"

"No Tobey, it's me," said Denton.

Tobey looked as if the words he'd just heard were just beyond his comprehension, words he had never heard before.

He ripped off his headset and flung it away from him as if the thin wires that formed the headset were thin, poisonous snakes.

"Tobey," said the tiny, patient voice coming from the headset. "I know you're there. Tobey: Answer me. Tobey, pick up . . ."

The tiny words kept on going, threatening to drive him insane. So Tobey gathered himself. He took a deep breath. He checked the porcelain gun he still had on him, and then closed his eyes. He rubbed his scalp. Then he looked at the headset lying on the floor.

"Tobey," said Denton's tiny voice, "I know you're there . . ."

Tobey picked up the headset and put it on.

"Yes, Mr. Denton," he said.

"Tobey," said Nicholas Denton. "You can come out now."

"I can?"

"Yes of course."

"What about the others?"

"They're dead. They're all dead. So come on out; nothing will happen to you outside."

The last phrase flipped through his mind like a card tossed off by a clever magician: *Nothing will happen to you outside.*

"You're wrong," he told Denton.

"I can assure you, they're all dead," said Denton. "So you can come out now; I guarantee your safety: There are two-dozen FBI out here, none of them will touch you; none of them will let anybody touch you."

"What, and I'm going to go back into the fold?"

"The fold? No," said Denton. "No, you're way past that. But you delivered Acrobat: You can walk away."

"And then?"

"And then what?" said Denton.

"And then what will I do?"

"Live out your life—"

"You weren't supposed to know we'd be here! I didn't tell

you that we'd be here!" said Tobey with an odd and sudden petulance.

"I guessed," said Denton.

"Oh," said Tobey, nonplussed. "All of them?" he then asked fitfully. "They're—they're all dead?"

Denton sighed. "Monika Summers is dead—I'm looking at her corpse right now. Ljubica Greene's car exploded just shy of Georgetown."

"But you haven't caught Duncan—"

"Jerome Duncan Idaho was shot earlier tonight, around four o'clock in the morning, just when you and the others were breaking in here," said Denton, without a hint of any emotion. "He was shot and killed on a small access road in McLean, Virginia. His body was positively identified by Arthur Atmajian, head of Physical Plant Security."

"You're lying."

In the background, Tobey heard someone say to Denton, "Ask him to undo whatever it is he did to the vault door."

"Open the door and I'll take you to the morgue and show you," said Denton.

"Dunc— . . . ," he hiccoughed, unable to get his mind around the hard truth. "But Russell got away. Not everyone's dead; Russell got away."

"Yes," said Denton calmly. "Russell Orr got away."

Outside, thought Tobey, seeing him in his mind lost in a jungleland, unable to see where the next—

"If he's ever spotted, Russell Orr will have no life—but you will, Tobey," said Denton.

Tobey said nothing, listening.

"I know what happened," said Denton. "You got too close and lost sight of what you were doing. But that's okay, I've got no hard feelings. You did more or less what you were supposed to do. You can walk away."

"Oh, so I'm guessing you'll let me live even though I know about you and all that money you took, huh?" said Tobey, a little hysterically.

Denton gave a start. "What are you talking about?" he said, sounding confused.

He's playing dumb for those FBI out there—"The money you took from the Chinese? Come on, Mr. Denton, don't play dumb with me, okay? I have a brain, I use it. We've been tracking you for months, trying to figure out ways you could bring in that money that you got for all those Skunk Works secrets? The sixty million? I know all about it, Mr. Denton—I know all about *you*."

"Tobey, what are you—what is—what are you *talking* about?"

"How are you gonna let me go if I know all about what you've been doing?"

Denton paused, as Tobey in the background heard someone say, "What is he talking about?" Through his headset, Tobey heard Denton's muffled answer, "I don't know," Denton sounding as if he were covering the transmitter.

"Huh?" asked Tobey. "You'll want me *dead*. I know about you."

"You know about me, is that right?" said Denton—

—then out of the blue he asked, "Tobey, why do you think Acrobat brought you in?"

Tobey frowned, confused by the direction of the question. "What? Why did—I-I—what do you mean?"

Denton was patient. "Of all the people to bring into their operation, Acrobat brought in one of the best finance people in Langley. And what did they make you do? They made you look for a payment of sixty million dollars the Chinese made to someone inside Langley."

"Yeah, that's right. They brought me in to investigate *you*—"

"Yes of course, but Tobey, my point is, did you ever investigate *my* bank accounts? Did you ever do a scan of *my* Social Security number?"

Tobey didn't speak.

Denton went on. "Of course you didn't. You taught each and every member of Acrobat how to track money, how people could launder it, how people transferred it, how to get money to do pretty much anything anyone would ever want it to do—but Acrobat never assigned you to investigate *me*, the prime suspect of this corruption scandal." Denton sighed. "To-bey, don't you see? They weren't investigating anybody. They were using you to figure out how to get away with—"

"Bullshit," said Tobey. "Bullshit, you lie!—you *lie!*—Jesus, Mr. Denton you're such a *liar!*"

"Alright, I'm lying—so what about Skunk Works," Denton pressed on.

"Skunk Wo—Wha-What about it—What about it?"

"Why did Acrobat have to break into Skunk Works?"

"To get—to get evidence, evidence against *you*," said Tobey, gathering steam, getting on the offensive. "You—*you* . . . You were selling Skunk Works secrets, we had to gather the evidence—"

"Yes of course I was selling Skunk Works secrets, but why did Acrobat have to *go* to Skunk Works?" Denton quietly insisted. "Spectacular scoring run, don't get me wrong—but why did Acrobat have to do it? If Acrobat was investigating *me*, why didn't they break into *my* office? Why didn't they put a surveillance on *me*. What was there in Skunk Works that they just *had* to get at?"

Tobey stopped breathing, staring off into space as his fingers gently touched the microphone at his lips, as if he were afraid it might turn alive.

"You're lying—you're *bluffing*—you're just trying to-to-to-to-to screw with my head!"

"The moment you—"

"You're *lying*—"

"The moment you—Tobey, *listen*: The moment you tipped them off that I was coming for them, Tom Carr and his kids all went underground. And since then, their number-one priority has been to get to that safety deposit box. Why?"

"Huh?"

"Why," said Denton. "It's a simple question. Why did they run? Why didn't they go to the FBI, or the press, or *anyone*. Why did they just *run?*"

Tobey blinked. "I don't, I don't—"

"What do you think you'll find in the box?" Denton suddenly asked him.

"What?" asked Tobey, thrown by the question.

Denton took a slow breath. "Inside the vault you're in, in that safety deposit box. A lot of people died to get at that box. What do you think you'll find inside?"

"I-I-I'll find the fake IDs, the fake credit cards, the papers that will get us out of here—"

"You told me Ljubica was a shopper, so why couldn't she shop around for another set of IDs?" asked Denton. "She could find weapons and gear for you whenever she wanted to, in just a couple of hours—so what's so hard about finding some fake passports and bogus credit cards?"

"She, we never brought it up; it just never *occurred* to us—"

"What's in that box, Tobey? What's *really* in that box?"

Tobey didn't say a thing, shaking his head in the empty vault as if Denton could see him and react. "You lie," said Tobey. "You lie—you're a liar—you're *lying!*" he screamed hysterically.

"Am I?" said Denton.

Tobey tore off his headset and raced to the wall of safety deposit boxes, looking for the right one, looking for 27-13, looking, looking, 11-18, 12-18 a blur of columns of boxes, 28-19, backtracking, 27-20, looking down, 27—

He found it: 27-13, the biggest box in the vault. Like all the other boxes, though, two keys were needed to open it, the handle between the locks looking back at him like a smiling clown with a secret.

Tobey patted his fisherman's vest until he felt the lock-breaker he'd used for the vault's two key locks. He turned to smiling, secretive box 27-13 that looked as if it had begun to leer at him, and drilled both locks, the lock breaker piercing them as easily as an awl through an eye. When he was through, he twisted the lock-breaker, trying to get it to catch the locking mechanism and pop the locks, just like Yuvi had taught him, fiddling and jiggling them until both locking mechanisms popped open—first one, then the other.

Tobey stood there, unable to believe it had been done so quickly, surprised at his own desperation.

The drilled locks looked back at him like the punctured eyes of the blind, the metal handle no longer a smile, or a leer, but a tight frown, or a scream.

Before he could stop himself, Tobey opened the door, grabbed the handle of the safety deposit box within, and pulled with all his strength, ripping the box out of the wall.

The box was heavy. Heavy and long. As he pulled it out, in his carelessness, it swung out of its slot to the floor, its weight breaking out of his grip, the box falling onto its side in the middle of the vault floor.

Tobey looked down at it—a gray-brown box, two feet by two feet by three feet, lying amid white formica flooring. He knelt down beside it and turned it over right side up, its lid still secure.

Then he popped the lid and opened the box.

On top there were six U.S. passports and a five-inch stack of credit cards, each bundle carefully held together by rubber bands. Paper-clipped together were six birth certificates and six Social Security cards.

All these documents floated on a sea of money.

"No," said Tobey. "No, no, no."

They were hundreds, in bundles of ten thousand. The bills were all old, used, wrinkled—the bills had been around.

Tobey stared at the money, then reached in and pulled out a stack of it, then another, and another, gathering all the stacks on the floor beside him, a little mountain of money growing on the ground beside him—

—but there weren't that many stacks. Only a couple-three stacks of ten thousand covered the surface of the box's contents.

Quicker than he thought possible, Tobey added up all the money, quickly multiplying the stacks in his head, adding it all up and coming out with a round figure: Three hundred thousand dollars, cash.

Walking-around money, Tobey thought, knowing that three hundred thousand wasn't that much, comparatively. It was only four years of his own CIA salary, barely.

It's just walking-around money—it's not real money! Tobey thought triumphantly.

But beneath the bills, there was more.

Looking back into the safety deposit box, filling most of it, there was a cardboard box with GEORGIA PACIFIC printed on top. It was one of those boxes that were used to store reams of photocopying paper, the box wrapped shut with clear packing tape which had been doled out in such a way that the tape formed two convenient handles on the top. It fit snugly inside the safety deposit box—all Tobey had to do was reach in and pull it out.

So that's what Tobey did: He reached in and pulled out the box.

It was very heavy, forty pounds at least, enough to make Tobey grunt unconsciously as he pulled it out of the safety deposit box and dropped it besides the cash on the floor. Ripping at it with his fingers, Tobey pulled at the plastic tape, trying to tear it open—but it wouldn't give.

"Come on, come on, *come on, open up, you stupid motherfucker!*" he screamed in frustration, eventually leaning down and using his teeth to rip open the plastic tape, ripping it open—

The tape gave, Tobey ripping it away and flipping the top off of the box. Inside, there were two stacks of plastic security envelopes, fit snug into the cardboard box, the envelopes too without any markings. Tobey grabbed one of the envelopes and yanked it out, the envelope the size and shape and feel of a ream of paper.

He ripped the envelope open and discovered what had been so carefully packed inside.

They were documents, documents Tobey had never seen before, not in real life anyway. A whole stack of these documents twice as thick as ordinary paper, maybe two hundred of them in the envelope he had in hand, all printed with elegant scrollwork on the margins, all with fine ink engravings of Ulysses S. Grant in a pose Tobey had never seen before.

At the top of each of these documents, flying on an ink-drawn ribbon, were the words TREASURY OF THE UNITED

STATES OF AMERICA. At the four corners of each of the documents was a number: ten thousand. And at the bottom of each, written in hard yet dynamic Ionian script, the words TEN THOUSAND DOLLARS. *Bonds,* Tobey thought clearly, with the detachment of surprise and comprehension, finally understanding how the money had been moved from one country to the other. *Negotiable bearer bonds, as anonymous as currency, and just as liquid.*

"No-no-no-no-no-no," he whispered as he reached in and grabbed another of the plastic envelopes, ripping it open again, again finding more of the Treasury bonds.

The Georgia Pacific box seemed to have an inexhaustible supply of these heavy-duty plastic envelopes, as if some machine somewhere had manufactured them all and carefully packed them before shipment.

Tobey slumped to the ground, letting the bearer bonds he had in hand slide out of his fingers and to the floor around his knees. There were so many of the bonds, he felt suddenly as if he were drowning in a sea of them.

The passports lay there in a neat little bundle, so Tobey picked them up, barely seeing them as he cried, ripping off the rubber band that held them together and going through them one at a time.

Tommy, Monika, Russell, Ljubica, Duncan—passports for each of them. There was even a passport for him, all of them with random aliases, their new identities: Fred K. Kolber, Ariel F. Marianni, Adam-Garth Velazquez, Elyse Koestler. Tobey discovered that his own fake name would have been Gregory B. Vernice.

Greg Vernice, he thought, looking at his passport, remembering how Monika had told him just a week or two before they'd scored Skunk Works that she needed a passport photo. "For Personnel records," she'd said. How everyone around the Acrobat cubicles had shot each other glances. Tobey remembered Duncan had given him a pat on his shoulder, where he'd gotten his acrobat tattoo, and Tobey had winced, telling him to watch it.

Opening all the passports to their picture pages, Tobey

spread them all out on the floor in front of him. They tried to
snap shut when he left them open on the floor. So having
nothing else to hold them open with, Tobey used stacks of
walking-around money to keep the passports open. He opened
them all save his own, staring down at them all, looking from
one to the next and back again, his eyes skipping from one to
the next, trying to take them all in as his crying stained the
insides of his glasses, tears collecting on the inside of his
lenses, and then dripping off.

Monika smiled back at him, her face tilted up a bit, her
teeth eager and white. Duncan's face was tilted slightly down,
his eyes up, looking directly at the camera, looking like he
was sizing up the viewer. Ljubica looked aloof, her face ever
so slightly turned to her left, her mouth serious, curving
slightly at the corner. Russell was bored, his head tilted
slightly forward, the curve of his brown brow enormous, his
mouth set and serious.

The most surprising was Tom Carr. Tom Carr looked as if
he knew—deep down—who would ultimately get to see this
picture.

*They were gonna bring me in on this. They were gonna
bring me in, bring me in all the way. . . .*

"Why?" Tobey whispered to the mute passport pictures.
"Why did you go and *do* this? Why? Why did you have to
take us here?"

Tom Carr gave no answers. Nor did Ljubica or Russell or
Monika. Not even Duncan.

"Tobey," he heard Denton's tiny voice coming through his
discarded headset. "Tobey, pick up. Tobey, please, pick up."

Tobey sniffled a bit, then wiped his face. He crawled over
and picked up the headset.

"Tobey, pick up."

Tobey put on the headset. "Yeah," he said, broken.

Denton tsked. "Aaaah Tobey. Tobey, Tobey, Tobey," he
said. "Remember on your first day with Acrobat? Remember
how you took a package to the Chinese Embassy? For eight
months, every single week, you delivered packages. Some-

times a big box, sometimes just a little envelope. But you never retrieved anything, now did you?"

"What was I delivering?" Tobey asked like a moan.

"Langley secrets," said Denton. "Strategic intelligence assessments, digests, source materials. Secrets Acrobat stole, and then sold for money." Denton sighed again, Tobey hearing as he lit a cigarette. "Then there was that PCB board in Manhattan, the one you fried with that microwave bomb—weird how Tom Carr knew exactly where it was, hmm?"

Tobey sniffled. "Did he put it there?"

"Yes of course," said Denton dreamily. "We were on to him by then. He'd scored the PCB board for the Chinese, from a lab out in New Jersey. Up and did it all by himself. Amazing. A truly gifted roadrunner. He himself put the PCB board in that bank vault in Manhattan. But then somehow, Tom figured out that we might be on to him. So he had the Acrobat workgroup scotch the exchange. Suspicion on him was instantly deflected; he got a big chit in the game. Ironically, *I* got into trouble because one of my work-groups was playing cowboys and Indians. And Acrobat and Tom Carr skated off to Michaelus's Directorate, making it that much harder for me to keep an eye on him." Denton sighed long and leisurely. "Tom Carr . . . ," he said, then let out a long, low whistle. "He had it coming."

Tobey Jansen just cried as he stared at all the passports.

"Unblock the door," said Denton. "Whatever you did to it, undo it."

"Why?" he cried. "Why did they do this?"

Denton paused, sounding surprised. "Because they were traitors, Tobey. That's why I sent you to join them—I needed someone who could watch them. Because they decided that they didn't need us. They decided they could make it on their own."

"What did they want, what were they doing?"

"They were doing—"

"Why did they do this?" Tobey screamed.

Denton said nothing.

"Why?" said Tobey. *"Why?"*

"I don't know," said Denton after a moment, sounding as if he were really thinking about this question. "I . . . I don't know. Maybe . . . maybe Tom didn't like being stuck on the promotions ladder, or maybe he got tired of answering to his peers, I don't know—I could bullshit you all day. But I really have no idea." Denton paused, as if surprised. "Why do people do anything?" he said finally.

Neither spoke for a bit. Tobey sat back and looked at everything he'd found in the box: The stack of negotiable Treasury bonds, the walking-around money, the stack of credit cards, the passports—

"Fuckit," said Tobey, ripping off his headset.

"No, don't—shit, he's gonna shoot himself. . . ."

From his fisherman's vest, Tobey pulled out his porcelain gun, put the muzzle to his ear, and fired.

EPILOGUE

What We Sacrifice Each and Every Day

James Jesus Angleton: THAT *was someone to take seriously. A spy and a saint and a crazyman and a killer. A truly dangerous man. Compared to him, the jokers and jesters we're dealing with today are just that: Clowns.*

Atmajian shrugs. In all fairness, Nick, guys like Angleton were playing for real stakes. We practically have to manufacture our enemies.

Denton stares at him, with such force that Atta-boy is surprised to find himself squirming.

Don't kid yourself, he says. Maybe Angleton fought a war, but we're defining the peace.

Denton's original lie—that the work-group Acrobat were all a bunch of bank robbers, plain and simple—made things remarkably tidy at the end of the day. The next Wednesday, Mario Rivera himself gave the news conference, explaining how the five suspects, Ljubica Sarah Greene, Tobias Richard Jansen, Jerome Duncan Idaho, Russell Orr, and Monika Patricia Summers, were believed to be responsible for the raid on the Chase Manhattan Bank in lower Manhattan last November, as well as the stickup of the Western Union in Camp Springs late last week. Rivera further explained that an anonymous tip had led the FBI to mount an ambush at the gang's next target, the Riggs National Bank on DuPont Circle. Three of the suspects were shot and killed by FBI SWAT personnel; one of them was involved in a high-speed car chase that ended in a shoot-out with the FBI in McLean, Virginia. (Arthur Atmajian was pretty pissed about the FBI getting the credit. "Let it slide," Denton wisely advised him.)

Mario Rivera said that the fifth suspect, Russell Orr, was still at large and being actively pursued. Orr was placed seventh on the FBI's Most Wanted list, and Rivera assured the news crews that they would be making an arrest shortly.

There was no mention of Skunk Works.

Rivera gave good press—with his sad eyes and huge arms and self-deprecating manner, the reporters thought he was pretty cool, and they liked his "Just the facts, ma'am"-approach to briefings. That's why the press didn't ask any questions Rivera couldn't handle—they liked his demeanor so much they were willing to trust his facts, no matter how flimsy.

Only one person made a stink about the affair: Barry Greene. A respected Los Angeles businessman involved in real estate, Mr. Greene said there was no reason for his daughter, Ljubica, to have robbed any banks or to have been involved in any such trouble. "I'm a wealthy man. I give my daughter money whenever she needs it, whenever she asks me for it," he said, forgetting his tenses.

He was just one man, but he had plenty of friends and a lot of money, so he very well might have caused some bad migraines all around.

But then Mr. Greene blundered: Bizarrely, he claimed that his daughter had in fact worked for the Central Intelligence Agency.

Of course, nobody believed him after that. Soon enough he became an embarrassment to his well-connected friends and an annoyance to the reporters who had been foolish enough to listen to him in the first place. Once Mr. Greene mentioned the three little letters, his credibility evaporated.

"Love those conspiracy theories," Nicholas Denton told Arthur Atmajian a few days after Rivera's press conference. "Crying 'wolf' and all that."

Quite true.

The Senate Intelligence Committee, though, didn't let things lie. They started probing the Ombudsman's Office. They wanted to know exactly what had happened with Acrobat, and they wanted to go through Bart Michaelus's office with a fine-tooth comb, not resting until they'd accounted for every bit of dandruff.

Phyllis Strathmore was the Ombudsman. She was also Denton's friend. It wasn't hard for the two of them to maneuver the committee into concluding that Michaelus had masterminded the whole Acrobat/Skunk Works mess. And Michaelus's death? A falling-out among thieves! The fact was, Michaelus had been involved in so many shady deals and misuses of CIA personnel that one of the Intelligence Committee staffers told Nicholas Denton privately, "I know it sounds awful, but thank God Acrobat bumped him off. Can you imagine the scandal if he were still alive?"

"Yes," said Denton. "I can."

Nicholas Denton lived in a locked world, a world he'd built for himself brick by brick.

Sinatra, the Denton family's dog, died that summer, a devastating blow to Karen and the kids. In the last few months, his glaucoma turned him almost completely blind, and then in the space of a couple of months, gout and arthritis set up shop and proceeded to ravage him good. The poor guy was in pain, and it wasn't fair. So one Sunday morning in early July, Denton and Karen called a family meeting and they all had a talk about Sinatra: About how much he was suffering, about what a good dog he was, about how loyal and brave he'd always been. Sinatra blindly wagged his tail as he heard his name being bandied about. But he kept his head between his paws, too tired and hurting too much to get up and demand affection from the kids like he had just a few months before.

So on Monday morning, Denton took the day off and they all drove down to the vet's office. Everyone was crying when the vet gave Sinatra the shot. He didn't even flinch at the sting of the needle. As if he knew what was going on and sensed that it was okay.

Other than that, life went on.

The Dentons had a lot of barbecues over the summer, especially when the kids got shipped off to camp in Maine. The poor Macintoshes, whom the Dentons had blown off for so long, finally came over, as did all the rest of Karen's friends: The Feinbergs, the Joyces, Jim and Darcy Leyden, the Dominicks, the Mitchells, and of course the Atmajians.

"God*damn* that was messy," Atta-boy chided Denton when they had a minute alone, the two of them having a beer over the barbecue grill, referring to Acrobat. "Let's hope there's no next time," he said.

Denton scoffed. "There'll be a next time," he said. "There'll be plenty of next times."

Atta-boy blinked, not understanding.

Denton flipped a burger and took a drag on his cigarette. "This is just the start, Atta-boy, you just wait. We're going to have Acrobats sprouting up like weeds."

Atta-boy stared at his best friend. "You're wrong," he said simply.

Denton smirked. "Watch."

"Whatcha all talkin' about?" asked Gavin Joyce, married to Portia, Karen's friend since God knew when.

"Football," said Denton with a smile, intensely disliking Gavin but keeping that thought to himself, one of the little compromises of his marriage.

Lots of compromises. Nicholas Denton despised barbecues—Karen was the one who liked them. Denton himself was more into meeting friends for dinner in formal restaurants in the city, which always made Karen nervous. Being as big a woman as she was, she always felt elephantine around the sleek company her husband always surrounded them with whenever they went out.

"I don't know why we have to go out—why don't we have a barbecue?" Karen would invariably ask whenever they went out.

Denton just sat there behind the wheel of his Mercedes, thinking, *In one ear, out the other—be Zen.*

The summer rolled along.

While in camp, little Artie suffered a severe concussion while playing right field. It seems he had been staring at the seams of his baseball glove while in the middle of a pleasant daydream when somehow—unbelievably—impossibly—a wild pop fly zonked him squarely on the head, knocking him out cold. When Denton got the news at work, his ulcer flared so bad he wasn't sure if he was going to puke blood or merely shit it out.

If it had been up to him, he would have been on the next flight to Maine. But work got in the way. He had a liaison meeting with his counterparts from the Defense Intelligence

Agency and the Treasury Department, and then he had to finesse the ranking Democratic senator on the Senate Intelligence Committee. The old fucker kept floating his dentures whenever he took a sip of his drink—Denton could have screamed. But he smiled and bided his time, then nearly plowed his car into the Potomac as he tried to make it to the airport.

The doctors said Artie would be fine. The biggest problem was reassuring the kid—Artie felt guilty and upset at having disturbed his parents with his misadventure, a reaction Denton had noticed all children had whenever they were involved in a genuine mishap. Karen and Denton had to climb up into his hospital bed and sandwich him with reassurances before Artie got over it.

"Look at your head!" Karen told Artie, trying to distract him. "You look like a mummy!"

Artie had looked in the mirror of his mother's compact and been very impressed, as impressed as he'd been when he saw the magnetic resonance imaging machine at the hospital.

"They took a picture of my *brain*—from the *inside*," he told his parents wisely.

"Yes, but did they find anything?" Denton teased his son.

"Nicholas!" said Karen.

In the fall, now that they were old enough, Denton started taking both Artie and Nicky Junior to play squash with him and his friends. With the new administration taking over the management of the store, Denton was a busy boy during most of the winter and the following spring, making new friends, taking a lot of lunches, sewing up contacts like a tailor embroidering rhinestones. The best time to network was really during the weekends, but then that was when Denton liked spending serious time with the boys. So he compromised, taking them with him to the Racquet Club and teaching them himself whenever he could.

It made Claire furious.

"Why can't *I* go!?!"

"Because you're *five*. When you're seven, you'll get to go."

"If I was a *boy* I'd get to go," she'd claim angrily, making

Denton feel very guilty as he and Nicky Junior and Artie got in the car and drove off.

One time in the locker room, after they'd played for a couple of hours, Denton and the boys were going to the showers when Denton was stopped by Douglas Bratts.

"Got a minute?" said Douglas, as he was finishing getting dressed.

"Uh—sure," said Denton.

Bratts was one of those verbose men you want to throttle on general principle: It would improve the economy of speech of the species as a whole if he was put out of his misery. But instead, he shared his misery with Denton, going on and on about some problem with the new administration and blah blah blah blah.

Denton couldn't throttle the man, no matter how satisfying he could imagine that would be. Instead, Denton had to stand there with just a towel around his waist, listening to this dickhead and smiling at all his stupid jokes because he happened to be the undersecretary of the Army, and Denton was trying to use him to control the general in charge of Army Intelligence, Frank Crosby.

Denton knew everybody, and everybody knew Denton—and he was always the same: He was always charming; he was always smiling. He couldn't afford to frown and shake his head and tell Douglas Bratts to fuck off, just as he couldn't afford to spend the time with Frank Fierstein—the funniest guy Denton had ever met. Not only that, Frank was sharp and thoughtful, a truly insightful thinker with some of the most interesting ideas about the future of American Intelligence. But Fierstein was also the least influential man in Washington. So no matter how much he might like him, Denton couldn't afford to be friends with Frank because he simply couldn't afford to be careless with his time and person. He had to cultivate the right people, people like this moron Bratts.

". . . he tells me how he's on top of it, but Nicky, please, I can see right through him; so I tell him, 'Barnes, don't shit a shitter. Your figures are *way* off the mark, and if you think *I'm* going to authorize something like that . . .' "

Denton kept smiling as the endless anecdote went on. People were process, the rungs on the endless climb to keep himself secure and in control of his little corner of the universe. If he had to make sacrifices and compromises, well: He'd built a secure place for himself and his family in this world. They were safe, they were secure, all Denton had to do was make a few sacrifices, cut a few corners, hold himself in check, and keep an even keel, no matter what he might want, no matter how much he'd like to tell the whole world to go kiss his fat white hairy ass—

"Daddy?" said Artie, tugging at his father's hand as he danced around. "Daddy?"

"Hmm?" said Denton, breaking Douglas Bratts's flow.

"Daddy, I gotta *go*—I gotta go *pee*."

"Okay Artie," said Denton, turning to Bratts. "We'll talk soon?"

"Sure-sure, Nicholas, I'll give you a call early in the week."

Denton and the boys walk-skipped to the back of the locker room, where the toilets and showers were. He was about to turn left into the toilets when Artie tugged his hand again.

"What?" asked Denton.

"Aren't we gonna take a shower?" Artie asked.

"I thought you said you had to go?"

Artie grimaced painfully. "That man talked too much," he said simply, Nicky Junior agreeing with a nod and a heartfelt "Yeah" as he and his brother trooped into the shower like soldiers after a long march.

Denton was impressed.

In September of 2001, on the day before the Twin Towers were leveled, Nicholas and Karen Denton watched Claire blithely blow them off as she trundled into her kindergarten classroom. Her parents watched from the threshold of the door as Claire took a cool look around at the other little boys and girls and instantly made a place for herself. Karen cried and said she wanted another baby. Denton uncharacteristically mumbled that that might not be such a good idea; maybe they should just get another dog instead.

By Christmas, she was pregnant again. The new puppy's name is Kandinsky.

And as for Russell Orr, well: He was no longer undecided. He had decided to drift.

He didn't spend the rest of his life wandering through the streets of Washington, of course. By Sunday morning, as he read an account of all that had happened, he knew he couldn't stay in D.C. Sooner or later someone would spot the big black man with the shaved head and the tiny little non-prescription glasses. After all, his picture was in the papers.

So he caught a train to New York, where the city is so big and the people are so worried about their own survival that no one would notice him. He ditched his glasses and let his hair grow out, a modest, half-crown Afro sprouting like kinky black broccoli in just a couple of months. For a while, he worked for a moving company out of Queens, living by himself in a tidy apartment in the Bronx. Nobody bothered him during all that time, and he was careful to stay out of Manhattan, where he might run into someone from his previous life.

But the city weighed on Russell. It scared him a little, and he didn't like the grayness of New York after all the southern green of D.C. So one day, near the end of summer, Russell woke up and decided to leave it all. He dressed in his sturdiest and most inconspicuous clothes, took the cash he had hidden behind one of the drawers of the kitchenette, and left his New York life behind with nothing in hand.

That's how Russell remained—he drifted.

From New York, he moved on to Detroit, which he liked enough to stay there for a couple of years. Then, out of the blue one day, he walked away from his Detroit life, leaving behind a whole houseful of furniture and clothes and the personal debris of a life. In fact, he even left behind the incredibly well-constructed identity he had built for himself in Detroit, heading out West without any clear sense as to what he was looking for or where he was going. All he knew was that he had to just *go,* driving along on a motorcycle he'd bought under a fake name he manufactured on his last day in Detroit. It hadn't been his specialty while at Langley, but Russell's gotten good at inventing fake lives. There's no trick to it, really. In a free society, people pretty much take you at your word.

He drove around for over a year before he settled in Texarkana for a time, working on oil derricks and calling himself Big Jim Fulton, claiming to be an oil rigger from Alaska via Washington State. But then one day, some federal marshals came snooping around, asking questions and generally making their presence felt. The marshals were looking for a key link in a drug supply line, but Russell didn't know that. All he knew was that someone was snooping around. So before he had the chance to become better informed about the situation, Russell Orr was on the go, discarding his Big Jim identity like a cheap mask.

He was on the move for quite some time, zig-zagging up and down the country, generally heading west as he pretended to himself that he was only trying to shake the Federal Marshals who had almost caught up with him in Texarkana. But he knew he was fooling himself. He just liked being on the run.

Finally, out of some atavistic sense that he ought to settle down, Russell stopped in Santa Fe, New Mexico.

He's been there for a while now. He has a job working at a department store, in their storage facilities. He drives a forklift, keeping to himself mostly, reading buckets of books and watching television alone on his days off, or sometimes watching it at the neighborhood bar, where they call him Buddy Reece. Like in New York and Detroit, like on the road and in Texarkana, like in every place he'll ever go to, Russell doesn't have any close friends, much less anything approaching a family—Russell has no tether. He has nothing to tie him down, like he had with Acrobat.

Occasionally someone will take a liking to him, an interest. Occasionally some woman will start looking at him. Russell allows this, but he doesn't let it touch his heart. He smiles and nods and, ever so imperceptibly, he takes a step away.

Sometimes, Russell thinks about the plan they'd had, the pact they'd made. It had been such an easy sell, Tom Carr hadn't even had to make much of an effort at getting them to buy it. Why would he: The plan represented freedom. That was the whole point of it. All the freedom this world had to offer, bought and paid for with just a petty betrayal. And they were all petty, no matter how monstrous the betrayal.

Sometimes, just before he sleeps, he allows himself to think of Ljubica. He lets himself be fooled by the notion that Ljubica knew how it would all end and was actually trying to save him. He tells himself the blatant lie that Ljubica loved him so much, she was willing to part with him in order to let him live.

Comforting lies that allow him to sleep.

And when he dreams nightmares, he dreams of his mother, his only living kin. She's sitting in her chair in Seattle, watching the world go 'round, without any money or the protection it buys. He hasn't made any move to contact her in all this time, and he supposes he never will. He can't risk it, he tells himself; and while that's true on the one hand, it's a lie on the other. He imagines her sick; he imagines her dying. He pictures her pleading, watery eyes asking him for the help and kindness he owes her.

But all this drifting has made his heart hard. Hard, and restless.

He hasn't been in Santa Fe that long, but surprisingly, he's getting impatient. In the afternoons, driving down the highway, the orange setting sun making his eyes squint to slits, he finds his mind drifting west, toward California maybe, or maybe some place farther still. He's not looking to catch sight of a federal marshal, but then he wouldn't be unhappy if he did. He almost feels happiest when he's on the go—it's as if he feels at home when he's on the run. Running always to the West, drifting into the wide open spaces of the most austere isolation. He has no one who can hold him back even for just a little bit. It's so lonely, this freedom is, and it's so frightening. But it's addictive, too, and it feels natural. Normal. As true as apple pie.